A CLEAN

AUDREY DAVIS

TANZANITE BOOKS

CHAPTER 1

Young people in England are the most illiterate in the developed world and are floundering in maths, according to a global ranking.

'It's not only the young ones,' mused Emily as she put her laptop to sleep and headed upstairs for a shower. Every day she cringed as she scrolled through her Facebook page or flicked through the comments section of the *Daily Mail*. If she had a pound for every "definately", "should of" or incorrect use of its/it's she could feast on sirloin steak instead of rummaging through the Value section of her local Tesco. She was equally appalled at people's inability to do the most basic arithmetic in their heads. Surely it wasn't rocket science to calculate that if an item cost 84p and she proffered £1 then 16p change was due?

Jim had always scoffed at her devotion to the trashy world of tabloid journalism. He was a *Telegraph* or *Times* man. 'Real news, Emily. Honestly, your brain will rot reading all that nonsense.' Then he'd settle down for his nightly dose of Channel 4 News, while she wondered if she could catch up with Kirsty and Phil once he'd retired for the night. She loved Kirsty. All womanly curves and clipped vowels. Which brought her back to the *Daily Mail*. It might not be highbrow – more articles on which brow shape was currently in vogue – but it did raise some interesting questions. Like how a woman could build a multi-million dollar empire purely by virtue of having an unfeasibly enormous bottom. Emily's rear was far from superstardom status but it did seem to grow in direct proportion to the shrinking of her grey matter. Einstein could probably have created a mathematical equation to address the conundrum.

Twenty minutes later she was sitting at her dressing table, dragging a comb through her hair. The reflection that stared back at her wasn't too bad, at least for a fifty-two-year-old. High cheekbones, thick hair and good skin, kept in check with liberal applications of whatever cream or serum promised to work miracles. Her bathroom cabinet resembled a suburban branch of Boots. Yes, she had a few fine lines but failing eyesight had its compensations. She had reading glasses stashed everywhere – bedroom, kitchen, bathroom – but she happily applied her make-up without visual enhancement. Her daughter had bought her a magnifying mirror for Christmas which still languished in its box. Some things didn't need to be brought into sharp focus. A gentle blurring of the edges was just fine.

'Mum! Are you there?'

Emily started at Tabitha's voice from downstairs, the front door slamming behind her. A minute later she bounded into the bedroom, all blonde curls and breathlessness. Sometimes her daughter made her think of the Duracell bunny on amphetamines, ricocheting from one crisis to another, bumping and crashing her way through life at full pelt.

'Washing machine's on the blink again, brought some laundry round, hope you don't mind.' Tabitha threw herself down on the bed. Today she was wearing tight red jeans and a floppy black sweatshirt emblazoned with 'Don't walk, dance'. She kicked off her ballet pumps and regarded her mother with blue eyes the shade of stone-washed denim. Emily was quite partial to skinny jeans herself, despite reading several articles declaring that certain outfits were off-limits when one reached a certain age. Bollocks to that! She still wore cut-off shorts in the summer when the sun decided to put in an appearance and had yet to witness anyone fainting in horror or disgust.

'That's fine, darling. We'll pop it on in a little while. Fancy a cuppa?' Emily got to her feet, smiling as Tabitha leapt off the bed and headed back downstairs. She'd already done a few stretches and yoga positions, part of her daily routine. Luckily her faculties were still intact. She knew of at least two friends of friends who had been diagnosed with dementia in their forties. Her morning Sudoku and crossword puzzle were her way of kick starting her brain, although there were days when her thoughts bounced around like globules in a lava lamp, connecting then dispersing in no apparent pattern.

In the kitchen Emily flicked on the kettle. She liked her kettle – bright orange to match the toaster and bread bin – bursts of colour in an otherwise bland environment. Wall-to-wall cream cupboards and grey floor tiles. They'd been Jim's choice, a man whose idea of daring was to swap his usual butter-slathered toast for a muesli mix in a concession to healthy living. She couldn't abide the stuff – like sawdust mixed with unidentified animal droppings – preferring a boiled egg or some fresh fruit. Not that his muesli had done much good. Found slumped over his desk four years ago when he should have been presenting at a strategic planning meeting.

Emily nursed her cup of instant coffee and watched as

Tabitha began dragging out miscellaneous clothing from a black bin liner and stuffing them haphazardly into the washing machine. The cycle started, she pulled up a chair and launched into a rapid-fire summary of her escapades that week. She often thought of Tabitha – thirty next birthday – as a human whirlwind, constantly teetering on a precipice of euphoria or despair. Today was a good one, her smile like sunlight breaking through the clouds, words tumbling from her mouth and tripping over each other in the way of toddlers with only a basic grasp of walking.

'How's Tom?' she asked. Tabitha's boyfriend of more than a year seemed a decent enough sort. Easy on the eye, unfailingly polite and hugely appreciative of her Sunday roasts. Particularly since her daughter's recent evangelical conversion to all things organic and wholesome. And gas-producing. A good fifteen to twenty-minute gap was necessary before entering the bathroom after Tabitha. She could rival napalm in the toxicity stakes. *Apocalypse Now,* or certainly a short while after a nut roast had been consumed. Emily sometimes found herself humming "The Ride of the Valkyries" as Emily emerged from the loo. She hoped it was a passing phase. Her daughter had been through more phases than the moon. With a few total eclipses along the way.

'He's good. Busy at work.' Tom worked for a small but niche travel agency on the High Street in Little Hambledon, a picture-postcard village a few miles away from Emily. She and Jim had bought their seventies-built detached property just over twenty years ago. It wasn't exactly a candidate for a *Country Living* double-page spread – too boxy and functional – but its location in Tattler Green was considered highly desirable. Easy access to the motorway and Heathrow airport, the village itself boasting a pretty common with duck pond and various pubs and small shops. They'd done a lot of work to it over the years; new bathrooms to replace the hideous sludge-brown suites and even darker tiles, the aforementioned bland but eminently practical kitchen, polished oak floorboards throughout instead of swirly shag pile in shades of mud brown and fluorescent blue. Emily had wondered if there had ever been a study into why so many people in the 1970s had been so utterly devoid of taste. Or simply had severe eyesight problems. 'Ooh, this is a tiny little bathroom with barely any natural light so let's give it an avocado green loo and matching basin shaped like a shell. And tile it wall to ceiling in khaki with a hint of pink. Lovely!'

'So what's new with you, mummy dearest? Any deep, dark secrets I should know of? Like a hot man, perhaps? You really need to get back in the saddle, so to speak. Can't spend all your days cloistered away turning verbal diarrhoea into something readable!'

Tabitha was always teasing Emily, both about her part-time work proofreading and editing short stories for women's magazines and her lack of a love life. She didn't mind. The former brought in a bit of extra cash, the latter she tried to ignore. In the years since Jim died she'd had a handful of dates – chiefly with men around his age and also widowed – but had failed to click with any of them. She had a nice circle of friends but was happy being on her own a lot of the time. She certainly wasn't prepared to hook up with any old codger just for the sake of it.

'For your information, I've been having *amazing* sex with my car mechanic for weeks now. And no cracks about my big end, thank you!'

Tabitha snorted in laughter. She knew very well that Ken Crompton was nearing retirement age and had all the wit and warmth of a dead haddock. The only reason they both used him was because he was cheap and reliable, unlike many of the other garages in the area.

'Ha ha, very funny. Seriously though, you should think about on-line dating. There's tons of websites out there and they can't *all* be mad stalkers or porn-obsessed saddos. I can check some of them out for you if you like?' Tabitha looked imploringly at Emily, who scowled back in exasperation.

'Tabitha, I am perfectly capable of sorting out my own love life. If I choose to. And right now, I choose *not* to. I am quite happy with my life as it is, even if it seems deadly dull to you.' Cue massive eye roll from Tabitha, before she began rummaging in the fridge in search of a snack. 'If I happen to meet someone and it feels right then I'll take it from there. Until then – don't you *dare* scoff my last piece of Cheddar – I'll continue with my vows of celibacy and get my thrills from my work. You have no idea the shenanigans some of these characters get up to. Gets me hot under the collar sometimes!'

* * *

ALMOST AN HOUR later and Tabitha had departed, washing duly going through its cycle and barely enough Cheddar to satisfy a mouse left in the fridge. Luckily all the really good stuff was hidden away in the overflow fridge in the utility room. Tonight it was Emily's turn to host book club and she'd shopped earlier for the requisite canapés – devils on horseback, mini spring rolls, a platter of French cheeses – as well as an assortment of sweet nibbles. Under pressure from her older sister Celeste she'd agreed to join the merry-go-round of monthly meetings where novels were analysed, dissected and discussed in depth, the focus being on literary content, intellectual stimulation and relevance in today's multi-cultural society, Or, as Celeste's husband Michael put it, 'Ten minutes on the book, the rest shoving nibbles and booze down their necks and bitching about some poor soul or other.'

As she skimmed a duster over the coffee table and gave the bookcase a quick once-over, she smiled at her large collection of paperbacks. Most people she knew, herself included, downloaded everything on to their Kindles or similar devices. Certainly a lot less baggage weight when going on holiday, but there was something special about turning the pages of a much-loved book. Her fingers came to rest on one. A present from Jim. *Blood Angel – A Tale of Gory Revenge.* About as far removed from Emily's tastes as possible. Pushing it back into position she realised with a jolt that today would have been their thirtieth wedding anniversary. Thirty years since Emily had turned to Jim and said, 'I do'. When a little voice in her head had been whispering, 'Are you sure? Really, really sure?'

She'd only been twenty-two when they'd got married, Jim five years older. Far too young to be trussed up in white taffeta that stretched uncomfortably against her slightly protruding stomach. Yes, caught in the age-old trap of finding herself pregnant just a year after finishing university. They'd met there, at the students' union, a rather tipsy Emily flattered by the attention from this rather earnest postgraduate with his unruly brown hair and tattered Jimi Hendrix T-shirt. He drank wine rather than beer – which she thought the height of sophistication – and had a vinyl collection that filled his parents' spare bedroom.

In the early days of their burgeoning romance, Emily felt safe and a little smug as her singleton friends bed-hopped around the campus. Moaning continuously about their scruffy student boyfriends with their bacteria-gathering bathrooms and mountainous heaps of dirty washing that festered in corners of their cupboard-sized rooms. Jim was different, a grown man with a future in marketing already mapped out. He owned his own place, thanks to a legacy from a dotty old aunt who'd secretly stashed away a fortune betting on greyhounds, and took her to nice restaurants. Dependable, devoted, financially secure, what was not to love? Except Emily couldn't help wondering sometimes if something was missing. Passion, perhaps? That feeling of a delicious fizz of anticipation when you were waiting to see the supposed love of your life. The sex was fine – well, *OK* – not that she had much to compare it to. Apart from the odd steamy novel or TV show that had her dad coughing furiously and her mum rocketing out her chair to deal with some suddenly urgent matter in the kitchen. Not so much a fizz, perhaps, more like a glass of two-day old Lilt. Still drinkable but lacking sparkle.

For their silver wedding anniversary, Jim had bought her a pretty pair of earrings. Shame he hadn't noticed in all these years that she'd never had her ears pierced. Her mum deemed it akin to self-mutilation – 'You might as well get your neck stretched like those African women!' – so she'd never got around to it. She, in turn, had searched the internet for the perfect decanter with a delicate silver base in a pattern of intertwined grapes and leaves, Jim's love for wine and all things tastefully alcoholic having blossomed over the years. He would sniff, swill and pontificate on its provenance, whereas Emily just liked the way it made her feel mellow and couldn't care less if it came as part of a 'dine in for a tenner' deal.

What was the symbol for thirty years? Pearl? Couldn't imagine Jim fishing a tantalising little faux-suede box out of his pocket, nestled inside a single lustrous drop on a fine gold chain. Not one for romantic gestures, his gifts had been of a more practical nature. Like the Christmas before he died. She'd bought him a bottle of vintage Armagnac produced in the year of his birth. He'd given her an electric foot file designed to slough away dead skin and callouses. 'Look, Em!' he'd exclaimed as she attempted to generate some kind of enthusiasm. 'It's got real diamond crystals!' Try as she might, Emily couldn't imagine Eartha Kitt purring with pleasure over finding *that* in her stocking. Poor old Santa Baby would most likely have been shoved unceremoniously back up the chimney.

Speaking of chimneys, it had been more than four years since her own one had been lit. Metaphorically speaking, more like ten years since any kind of flame had smouldered in Emily's life. After Tabitha was born – and both she and Jim had been smitten by their daughter from day one – she had hoped to expand their little family. However, it was not meant to be. No clear-cut medical reason, the doctors said. And as the months and years passed and Jim retreated to his own study/guest room at night – 'hate to keep you awake with my snoring, my dear' – her dreams of a brother or sister for Tabitha faded along with her libido. A perfunctory peck on the cheek or the lips, the occasional pat on the bottom, the very occasional coupling which lasted as long as a TV ad break. And usually followed a fine bottle of St Emilion Grand Cru if Jim had been celebrating a particularly successful campaign.

There was still a basket of logs next to the fireplace. And, if her memory served her correctly, a box of firelighters on a shelf in the garage. Jim had disapproved of firelighters.

'That's the cheat's way, Em. It's all about arranging the kindling correctly, a few scrunched-up pages of *The Telegraph,* and Bob's your uncle!' Then he'd huff and puff and almost blow the house down as the flames failed to take hold. On the odd occasion when Jim was travelling, Emily took gleeful delight in lighting the fire herself. With the aid of the illicit firelighters it took her approximately five to ten minutes to produce a roaring hearth. Curled up with her Kindle and a glass of passable plonk she'd congratulated herself on a job well done, and with the minimum of fuss. Then made sure to clear away the evidence before Jim's return, lest his masculinity be reduced to a pile of cold ashes.

It was just after seven and Emily had set the stage; the fire ready for the touch of a match, the food artfully arranged on plates adorned with seedless green and red grapes. Candles burned on every surface, suffusing the air with a hint of wild berries and cinnamon. The lamps were turned down low, both for atmosphere and because women in their fifties and sixties preferred the subtler approach of ambient lighting. Going into a brightly lit changing room these days was akin to torture; every lump, bump and line thrown into sharp relief by the brutal glare and wall-to-wall mirrors.

First through the door was Celeste. At almost sixty she was remarkably well preserved, like a plump Christmas ham glistening under the hallway light. She'd recently taken to having hair extensions after complaining that her once-crowning glory was thinning at an alarming rate. 'I'll be damned if I end up with a bloody comb-over like that Bobby Charleston!' she'd decreed, before emerging from the salon more footballer's wife than footballing legend.

One of her sister's more endearing traits, in Emily's view, was her proneness to malapropisms. Hence the Charlton/Charleston mix up.

'Hello, darling! You look fabulous! Haven't seen that top before, is it new?' Celeste clamped her sister to her bosom, nearly asphyxiating her in a cloud of La Vie est Belle. Emily smoothed down the simple but fitted teal blue number with its daring – for her – halter neck. At a time in life when women were forming campaigns like twenty-first century suffragettes to bring back sleeves she was inordinately pleased that she had succumbed to neither bingo hall nor bingo wings. And, with hopefully a real fire to keep them warm this evening, she felt a little flesh-baring wasn't too over the top.

Celeste followed her sister into the kitchen, opening the fridge and retrieving a bottle of Pinot Grigio. Pouring herself a generous measure, she sank down on a counter stool and scooped up a handful of Bombay mix. Duly chewed and swallowed, she surveyed Emily with an appraising eye. 'A bit outré for book club, ma petite?' Celeste had briefly taken a French course at night school and liked to toss in a few Gallic phrases in a bid to impress. 'Shame we don't have any male members, I'm sure dear Arnold Pettifer would be quite smitten with your defoliage.' As Arnold Pettifer was nudging seventy and had a smile reminiscent of yellowing tombstones – with an odd familial gap or two – Emily didn't feel it too much of a loss.

'Did you enjoy the book? Found it a bit boring myself. All that weeping and wailing and endless doom and death! Give me a good Sheila O'Flanagan any day of the week.' On this, Emily had to reluctantly agree, even though it had been her selection. Over 700 pages of painstakingly researched historical fact/fiction did not make for a light bedtime read. It might have won several major prizes but to her it served only as a more effective sleeping pill than those prescribed by her GP. She'd managed a quarter before giving up and downloading something frivolous but eminently more entertaining.

'Last month was really interesting, shame you couldn't make it,' continued Celeste, as her sister looked at her watch and wondered if anyone else was going to show up. 'Not my usual cup of tea, but I'm now an Ernest Hemingsworth devotee.' Oh help, thought Emily, wondering where this particular train of thought would crash spectacularly. 'Alice chose it, she's always been a bit pretentious, but I found it quite fascinating. All about bullfighting in Spain. You know, the tradition behind it, the way those men saw themselves as warriors fighting a noble cause. You really should read it, Em. Here, I've written down the name for you.' Celeste scrabbled in her bag, produced a tiny notepad with a flourish worthy of Paul Daniels at his peak. *'Murder in the Morning!'* she pronounced. Emily simply prayed for the doorbell to ring. Which it did.

* * *

HALF AN HOUR in and book club was in full flow. Emily's living room was filled with the thrum of ceaseless chatter. Glasses chinked and plates clattered as oozing wedges of Brie were spread on crackers, spring rolls dipped in sweet chilli sauce, horseback thingys taken apart to cries of 'Ooh, it's a date, thought it'd be an oyster! Or is that the angel version?' Michael – damn him – had been proven right as this month's weighty tome had barely warranted more than five minutes of their time.

'Watching paint dry would have been more fun,' said Esther Thompson, licking a particularly gooey St. Augur from her fingers.

'Too true,' chipped in Susan Wainwright. She had sped her way through the savouries like an Olympic athlete with an eye on the gold, which in her case was Emily's fabled mini cheesecakes. With a crumbly butter biscuit base and meltingly creamy in the middle, they were topped with a layer of sweet but tangy blackberry compote. Emily felt slightly miffed that her book choice had failed to captivate her fellow members. Still, at least she'd got beyond the first chapter.

'Oh, I really shouldn't, but ...' Susan bore the expression of a woman who'd just spent the past hour in the throes of ecstasy with George Clooney/Brad Pitt/take your pick of desirable males as she grabbed another cheesecake. Her third, Emily noted, relieved that she'd made a double batch. Susan then launched into a blow by blow account of what some random woman she knew was up to these days. Which involved latex, whips and something about the headmaster of the local secondary, who'd always seemed a perfectly nice man to Emily, if you discounted his fur-lined anorak and encyclopaedic knowledge of feathered creatures.

Nancy Edwards, a mousy little soul who had barely contributed a word to the proceedings, was currently fanning herself with a copy of *Good Housekeeping* purloined from Emily's magazine rack. Gosh, it was a little hot in here, thought Emily. Even with her wispy Arnold-attracting top. Taking a large gulp of water, she glanced at the fireplace and realised her fire was more than blazing. It was now raging like a mini Hades and belching out eye-watering plumes of smoke. Esther was in the midst of a spectacular coughing fit, Alice's face was turning a vivid shade of scarlet and Susan had put down her dessert plate and looked vaguely distressed. And not just because the cheesecakes were finished.

'Emily!' squeaked Celeste, having just returned from a nose-powdering session in the cloakroom. 'I think we have a problem!' No kidding Miss Marple, thought Emily, as smoke continued to billow around the room. All the women were now convulsed in a cacophony of honking and spluttering like consumption sufferers in a modern-day sanitarium. What to do? Call the fire brigade? Much as the thought of hunky hose-wielding men storming her semi gave her a little frisson of excitement, it seemed to her that the problem was more to do with a blockage in the chimney than an out-of-control inferno.

'What the hell's going on in here?' Through the pall of

smoke emerged the robust figure of Celeste's husband, Michael. Often on taxi duty – Celeste never knowingly under drank – he forged a path towards the fireplace, pausing only to grab a vase of fast-wilting tulips. Tossing aside the blooms, he chucked the water on to the smouldering embers. Which hissed, spat and emanated an astonishing amount of steam. *From hellfire to hammam,* thought Emily. All we need now are fluffy white bathrobes and a reflexology session.

A short time later, the book club ladies said their goodbyes.

'Most excitement I've had in a long time!' Nancy gave Emily an uncharacteristic hug, her usual lavender and old lace fragrance tinged with a hint of charcoal.

'Wait until I tell the women at yoga about tonight!' chirped Susan, although Emily suspected they already knew, had seen the high definition footage and were on to the next domestic drama-to-be.

Michael, a pink-faced and slightly droopy Celeste clinging to his arm, paused at the front door. 'Have you ever had your chimney swept, Emily?' For some reason – maybe one too many glasses of Pinot consumed or just the sheer exhaustion of it all – Emily couldn't help but giggle. Not recently, she wanted to retort, but thought better of it. Michael was solid, reliable and adored her older sister but he was not over-endowed in the sense of humour department. Particularly the section marked 'slightly smutty'. 'Well, I think you should call someone in. Have a look on Google. Could well be something dead up there. Goodnight then.'

Emily, having cleaned up the kitchen, sprayed liberal doses of air freshener around the living room and taken a shower to wash away the stench of smoke, sank down on her bed. A chimney sweep. Did they even exist anymore? Suddenly her head was filled with pictures of Dick Van Dyke dancing with penguins, alongside Julia Andrews being practically perfect in every way. 'A spoonful of sugar makes the medicine go down ...' She shook her head forcefully. The last thing she needed right now was a night's sleep plagued by Mary flipping Poppins. She'd investigate the existence of men with long brushes and soot-smeared faces tomorrow.

CHAPTER 2

Back home after several cups of coffee with her mum, Tabitha sank down on the loo seat. What a relief! It was all very well drinking the recommended eight glasses of water a day (plus tea, coffee, wine etc) but not if your bladder was the size of a peanut. OK, it was probably perfectly normal sized for a twenty-something female but it always seemed to scream 'time for a pee!' at the most inopportune moments. Like ten minutes into a movie when she was squashed into the middle row of the cinema between a man the size of Magic Johnson and a woman the width of a small bungalow. Both nursing buckets of popcorn that could have fed a small African nation for a week. And as reluctant to budge as a soon-to-be neutered spaniel on its way to the vet. Or – even worse – on a rickety old bus in the middle of nowhere in Indonesia where the choices were behind a bush where goodness knows what creatures lay in wait or a delightful hole in the ground with strategically placed foot markings on either side. That was a memorable trip, thought Tabitha. She'd been proud of her pelvic floor, lasting two excruciating hours until the relative luxury of the backpackers hostel.

She'd read somewhere, the *National Geographic* perhaps, that an elephant could urinate around 160 litres in one go. Or was it David Attenborough? Not who could pee so copiously, of course, just where that little gem of knowledge had come from. Apparently the average human managed a mere 600 to 1000 ml. Which was only a bottle of Sauvignon Blanc, give or take. What was *really* fascinating, however, was that both elephant and human took about the same time to empty their bladders. She found that hard to believe. Ah well, the miracles of nature. A quick dry off, up with the pants and jeans, hands washed, time to make something to eat. Quinoa with feta and lentils, part of her new health kick. Although egg, chips and beans might be quicker. And tastier. She grabbed the door handle, turned it and ... shit, no. Oh, damn and bugger! Tabitha gazed in horror at the handle, now detached and in her squirty soap-scented hand. She rammed it back on the sticky-out spindle thing and tried again. Nothing. It wouldn't budge. Not an inch. She was locked in the lavatory, just like the old ladies in the song.

Right. Tabitha took a long, deep breath. Don't panic. Stay calm. She checked her watch. 5.30pm. Barring hold ups, Tom should be home in half an hour. She can't call him as her mobile is in the kitchen on charge. I mean, who takes their phone to the loo? She remembered giggling when her former boss Denis related the tale of his tumbling into the bowl mid-stream. No amount of drenching it in rice grains saved that poor Nokia. An ignominious end.

But wait a minute. Didn't Tom mumble something this morning over his Shreddies that he might go for a pint – or two – with Clive and Keith from work? Maybe even a curry if they hadn't put the Premier League to rights in the pub? Tabitha, sitting at the kitchen counter with her tongue sticking out as she applied her mascara, had barely been listening. She'd had a long day ahead – sorting out new stock, packing up internet orders, listening to the latest tales of dating disasters from her boss – so Tom's after-work movements hardly warranted more than a cursory 'whatever'. He could be at least an hour, probably more like two – or three – or …

Feeling her heart racing faster than Usain Bolt, Tabitha attempted to clear her mind, particularly of the image of two lightly fried eggs, crispy golden chips and a side of Heinz's finest. She could survive without food for a few hours. Might even help lose some of that excess flab she packed on over the Christmas holidays. But water? Wasn't the maximum survival time something like a week, less if you were in the baking heat of the Australian outback? Which, of course, she wasn't but the bathroom was pretty warm. What if Tom, strolling back from a tasty chicken tikka Balti and garlic naan, got hit by a bus? Or an asteroid? Or collapsed with an undiagnosed brain haemorrhage? And, having left his wallet in the Delhi Delight, was now lying in intensive care while staff desperately tried to trace his next of kin.

Tears began to well in Tabitha's eyes, then spill down her cheeks. Which made this morning's mascara – a departure from her usual brand – join the cascade. Blinking hard, for there was now a nasty stinging sensation, she squinted painfully at the mirror. Great, just great. Now she resembled a blinking giant panda. As she turned on the tap and grabbed a wodge of toilet paper to wipe away the smudges she ever so slowly registered the trickle of water that gradually became a steady flow. OK, so she might not die a horrible death by dehydration just yet. Or be accepted as a member of Mensa anytime soon.

* * *

THE MORNING after the night before and Tabitha unlocked the door of The Little Shop of Treasures, plonked her handbag on the counter and wandered through the back, the beaded curtain jangling behind her. Her boss was already there, opening boxes of greeting cards and sorting them into neat piles. ABBA's 'Take A Chance on Me' played in the background and the air positively reeked of a consignment of scented candles meant to enhance a romantic evening but more likely to bring on a migraine.

'Darling, you're late!' Meryl tapped her watch pointedly but with a smile. Clearly last night's blind date had gone well. A blow by blow account would follow, but for now it was time to get the shop ready to open in thirty minutes.

Tabitha had worked there for almost eighteen months now. It wasn't quite what she'd had in mind when she'd graduated with a degree in events management. She'd stood there proudly on the stage, clutching her empty cardboard tube (for photo purposes only), and beamed at her mum. And begged her silently not to leap to her feet and scream 'Love you!' hysterically like a pubescent One Direction fan. Sadly, her fantasies of micro-managing high-end parties, teetering around in Jimmy Choos and barking orders at minions laden with hideously pretentious canapés – sautéed snails a la croûte, anyone? – and balancing trays of Pol Roger had not been realised. She'd managed a couple of corporate events, but these were more vol au vents, paint-stripping wine and a couple of unfortunate incidents involving ageing executives with bad breath and wandering hands. The closest she'd got to celebrities was assisting at the end-of-season wrap party for reality TV show, *Scots Wa Hae.* This featured a delightfully colourful cast of Glaswegians being filmed going about their day to day lives. There was Wee Jock, a six foot three bundle of tattooed joy, who claimed to be in the *Guinness Book of Records* for most pints of Tennents Lager consumed in one minute; Senga, boasting of bedding half a Scottish third division football team (presumably not all on the same night), and Big Tam, her personal favourite. A die-hard *Braveheart* fan, he had watched the film a mind-boggling 250 times and still blubbed like a baby whenever Mel made his 'freedom' speech. A surprise nationwide hit – with subtitles, of course – the show was scheduled for a second series. So a rather inebriated Tam informed her, his blue-striped face coming perilously close to her crisp white blouse. 'Aye, hen, we've had better ratings than *Emmerdale* and *Corrie* put together.' Swaying slightly, he proffered a congealing plate of deep-fried Mars bars. Tabitha politely declined.

So here she was, hardly in the job of her dreams but it paid the rent and she was very fond of Meryl. Somewhere in her mid to late forties, she'd never been married but still believed the perfect man was out there somewhere. Her real name was Beryl but she'd changed it in homage to her favourite actress who also happened to star in her number one movie, *Mamma Mia*. Such was her devotion she frequently sported dungarees and would burst into ABBA songs at the drop of a hat. Unfortunately, Beryl/Meryl made Pierce Brosnan sound like Alfie Boe.

'If you change your mind, I'm the first in line,' warbled Meryl. Tabitha looked at a display of hand-painted wine glasses and wondered why they didn't shatter as her boss did a passable impression of a cat being administered an enema. Grabbing a Stanley knife, she began attacking a box of cutesy fridge magnets bearing such slogans as "Cleaning the house while the kids are still growing is like shovelling snow while it's still snowing". As she began to arrange them on their special board, Meryl – thank you, God – switched off the CD player.

'Time for a brew, methinks, before the hordes descend.' Tabitha nodded in agreement. She'd overslept this morning, still traumatised by her near-death experience in the loo. Luckily, Tom was home sharpish as Clive had been off sick and Keith under threat of castration from his missus if he wasn't back in time for the kids' bath and bedtime story. Once he'd released her from captivity – and stopped laughing long enough to put the oven on – she'd felt vaguely sick and more than a little miffed at his lack of sympathy. Then her sleep had been peppered with vivid nightmares involving killer toilet brushes and lakes of elephant wee.

'So, how was last night?' she asked, sipping her builder's brew. Meryl had recently joined an online dating service. She'd only been on four dates so far – including this one – but the first three had been unmitigated disasters. The first, with recently divorced car salesman Dave, mainly involved him weeping openly about how his wife had run off with his best friend. The second – Nathaniel (call me Nate) – started more promisingly until she discovered his passion for taxidermy. 'Just finished the most amazing ferret. It's getting the eyes right, that's the tough bit,' he'd enthused, eyes glittering with all the fervour of a mass murderer. Slapping down a fiver for her drink, she'd fixed him with her own beady stare and the parting words, 'Get stuffed.' Which she was really rather proud of. Date number three – accountant Alan – might have had potential if he hadn't so blatantly lied in his profile about his height. His alleged five foot eleven could only be achieved if he carried around a large crate to stand on. More like five foot two, and she suspected even then that he had lifts in his highly polished brogues. Which meant, standing up, his nose came perilously close to nesting in her not-inconsiderable cleavage. Admiring her décolletage was one thing, but using it as a set of well-padded earmuffs was quite another.

'It went really well!' exclaimed Meryl, more than a hint of joyous disbelief in her voice. 'We hit it off straight away. So many things in common. He loves going to the movies and cooking and he was really interested when I told him about the shop. His name's Miroslaw, from Poland originally, but lived here for yonks. Still got a hint of an accent – quite sexy, actually – and he looks a little bit like a younger Al Pacino. Honestly, Tabbie, I think I might have hit the jackpot this time! He runs his own building business, mainly fitting conservatories, new windows, that kind of thing, *and* he drives a Range Rover!'

Tabitha smiled, genuinely delighted for her boss, who she also considered a friend despite the age gap. She was one of the few people Tabitha tolerated calling her Tabbie, an abbreviation she hated as it made her feel she should be coughing up fur balls and depositing dead birds on her neighbours' doorsteps. Her mum had chosen the name because of her love for the old US TV show *Bewitched*, in which the main character Samantha's daughter was similarly monikered. She generally insisted that it never be shortened – Tom once called her Tab and was lucky he'd ducked in time – but for some reason Meryl was incapable of getting it right. Shame she hadn't also inherited the character's ability to perform magic by twitching her nose. That would have come in useful last night. Both to escape the lavatory and to have zapped a zipper across Tom's guffawing gob.

'Sounds too good to be true! Are you sure he's not married, or gay, or just has appallingly bad eyesight?'

Meryl swatted at her young assistant with a copy of the local free newspaper. 'Less of your cheek, young lady! He was the perfect gentleman. All holding doors open and pushing in chairs. He said he'd nearly been married once, about twenty years ago, but it didn't work out. And he can't possibly be gay, I'd have spotted the signs right away!'

This from the woman who for years had been adamant

that Graham Norton was straight and only holding out for the right woman to cherish his impish Irish charms.

'So when are you seeing the incredibly manly Miroslaw again?' asked Tabitha. She was now ripping open cardboard boxes of newly delivered merchandise, cursing as yet another fingernail snapped in the process.

'Tomorrow evening. We're going to see the new Meryl Streep movie then have a bite to eat at that nice tapas place. What do you think I should wear? I've got a lovely new little floral dress I picked up at Bab's Boutique the other week. Or should I play it down? Maybe jeans and a fitted top?'

Tabitha eyed her boss carefully. Anything but bloody dungarees, she thought. Also, taking into account Meryl's sizeable bosom, she'd err on the side of caution when it came to anything too fitted. Lest a button popped and took out poor Miroslaw's eye.

'The dress sounds good. Maybe play it down with your nice denim jacket and those cute suede boots? So, when will I get to give him the once-over? If he doesn't pass the Tabitha Five Point Test then I'm afraid it's *'do widzenia'*.'

'Do what? And what is the Tabitha Five Point Test when it's at home?'

Tabitha prided herself on knowing how to say a handful of key phrases in around ten different languages. Not that *'donde esta el bano'* (where is the bathroom in Spanish) had served her particularly well since she'd never been to Spain. Still, one never knew when these little nuggets of knowledge might come in handy.

'It means 'goodbye' in Polish. The Tabitha Five Point Test is just something I came up with after dating a couple of real duds a few years ago. It's pretty simple. If they can meet the following criteria then they're worth considering.'

- *Must have good teeth. Preferably their own. Dental hygiene majorly important.*
- *Absolutely no nail biting. Chewed nails and gnawed cuticles are a no-no.*
- *A nice head of hair is good, but will accept partial or full baldness if done with taste. Grey is fine, dodgy dye jobs not.*
- *Should be polite, attentive and have a good sense of humour. An ability to cook would be a bonus but not essential.*
- *Doesn't have to be a genius in bed (although that would be lovely) as long as he knows which bits go where and considers his partner's satisfaction equal to his own.*

She ticked off each item on her fingers, Meryl gaping either in awe at her wisdom or disbelief at her *actually* having a list compiled. Tabitha was pleased to note that Tom generally complied with all the above, although cooking wasn't his strong suit and sometimes his humour was gained at her own expense.

'Gosh, Tabbie. You've got it all worked out, haven't you? Mind you, having met Tom I can see he fits the bill. How is he, anyway? He hasn't dropped in here for a few weeks now.'

Meryl was minutes away from turning the shop sign to 'open'. Tabitha deposited the contents of her final box on the counter, a selection of magnifying reading glasses in funky patterns and prints.

'He's good. Business has been a bit ropey lately but hopefully things will pick up soon. Listen, I was going to invite a couple of people over for dinner next Friday. How about you come too and bring lover boy? I'd love to meet him. Promise I won't give him the Spanish Inquisition. Just want to make sure his intentions are honourable!'

Meryl beamed a smile at the first customer of the day. A

young woman clutching the hand of a toddler and attempting to push a pram at the same time.

'I'll run it by Miroslaw but I'm sure it'll be fine. Just let me know what time and if I can bring anything. And promise me you won't put him on the rack. Even the dish-drying one!'

Tabitha cackled in her best Monty Python impression. 'Nobody expects the Spanish Inquisition! Now let's get this show on the road. Good morning, how can we help you today?'

CHAPTER 3

The next day, to Emily's surprise, she found several chimney sweeps listed in her area. With no clue which one to choose she decided to go for her usual modus operandi, opting for the catchiest name. Up Yours Chimney Services. A bit rude, maybe, but Emily was no prude. And they were members of the European Federation of Chimney Sweeps, which sounded very impressive. Perhaps they all met up once a year in The Hague or Brussels. She imagined a giant table around which sat dozens of men – perhaps women too – comparing brush lengths and discussing the merits of coal versus wood. Maybe having a sing along in Mockney accents. She shook her head. Now she was just being silly.

A few minutes later, having spoken to a charming lady on the phone and arranged a visit for early afternoon, Emily decided to head to the shops. Gathering up her bag and keys, she slung on her fleecy coat – there was a distinct glitter of frost on the driveway – and went into the garage. Her little Mini Cooper awaited her, custard yellow with broad white stripes on the bonnet. She adored her car, even if it was getting on a bit. The last garage bill had been a shocker, but she couldn't bear to trade it in for something newer.

'It's a Hamish,' her friend Kirsty had pronounced when she first clapped eyes on Emily's pride and joy almost ten years before. Kirsty was a slightly mad Scot – but in a good way – with a passion for expensive single malts and a doting husband, Dave, a strapping Aussie ex-rugby player. They'd moved to Oz almost five years ago, and Emily missed her friend terribly, but they chatted regularly on Skype. 'Och Em, I've been fair scunnered this week. Been on that 5:2 diet but havnae shifted a pound. And there's Dave's niece's wedding coming up in two months. I dinnae want to get wedged in a pew!' Despite having left Scotland in her late teens, Kirsty still spoke in the local vernacular. A particular favourite word was 'jobby' which literally meant 'poo' and was used in a variety of situations. Such as, 'That film wis pure jobby.' Or in the context of a joke, which had often left Emily weeping with laughter. 'Three jobbys in a row, which one is the musketeer? The dark tan yin!' So, Hamish it was, a daily reminder of friendship and fun and an absolute joy to tootle around in.

As she pulled into a parking spot, her mobile rang. Celeste's name flashed up on the screen. No doubt checking up on the aftermath of the book club, thought Emily.

'Hi, Celeste. I'm just about to hit the shops so …' She paused as she realised her sister was snivelling down the line, albeit in a rather forced manner.

'Oh Emily, it's simply *awful*! I just heard, that lovely, lovely Tom Jones – no, silly, not the Welsh one that sings and gets pelted with underpants – the butcher on the high street. Made the best Cumberland sausages and his chicken and leek pies were to *die* for! Well, not literally, of course.'

Emily realised she'd parked right outside the butcher's in question. She hadn't been there for weeks but had decided to treat herself after landing a decent commission on a series of young adult books she'd edited. A distinctly unladylike sniff of warthog proportions came down the line, followed by: 'He died!' Emily was unsure how to react. Mr Jones had seemed a perfectly nice man but admiring his bangers and deft ways with flaky pastry hardly warranted such extreme emotion. Still, Celeste was nothing if not overly dramatic.

'I'm sorry, Celeste, that's very sad. How did he die?' Banishing images of the poor man taking a tumble into the mincing machine, she waited for a response.

'Cancer, I'm afraid,' said Celeste, injecting just enough tremor into her voice. 'I think it's quite a rare one. What's it called again? Oh, yes. Now I remember. Cancer of the asparagus.'

* * *

Stepping into the shop, Emily noticed that the staff were all sporting black armbands. And deeply sorrowful expressions as they dismembered some poor beast, the occasional tear threatening as they recalled his prowess with pork chops, his legendary French-trimmed racks of lamb. His son, Alistair, appeared to be at the helm. An unassuming sort with bulging forearms and a tattoo declaring 'meat is the answer' (take that, Morrissey), he looked up as Emily approached the counter. 'Morning, Mrs H. What can I get you today?' Emily looked at her list. A complete blur. She wrestled her reading glasses from her head. Better. 'A pound of your pork sausages with fennel and chilli, please. And two rib-eye steaks.' Blow the cost. At least she could share them with Tom the next time he and Tabitha dropped in. And leave her daughter to her marinated mung beans and other monstrosities. Duly wrapped and paid for, Emily headed next door to the deli. The book club ladies had devoured every last morsel of her truffle-infused Brie, and she fancied some of their totally scrummy sun-dried tomatoes infused with garlic oil for a salad recipe tonight. As she waited to be served, she felt a tap on her shoulder. Susan Wainwright was right behind her, wicker basket slung over the crook of her arm.

'*Such* fun at book club last night! Well, apart from the house nearly burning down, of course.' Slight exaggeration. Although word had no doubt swept through town faster than a Californian wildfire of their near-death experience.

'Glad you enjoyed it, Susan,' Emily replied. 'It's your turn to host it soon, isn't it? I've forgotten the name of the book. What is it? I'll download it later today.'

Susan shifted the weighty basket from one arm to the other, Emily catching a glimpse of a large box of colourful macarons from the patisserie at the far end of the high street. '*Beyond the Blindfold*,' announced Susan, beaming broadly. 'Thought we needed a break from all the heavy stuff. I just read a little snippet about it on Amazon, but it sounds intriguing. All about a middle-aged housewife who meets a much younger man on a package holiday to Greece. All kinds of kinky cavorting to follow!'

Maybe she'd invent a minor ailment that evening. Ingrown toenail surgery or varicose veins stripping. The thought of reading about some menopausal woman getting tied up and spanked by some hunk called Georgios while smeared head to toe in baklava didn't really appeal. Would remind her too much of her own sad single status and unlikelihood of being smeared with anything exciting in the foreseeable future. Unless you counted Nivea body lotion.

Both women having made their purchases – mini samosas and a tub of salmon pate for Susan – they headed outside together. 'Love to chat more, Emily, but I've got an appointment now so better get a wiggle on. See you soon!' With a flutter of her free hand Susan disappeared around the corner. Emily looked at her list again. Just a couple of toiletries from Boots and she was done.

* * *

She was just finishing her lunchtime sandwich and glass of water when the doorbell went. Glancing at her wrist, she was impressed that the chimney sweep was on time. Punctuality was a big deal for Emily. She hated when people turned up to things half an hour or more beyond the appointed hour. With no plausible excuses, like broken down cars or cancelled trains. Just an airy, 'Gosh, just completely lost track. Sorry!' As if every watch, clock and device in their home had been inexplicably sucked into a black hole designed specifically to thwart their chances of being prompt. Placing her empty plate and glass in the dishwasher, she made her way to the door. Opened it, a warm smile of welcome on her face.

'Hi there. Mrs Hardwick? I'm Joe McKenzie. The chimney sweep.' He held out his hand. Emily gaped at it. Long, slightly tanned fingers. Well-groomed fingernails. Not so much as a speck of dust to be seen. She shook his hand, admiring his firm grip. Allowed herself a moment to take in his quite remarkably handsome face. He was smiling back, albeit a little quizzically. Help, she was still holding his hand. 'Come in, come in!' she twittered, feeling a bit like a character from that Harry Enfield sketch when two lecherous old dears scared off the gas man. *'Ooh, young man!'* He followed her into the hallway and through to the living room. 'Here's the fireplace,' she said, pointing to what was – quite obviously – a fireplace. Joe approached it, knelt down on the hearth and – taking a small flashlight from the breast pocket of his light grey overalls – peered upwards. He said nothing, just switched off the flashlight and got to his feet. 'OK, I'm guessing there's some kind of obstruction, but I'll need to get my tools out of the van and take a closer look. Won't be long.' He strode off towards the front door, Emily noting his long, muscular legs and broad shoulders. For goodness sake, woman, she chided herself. Talk of Susan's torrid book choice had filled her head with inappropriately lustful thoughts towards innocent young males. She'd be fantasising about being tickled by feather dusters next.

For the next hour or so Joe worked away at discovering why Emily's fire had temporarily transformed the room into a smoke-filled version of the *Phantom of the Opera's* underground lair. He laid out dust sheets on the carpet, covered his sturdy work boots with plastic protection and produced what looked like a steroid-pumped vacuum cleaner. With the aid of various connecting rods, he inserted a lengthy brush into the chimney, then took himself back outside and onto the roof using an enormous, sectioned ladder. Emily, meanwhile, had nipped upstairs to tidy up her hair and check her make-up. Which she'd have done anyway, she reasoned, even if Joe had looked like her *actual* gas man. Who was very sweet but less babe magnet, more Neanderthal man. Pleasant enough, if you discounted his hairy knuckles and peculiar grunts when dismantling the boiler, but not quite the stuff of erotic daydreams.

'This was the cause of the problem.' Joe proffered a soot-stained canvas like a proud mum showing off her new-born. Except the swaddled bundle was actually a blackened carcass with just a few pathetic feathers still clinging in places. 'Sorry, didn't mean to upset you,' he stuttered as Emily took a step backwards, hand clamped over her mouth. He hurried outside to dispose of the rotten remains, returning within seconds. 'Mind if I wash my hands?' Emily nodded in the direction of the downstairs loo. She heard the tap running then he was back, looking a little embarrassed. 'A pigeon, I reckon. Probably got stuck weeks or even months ago. Happens a lot.' He ran a hand through his raven-black mane – help, she was now totally bird obsessed – and stared at her. Probably because she hadn't uttered a word for several minutes. 'Cup of tea?' she asked, having finally regained the power of speech. 'Great. Milk, two sugars. I'll just pack away my stuff.' Emily nodded again – feeling a bit like one of those stupid dashboard toys. What was *wrong* with her? So, her chimney sweep happened to look like a latter-day matinée idol, all chiselled cheekbones and eyes like molten chocolate? Even in overalls and a smudge of black on his nose, he exuded sex appeal. Stop! You are a fifty-two-year-old widow. He is a twenty-something hunk who wouldn't look twice at someone old enough to be his mother. Cougars, wasn't that what they were called these days? Except Emily felt she was about as predatory as an ancient feline who craved nothing more than a saucer of milk and a good ear scratch.

Emily nursed her own cup of rapidly cooling tea as Joe clattered around next door. She thought about the poor pigeon and its untimely demise. It evoked memories of trips to Belgium with Jim for gastronomic weekends. Usually during the game season when wild boar, hare and pheasant would feature heavily on the menu. He'd relish every morsel, be positively euphoric when he spat out a mouthful of lead shot. She'd enjoyed those trips too. Travelling by car with friends, sharing night caps and nonsensical chatter into the wee small hours. Good times. She felt a little misty-eyed for a moment. There *had* been good times, hadn't there? Life wasn't like the movies, full of happy endings and sex scenes of mind-boggling athleticism. She'd looked up some 'positions' once on the internet many years ago. Just to see if they could inject a bit more spice into their intermittent bedroom activity. Jim had simply looked at her as if she'd suggested a threesome with the local vicar when she'd tentatively proposed a few risqué moves. Probably just as well. Emily had never been renowned for her flexibility or sense of balance. She'd tried a Pilates class at the gym once. Gave up when she kept falling off the Swiss ball.

'Hi. Thanks for the tea.' Joe handed over his drained mug.

'You're welcome,' replied Emily, feeling the beginnings of a flush rising into her cheeks. He really was quite gorgeous. And probably had an equally gorgeous young girlfriend who would have no problem with a Swiss ball. Or bending herself into impossibly complex positions in the bedroom.

'So, is everything fine now?' Clear your mind, Emily. Think clean thoughts. Take a mental brush to your grey matter and give it a good old scrub.

'All good, except I think you need a special guard to make sure this doesn't happen again. I've taken some measurements but I'll need to check back at the office, order the piece. If that's OK with you?' Joe regarded her questioningly.

Am I OK with this vision of absolute loveliness paying me another visit? Brightening up my dull little existence? Is the Pope Catholic?

'Of course! Wonderful! Just let me know when you've got it. Any time. I'm always around.' Great, now she sounded like a right saddo. Sitting around all day crocheting blankets and watching the *Jeremy Kyle Show*.

At the front door, Joe shook her hand again. She managed to let go this time. Gorgeous, punctual and polite too. 'I'll be in touch. Should only be a few days. Nice to meet you, Mrs Hardwick.'

'It's Emily. Please, call me Emily.' He smiled that heart-melting smile. She felt her insides flutter like a just-landed trout. 'Right you are, Emily. See you very soon.' And off he went, clambering into his van with 'Up Yours' emblazoned on the side in jaunty black and gold lettering. She closed the door and leant against it. Feeling ridiculously light-hearted and giddy with a flood of emotions she didn't really want to analyse too deeply.

* * *

Seated in his van, Joe swiped through his iPad agenda, figuring out where his next appointment was. He looked at the details but his mind was a million miles away. No, scrub that, his mind was a matter of steps away, behind a glossy black front door where he'd just carried out a routine job. No different to any other except … for some reason, his newest customer had had a most unexpected effect on him. *Emily*. He said her name out loud, relishing the way it sounded, then gave himself a whack on the head with his iPad. OK, so she'd greeted with the most bewitching smile. Most of his customers smiled at him, apart from the miserable ones who resented having to part with a penny for his services. But none had ever affected him in *this* way. He realised how much he was looking forward to seeing her again. There was just *something* about her. Not just how she looked, although she was undoubtedly attractive. Tousled blonde hair, a pretty heart-shaped face with piercing blue eyes and a very nice figure. This time Joe bounced his head off the steering wheel. Ouch! Since when did he describe women as having 'heart-shaped faces'? He was a chimney sweep, not a frigging *Mills and Boon* author. And she was clearly quite a bit older than him. Maybe fifteen years or so? He'd always been rubbish at guessing people's ages. 'Go on, how old do you think I am?' some female he got chatting to in a bar would ask, giggling coquettishly. Joe usually erred on the side of caution, pitching his estimate much lower than the evidence before him suggested, for fear of having his pint poured over him if he went too far in the other direction.

This wasn't how his day was supposed to pan out. He quickly typed a note to remind him to order the part, checked the address for his next call, and started the engine. With only a fleeting glance behind him he put the van in gear and sped off.

CHAPTER 4

Susan drifted the mile or so back home in a complete daze. Her basket was heavy, her heart even more so. It had started to sleet, but she barely noticed. Didn't pause to tug her hood over her head. Just kept trudging along, one foot in front of the other, oblivious to everyone and everything.

'Watch out, missus!' hollered a teenage lad on a skateboard, weaving his way in and out of the pedestrians. She'd almost walked into him. Muttering an apology, she stepped up her pace. Another five minutes and she'd be there.

In the warmth and dry of her little cottage Susan dumped her groceries on the table. She shrugged off her coat and draped it over a chair. Slumped down and rubbed her hand across her still-damp cheeks. She should have been expecting it. Should have been more mentally prepared. But still the news had sliced through her like a razor-sharp knife. Or a scalpel.

'I'm so sorry, Susan. The biopsy has revealed you have breast cancer. But the good news is we've caught it early. So, it's eminently treatable.' Dr Adlington gazed at her computer screen, pearly-pink manicured fingers tip-tapping away at the keyboard. 'First things first, we're going to book you in for a small operation. As quickly as possible, although I'm afraid with the NHS things don't always move as fast as one would like.' She tapped away again, her pretty little nose scrunched up in deep thought. 'OK. I'll get a letter out to you as soon as I can with the date and time of the surgery.' She looked up and smiled at Susan. Who tried but failed to reciprocate. Her lips felt as if they were made of firmly set concrete.

'Will I need a ... a ... mastectomy?" She could barely speak, her mouth as arid as the desert.

'Let's not get ahead of ourselves, Susan. One thing at a time, eh? You'll need a pretty intense course of radiotherapy to follow up. Please try not to stress too much. I know that's very difficult but it's important to keep positive at times like these.' She stood up, signalling the end of their session. Susan picked up her basket and left, the doctor already preoccupied with the arrival of her next patient.

She'd discovered the lump a month ago. Had never really bothered too much with all the 'examine your breasts regularly' advice. To be honest, Susan wasn't really comfortable with scrutinising her body in great detail. She knew she was overweight. She always had been. A chubby child, a plump teenager, painfully aware of her size alongside her slim and svelte classmates. Never able to dress in the latest fashions. Hiding her flab beneath loose-fitting tops and elasticated-waist trousers. Into adulthood she'd sought refuge in her job and – behind closed doors – the comfort of food. Enormous slabs of cake devoured in one sitting. Mouth-watering pies and mounds of chips demolished as she flicked through the channels on the TV, tray on lap. Sometimes, in her darkest moments, she wished she was an alcoholic instead. A functioning one, who guzzled glass after glass both socially and privately but who could at least present an acceptable face to a harshly judgemental society.

Susan knew that people sniggered at her behind her back. She could feel their eyes appraising her as she forked food into her mouth.

'Doesn't she know when to stop? Doesn't she have any sense of self-esteem?' No, in fact, she didn't. She loathed herself, envied her friends with their trim figures and ability to decline dessert at the end of a meal. She'd tried diets, many different ones, over the years but always the siren's call of food lured her off the path of redemption.

It was her fiftieth birthday in just a few weeks. She hadn't planned a big party, maybe just a few friends round for cake and champagne. Not that she had very many close friends. She could probably count them on the fingers of one hand. Maybe – no, probably – because she came across as a gossip-monger, always at the front of the line when it came to scandal and salacious chitchat. What they didn't realise was that this was her feeble way of feeling connected in a world that seemed callous and indifferent to her inner demons. By being the first to impart knowledge she felt some small sense of power. Ridiculous, she knew, but it instilled in her a feeling of being at the centre of something. When she so often felt side-lined and alone.

Would she have lost all her hair in six weeks time? No, that was with chemotherapy, wasn't it? She really should read up on what lay ahead. Then again, did she really want to know? Maybe she should just forget about celebrating that so-called milestone birthday. Susan was quite sure most people didn't even know her age. Anyway, fat and fifty? Why rejoice in that double-whammy of despair?

She'd often wondered if her life would have been different if she'd met someone. A nice man, who'd treated her with kindness and respect and made her feel loved. She'd had a few boyfriends in her late twenties and early thirties but she always sensed their repulsion at her size. Or did she simply project her own self-hatred on them? Force the decision before they even had a chance to get close that she simply wasn't worth it? There had been one man – Jonathan – who'd almost broken down her barriers. She could picture him still although it was almost twenty years since she had last laid eyes on him.

She'd bumped into him in the local bookstore. Quite literally. Susan had a pile of books stacked in her arms and was conscious that her handbag strap had slipped off her shoulder. As she juggled her weighty cargo and attempted to manoeuvre the strap back into position she collided with someone. Her intended purchases tumbled to the ground, a heavy hardback landing painfully on her big toe.

'Sorry! I'm so sorry. It was totally my fault. I wasn't looking where I was going. Are you all right?'

Aware that her cheeks were burning and her toe was throbbing, Susan looked at the stranger she'd crashed into. Her brain did a quick character assessment. Medium height, cropped brown hair, average build but with a friendly face. Nice eyes, hazel in colour, that were now observing her with concern.

'I'm fine. It's you I'm worried about. Did you hurt yourself?'

Susan realised she was hopping from foot to foot whilst simultaneously trying to gather up the books that lay strewn before her. He beat her to it, arranging them in a neat pile on a nearby shelf. He took her arm and gently steered her towards a chair, indicating she should sit down.

'It's nothing. My toe took a bit of a wallop but I'll survive. I'm sorry again. I really shouldn't be let out on my own!'

This was Susan's attempt to defuse an awkward situation with humour but also a reference to her mother's attitude towards her. She had always managed to make Susan feel like a failure, endlessly comparing her to friends' daughters with their perfect size ten jeans and adoring boyfriends/husbands. Susan had worked hard at university to obtain her accountancy degree but largely dodged the social scene. She'd stayed at home, cloistered away in her bedroom poring over textbooks and sneaking chocolates from her secret stash in her sock drawer. Her mother attempted to feed her healthy meals but her good intentions were undermined by the snide comments that accompanied virtually every mouthful.

'If you'd just chew your food a little longer instead of wolfing it down. There's no need to finish every scrap, you know. Margaret Connolly's daughter lost two stone recently. She looks absolutely amazing. You have quite a pretty face, Susan, shame you can't really see it under all the fat.'

Her mother had died three years ago. A sudden stroke which left her hospitalised for almost two months until she finally slipped away in her sleep. Barely able to speak in her last days, she still managed to convey her disappointment in Susan through pale eyes that always judged and always found wanting. Her father had passed away when Susan was only fifteen. Her memories of him were faded and worn around the edges but he had been warm and supportive, never commenting on Susan's size.

'Need a hand with your homework, love?' he'd inquire after a day at the office. They'd sit together at the kitchen table, cups of tea and rounds of hot buttered toast before them as her mother rinsed salad leaves and chopped cucumber, disapproval evident in the set of her rigid shoulders and tightening of her thin lips.

'You shouldn't be encouraging her to eat garbage,' she'd remonstrate later, as Susan sat at the top of the stairs, knees hugged to her chin. She knew her father would come to tuck her in, kiss her on the tip of her nose and tell her she was beautiful.

'Your mum means well, my love, but you mustn't fret. It's just puppy fat. One day soon you're going to emerge like a butterfly and then I'll be beating off the boys with a big stick!'

Neither things had happened. Susan remained an overfed and overweight chrysalis and her devoted dad had died of a heart attack before she'd even had her first, tentative kiss.

* * *

Back to that day all those years ago. Her knight in shining armour, or rather jogging bottoms and a fitted black T-shirt that showed off a decent chest and arms, was now scrutinising her big toe. In a concession to the heat of a half-way decent day in May she'd put on a pair of flip flops. And now wished she hadn't, horribly aware of her plump little feet devoid of manicure and with the injured toe turning pinky purple and swelling alarmingly.

'Did you drive here? OK, I think the best thing is to go pay for your books and I'll give you a lift home. No, please, it's the least I can do.'

He waved away her protests and took her books up to the counter, returning to lend her an arm as she hobbled over to pay. Transaction done, he hoisted up the plastic bag of goodies and helped her outside, gesturing to a dark green Volkswagen Golf parked at the pavement. As he took out his key and unlocked the door, he hesitated. Smiled and shook his head.

'Here's me about to drive you home and we haven't even introduced ourselves. I'm Jonathan, I work as a chartered surveyor at the local council, I normally cycle everywhere but my bike had a flat and I needed to pick up some shopping anyway. I'm not an axe murderer, I'm not married and I can't bear to see a damsel in distress. Oh, and I love reading, hence the visit to the bookshop. Your turn!'

Susan felt completely tongue tied. She simply wasn't well versed in the art of small talk. Since starting her own home-based business a few months ago her social interaction was limited to talking to clients on the phone or brief exchanges with shop staff when she was stocking up for the week. It pained her to admit it but her longest chats recently had been with the proprietor of the artisan patisserie in the next town.

'My name is Susan. Erm … I live alone and run my own business. Keeping accounts for small companies, that kind of thing.'

And I'm enormously fat and hideously lonely and I know you're just being nice. But I'll take that for now. Besides, my toe hurts like hell and refusing a lift would be churlish. None of which she said aloud.

Jonathan proved to be every inch the proper gentleman, driving her home and making sure she wrapped a bag of frozen peas around her tender toe. He unloaded her books, lining them up neatly on a shelf on her bookcase. Boiled the kettle and made them both a cup of coffee. Stayed for over an hour, chatting about this and that and urging her to call him if the swelling got worse.

'I'm pretty sure it's not broken but I'll happily take you to A & E tomorrow if you're at all worried. Here's my number.' He scribbled it down on a scrap of paper. Susan gazed at it in awe. When was the last time a man had given her his phone number? Probably not since she was about eighteen and the fellow in question had obviously made it up as she'd never been able to reach him.

In the end she didn't have to call him. He'd dropped by the next day, bearing a small but exquisite bunch of flowers. He'd insisted on examining her toe which, by then, was mottled but clearly on the mend. Then he'd suggested they went out for a meal which they did. To a little Italian restaurant where they shared bruschetta and platefuls of carbonara, Susan attempting to nibble rather than gobble it down as if her life depended on it. She was so used to eating alone and giving little thought to the actual process that it was a genuine surprise to dine with someone. To actually punctuate mouthfuls with conversation and even align her cutlery on the plate when some remnants of food remained.

To her even greater surprise, Jonathan asked if he could see her again. She agreed, trying not to show the sheer joy coupled with disbelief that his request created inside her.

'How about you come round to my place? I've got a pretty amazing video collection and I can make us something to eat. Steak and salad? Or I do a very nice chicken curry.'

And so it began. A night of movie watching and a delicious home-made chicken tikka masala lead to their first, hesitant kiss. Susan was petrified as Jonathan moved closer on his squishy two-seater sofa. She hadn't kissed anyone in almost a decade and wished she had a) swotted up on technique and b) didn't stink of garlic and spices. As his arms closed around her she wished for the millionth time that she wasn't all flab and jiggly bits. Breathing in didn't help one iota. It just made her feel a little dizzy although that could also have been a reaction to his lips tentatively touching hers. As the pressure increased, Susan felt something she hadn't felt in a very long time. The awakening of her long-dormant libido and something else. The faintest fluttering of butterfly wings that signalled her long-buried self confidence was kicking off the mud and making a bid for freedom. As Jonathan took her by the hand and led her upstairs she raised her eyes to the heavens, blinking away a few unexpected tears.

'Thanks, dad. Maybe I've finally got my wings.'

It had been lovely in the beginning. Jonathan was kind, attentive and thoughtful. He never complained when she locked herself away for hours on end dealing with difficult clients and juggling tricky numbers. He'd roll up on his bike, plonk his helmet on the coat rack by the front door and squeeze her tight.

'How was your day?' he'd ask, smoothing his thumbs over her scrunched up brows. They'd make their way to the kitchen, pausing for a prolonged kiss or two. Susan tried so hard on the dietary front, conjuring up healthy but satisfying meals she found in the many cookbooks she'd accumulated over the years. Not that Jonathan ever criticised her size. Not once. When she tried to raise the subject herself he silenced her with a lip caress that rendered her speechless.

'Susan. Please, don't. I love you just the way you are. If it would make you happy to lose weight then I'd support you one hundred percent. You know that. But what I see is a beautiful and smart woman who makes me feel great and I don't calculate your worth to me in pounds and ounces. I think we're good together. Don't you?'

Susan had nodded numbly, still unable to speak. Unable to fathom why this lovely man would choose her over all the slim and trim women he could have. Still shamed beyond belief that she retained an illicit stash of chocolate in her handbag. And delved into it when she faced herself in the mirror and loathed what she saw reflected back at her. Fat and unworthy. He said he loved her, but what use was that when she could barely stand the sight of herself?

Six months into their relationship and Susan woke up with a start. She'd had a vivid dream – nightmare – of being confined to a wheelchair. Obese to the point that she could no longer walk unaided. Behind her had been a grim-faced Jonathan, pushing away, the effort ingrained in his twisted features. Drenched in sweat, she rolled over to where he slept, oblivious to her angst. Sweet features arranged in blissful repose.

'Jonathan. *Jonathan*!'

She'd nudged him awake, confusion contorting his face as he rubbed at sleepy eyes. He'd gazed at her for an explanation as to why she was rousing him a good two hours ahead of the alarm call.

'I'm sorry. God, I'm just so sorry. It's just ... I can't do this anymore. I can't be with you. It doesn't feel right anymore. It's not you, it's me.'

Susan had cringed at her wording, so trite and cruel for a man who had tried so hard to make her happy. Make them both happy. What was the song again? If you love someone, set them free. That was what she was doing, she persuaded herself. Almost.

'I don't understand. Susan, please talk to me. I can change. If there's something about me that pisses you off, then tell me! I really thought we had something. Tell me what I need to do.'

She'd looked at his broken, uncomprehending face and wished with all her heart she could take it back. Make it right. But Susan knew she had to let him go.

'Jonathan, you're lovely. You've been such an amazing part of my life. But it's over. I just don't see us going any further. I'm sorry. Truly, I am.'

He'd left, gathering his pathetic detritus of belongings – razor, deodorant, a few pairs of underpants – and pedalled off. Susan stood at the front door and began to sob. Her sobs continued for several hours.

* * *

SHAKING herself out of her reverie, Susan gazed out of the window. It was getting darker outside, the earlier sleet turning to flakes of snow. She got slowly to her feet and began emptying her basket. She lifted out the box of macarons with its cellophane window. Pink ones, green ones, yellow ones. An abundance of sugary heaven. Raising a fist, she brought it down hard on the box, feeling them crumble and disintegrate beneath the force of her blow. Then, the tears began to fall.

CHAPTER 5

In the end it had taken three days for Emily's part to arrive. Three long days during which Joe tried – and failed – to push her from his mind. It was boxed up in the back of his van. He'd rung her an hour ago to fix a time to drop by. She'd answered quickly and assured him she would be home all afternoon. In the meantime he had a few calls to make. First on the list was a couple of miles away in the Holsworth estate. They were regulars, devoted to their log-burning fire in the winter months. And not averse to sparking it up in spring or even summer if the good old British weather proved as unreliable as ever. Joyce and William Meadows believed in a clean chimney as much as they believed in an afterlife. Which had led to some interesting conversations over the years.

'So Joe, when you come back to this spiritual plane, having shed your existing form, what do you imagine your reborn life as?' Joyce had smiled at him quizzically one memorable day, plonking a cup of tea in front of him. Joe had massaged his head, partly because he had no bloody clue how to respond and also because a lump of blackened gunge had smacked into his cranium on an earlier job.

'Erm, not sure really. Maybe as a goldfish? Just swimming around in a bowl all day. Not much to worry about. Just a sprinkling of fish food. Easy to please.' He really didn't know how to answer. At thirty-one Joe liked to think the afterlife was a long way away. Like prostate problems and false teeth. He was still young, and thoughts of death rarely crossed his mind. OK, that wasn't *entirely* true. He'd seen death up close but thoughts of his own mortality rarely troubled him.

'Oh no, absolutely not!' William had countered. 'I see you as a leader of men. You have great presence, charisma, charm. A bit like the Dalai Lama. Maybe not quite as influential, but still ... enigmatic.' He'd stared at Joe, something slightly unsettling spreading across his ruddy cheeks.

Joe was mightily relieved when he climbed back into his van after *that* visit. William had kept staring at him as if he expected him to reveal the meaning of life, instead of sweeping their chimney. No saffron robes or tinkling bells for him. He didn't feel remotely enigmatic. More like vaguely knackered.

Just two more calls, a quick break for a sandwich, and he'd head to Emily's. It wasn't a particularly busy day and he'd already cancelled plans to meet someone for drinks in the evening. A twenty-something called Abigail whom he'd met at a party a couple of weeks ago. Nice enough if you were into eyebrows that looked like inked-in colons and conversations revolving around reality TV shows, but not really his type.

He hadn't done serious for a long time. Quite content to bounce from woman to woman, no undying love declared, no promise of commitment. They went along with that – for the most part – no one expecting too much once the cards were laid out on the table.

His last relationship, with Caitlin, had set his thoughts off in a different direction. She was undoubtedly stunning, with a gleaming auburn bob and a body that had men's heads swivelling in true Exorcist fashion. She was good fun, sharp-witted and a devil in the bedroom. They'd bonded over a mutual love of *When Harry Met Sally* at a friend's birthday party. Fuelled up by a glass or three of home-made punch. Or rocket fuel. They'd tumbled into bed that very same night.

'Best scene in a movie *ever*. The fake orgasm. So convincing. Don't you agree, Joe?' He'd agreed, eager to please, eager to take things to the next level. And absolutely sure that her gasps and groans were one hundred percent genuine.

Caitlin managed a high-class beauty boutique selling must-have lotions and potions at prices that would secure a small property up north.

'£150 for a face cream? You have to be frigging joking!' Joe had only dropped in a couple of times but he was totally gob-smacked at what people would pay in the quest for eternal youth. De Luxe catered for an elite clientele hell-bent on giving the two fingers to Mother Nature and her wrinkles and crows' feet. How his mother would have laughed, lobbing her supermarket own-brand creams and serums into her trolley, alongside the weekly groceries. She'd looked amazing, until the cancer got its grip and her skin took on a yellowed hue, cheekbones slicing through hollowed flesh. It had been five years since she'd died, but Joe felt her loss keenly each and every day. He still talked to her in his head, imagined her chortling over his reincarnation as the Spiritual leader of the Tibetan people. 'Oh, Joe, you're more likely to come back as a mangy alley cat, the number of women you've got through!'

Oh shit. He was getting a bit teary, as he often did when he thought of his mum. He wondered what she would have made of Caitlin. If the two women would have got along, or if his mum would have considered her too showy, too high-maintenance. He suspected the latter. Not that it mattered now anyway.

They'd been together for almost a year, Joe smitten in a way he'd never thought possible. He'd even found himself, on quite a few occasions, wondering if he really had found The One. The problem was, as Joe allowed himself to daydream about the perfect engagement ring and a simple but sensational wedding on a sun-kissed beach, Caitlin had other ideas.

'I'm so sorry, Joe, but I've met someone else. I guess I should have told you before but … ' Joe, still in a sex-glazed euphoric state, looked at his partner. And thought, yes, perhaps it would have been better when fully dressed rather than post-coital and gleaming in after-glow sweat. It turned out she'd been seeing a chap called Arthur who owned a chain of fitness centres in the area. And was a regular customer at De Luxe. Joe refrained from asking what his cream of preference was and why she'd waited until now to enlighten him. It was only after she'd wiped away a tiny tear, slithered into her slinky undies and slunk out the door that he wondered if had all been completely fake after all.

Right. Enough wallowing in the past. Joe gave himself the mental equivalent of a duvet shake. Get rid of the lumps, bumps and creases and get on with the day. He'd stop at the bakery in town, grab a tuna baguette and Diet Coke, then head to Emily's. That thought alone coaxed a smile on to his previously frown-filled face.

* * *

EMILY WAS TWITCHY. She'd spent the morning working on editing short stories for the magazines she had on her limited roster of freelance jobs. Some had been relatively easy but dull. A bit of cropping here, a grammatical correction there. She'd enjoyed a tale involving a dead husband who'd come back to haunt his cookie-baking wife and her weed-whacking lover. Boy, could that guy lick a garden into shape, and make a woman feel the need to produce a trayful of something hot and sweet. Like chocolate brownies. Which she'd just happened to rustle up this morning. To go along with the tea which she'd offer Joe. As a politeness, no less. OK, she was morphing into a character from *Gone With the Wind*. Scarlett O'Hara. Get a grip, woman!

Just time for a quick scroll through the *Daily Mail*. The usual antics of various reality TV show celebs Emily had never heard of and couldn't care less about. Ooh, here was an interesting story.

'Two complainants have failed in their attempt to get Germany's constitutional court to reconsider the laws banning sex with animals.' *What?!* Emily read on, goggling in disbelief.

'The two unnamed individuals say they are sexually attracted to animals.' Truth is indeed much stranger than fiction, she thought. What kind of a person would look at a pig … or a goat … or a donkey and think – I fancy getting jiggy with you? Not that it mentioned anywhere exactly what type of animal these total weirdos found irresistible. Maybe they preferred domestic pets, a cat or a dog. Oh great, sighed Emily. I'll never be able to listen to Donny Osmond's 'Puppy Love' in quite the same way again. Not that she listened to a lot of Osmond music. Although she'd had a bit of a childhood crush on the toothsome one, even used her pocket money to join his fan club.

Joe was due to arrive in less than half an hour. Emily's heartbeat quickened at the thought. You silly, silly woman, she reprimanded herself. Perhaps she should take a cold shower. Answer the door in her most ancient, unflattering pyjamas with hair standing on end and completely bare-faced. That would have the poor boy scarpering the second he'd finished the job. Not that he was likely to hang around anyway. He no doubt had a long list of calls to make and hanging out with a woman old enough to be his mother probably didn't figure highly on his afternoon agenda. Although, maybe he was older than he looked. She'd just happened to be browsing an article on Facebook yesterday featuring a roll call of women either dating or married to much younger men. Catherine Zeta-Jones and Michael Douglas, twenty-five years' age difference. J Lo and her on/off boyfriend, Jasper or Casper something, an eighteen-year gap. And didn't Kylie Minogue get engaged to someone almost twenty years her junior? So, it wasn't outside the realms of possibility. Even if they were all impossibly glamorous stars and Emily was just a boring old housewife unlikely to be waltzing down a red carpet any day soon. Still, there was no harm in checking that she didn't look too frightening. Maybe a dab of lipgloss and a hint of mascara. Nothing wrong with that, was there?

When the doorbell chimed, a few minutes ahead of schedule, Emily was ready. The kettle had just boiled – in case he needed some refreshment. The brownies were baked – in case he was feeling a little peckish. And Emily had her second-best set of matching underwear on. In case ... what? He felt the overwhelming need to down tools and bend her over backwards for a few hours of afternoon ecstasy? Unlikely. But the very thought heated up her cheeks.

'Hi. How are you? Sorry if I'm a bit early.' Joe gave another of his knee-trembling smiles that seemed to light him up from within and gave Emily the sensation of curling her toes around a just-filled hot water bottle.

'Not a problem. Come on through, or do you need to

work outside first?' She hesitated. Should she offer him tea and brownies first, or would that seem rather forward? Joe, fortunately, took the lead. 'I'll just get my ladder out, should only take me a few minutes to fit the guard. I'll come back in when I'm all done.' And off he went, striding back to his van like the hero in a Western, all swagger and sex appeal. If he'd had a gleaming black stallion waiting instead of a slightly beaten up Transit Emily's head might have combusted with lustful thoughts. As it was, she felt all a-flutter, butterflies whirling and diving in her stomach. She hadn't felt this giddy – now she was all *Gone With the Wind* again – since who knows when. In fact, she couldn't actually recall ever feeling this way in her entire life. Which either suggested her life had been woefully lacking until now or that she was in danger of losing the plot completely. Neither of which could be described as best-case scenarios.

When Joe reappeared, a little grubby round the edges but still ridiculously attractive, he headed immediately to the loo for a quick clean up. By which point Emily had re-boiled the kettle, made a pot of tea and was leaning back in a pseudo nonchalant fashion against the worktop. 'Thought you might like a cuppa. And I made some brownies earlier. If you fancy one?' *Or me, said the devilish little voice in her head.* He nodded enthusiastically, pulling up a chair and placing a brownie on the side plate Emily had thoughtfully positioned next to his mug. She poured his tea, proffered the sugar bowl and milk jug. Lifted a brownie on to her own plate and took a delicate bite.

'So, Joe. Are you married?' Well done, Emily. Talk about going in for the kill. Why not just hand him a bloody questionnaire and be done with it? Memo to self, engage brain before opening mouth. Joe, to his credit, didn't seem overly taken aback at her directness. 'Nope. Not married. Not seeing anyone at the moment. And you? I mean – sorry – I'm guessing you're married but I couldn't help wondering, noticing . . .' His voice tailed off, embarrassment obvious as he fiddled with his spoon and took another mouthful of cake. Emily hesitated. She felt they were venturing into uncharted territory where each revelation could alter the dynamics of their relationship. Not that they *had* a relationship. But she'd certainly never shared anything remotely personal with the gas man. And he hadn't been offered as much as a plain digestive or glass or tap water.

'I was. Married, I mean. He died four years ago. It's fine. I mean, it's not fine but you just get on with it.' Emily raised her eyes, saw the predictable sympathy in Joe's expression. And something else. Something that looked a bit like – anticipation? A tiny glimmer of interest? Or was she simply reading far too much into what amounted to a young man being friendly and sociable?

'I'm sorry. That's tough. I can't imagine ... well, I can, in a way. My mum died five years ago and I miss her every single day. I'm sure you feel the same way about ...' The question hovered in the air, as choking as the fumes that had billowed through her living room just days before.

'Jim. His name was Jim. Yes, I miss him. Of course. But life goes on. I keep busy.' She fingered her necklace, smoothed down a stray strand of hair that had come loose from her scrunched-up topknot. She gazed at him over the rim of her mug. He shifted in his seat, took another brownie, eyebrows raised as if to query the wisdom of having another. She nodded and smiled as he took a bite then leaned back, chewing thoughtfully.

'I couldn't help noticing, in your bathroom, the tap's dripping a bit. Probably just needs the washer changing. I don't have the right stuff on me now, but I could easily fix it for you. If you like. I'm not too busy tomorrow morning so I could drop by. No charge. Be glad to do it.' His words came out in a rush.

'But that's a plumber's job!' Emily had known for weeks now that the tap was a nuisance but had pushed it to the bottom of the pile of jobs that needed doing. Like her taxes and shaving her legs. Suddenly the latter seemed much more pressing.

'It's really no problem. I'd like to do it. I'm not too bad at things like that. Small repairs around the house. Got any shelves you need putting up? Or tiles that need laying?' Joe got to his feet and stretched, muscles clearly defined in areas Emily tried very hard not to focus on. She wished he hadn't used the word 'laying'. Too many ulterior interpretations. Or was that just her filthy mind twisting and distorting the most innocent of remarks?

'That's so kind of you. If it's not too much trouble. And I'd pay you, of course!' Emily walked with him to the front door. She wished she could slow down time, rewind a little, not come across as a desperate housewife who needed a crumb of interest thrown her way.

'I'll ring you tomorrow. I can probably swing by mid-morning, if that works for you. It'd be nice to see you, Emily.' He raised his hand in a goodbye gesture and closed the door behind him. Emily leant against it, his parting words rendered her both speechless and convinced she'd fallen asleep and was in the midst of an amazing but improbable dream. Involving both Joe and maybe a few sheep or cows too. Hell, if she was going down, she might as well go out in a blaze of glory. Or a fantasy of epic farmyard proportions.

CHAPTER 6

A long, hot bath. That was what Tabitha craved right now. With a liberal slosh of scented oil drizzled under the running tap. She'd been on her feet all day, dealing with customers in the shop. Most charming and happy to spend several quid on quirky greetings cards or little trinkets for beloved nieces/nephews/grandchildren. And a few not so charming. One old crone – who really should only have been let out at Halloween – had spent almost half an hour slathering the 'try me' samples of organically produced hand creams on her wizened claws. Then complained that the smells were 'quite obnoxious'. As she scuttled off back to her broomstick Tabitha resisted shouting after her that six different fragrances mixed together didn't necessarily make for olfactory heaven. Maybe eye of newt and tongue of bat would have been more up her street. Up yours, Endora.

As she waited for the bath to fill, Tabitha perched on the edge to peel off her undies and – ouch! Something sharp pierced her upper thigh and she leapt up and whirled around to identify the culprit. Oh joy. Tom had obviously been tending to his tootsies again. A neatly arranged montage of toenail clippings lined virtually the full length of the tub. Grabbing a wad of toilet paper, an exasperated Tabitha scooped them up and tossed them in the bin. Tom, not known for being particularly artistic, could rival Tracey Emin when it came to displaying the most unsavoury objects. Even his beard trimmings seemed to form impressionistic patterns in the wash hand basin. Clearly incapable of rinsing them away, he would look at her with wounded innocence when she railed against his revolting habits.

'Lighten up, Tabitha. It's only a bit of chin fluff. At least I put the toilet seat down – well, most of the time.' This was true, but today was miraculous insofar as there was actually a roll of toilet paper to hand. Correctly positioned on the holder. Usually it was lying dejectedly on the floor or conspicuous by its total absence. It reminded Tabitha of the old joke, 'How many men does it take to change a loo roll? No one knows, it's never been done.'

Ah, bliss. Total peace and tranquility. Not much couldn't be put to rights by a proper soak. Showers were all well and good when you were time pressed but you couldn't beat a bath. Just a drop more from the hot tap. Perfect. As she lay back, hair slathered in a deep-moisturising treatment covered with a plastic shower cap pinched from a hotel, she sighed. Her life was good, but was it good enough? Career going according to plan? Not really. Love life on track to happy ever afters? Jury definitely out on that one. And she worried about her mum. Only in her early fifties and already resigned to being alone with nothing but her Kindle and rewriting trashy 'true life' tat for bored housewives to keep her afloat.

Tabitha determinedly fired off her CV on a weekly basis to various companies in the hope of securing something more in keeping with her youthful aspirations. The outright rejections were hard to take, the 'no replies' even more soul-destroying. For now, she'd keep on beaming broadly at Meryl's motley clientele and pray that Endora wasn't part of a larger coven.

She'd been with Tom for almost eighteen months now. Had actually met him in the shop. He'd dropped in to buy something for his sister's birthday.

'What do you buy the girl who has everything? Nothing!' he'd chortled, his hazel eyes twinkling across the counter. Tabitha had taken in his broad shoulders, nicely fitted jeans that emphasised a bottom worthy of serious ogling and been fairly smitten on the spot. She'd sent him off with a beautifully gift-wrapped silk scarf in shades of turquoise and lilac, her phone number attached on a yellow Post-It note. He'd rang that evening.

They'd dated, she laughing uproariously at his filthy jokes, he bolstering her fragile ego and assuring her that one day soon she'd be the darling of events featured in gossip columns. In the bedroom, he was both boisterous and tender, trailing butterfly kisses the length of her body, then wrapping her in his solid arms until she drifted off. He'd moved in with her after six months, his landlord having announced he was putting the flat up for sale. Tom didn't earn a fortune but he contributed to the rent and even did the odd repair job. OK, changing a lightbulb or replacing a washer wasn't *quite* in the Grand Designs league but his heart was in the right place. As were his other essential organs.

So, what was missing? What did Tabitha want out of a relationship? It wasn't his unhygienic habits that were a deal breaker. Since her recent health kick, featuring a hearty intake of beans and pulses, she'd developed her own distinctly unattractive side. A propensity to wind measuring high on the Beaufort Scale.

'Duvet hovering again?' quipped Tom the other night after a high-octane meal of Puy lentils and chickpeas in a spicy sauce. He'd sauntered off into the bathroom, singing loudly about magic carpet rides.

What she absolutely *didn't* want was to end up like her parents. She missed her dad but knew her mum didn't. Well, she *did*, but more in a practical way. Not in a *heartbroken, my life has ended, there'll never be anyone else* way. Since she was old enough to notice, Tabitha had observed how they'd exchanged polite conversation, with very little physical contact. Hugs galore for her from them both. Hugs between them reserved for special occasions, even then minimum body contact. Separate bedrooms. Separate interests. Separate lives. Jim never happier than when signing for a case of carefully selected wines from his vintner club or clearing up leaves in the driveway, blower strapped to his back like a horticultural version of Bill Murray in *Ghostbusters*. But not as witty.

Feeling less relaxed than she'd hoped, Tabitha eased herself out of the bath. Grabbing a towel from the rail and a smaller one to wrap round her head she wandered into the bedroom. A quick, upside down blast of her hair, a liberal coating of body lotion and she was almost ready. Trackie bottoms and a baggy T-shirt would suffice as she wasn't venturing further than the kitchen or living room this evening. And Tom never complained if she looked less than immaculately groomed. There, a big plus point in his favour. She had a couple of girlfriends with partners who visibly recoiled in horror if they emerged with less than a full face of make-up and salon-perfect locks. As neither were contenders for Adonis of the Year themselves, she reckoned they should have been kicked into touch a long time ago.

Tom was due home in less than an hour, and Tabitha had a treat in store. Well, she *hoped* it would be a treat. A self-confessed gadget junkie, she had accumulated all manner of gizmos both for self-titivation and culinary improvement. Appliances to rip the hair out of your legs, buff your face like a miniature sand blaster, wobble your midriff into a semblance of a six-pack. While eating pizza and doing the ironing. Her latest purchase was an addition to the kitchen collection. A spiraliser. She'd first read about it on the website ScrumptiouslySophia which featured an unfeasibly gorgeous young woman doing amazing spirally things with all manner of vegetables. Which replaced your need for horribly fat-producing pasta. Her recipes featured such ingredients as chia seeds, organic coconut oil and nutritional yeast. How that differed from ordinary yeast Tabitha didn't have the foggiest, but courgetti sounded good. Just like pasta but without all those evil carbohydrates. You just shoved the courgettes in the machine, twirled the handle a few times and – voila! Twisty, spirally bits of green vegetable. After sautéing them for a few minutes, she would mix them with a sauce packed with mushrooms, various seeds and lots of spinach. Yum.

Sitting at the table, Tom stirred his courgetti around. Then stirred it around again. He scooped up a little on his fork then put it back down again. 'Tabitha, what on earth is this?' His face bore the pained expression of a man expecting a T-bone steak and being served earthworms coated in dung instead. Which, come to think of it, wasn't too far off the appearance of tonight's dinner. Tabitha glowered at him, hoping he hadn't quite noticed her own lack of enthusiasm at the plateful before her.

'It's healthy!' she retorted.

'It tastes like crap', replied Buckinghamshire's answer to A A Gill.

'Fine, don't eat it then.' She snatched away his plate and scraped its contents into the bin with savage ferocity.

'I'm starving. Didn't have time to stop for lunch today. Think I'll head out to The Right Plaice, get a nice cod and chips to take away. Want one?' Picking up his keys he headed for the front door. 'No, thank you, I'm trying to eat more healthily, in case you hadn't noticed,' sniffed Tabitha. She waited until she'd heard his car drive off before dumping her own plateful. And reaching into the biscuit barrel for a fistful of chocolate digestives.

* * *

'So is it me or is he just an ungrateful git?' Tabitha had devoured all the biscuits and rung her friend Fiona. They hadn't seen each other for a little while but – as good friends always do – they picked up the pieces and offered advice when asked for. Sometimes when not asked for. Which was definitely the sign of a solid friendship. Unsolicited counselling could be the undoing of a seemingly strong bond.

'Calm down, girlfriend. He hated your spirally shit. Which, incidentally, *sounds* like shit. Hardly grounds for changing the locks, is it? Just feed him carb-loaded crap washed down with beer and he'll worship you forever. Simples!'

Tabitha thought the world of Fiona but felt indescribably depressed at the scenario she'd presented. How to keep your man. Fill him with pasta/pizza and gallons of ale and all would be hunky dory? The way to a man's heart was apparently through his stomach but she was aiming a little higher. If she connected with someone on a more *intellectual* level then they could compromise on the food front. On many fronts. Not that she claimed to be an intellectual herself – flashback to the toilet episode – she just wondered if the spark of attraction that had brought her and Tom together was slowly being doused by the mundanities of life. She was almost thirty and visions of the two of them settling down and starting a family seemed increasingly as likely as her winning the National Lottery. Or even landing the job of her dreams.

'You still there, Tabitha?' She realised Fiona had been rabbiting away while her mind had wandered off to darker places. And there was still no sign of Tom and his cod and chips. No doubt he'd bumped into one of his mates and was probably chugging back a pint or two at the local pub. Damn, and she'd be hoping to sneak in a chip or two when he wasn't looking.

'Sorry, Fiona. What were you saying?'

Brought quickly up to speed on the latest goings on in Fiona's life – still totally loved up with her boyfriend, Pete, and in line for a promotion at work – Tabitha agreed a girls' night out was overdue.

'I can do Saturday but not Friday, I'm afraid. I've invited Meryl and her new man over for dinner, plus another couple. Hey, why don't you and Pete come too?' As Tabitha only had six dining chairs she had a momentary panic as to how she'd seat any more people. Luckily, Fiona said she already had plans for Friday but was free Saturday.

'I'll buzz Derwyn too, shall I?' she asked. 'It's been ages since the three of us went out together. It'll be great!'

Tabitha felt a pang of guilt. Pre-Tom she'd seen her friends on a regular basis, but their meetings had dwindled as she'd embraced coupledom with a vengeance. Now that the gloss was wearing off she regretted her withdrawal from the social scene. A night out could be just what the doctor ordered.

Plans made, they said their goodbyes and Tabitha – still ravenous – made herself a cheese sandwich. Surprise, surprise, a message had pinged on her phone from Tom, saying he was just having a quick drink with Clive who'd been picking up a battered saveloy with a side of onion rings. Why he felt the need to share Clive's menu choices was anyone's guess. Probably as retaliation for her serving him something that wouldn't clog his arteries. Bugger, she could *murder* a plate of onion rings right now. And Tom too.

CHAPTER 7

Celeste was cleaning out her cupboards. Once a year or thereabouts she liked to have a good old purge – out with the old, in with the new. Or something like that. Tatty old pots and pans, beyond salvaging with a Brillo pad; ageing towels which had lost their fluffiness, magazines she'd kept for some delicious recipe or scoop on the latest must-have rejuvenating cream but now couldn't be bothered flicking through to find them, and – her favourite – clothes. She found it incredibly therapeutic to fill bin bags with blouses, skirts, dresses and so on that had lost their appeal. The lady at the local charity shop always looked ready to explode with joy when Celeste staggered in with her armfuls of booty. Chiefly because Celeste only wore high-end fashion. Maybe not quite Dior or Balmain but certainly a million high street miles from most of the threadbare junk that landed on the shop doorstep. Literally abandoned overnight like an unwanted puppy, usually unwashed and with more holes than a leaky sieve.

'Sorry, my darlings, but you just don't do me justice anymore, do you?' she murmured apologetically to a pair of fine wool trousers in a pale dove grey. In truth, she couldn't quite do up the button anymore but Celeste wasn't about to let that stark little reality rain on her parade. So, she'd gained a few pounds? Better that than to be rail thin, all jutting bones and turkey necks. She prided herself on her curves. Michael always said he liked a bit of meat on her, couldn't be doing with those scrawny creatures with no arses and shoving lettuce leaves around their plates, whilst drooling over their dining companion's coq au vin and butter-laden mash.

She really was so lucky to have Michael, she thought, shoving a purple chiffon blouse into a bag. He never complained when she returned from a shopping spree, laden with expensive-looking purchases. 'Got some nice things, sweetheart?' he'd ask, peering at her over his glasses from the comfort of his Eames lounge chair. He'd retired a few years ago, well set-up after a lifetime with a private bank dealing with clients who wouldn't be seen dead in anything less than 'hot couture'. And he demanded so little, quite content to potter around at home, playing the stock market when the mood took him, always happy to drop her off and pick her up when a few sherries were on the cards.

Celeste had never really worked, at least not since her early twenties. She wasn't a natural at school, academically or on the sports field. Science and mathematics bored her rigid, English was OK but she knew she had a tendency to get words mixed up. 'My mum reckons I'm – what do you call it – anorexic?' she'd confided in Michael on one of their early dates. To his credit, he'd never laughed or mocked her. Just smiled indulgently and pulled her in for one of his life-affirming hugs.

Children weren't something she had ever wanted. She simply didn't feel the maternal type and Michael, luckily, was happy to concur. He had been married briefly once before.

His ex-wife was called Margaret but beyond that Celeste knew very little. Nor did she want to know. She considered it the past and firmly believed in living in the present. The only other thing she knew was that they had a daughter, Sophie, who now lived in Scotland and had two little ones of her own. Relationships were strained between father and daughter, the odd birthday or Christmas card sent or received. As far as she was aware they didn't speak on the telephone or communicate by email. She hadn't exactly demanded it when they met, or had she? She couldn't really recall. Whatever. By all accounts his ex was a total bitch and had done her utmost to cut Michael out of his daughter's life. This suited Celeste just fine. She didn't want to share Michael, selfish though that may be. She was happy with her life, happy with her husband, and anything else might cloud the picture. She got up every day, primped and readied herself and marvelled at the fact that she lived in a beautiful home with a husband who adored her and a lifestyle that made her the envy of many of her friends.

Although she had never had a career, Celeste considered herself the rock to which Michael anchored himself. She had supported him unquestioningly and resolutely throughout his working life. Always immaculately presented, with a home that glittered and gleamed as a beacon to their success and unity. Dinner parties were hosted, guests treated to lavish, multi-course meals. She'd listen enraptured to an important colleague's mind-numbing chatter, always with the perfect hostess smile on her perfectly painted face. She kept the yawns and face-pulling until bedtime, when Michael would laugh at her spot-on impressions and congratulate her on another outstanding evening.

Her only little secret – if you could call it that – was a hobby she'd taken up a few months ago. Out of sheer boredom, if she was completely honest with herself. Michael had

had his years of slogging away in the banking world, so could be forgiven for taking pleasure in doing very little, or nothing at all. Celeste was proud of what she'd achieved as a wife and home builder but nagging away at her over the past couple of years had been two small words. *So what?* She didn't have degrees or certificates or accolades from City high flyers. She'd never been quoted in *The Financial Times* (or even the local rag, come to think of it). She imagined her gravestone – sleek, polished marble – engraved with the words, 'Here lies Celeste Atherton. Wife ...'

Michael had tried to cajole her out of her dark thoughts when she voiced them. Which wasn't often.

'Sweetheart, if I'd wanted a ferocious lawyer for a wife I'd have gone looking for one. Then I'd never have seen her anyway and we'd have ended up divorced! And if that was her specialist field I'd have lost everything. I chose you. And I love you, just how you are.' He'd plant a kiss on her forehead then retreat to the sanctuary of his study.

She'd been flicking through a few tired-looking magazines at the hairdresser. Not her usual fare but getting her extensions redone was a long and tedious process. One in particular – *Tea Break* – had kept her reasonably engrossed as her stylist Steph clipped and sizzled her human hair add-ons into position. She'd just finished reading a piece on a woman who professed to still love her husband despite his fondness for dressing up as a baby – a twenty-two stone bearded one – when another article caught her eye. 'Ladies, do you have a steamy novel just bursting to get out? A passion for romance with just a hint of naughtiness thrown in? We're looking for new and previously unpublished manuscripts for our competition. The winner will receive £5,000 and have their story appear in instalments right here in your favourite weekly read!' Glancing around and realising that Steph had nipped off – probably for her nicotine fix – Celeste swiftly tore out the page and shoved it into her handbag. She spent a flipping fortune in here restoring what Mother Nature had decided to deprive her of. One poxy page of a tatty magazine hardly amounted to grand arceny.

* * *

'CELESTE? Just heading out for a walk. Probably be a couple of hours. Thought I'd try and up the ante a bit.' Michael peered around the bedroom door, already wearing his quilted jacket and sturdy shoes. 'No problem,' replied Celeste, tying a knot in bag number three. 'Enjoy, darling. See you later.' Ever since she'd bought him a fitness tracker for his birthday Michael had been obsessed with getting in his recommended 10,000 steps a day. Often this involved nothing more than a stroll to the shops and several circuits of the house – she swore he was wearing holes in the carpets – but more recently he'd taken to going on proper walks. Sometimes for hours on end.

So, she had an hour or two to get on with her project. That's how she liked to think of it, an assignment she'd set herself, with a fixed deadline. Only one week to go. The clock was ticking but Celeste was quietly confident she'd make it. And inwardly bubbling over with excitement at the thought of maybe – just maybe – seeing her work in print. With her name attached! Then she'd be somebody. And they could add 'writer' to her epitaph. Although she hoped she didn't pop her clogs before she saw her dream come true. Like that poor Swedish chap whose books became international best-sellers after he'd died. No fun in that.

At first Celeste had been hesitant to start, even though she'd always loved writing short stories when she was younger. She'd never shared them, just scribbled away furiously in a lined school jotter when she wasn't bogged down with hideous maths homework or trying to invent excuses to skip PE. Her sister, Emily, was always the more intelligent one, the one who went to university and studied English Literature. She'd ended up getting pregnant and married, her grand career plans derailed by motherhood.

There were two main reasons for Celeste to feel absolute terror at the thought of entering the competition. Number One – the submission had to be between 40 and 50,000 words. As these days, her writing was confined to grocery lists and the occasional email, she could not imagine producing that number of words. It would be like trying to scale Everest in stilettos. Except, to her amazement, she had found a flow and rhythm to her writing, some days clocking up 1,000 words or more. Number Two – Celeste was well aware of her tendency to use the wrong word from time to time. But with the aid of spell and grammar check on her computer she was confident she hadn't made any serious errors. Anyway, she was sure they had editors who would correct potential boo-boos. The key thing was that she'd produced something she believed was both steamy and readable. Perhaps not the next *Fifty Shades of Grey* but at least a few shades of blushing pink. Less props involved but her manly hero would hopefully seduce the *Tea Break* faithful with his impeccable pecs and mind-blowing stamina in the boudoir. Her most recent chapter had him going at it for thirty-seven minutes. Not including foreplay. Or after play. Luckily his playmate was a plucky soul with thighs of steel and a pelvic floor that could crush Coke cans.

Celeste booted up her laptop. Another day, another chapter. Maybe the second last one. What was the word, penintimate, something like that, anyway. Sounded about right, considering the subject matter. Her insatiable male character, who went by the name of Leo, had managed to vanquish all contenders for the hand and heart of his chosen one, the seductive yet sturdy Seraphina. Whose name came from the Hebrew language and meant 'ardent or fiery'. And she was certainly both, passionate to the point of making mere mortals weep and wave white flags of surrender and as likely to burst into flames as a well-tended hearth. Which reminded Celeste, she really should ring Emily and make sure she was all right after the book club evening.

She leant back in her chair and stretched her arms above her head. Writing was more fun than she could ever have imagined but it did give her sore shoulders and an aching neck. She twisted her head one way then another, wincing as she heard a loud click. Another 500 words or so and she'd take a break. A *Tea Break*, no less. Celeste gave a little inward smile as she imagined their readership getting in a right old flap as Leo and Seraphina hit orgasmic highs that could lift the roofs off ancient buildings and have the Gods reaching for their ear plugs. And eye masks. Yes, she'd created a little slice of mythological mayhem with a liberal dose of good old rampant sex which she was sure could be a contender for first prize. All she had to do was come up with an amazing climax – and there'd already been a few of those – and £5,000 could be hers. The first money she'd earned for herself since who knows when.

A cup of tea and a slice of carrot cake later, Celeste was torn between getting on with her writing and calling Emily for an update on her chimney crisis. She decided on the latter. Leo and Seraphina's final grunts and gasps could wait.

'Emily! Comment ça va?'

Celeste had quit her evening French classes on the grounds that they were too boring and full of earnest souls keen to grasp the finer points of grammar, whereas she just wanted to sound more alluring and be able to decipher menus in some of the posher restaurants Michael took her to. She'd never forget her abject humiliation when they'd dined at some Michelin rated establishment and she'd asked for 'conard'. The waiter had retreated with a purplish tinge to his face and even Michael had almost choked on his mouthful of lightly bodied Burgundy.

'What? What did I say?' she'd demanded. Although she already knew she had come up with another Celestism, as they had come to be known over the years.

'Sweetheart, you just ordered an arsehole. The French word for duck is 'canard'.' Michael had wiped his eyes on his napkin, patted her hand affectionately. Celeste had withdrawn her hand abruptly, mortified yet annoyed that the understandable swapping of one vowel sound should cause such mirth at her expense.

'Obviously, I didn't need to order an arsehole when I have one sitting right opposite me,' she'd retorted, in a rare moment of biting back. Michael looked suitably stunned for all of three seconds, then reached for her hand again.

'I'm sorry, I didn't mean to upset you. It's an easy mistake to make. Forgive me?'

He'd looked at her with his earnest, dark brown eyes and she'd felt her humiliation melt away, thawed by his kindness and devotion.

'You're forgiven. As long as I can have the trio of chocolate desserts with a liqueur coffee for afters.'

Celeste realised her thoughts had drifted away and Emily had been speaking for quite a few seconds. She snapped back to the present, banishing thoughts of arseholes and divine chocolate tortes from her head.

'Sorry, darling. What was that? I was just ringing to see how things were, if you managed to sort out your chimney problem?'

'Hi Celeste. I just said everything was fine. Yes, I found someone online, he came round the next day and retrieved a dead bird. Michael was right – well, he usually is, isn't he? All it needed was a good clean then he dropped by yesterday to fit a special guard to stop it happening again. So, all good. Fantastic. Couldn't be better, really.'

Strange. Her sister seemed incredibly enthusiastic about having her chimney swept. Although she supposed that living on her own meant she got lonely sometimes, so even a humble tradesman dropping by might brighten an otherwise dull day.

'What was he like then? I can just picture him now. A stocky little fellow, all sooty jowls and cap-doffing. Did he have a cockney accent? I mean, a real one, not like Dick Van Drake in that movie? What was it called again? Honestly, my memory's getting worse these days.'

Emily smiled, both at how completely wrong Celeste was in her imagining of Joe and the thought that he would hopefully ring her soon to arrange a time to drop by. It was already ten o'clock and she didn't want the line to be engaged when he called. She wished now she'd also given him her mobile number, but she could do that when he arrived. Or would that be way too forward?

'*Mary Poppins*. The film you're thinking of. And, no, he didn't look like that at all. His name's Joe and he's maybe around thirty and quite good-looking, actually.'

She refrained from saying 'drop-dead gorgeous' as she knew it would pique Celeste's curiosity no end. She'd probably pester Emily for his number and call him around for a quick inspection. Of him, not her fireplace, as she and Michael had a fake gas-burning one.

Just then her phone made a buzzing noise, indicating another call was coming in. Damn! Time to get Celeste off the line, pronto.

'Sorry, Celeste. I really have to go. I've got a pile of stories to edit and deadlines approaching. You know how it is. Well, you probably don't but ... must dash. Chat soon. Bye!'

Celeste was a little taken aback at Emily's curtness. She'd been all set for a good old chinwag. A distraction from Leo and Seraphina and their wanton ways. Which made her smile inwardly as Emily had absolutely no idea her flighty big sister was a few knee-trembling moments away from completing her own slice of fictional rumpy pumpy. So, just one more sliver of cake and maybe a tiny glass of bubbly – the sun was definitely over the yardarm somewhere on the planet – and she'd settle down for the mind-blowing finale.

* * *

'Hi Emily. It's Joe. The chimney sweep.' As if she could possibly have forgotten his name or got him confused with *another* Joe.

'Hi Joe. How are you? Listen, I really appreciate you calling and offering to fix my drip...'

Why did everything she said seem laced with double entendres? Yes, I am a leaky and sad old woman who needs a good servicing. Preferably more than once a year and without call out charges. Or replacement parts. Although lately her hips hadn't been so much as lying as protesting that she wasn't the bouncy young thing of days gone by. When she could gyrate on the dancefloor to the sounds of the eighties, handbags stacked in the middle, would-be suitors circling like pimply predators. Acne to acne, pus to pus. Sorry, Mr Bowie.

'No problem. I'll be with you in fifteen minutes, if that's OK?'

More than OK. If George Clooney himself had just rang to say he was stopping by for a quickie she couldn't have been more delighted. Or excited. And just a tad petrified.

'Great! See you soon!'

Emily put down the phone, praying that her enthusiasm

didn't betray the fact that she had a serious case of the colly-wobbles. Her stomach was churning, and also making embarrassing rumbling noises. She knew she should have forced down some breakfast but her appetite had been non-existent. Too late now. She poured a glass of tap water and willed herself to calm down.

She didn't even wait for him to ring the bell this time, opening the door the second she heard his van pull into the driveway. She watched as he eased his long legs down from the seat, reaching across to pick up a small toolbox.

'Hi, Emily. Gorgeous day, isn't it? Too nice to be stuck indoors, eh?'

As she stood back to let him in their arms brushed, and Emily felt as if several thousand volts had passed through her. She couldn't be sure but – judging by Joe's slightly flustered expression – he had felt it too. He paused for a second, as if he was about to say something, then continued along the hallway.

'So, can I get you anything? Or would you just like to get down to it?'

This time Emily's face flamed red. She had luckily escaped the dreaded hot flushes of the menopause but imagined this was how it felt. Except she couldn't blame her hormones, just her propensity for unintended innuendo.

'You know, a coffee would be great. I'll have that washer changed in a jiffy then we can have a chat. If you've got time, that is.'

If he'd picked up on her double meaning then he was too gallant to mention it. Although there was a definite mischievous twinkle in his eyes before he bent down to retrieve the necessary bits from his toolbox.

Leaving him to it, Emily hastened to the kitchen to boil the kettle. Her face had cooled down but her insides were still a knot of mortification laced with a liberal dose of lust.

Did she really believe that Joe could possibly be interested in her, when he could have his pick of lithe lovelies? With not a stretchmark or wrinkle in sight, and at least two decades away from their half century.

As she spooned coffee into the pot, a terrible thought struck her. What if she reminded him of his dead mum? A kind of twisted version of Oedipus complex, his desire for his deceased mother transferred to Emily instead? Or maybe he just got his kicks toying with the affections of middle-aged women, secretly laughing behind their backs as they lapped it up? He must encounter quite a lot of desperate and sex-starved housewives in his trade, probably greeting him in flimsy negligees and deliberately flaunting their saggy bosoms. Perhaps he enjoyed the odd romp between the sheets, saw it as a service to the old and needy. Like meals on wheels or changing dressings on weeping, ulcerated legs. OK, maybe a bit more pleasant, but still. She shuddered at the thought of Joe bed-hopping his way around the county, leaving a trail of heartache in his wake.

'All finished. No more drips. Ah, thanks, just what I need.'

Joe smiled warmly as Emily handed him his steaming mug of coffee. She smiled back, mentally remonstrating with herself for thinking such dark, evil thoughts. He was as much a serial seducer of housewives as she was prone to pouncing on unsuspecting workmen. And she wasn't wearing a diaphanous nightie, just a plain black vest top and jeans. Plus her undies were several years old and hardly likely to inflame a young man's desire. Any man's desire, for that matter.

'Listen, Emily. I meant it when I said I'd be happy to help with any other jobs you might need doing. I know you're uncomfortable with not paying me but I don't want anything for the tap. That was nothing, honestly. The truth is ... well, I don't want to seem forward or make you feel awkward but ... I really enjoy your company. I think you're a lovely lady and

… I wondered would you like to maybe go out some time? With me?'

If Emily had been speechless at the end of his last visit, she was positively struck dumb now at Joe's words, particularly as he was gazing at her with an expression both bashful and hopeful. And the other five dwarfs, although definitely not grumpy. She certainly didn't feel remotely like Snow White, more Sleeping Beauty woken from years of slumber by a kiss from a handsome prince. Not that he'd kissed her – yet – but he'd asked her out! On a date! Which usually led to…

'I'd like that. Very much.'

Emily managed to control herself and her tendency to babble when placed in an awkward situation. Chiefly because it didn't really feel awkward, not when Joe looked ridiculously pleased at her response. He set his mug down and reached for his phone.

'Give me your mobile number and I'll text you later. I just need to check my agenda back at the office. We sometimes get evening call-outs but I'm pretty sure I'm free this Friday, if you are. There's a nice little bistro a couple of miles away that opened recently and I've heard it's really good. Chez Jacques it's called, does these amazing steaks on hot stones. And lots of other things if you're not big into meat. What do you think?'

Emily thought she had died and gone to heaven. Or maybe she was destined for the hot, burny place but right there and then she didn't care if Lucifer himself materialised and signed her up as a horned minion.

'That sounds wonderful. Here's my number.'

She reeled it off, Joe typing away with his tongue snagged between his pearly whites in the most adorable fashion.

'All done. So, I'd best be off for now but I'll be in touch to confirm. Say, 7.30 and I'll swing by and pick you up?'

Emily nodded her assent, rising to her feet to see him to the door. He stopped for a moment, raised his hand and touched her lightly on the cheek.

'See you soon, Emily.'

And then he was gone. Leaving her with the sensation of being scorched inside and out. The fire had been well and truly lit and she had no idea what the flames had in store.

CHAPTER 8

'I mean, what a totally *useless* present! Honestly, the man is completely clueless.' Derwyn banged down her wine glass for emphasis, some of its contents sloshing on to the table.

'So, what was it then? Don't keep us in suspense!' Tabitha knew her friend could keep a story going longer than a Tolstoy novel. And she was bursting for the loo – as usual – after three much-needed lager shandies.

'Only a bloody gadget for sucking the air out of a champagne bottle, so you can keep it fresh for another day! What kind of person would even consider not polishing it all off? I told him where he could stick his fizz preserver.'

Tabitha laughed, picturing poor Ed's face. He'd probably spent hours browsing for what he thought was an imaginative gift for Derwyn's birthday. When he'd have been better off buying a case of Moet et Chandon, complete with supersized champagne flute.

Early Saturday evening and Tabitha was out with her two closest friends, Fiona and Derwyn. It was lovely to see them, the drinks flowing as freely as the laughter. Normally she'd be doing something with Tom but she'd decided if he could skip off for drinks at the drop of a hat with his mates then so could she. Plus, he was officially in the bad books. Relegated to the naughty step after last night's fiasco.

She'd had another tiring day at the shop. Business had been brisk with Valentine's Day just around the corner. Spotty teenage lads buying cute cards and cuddly toys for their girlfriends. A few older women browsing a selection of rather saucier fare, giggling and blushing at the cheeky messages inside. At one point she and Meryl had had to retreat to the backroom in order to conceal their mirth when a gentleman of around seventy or so had been perusing some merchandise that had only arrived that morning. Skimpy panties in lurid hues of crimson, hot pink and boudoir purple. Each embroidered with such messages as 'It's Your Lucky Day' and 'All You Can Eat'. When he'd sidled up to the counter clutching a pair bearing the legend 'Too Hot To Handle' they'd barely kept it together. Tabitha had feigned a coughing fit as she took his money and stuffed the knickers into a gift bag.

'Crikey, someone's in for a bit of a surprise, I reckon,' Meryl had snorted, wiping tears from her eyes as the ageing sex bomb exited with great haste.

'Hey, you never know. He might have a much younger lady friend. Or maybe he and his missus just happen to have a fantastic sex life. Just because you're old doesn't mean you can't still get it on. Isn't that right, Meryl?' At which point Meryl gave her young assistant a sharp nudge in the ribs.

'Less of your cheek, Tabbie! I'll have you know I'm only forty-four. Well, that's what I'm admitting to, anyway. And even if I was twenty-four I'd much rather a massive bouquet of red roses than some tacky nylon thong. You'd probably get friction burns wearing one of those!'

Back to last night. OK, maybe she'd overreacted a bit, but

increasingly Tom was sliding down the Ideal Man scale, faster than Bridget Jones on a fireman's pole. She'd arrived home feeling weary and with a boot-load of shopping she'd picked up after a mad dash around the supermarket.

'TOM! Are you upstairs? Could you come down and give me a hand?' A deafening silence. She'd sighed heavily and plodded her way up to the bedroom. Could make out the distinctive theme tune of *Top Gear* as she neared the door. She opened it and took in the delightful sight of her man sprawled on the bed, remote control in one hand, bottle of beer in the other. A balled-up pair of socks lay inches from the laundry basket in the corner. Magic Johnson obviously not on top form then.

'Hey, Tabitha. You all right?' He'd barely glanced away from the screen, Richard Hammond wittering on about the merits of the latest Ferrari. Tabitha had taken a deep breath. Then another.

'Actually, Tom, I'm absolutely knackered. And I was shouting on you to help me unload the car. If that's not too much trouble.' Her sarcasm had failed to register. Tom had simply pressed 'pause', slid off the bed and made his way downstairs behind her at a pace that made snails look like Formula One drivers.

'Christ, that's a lot of food for just the two of us. Are we expecting the bomb to drop or something?' He'd looked at her in vague amusement. She'd glared back in increasing frustration. Then the penny had finally dropped.

'Shit, Tabitha. I'd completely forgotten. We're having people over for dinner, aren't we? And I was supposed to pick up some pork fillet from the butcher's. Which I didn't. Sorry.' He'd looked at her with pleading eyes, like a stray at Battersea Dogs Home intent on finding a lovely new home. Right then he was more likely to find himself on the menu at some dodgy Korean restaurant where pooches were considered a delicacy.

In the end Tabitha had rushed back to the butcher, picked up the meat and chopped, marinaded and cooked for the next two hours. She had barely made it in and out of the shower before the guests arrived. Meryl and her new beau along with a woman called Jessie who she'd worked with a couple of times at events. And who'd subsequently bombarded Tabitha with texts saying *We must get together soon!* Or *Would love you to meet my new man! He's a - maz - ing!!!!* Caving in under the pressure, Tabitha had invited them around. And been totally underwhelmed on both counts. Jessie could talk the proverbial hind legs off a donkey. On the most boring of subjects. Her new man, Jake, was a fanatical comic collector. 'Actually, the correct terminology is "graphic novel" but let's not be pedantic,' he'd intoned, doing that quotation mark finger waggle that had Tabitha wishing she could slice them off with a cleaver.

Meryl had, thankfully, been on good form. Relating tales from the shop and only once bursting into song when 'Super Trouper' came up on shuffle. This had prompted a rather bizarre discussion as to why the lyrics were, 'When I called you last night from Glasgow.'

'Surely it would make more sense if they said, 'last night from Oslo'?' queried Jessie, who was making heavy inroads into the third bottle of red. 'After all, they're from Sweden, aren't they?'

Tabitha had resisted pointing out that Oslo was, in fact, the capital of Norway and the whole point was about touring the world and missing someone while on the road. Jake was too busy yapping on about his graphic novel collection to Tom, whose glazed expression suggested complete and utter indifference to the subject and Meryl was giggling at something Miroslaw had said.

Her new man had been quiet but attentive throughout the evening, topping up glasses and giving Meryl the odd under-table hand squeeze when he thought no-one was looking. Tabitha wasn't sure about the Al Pacino resemblance but he was still attractive in a slightly swarthy way. He'd brought Tabitha a beautiful bouquet of flowers and had insisted on helping when it came to serving each course. So, not a total disaster but Tabitha had been hugely relieved when it came to an end.

Tom had loaded the dishwasher, still giving sheepish looks that had failed to penetrate Tabitha's icy exterior. She'd stomped off to bed, an Arctic blast trailing behind her. He'd attempted a cuddle when he crawled in beside her, but retreated when frostbite threatened to infiltrate his nether regions.

* * *

Back from the toilet, lipstick freshly applied and another drink in hand, Tabitha rejoined the conversation.

'I wasn't totally convinced, but Jen persuaded me to give it a try. Now I'm a complete convert! Honestly, you two, it just feels incredible. And Pete absolutely loves it!'

Tabitha looked from Fiona to Derwyn, a little baffled as to what the current topic was. She knew that Jen was Fiona's beautician and that Fiona was a regular at the salon, always keen to try the latest treatment. Maybe she'd had a new facial, even a few needles stuck in here or there? Although she was only thirty and had a complexion that made babies' bottoms look a bit rough.

Fiona leaned in closer. Spoke in a loud stage whisper.

'Got all my pubes whisked off. Not a hair left. Apparently it's the way to go these days. Much more hygienic and so much nicer when, you know...' She broke off, grinning from ear to ear. Both Tabitha and Derwyn were gawping at her. And trying not to visualise their friend's newfound hairlessness down below.

'Isn't it a bit – sorry, don't mean to be gross – but a bit, *childlike*? I mean, aren't we supposed to have some hair down there?'

Tabitha hadn't ever really given her pubic area much thought. She knew about Brazilians and landing strips and even trimming one's bits into intricate patterns like love hearts. Topiary for the brave and the brazen. She'd always been quite content to give it a little trim when it began to escape the edges of her panties. Tom hadn't complained and she'd certainly never demanded that he whip off hairs in his own private parts. She did her legs – at least in the summer – and she considered underarm hair removal as an essential. But waxing or shaving everything away? Wouldn't it itch like fury when it started to grow in? Having a good old scratch of the groin was surely something best left to the menfolk.

'Not for me, I'm afraid,' said Derwyn. Which made Tabitha feel a huge amount of relief. At least she wasn't alone in wanting to keep her hairy bits intact.

'Tried it once. Hated it. So did Bob.' Bob was Derwyn's ex, a man so hirsute he made ZZ Top look clean shaven.

'He said it looked creepy. Wouldn't sleep with me again until it had grown back in. Then the bastard ran off with a Sinead O'Connor lookalike. Go figure.'

Derwyn wasn't wearing the expression of a woman heartbroken and crushed. Quite the opposite. With her tumbling auburn curls, sparkling hazel eyes and wickedly contagious laugh she exuded sex appeal. Coupled to a Swansea accent unchanged by years in England she attracted attention wherever she went. And always spoke her mind, invited or not. She'd only been with Ed a few months and Tabitha wasn't sure he was a match for her friend. Definitely punching above his weight, if she was totally honest.

'So, Tabitha. How're things with Tom? I'm surprised he let you out tonight. Shouldn't you two be getting hot and heavy between episodes of *Game of Thrones*?' Derwyn leaned back, creamy cleavage thrust forward. A chap at the bar did a dramatic double-take, narrowly missing tossing his drink into the lap of his unamused girlfriend.

Tabitha fiddled with the ends of her scarf and took another swig of her drink.

'OK, I guess. Well, not really OK. More like a bit rubbish to be honest.'

To her dismay she felt tears brimming. Where had they come from? It wasn't as if the relationship was on the rocks, was it? Just a few lumps and bumps which was perfectly normal. Except, more and more she wondered what the future held for them. If, in fact, they had one.

'Gosh, Tabitha, I had no idea! Why didn't you say something before?' Derwyn squeezed in next to her friend and gave her an enormous hug, producing a packet of tissues from her pocket.

'I don't know. Maybe I'm just being silly. I mean, Tom's lovely really. At least, he is when he isn't forgetting important things or leaving his toenail clippings lying around for me to sit on.' Derwyn and Fiona both giggled, well versed in Tom's quirks and foibles.

'But he's just so lush!' exclaimed Derwyn in her husky Welsh tones. 'You look so great together. Is there something you're not telling us? Does he have a dark, violent side? A serious porn addiction? Or does he like dressing up in your bras and panties?'

Tabitha let out a snort of laughter. The thought of Tom squeezing his muscular frame into her minuscule undies wasn't an appealing one. He was certainly not the violent type, laid-back to the point of being horizontal. Which he often was when glued to his only real addiction, *Top Gear*. He smoked the odd cigarette but that wasn't enough to justify dumping him. So, what was the problem? Was she just being too picky? She knew she was a million miles from perfect. She wasn't seeking perfection, just a sense that she had found the person who brought out the best in her and who made her feel special. And the same in reverse.

'None of the above, thankfully. Sorry guys, just having a wobbly moment. Must be the time of the month or something.'

Tabitha knew she couldn't properly explain to her friends where her doubts were coming from when she had trouble rationalising them herself. Better to keep quiet for now. She glanced at her watch. Only 10.30 but she was already sleepy and suddenly wanted to go home and be with Tom. Snuggle up on the sofa watching some crap TV and reassure herself that all was fine. No need to panic. Everybody had their ups and downs and they'd get through this, recapture some of the early magic when they couldn't keep their hands off each other. When trivial matters didn't even scratch the surface of their shiny, new togetherness.

'Sorry girls, but I'm going to call it a night. Catch up again soon?'

Tabitha shrugged on her coat, hugging each of her friends in turn and assuring them that all was well. With promises to arrange another get together in the next couple of weeks she left the warmth and buzz of the bar for the short walk home.

* * *

'HELLO! I'm back already! Did you miss me?'

The house was deathly quiet. The small table lamp was on in the hallway, but the lounge was in total darkness. Tabitha called upstairs but there was no reply. She wondered if Tom had gone to bed early but that would have been completely out of character. He often stayed up until the small hours of the morning watching TV or flicking around on his laptop. The only time she could recall he'd retreated to bed before midnight was when he'd had a serious bout of man flu. That had been fun, listening to him sniffling and coughing and complaining that death was just around the corner. She'd imagined the Grim Reaper waiting patiently, scythe in one hand, box of Lemsip in the other.

In the kitchen, she flicked on the overhead light and saw a note propped up against the bread bin. She picked it up and read it.

Hey, Tabitha. Hope you had a fun evening. Clive and Keith invited me out for a few pints. Might crash at Clive's. He's got the entire box set of The Sopranos. Tried your phone but it was switched off. See ya. Tom x

Tabitha pulled out her phone. She hadn't realised it was off. She switched it back on, saw three missed calls from Tom and one from her mother. She debated calling her back then noticed there was also a text message.

Hello darling. Hope all ok with you. Just wanted to catch up. Nothing urgent. Chat soon. Love you. Mum xx

Trudging upstairs Tabitha felt wearier than ever. She didn't have a problem with Tom going out with his mates. She didn't mind if he stayed out all night and watched back to back episodes of mobsters going about their day to day brutal existences. What she did mind was the hollowness she felt deep in her core. The feeling she couldn't shake that there should be more. Much more.

Once she'd brushed her teeth, scrubbed off her make-up and clambered into bed, Tabitha realised what had been niggling at her from the moment she'd read Tom's note. 'See ya', he'd signed off. With only one kiss. Almost eighteen months together and neither of them had ever used the L word. Why? Tabitha was a naturally affectionate person and scarcely a day had gone by when she hadn't said 'love you' to her mum, either in person or by phone or text. She'd never really thought about it until now. Tom always called her 'gorgeous' or 'beautiful' or, occasionally, 'grumpy pants' when she was in a strop about something, but he'd never actually said he loved her. And she had never said she loved him.

Tabitha turned off the bedside lamp. She often drifted off with some random song playing in her head – earworms, wasn't that the term? – and tonight was no exception. 'Time To Say Goodbye'. She rolled over and prayed for sleep to come quickly.

CHAPTER 9

Michael sat by the window of the café. Or rather, the greasy spoon dive where truckers dipped doorstops of bread into underdone eggs, the aroma of frazzled bacon and blackened sausages battling against the underlying stench of sweat and cheap aftershave. He looked at his watch – a vintage Patek Phillipe – and placed a hand on his trembling left leg. She was late, only five minutes, but he was sure she wasn't going to come. His cup of tea cooled before him, in contrast to the beads of sweat that pooled on his forehead and made his underarms damp and clammy.

He hated this place but couldn't take the risk of meeting somewhere nicer, more upmarket, where Celeste or one of her friends might stumble upon him. They lived in a tight knit community where one man's indiscretion was fodder for weeks of breathless speculation and hearsay.

He was on his second cup. Fifteen minutes late now. She wasn't coming. He should have known. After their last meeting, when she'd burst into tears and fled, tattooed drivers looking up from their congealing breakfasts in fascination, he'd very much doubted she would come. He drained the dregs of his tea and stood up. At which point the door opened and she walked in.

She looked nervously around her, eyes alighting on Michael, who'd hastily sat down again. Ignoring the stares of the curious workers she made her way over to him.

'I'm so glad you came. I thought ... I mean, I was worried ... after the last time.' His words tailed off as she slipped into the seat opposite him, shrugging off her pale beige raincoat and folding it neatly behind her.

'I wouldn't have just stood you up. You know me better than that. I got stuck in traffic, that's all. I'm sorry.'

A plump waitress with a food-smeared apron materialised, notepad and pen at the ready. He looked tentatively across the table.

'Just a coffee and a round of toast, please,' she responded.

'I'll have another tea, thanks,' added Michael, waiting until the waitress shuffled back to the kitchen to fetch their meagre order.

She was silent, fiddling with the laminated menu card offering a host of artery-clogging delights. At the next table a group of men in grimy overalls burst into raucous laughter. He watched her, taking in her solemn face framed by fine dark blonde hair which fell to her shoulders. Large grey eyes that had yet to make proper contact with his. So achingly familiar, yet time and distance meant they really didn't know each other at all. And he wasn't sure how – or if – they could breach the chasm between them.

'So, how have you been?' Great, thought Michael. They'd met up five or six times already and still their conversation was limited to polite small talk. He desperately wanted to know everything about her, her life over the past twenty-six years. What her likes and dislikes were, her hobbies and passions, why her own marriage had fallen apart in much the same way as his own brief liaison all those years ago. History repeating itself, except she had two young children to raise on her own instead of one. He had seen photos of them – two small boys named Edward and George – fair like their mother but with their father's strong cleft chin and sturdier frame. Had actually met them once, but hardly in the best of circumstances.

'Fine, I guess. Still struggling to sort out the settlement. He won't agree to anything until he runs it by his solicitor countless times. The place I'm renting is tiny but it's all I can afford at the moment. It's so hard on the boys. They're too young to really understand and keep asking when we're going home to Daddy.'

Michael felt his gut clench as her eyes filled with tears. She hastily lowered her head and searched for a tissue as the waitress appeared with their order. He waited until she departed before speaking. 'You know I want to help you. Please, let me give you some money. It's the very least ...'

She cut him off in mid-sentence, straightening up in her chair with an air of stubbornness and defiance he recognised so well. She was, indeed, her father's daughter. 'I don't *want* your money. I've told you that over and over again. I'm not even sure if I want to see you. Every time I agree I beat myself up about it. You left us when I was just a baby, and now you expect to fix everything with a blank cheque and empty platitudes. All those years of absolutely nothing and now you want to be the perfect Dad. Well, in my experience there's no such thing. I never had a dad growing up, just a mum so bitter and twisted she could barely speak your name. But you could have tried to keep in touch, if you'd wanted to. And now my bastard of an ex is inflicting the same pain on my precious boys. It's just a bloody mess.'

His beautiful, proud and pig-headed Sophie looked

momentarily shocked at her own words, probably the longest sentences she'd uttered since they'd started seeing each other six months ago. It had come as a total shock. He'd had no idea her marriage had broken up, and certainly no clue that she'd fled Scotland with the boys and set up home in the village of Cliffdown just twenty miles away from where he lived. How could he have known? Aside from the odd card she had rejected all contact with him. He had no telephone number, no email address. His ex-wife Margaret loathed him and had gone out of her way to administer a steady drip-drip of poison against him as Sophie grew up. It was only when she reached her late teens that she'd somehow discovered his address and made contact. By then she was studying in Edinburgh, sufficient distance between her and her mother to allow this tiny breakthrough in communication. But only on her terms. She'd made it very plain she didn't want to see him, yet a tiny part of her clearly couldn't sever the fragile parental bond entirely.

'I know I could have tried. I *should* have tried. I've tried to explain but it was all so complicated. There wasn't a day I didn't think of you, you must believe that. You were my daughter. Only your mother made it so, so difficult and then I met …'

Michael's voice faltered, diluted by a wave of shame and guilt that had tormented him for almost a quarter of a century. For the truth of it was, from the first day he met Celeste he had realised two things. One, that he had met a woman who could make him happy and who considered it her life's purpose to supporting him and his burgeoning career. And, two, that she had no interest in knowing anything about his previous marriage or child. Indeed, she made it perfectly clear from the outset that children played no part in her future plans. Conveniently, Margaret had fled the country with Sophie shortly after they split, settling in

Guernsey where her parents ran a highly successful bijou hotel.

He had been totally smitten by Celeste, who was working as a receptionist for a small law firm near his own offices when they met. She was the very antithesis of Margaret, who had been as ruthlessly ambitious as he, albeit in the hospitality industry. She had little time for schmoozing with his banking colleagues, even less time for creating the perfect home. Her job was her passion, and Michael came a poor second-best. He realised very quickly after they'd wed that they had made a mistake, that what he mistook for love was more like inflated egos combining to make a giant balloon of self-conceit that was destined to pop. A bit like the failed condom that resulted in Sophie, as Margaret had made it clear she wanted a child but not until her career was on a steady upwards trajectory. But she didn't let a little thing like an unplanned pregnancy get in the way, working until the day before Sophie emerged into the world. Michael could still vividly remember looking at his newborn daughter's crumpled little face and thinking, 'We made you, but I can't keep up this pretence anymore.' Sophie was only six weeks old when he announced he was leaving, Margaret screaming abuse at him while Sophie slept upstairs, blissfully unaware of the tempest that raged below.

'And then you met her. That woman who twisted you around her little finger and whispered in your ear that you shouldn't have anything to do with me. Who beguiled you so much you chose to turn your back on your only child. No, do *not* interrupt me.' Sophie held up her hand, silver bracelets jangling as she brought it down hard on the table. The impact sent her untouched coffee slopping over the cup, her cold toast leaping from the plate. More curious stares from the other customers, although there were only a handful left after the breakfast rush. 'Yes, you've tried to explain but I find it rather difficult to accept that you would just roll over and agree to whatever she wanted. What, was she some kind of enchantress or something? Did she cast a spell on you? What kind of a woman would ask a man to cut all ties with his daughter? A completely selfish cow, that's who. And you, what does that make you? A weak and spineless man who put his own self-obsessed lust ahead of his fatherly duties.'

Again, Michael tried to cut in, his heart pounding as Sophie's fury reached a crescendo. Again, she signalled that she had not finished with him yet. 'I know Mum did her utmost to keep you away from me, but what I'll never understand is why you chose another woman over me. You should have been hammering on the door, demanding to see me. Tried to mend some bridges at least. But you just walked away. And I really don't know if I can ever forgive you for that.'

Michael knew that every painful word Sophie said was true. On previous meetings they had tiptoed around the subject, both too afraid to voice their deepest, darkest thoughts. He had been stunned beyond belief the day he spotted her in Cliffdown, wheeling a supermarket trolley around the local Waitrose, two small boys perched in front. He'd been visiting an old colleague for lunch and had decided to pick up a few bits and pieces to surprise Celeste with supper that evening. She wasn't a natural in the kitchen, preferring to either eat out or pick up a selection of high-end ready meals from M&S. Whereas Michael quite enjoyed pottering around, chopping this and marinating that, with a good glass of red to hand.

He'd recognised her from a photo she'd sent a couple of years earlier, slipped inside a Christmas card. A family shot, with a tiny Edward and George – only sixteen months apart in age – and a smug-looking Ralph, her erstwhile husband. He'd disliked him on sight, but his heart had jolted at the two angelic faces that beamed at him, his grandsons. At that time, he had no reason to believe, to hope, that he might ever meet them. Yet amazingly, here they were, just feet away from him. Unless he was mistaken. They lived in Scotland so why would they be shopping here, of all places? Of course, they could be on holiday or visiting friends. It was a now or never moment.

'Sophie?'

He had absolutely no idea what reaction to expect. Rage, indifference, or just an overwhelming urge to ram him with her trolley and gather up her boys before disappearing forever? He just knew he had to reach out, say something, to the daughter he'd cast aside in pursuit of an easy, self-gratifying and ultimately shallow life.

She'd stared at him, a whole gamut of emotions playing across her face. He didn't try to decipher them, just smiled and said the words he'd been waiting to say for the longest time.

'It's me. It's Dad. I can't quite believe … It is you, isn't it? I'm not hallucinating, am I? This is so surreal. Please, Sophie, say something.'

The boys were drooping in their seats, clearly in need of a nap. The trolley was piled high with groceries, toilet rolls and multi-packs of juice. Sophie looked beyond tired, greyness etched into her skin, eyes circled with dark shadows. She was only in her mid-twenties but she seemed to have lived several, interminable lifetimes. Had he done this to her? Created this careworn creature when she should have been in her absolute prime? Surely not. She was married now, although he'd questioned the wisdom of getting hitched at just twenty. But what right did he have to question anything? He'd given that up when he left, abdicating all responsibility and possibility of fatherly counsel.

'Oh God. I so didn't want this to happen. I knew it might,

I know where you live, but... George, stop poking your brother in the eye!' Sophie desperately tried to intervene as her sons tussled with each other. Edward began wailing plaintively, his brother's digit bruising his eyeball as boredom and exhaustion set in. Their cries rose in unison, with old ladies tut-tutting and cashiers looking up, any excuse to relieve the tedium of swiping barcode items and exchanging pleasantries with the local customers. They sensed some excitement, a little departure from the humdrum existence of the daily drudge. A slice of real-life soap opera drama. Older man confronting younger woman with two children. Tears on both sides. Wait until they shared that one at home!

Michael had managed to keep a grip on the situation. He'd guided Sophie to the till, paid for her purchases – despite her protests – and steered her and the boys out to the car park, fully aware of the close scrutiny of those behind them. He'd loaded her shopping into the boot of her car, helped her wrestle the still-sobbing duo into their car seats and parked the trolley in the closest bay. He'd waited until she was strapped in, then tapped lightly on the window. She wound it down, her face a mascara-streaked mess, a cacophony of snivelling and snorting emanating from the back seats.

'Can I see you again? Please? I know, I understand if you don't want to, but ... please.' He couldn't bear the thought of not seeing them again. Fate had decreed their paths would cross; now it was up to her if they were destined to meet again.

Sophie had simply looked at him with an expression that said she had no idea what the right answer was, but she nodded. 'You know the little café on the corner of West Street and Wendover Avenue? I'll meet you there next Tuesday. At 10am.'

And then she was gone. And Michael had driven home, knowing he couldn't tell Celeste a single thing. Why create waves, except he didn't particularly like the voyage he had set sail on. Rough seas ahead, he had told himself. But for now, he had Tuesday.

CHAPTER 10

Tom Hubbard leaned out of the bathroom window and exhaled a satisfying lungful of smoke. He'd quit five years ago. Allegedly. Nagged to death by his mother. Herself a former smoker and everyone knew they were the worst. Evangelical in their mission to rid the planet of their filthy habit. Funny though, whenever he'd snuck outside at a party for a sly puff there was always someone following like a tobacco-starved stalker. 'Don't mind if I blag one, do you mate? I've given up, but …' Then they'd suck away with all the fervour of a death row inmate who'd just chowed down his last supper and was on to the postprandial gasper.

His girlfriend, Tabitha, didn't smoke but tolerated his occasional lapse. As long as he didn't smoke in the house and not within an hour of going in for a passionate snog. Even then, an eye-watering breath mint or lengthy mouthwash routine was often required.

A quick check in the mirror. Tom wasn't a particularly vain man but he knew he scrubbed up reasonably well. At a shade over six foot, with broad shoulders and a trim waist, he looked the essence of a gym devotee. Except he rarely set foot in one. Considered them the modern-day equivalent of a lunatic asylum. Except with acres of lycra and barbells instead of straitjackets and shackles. His younger brother Jake sweated it out up to five times a week on the treadmill, with some serious weightlifting thrown in, and still looked more cuddly teddy than pumped man god. Life really wasn't fair.

Parked around the corner from his work, Tom took a sip of his steaming-hot cup of takeaway coffee. None of that skinny latte/soy milk/dash of vanilla syrup crap for him. Just black brain juice, with three generous spoonfuls of sugar. He needed a major caffeine injection this morning. Business at the specialist travel agency where he earned his meagre crust had been poor. People simply weren't interested in – or couldn't afford – the types of holidays they catered for. Africa, South America, Asia, with the focus on luxury and exclusivity. He sent up a silent prayer – despite his atheist leanings – for a good day.

'So, you'd like to go on a safari? No problem. We have lots of options, different locations, budgets to suit everyone.' Tom beamed at the couple sitting in front of him. They reminded him of characters from a Beatrix Potter book. Mr Otter and Little Miss Mousey. Or was he getting his books hopelessly mixed up? He'd never been one for reading. He much preferred to be out there *doing* than getting snared up in imaginary worlds where goblins did battle with fearsome beasts, or a Chardonnay-swigging spinster concocted inedible soup and dreamed of snogging Jane Austen-inspired heroes. All right, these two examples owed more to DVD-watching sessions with Tabitha than to actual reading but the sentiment remained the same. Books were a poor substitute for getting on with real life. Unless you counted anything written by Jeremy Clarkson. A pure legend, in Tom's eyes. His column in *The Sunday Times* had him positively howling with laughter. His dress sense might be a bit dodgy but the man knew his stuff and had made *Top Gear* compulsive viewing. Until he wasn't on it anymore.

'We were thinking, maybe, Kruger National Park?' Mr Otter – on account of his eyes being quite scarily set apart, almost creeping off the sides of his head – looked up expectantly. His wife – Mrs Otter – clung to his hand as if she thought he might suddenly dash off in search of a tasty small amphibian.

'Sure, that's great, but it's pretty expensive. Not that I think for a minute it's beyond your budget.' Tom could see his male client rear up slightly, a hint of defensiveness in his posture. 'Listen, there's a fabulous game reserve called Welgevonden, just three hours or so drive north of Johannesburg. So, a lot closer than Kruger. And they have some amazing game lodges – small, intimate, great food and hospitality. We've sent loads of clients there. Always come back full of praise. You can do a three or four-night package. All meals included and two game drives each day. Can't promise you'll see all the Big Five but …' At which point Mrs Otter gave a discreet cough. Or perhaps she was just clearing a frog in her throat. Right, Tom. Now is not the best time to give in to hysterical laughter. Especially as he hadn't had the best couple of months client-wise and his boss was circling like a Great White with a gimlet eye on his next prey.

'It's just … I'm not really that comfortable at getting close to wild animals. It makes me a little anxious. Are the sides of the Jeep thing closed in? And I don't really like the cold. I believe it gets really cold in the mornings. And we have to wear those horrible cape things. And lots of blankets. And hot water bottles.' She looked at him with wide, pleading eyes. Like an impala gazing down the barrel of a ruthless hunter's gun. Shame he didn't have one on him.

* * *

'ANOTHER ONE SLIPPED through your fingers, Tom?'

His boss Jonathan Mitchell – not so affectionately known as Jaws by his staff – bared gleaming white teeth which had reputedly cost him about the price of a high-end sports car. Of course, he also had the sports car, lived in a luxurious penthouse pad on the outskirts of town and was married to Lila. Tom didn't know her very well aside from the occasional day when she would drop by at the agency. If Jonathan was a shark then she was a leopard, sleek and shiny on the outside but with a ruthless streak a mile wide. Lila rarely spoke to the staff, a curt 'good morning' if she could be bothered, before she strode her way imperiously into her husband's office. They had two children – Jackson and Amelia – who had inherited their parents' charm genes, as witnessed the one time they had set foot in the place.

It had been a Saturday afternoon and relatively busy despite the decline in bookings in recent months. Tom was dealing with a young couple wanting to honeymoon in Brazil, his colleague Clive was deep in conversation with a group of young women planning an Asian adventure and Jonathan was schmoozing over a well-to-do gentleman keen on a safari/Cape Town combo.

Lila had entered the agency, the children trailing behind her. Jackson, who was around ten, was glued to the screen of the latest smartphone. Amelia, probably six or seven, was clutching a fistful of Barbies. Both mother and daughter were sporting matching fur jackets, which Tom was quite sure were one hundred percent real. Waving her hand dismissively around the room, Lila had settled herself in one of the waiting area chairs. She'd picked up a brochure and flicked through it, razor-sharp talons threatening to shred the pages at each turn. Jonathan, who was now ushering his client to the door, both looking extremely pleased with themselves, gave an apologetic smile to his wife. She responded with a look of such venom that he visibly shrunk in stature, more cowering cod than deadly predator.

'Darling, I thought we were supposed to be looking at a new car for me this afternoon.'

The word 'darling' was enunciated in such a way as to suggest that Jonathan's balls were about to be snipped off and used as earrings. Jonathan obviously felt the vibe too as he unconsciously clamped his legs together and winced slightly.

'Sorry, my sweet. Just got caught up with a client. A fantastic one, I have to add. Very happy with what I put together and definitely going to recommend us to lots of his friends!'

Lila looked singularly unimpressed. And totally oblivious to the fact that the children had bored of their activities and were now systematically pulling brochures off the shelves and lobbing them at each other like frisbees.

'The showroom's only open another hour. Can't we leave the children here and go take a look? You know I'm desperate to check out that divine little cabriolet.'

Lila's killer gaze swept around the office, landing with terrifying precision on Tom. He shrugged apologetically at the young couple, who were trying to narrow down the hotel choices in Rio.

'You. Tim, isn't it? I'm sure you wouldn't mind keeping an eye on the children for a little while? They won't be any trouble. JACKSON, stop pulling the legs off your sister's dolls! And Amelia, if I've told you once I've told you a thousand times, it is not lady-like to pick your nose.'

Jonathan was already tugging on his coat, keen to keep his privates intact and appease his wife. Tom's clients had gathered together a pile of print outs of possibilities and were now shaking Tom's hand, eager to escape the mayhem. Lila flounced towards the door, her parting words: 'Be good for Tim, my angels. We'll only be half an hour or so.' Then they were gone, leaving Tom in charge of Satan's spawn. Clive had legged it to the back room, having dispatched his group with an action-packed two-week itinerary. Tom glowered at his two young charges. Jackson responded with a raised middle finger. His sister kept hers firmly planted in her left nostril, excavation still in progress.

It had been almost an hour before they returned, Lila with a face like chiselled stone when she'd learned she'd have to wait four months for her new car. Jonathan looked slightly grey and nauseous, no doubt worried that his testicles remained in jeopardy. Tom had survived – just – but was surrounded by dismembered Barbies, half-drunk cans of Coke he'd offered in desperation from the staff fridge and fragments of Jackson's phone which he'd hurled across the room in a fit of temper when refused permission to photocopy his bare bottom.

'My goodness, children. You have been a little naughty, haven't you?' cooed Lila, her stilettos crunching through shards of an iPhone 6. Amelia was now sobbing, her face a sodden mass of tears and snot. Jackson glared defiantly at his mother, swivelling around like a miniature dervish in his father's chair.

Jonathan at least had the good grace to look sheepish as he patted Tom on the shoulder.

'Thanks for that. They can be a handful at times, but they're adorable really.'

Privately Tom thought they were about as adorable as a dose of genital herpes but wisely kept his thoughts to himself.

'No worries. Happy to have helped. Any time,' he replied

cheerfully, thinking when hell froze over was the most likely next case scenario.

With his boss, Lila and their brattish progeny duly departed, Tom reckoned it was almost time to shut up shop. Clive had already sloped off seconds behind them, muttering something about an anniversary and flowers. He started to gather together his things, mind whirring ahead to a nice evening with Tabitha. Hopefully not featuring slimy courgette strands or that quinoa crap that looked – and tasted – like frog spawn. Maybe even some sex if he played his cards right. Although lately he'd sensed that she was not as enthusiastic as before. There was a distinct coolness about her, in contrast to the heat they had generated in the early days. Quite often he'd head up to bed after her to find her either snoring gently – and he wasn't always sure if she was pretending or not – or with her nose stuck in a book and body language that screamed 'try anything and you'll regret it'.

Did all relationships end up this way? Tom had no idea. His parents had been married for over thirty years and seemed to amble along nicely enough. Not that he wanted to know if they were still 'doing it'. As far as he was concerned, they'd produced him and his siblings, and beyond that he required no further detail. His relationship with Tabitha was the longest he'd had, but surely eighteen months was a bit early to reach the flannelette nightie, cup of cocoa and '*Emmerdale* or *Corrie*?' phase? OK, slight exaggeration. Tabitha wouldn't be seen dead in a nightdress, their cocoa was more likely to be laced with rum and Tom would rather gouge his own eyes out that watch a soap opera, but still. He sighed heavily. Time for a crafty fag out back then he'd head home and do his best to charm his way into her affections.

He'd just wandered back in after his sneaky snout when the ding-dong of the door signalled a new customer. Great.

So much for calling it a day. Popping a mint in his mouth he plastered on his biggest 'aren't I just so pleased to see you' smile.

'Hi. Sorry, I hope I'm not too late. I know you close soon but I just wanted a little advice on something.'

Tom narrowly avoided choking on his mint as he took in the vision of loveliness before him. Poker straight hair, almost jet black, with a long fringe that framed eyes the colour of molten toffee. Skin lightly tanned, slender body encased in a vivid scarlet coat cinched in at the waist. She was shaking out an umbrella, also bright red, and appeared breathless as if she had sprinted some distance.

'Of course not. Not a problem. Please, have a seat.'

Right Tom, stop gibbering away and behave in a professional manner. He gestured to a chair, trying not to ogle as she crossed perfectly proportioned legs clad in sheer black tights, dainty feet sporting grey suede ankle boots with a wedged heel.

'So, how can I help you?'

Feeling reasonably composed again, Tom beamed at her in what he prayed was a warm and welcoming manner, as opposed to a lecherous leer.

'It's a bit embarrassing, actually. The thing is, I was supposed to be going on holiday with my fiancé in a few months.'

Tom felt his spirits plummet like an elevator in a high-octane movie. Damn, she was engaged to someone. Then he mentally berated himself. So what? He was living with someone and supposed to be on his way to her right now to whisper sweet nothings in her ear.

'Well, he called things off. Said he didn't feel the time was right. Gave me all the crap about there not being anyone else, how he wished nothing but happiness for me. Bastard.'

The last word was uttered with a mix of heartfelt

venom tinged with a hint of sadness. Tom resisted the urge to rush around the table and fling comforting arms around her. She looked so downcast and lost and incredibly desirable.

'I'd already booked two weeks off work and I can't change the dates. My boss is a complete bitch, heart of bloody stone. So … I was planning to go somewhere on my own. But I'm not exactly well travelled and I'm really not sure where to go. But I'd like to do something different. Maybe South America? Or somewhere like Singapore or Hong Kong? I just don't know where to start.'

Tom steepled his fingers in his best 'I am giving this deep and serious thought' posture. He leaned back in his chair as she leaned forward in hers, eyes fixed firmly on him.

'There are lots of places I could recommend but it would take some time to go through the options and work out what's best for you. It's not something you rush into. And I'm afraid I really need to be leaving soon but …'

It was a sliding doors moment. Tom could either fix an appointment for this enchantress to come back to the agency in the next couple of days, or—

'Look, I'm free tomorrow evening after work if you'd be OK to meet somewhere? More relaxed, informal and I could do some research and look through it with you. Sorry, I didn't even introduce myself properly. I'm Tom. And your name is?'

She gave a dazzling smile that made Tom wish he was wearing sunglasses and had some bromide to hand to dampen down his rocketing testosterone levels.

'Kate. My name's Kate. That would be lovely, if you're sure it's not too much trouble?'

He scribbled down the name of a discreet little bistro on the edge of town which he was pretty sure neither Tabitha nor her mates frequented.

'Does seven o'clock work for you? Or we can make it a bit later, if you like.'

Kate took his business card, got to her feet and extended a hand. He shook it, feeling its softness and warmth, inhaling a hint of musky perfume as the space between them decreased.

'That's perfect. Thank you so much! I'll see you then.'

She glided towards the door, pausing only to give a small wave and a smile that played havoc with Tom's privates. Not too much trouble? He suspected he was playing with fire *and* trouble with a capital T. For Tom and Tabitha.

CHAPTER 11

The days had seemed to drag by endlessly but, at last it was Friday. And only two hours to go before Emily went on a date. An *actual* date with an *actual* man. And not just any man but a genuinely drop-dead gorgeous one who just happened to be young enough to be her son.

OK, banish that thought right now. Emily chastised herself yet again for dwelling on the small matter of the age gap. Joe obviously didn't see it as a problem, so, why should she? Anyway, they were only going out for a bite to eat which was hardly tantamount to a marriage proposal, was it? Maybe he'd decide in the course of the evening that once was enough and he'd simply drop her home and that would be that. Or maybe …

To calm her nerves and try to speed up time a little Emily had met Tabitha for lunch. They'd chosen a sandwich bar close to The Little Shop of Treasures as she only had an hour to spare and Emily didn't want to eat too much ahead of dinner. As Emily had walked in she spied her daughter at a corner table, fiddling with her phone and looking decidedly down in the dumps.

'Hi, sweetheart. Everything OK?'

Emily sat down, noting that Tabitha had already ordered for them – a tuna mayo baguette for Emily and a falafel wrap with hummus for herself. Two glasses of freshly poured sparkling water bubbled away next to the plates. Emily took a sip of hers and waited.

'Hi, Mum. I'm fine. Sorry, was just texting Tom about something. All done now.'

She placed her phone on the table then took a hefty bite of her wrap. Emily followed suit, carefully watching her daughter who looked pretty as a picture as always in a sleeveless, lacy top and black skinny jeans. Her blonde curls were artfully clipped up in a loose knot in a way that Emily always envied. Whenever she tried a similar style she inevitably ended up looking like she'd been caught in a Force Nine gale. She smiled at Tabitha who smiled back, but it didn't quite reach her eyes. Oh dear, thought Emily.

'So, how's work? Meryl still keeping you on your toes? Maybe I'll come to the shop with you after lunch, say hello.'

Emily didn't know Tabitha's boss terribly well but she liked her and knew they were fond of each other which made for a pleasant working environment. She knew her daughter desperately wanted more out of life than being a shop assistant but she was proud of her and prayed every day that something more suited would come along.

'Yeah, work's fine. Well, apart from the odd nightmare customer.'

Tabitha proceeded to relate the tale of her witch-like nemesis and her dissatisfaction with the hand cream selection which had Emily in fits of laughter. Her giggles faded as she realised her daughter was still looking distinctly fed up.

'And Tom? Everything good with you two?'

Bingo. She'd hit the proverbial nail on the head. Tabitha's face grew darker as she tore a chunk off her wrap and chewed it with all the ferocity of a starving hyena. She swallowed quickly and wiped a dribble of hummus from her chin.

'You know, Mum, I'm really not sure. Some days everything seems fine but others— Or perhaps I'm expecting too much. He's lovely but there are times he drives me mad!'Another long anecdotal tale followed, beginning with the toenail clipping episode and ending with the disastrous spiraliser experiment. Tabitha had a knack of making even the most banal story seem like a work of comedy genius and Emily was soon doubled over with mirth. Although she had a secret sympathy for Tom regarding the courgetti which didn't sound terribly appealing to her either. She'd recently been subjected to some vile concoction of Tabitha's featuring chunks of tofu and other unidentifiable lumps which she'd managed to eat but not without considerable effort and acting skills.

'No man is perfect, Tabitha. Your dad and I ... well, we muddled along but there were many, many times I wondered if there should be more.'

Tabitha gawped at her mother across the table. It was extremely rare for her to mention her dad these days, even rarer for her to admit that their marriage had been less than idyllic. She knew it, of course, but they didn't talk about it. In any case, she felt that she and Tom were better suited than her parents had been – at least in a romantic sense – but still doubts niggled away at the back of her mind.

Emily looked flustered, probably regretting her unexpected outburst. She polished off her sandwich and gazed around the café, catching the eye of a passing waitress.

'Coffee, Tabitha? Can we have two lattes, please?'

Her composure regained, Emily reached across and squeezed Tabitha's hand.

'I really like Tom but at the end of the day only you can

decide if you're truly right for one another. Don't settle for second-best, Tabitha. You'll only end up regretting it.'

'What about you, Mum? You're still young – and beautiful – shouldn't you be moving on with your life? Getting out there and meeting some new men? Meryl's hooked up with someone and she seems really happy. Shall I ask her for details of the dating site she used?'

Whatever reaction she might have anticipated, the one she got took Tabitha completely by surprise. Emily was grinning like a Cheshire cat who'd not only got the cream but also the promise of a lifetime of tummy tickles. Come to think of it, she looked more content and – what was the word? – radiant than Tabitha could recall seeing her in recent years.

'Well, the thing is, my darling daughter, I don't think I'll be needing that dating site. Since I actually have a date. Tonight!'

So, she'd said it. It was out there now and she couldn't take it back. Since Joe had texted to confirm their rendezvous Emily had been torn between telling Tabitha about it or keeping schtum. Even as she entered the sandwich bar she still hadn't decided on the best course of action. Perhaps it was the suggestion that she join an online dating agency that had swung it. Ha, look at me, a fifty-something mother and widow, still able to pull without the aid of dubious dating devices. And not some dodgy old codger lying through his false teeth about his occupation, marital status or year of birth. Nope, she'd bagged a date with a bona fide hunk who genuinely liked her.

'Oh my God! Mum! You are one serious dark horse. Who is he? Where did you meet him? Is he a friend of Aunt Celeste's? Why didn't you say anything before?'

Question after question tumbled from Tabitha's lips, the two delivered cups of coffee ignored as she waited breathlessly for answers. Emily girded her loins – a favourite expression in many of the short stories she forced herself to read – and plunged in before her courage deserted her.

'His name's Joe. He's a chimney sweep – the one who came by after the book club incident, I told you about that – and he's lovely. Really nice and gentle and he asked me out. And I said yes. We're going for a meal. It probably won't come to anything but ...'

Now why had she said that? Why was she so hell-bent on nixing any future plans when they hadn't even got beyond a first date? Was her self-confidence so low that the possibility of going a step further was beyond the realms of belief? Too many years spent alone had clearly chipped away at her already fragile ego.

'So, spill the beans. What does he look like? Has he been married before? Or is he a widower too? Ooh, I can just about picture him. Tall, dark and totally handsome. In a craggy, mature kind of way. Maybe a bit greying at the temples? I don't mind grey hair, it can look really cool. Hasn't done Phillip Schofield any harm and he's well into his fifties now, isn't he?'

As Tabitha twittered on, an icy chill settled on Emily's stomach and she felt vaguely sick. Deep down she knew the real reason she had hesitated over sharing her news was because Joe was so much younger than her. Closer in age to Tabitha than to herself, and she was very afraid of what her daughter's reaction would be when she learned this unpalatable truth.

'Erm, he is pretty tall. And dark. And definitely handsome. No grey hair but that's probably because ...'

Before she could continue, Tabitha had manoeuvred her chair right next to her and engulfed her in a massive hug.

'Oh Mum, if he likes to dye his hair then that's fine! As long as he sticks to his natural colour, none of that artificial black or garish red-brown so many older guys seem to think looks good. Yuck! Better a few grey ones than something that looks like a dead animal perched on the head!'

Against perhaps her better judgement – or simply because of sheer cowardice – Emily decided now was not the time to share Joe's youthfulness. She wasn't sure *when* would be a good time but she sensed right now wasn't it. She couldn't imagine Tabitha being thrilled at the thought of her mum getting up close and personal with someone born in the same year as the Live Aid concerts.

'Sorry darling, but I really have to dash. I'll pop into the shop another time if that's OK? Give my love to Meryl and I promise I'll ring you and let you know how the evening went.'

Emily kissed Tabitha on the cheek and they went their separate ways, Emily silently vowing to provide only the scantiest of details when they next spoke. Where they ate, what they ate, how he escorted her home and … the rest would remain her secret alone. If she allowed her imagination to take flight then there was absolutely no way she would be sharing those details with her daughter.

* * *

One hour until Joe arrived and Emily was seriously nervous. She'd poured herself a glass of wine and knocked it back in a matter of minutes. Reaching for the bottle she'd paused then purposefully rammed the stopper back in place. Being greeted by a slightly sozzled dining partner was probably not the ideal start to a first date. She'd checked her appearance at least twenty times and was not displeased with her efforts. A simple black dress, not too revealing but emphasising her good bits. Hair reasonably groomed, make-up subtle yet designed to enhance her features. She'd recently bought some contouring pencils – a bit Kardashian, but what the heck – and learned through trial and error how to emphasise her cheekbones and highlight her brow-bone and other key areas. Once she'd mastered the art of blending the various colours she looked less Coco the Clown and more potential sex bomb. At least, she hoped she did.

Still half an hour to go. Or had all the clocks in the house conspired to grind to a halt? Nope. Emily checked both her watch and her phone and it was seven o'clock on the dot. She'd brushed her teeth again and given herself another squirt of Jo Malone perfume. Probably a squirt too far as she positively reeked of Pomegranate Noir now. Poor Joe would probably need a face mask if he got too close. What to do now? In the end, Emily decided a blast of music was what was needed to pass the time. She popped the latest Now album collection in her CD player and shimmied her way around the kitchen. *Now 92.* It pained her to admit it but she could remember when the first one came out. Obviously not on an annual basis or she was a whole lot older than she thought.

Emily was just busting a few moves to Justin Bieber when the doorbell rang. She quickly turned off the music and hurried to answer it. There he stood, all gleaming manliness dressed in cream chinos and a light denim shirt, sleeves rolled up to reveal taut and tanned forearms with just the right amount of body hair. Emily had always had a thing about forearms. And calves. The latter she'd just have to hope matched the upper parts. Which she had little doubt would.

'Hi Emily. You look fantastic. And I love your perfume. Ready to go?'

Joe had leaned forward and pecked her on the cheek, thankfully not asphyxiated by her overzealous scent application. She refrained from gushing that he looked utterly edible, instead smiling at the compliment and locking the door behind her.

'Your carriage awaits. I thought you'd prefer something a little more upmarket than the van.'

Joe was now gesturing towards a very nice VW Golf convertible with its roof already down. It was an unseasonably mild evening and luckily not a windy one, otherwise Emily might have suggested putting the roof up for fear of an epic hair disaster.

It was a short drive to the restaurant, Joe and Emily chatting amicably on the way about mundane matters. The weather, what they'd been up to that day, who would be the next James Bond. Trivia but the conversation was easy and relaxed.

Chez Jacques was owned and run by a slightly eccentric Frenchman with a hint of Scottish blood. He greeted them like long-lost kinsfolk, clad in a tartan apron and with an accent that was two parts Gallic to one part Highlands. Emily found herself struggling to understand as he explained the menu choices in his unique vernacular, like Charles Aznavour crossed with Billy Connolly. They seemed fairly limited. Sizzling steaks on hot slate slabs with a variety of sauces and a side of chips. Salmon with mixed vegetables. A few pizza options. Or a couple of salad choices, goats' cheese or chicken. All the wines were the same price and were mainly South American. Emily nodded her agreement when Joe suggested a Chilean cabernet sauvignon with a large bottle of sparkling water as well.

'I believe the steaks are pretty awesome, Emily. They come partially cooked then you slice them up and they keep on cooking on the stone. But if you'd rather have something else. I know the menu's not huge but ...'

Emily was not the biggest carnivore on the planet but the steaks did sound good. She nodded and Joe placed their order, their waitress arriving to pour the wine and water. She also popped a couple of paper bibs over their heads – 'the meat spits out a bit of fat, you know?' – which had Joe and Emily gaping in bemusement then spluttering in laughter at the image imprinted on their chests.

'It's a chef's hat! Honestly, that's what it's supposed to be!'

'Then why does it look like a penis? Seriously, I am wearing a picture of a man's tackle on my bosom. Please take a photo so I can share this with my friends.'

Joe duly obliged, snapping a couple of shots with Emily's phone. She uploaded one to her Facebook page, with the caption 'Is it just me or does that look downright rude?' She was still giggling when their platters arrived, exuding heat and spattering fat as predicted. They both proceeded to carve up their hunks of meat, dipping deliciously chunky chips into the salsas and flavoured butters that accompanied them. Emily took a satisfying mouthful of her wine to wash it down. Joe had barely touched his but as he was driving that was understandable. The meat now looked suitably cooked, still pink in the middle but that was how she liked it. Speared a piece on her fork, plunged it into her mouth and ... wow. If sex wasn't on the cards tonight she could at least lay claim to a virtually orgasmic dining experience.

'What do you think, Emily? I hope you're enjoying it. I know I'm enjoying being with you. It just seems so ... easy, if that's the right word.'

Joe looked apprehensive and utterly adorable, despite the phallic symbol emblazoned on his manly chest. Emily wanted to retort that she was completely easy, a total pushover in fact, but thought it best to keep her lack of willpower to herself. The night was young, maybe she wasn't, but things were going swimmingly for now.

'I'm having a lovely time, Joe. Thank you for asking me out. The food's amazing and the company even more so. I haven't had this much fun since ... ooh, I had my chimney swept!'

Joe raised his glass with a smile that would have made glaciers melt, and gave Emily some serious reverberations in the nether regions. She clinked hers in return and took another bite of meat. A little overcooked now but ... oh, shit ... why wasn't it passing through her throat? She tried to swallow but it was wedged firmly in place, effectively blocking her airway. She attempted a discreet cough but it budged not an inch.

'Are you OK? Emily, is something wrong?'

Joe was looking extremely concerned, although it was hard to tell as Emily's vision was beginning to blacken around the edges. The meat plug refused to shift and she felt both dizzy and nauseous. She tried to cough again but to no avail.

As if in slow motion Joe had materialised behind Emily and was wrapping his hands around her. One, two, three squeezes and the offending lump of steak was propelled on to the table in front of her. The other diners looked on in grim fascination, Emily wishing she could just disappear in a puff of smoke. How not to inject romance into an evening, part one.

'Christ, Emily. You really scared me there! I did a first aid course a few years ago, learned the Heimlich Manoeuvre, but never thought I'd actually have to use it. I'm so sorry. Maybe we should have gone for salads? Are you sure you're OK? Maybe I should get you home.'

Emily shrugged on her jacket as Joe settled the bill, her cheeks still burning at her near-death experience. Ah well, a lesson learned. Never bite off more than you can chew. Applicable to more than just dining experiences. Her throat still ached slightly but her humiliation far outweighed any physical discomfort. She had daydreamed wistfully of being encircled in Joe's well-honed arms but not while she was half choking to death.

'I'm fine, really. Just a bit embarrassed. Not what you want to happen on a first date, eh?'

And probably the last one, Emily pondered sadly. Oh well, it had been fun while it lasted. Admittedly not very long but when she was dribbling away in an old folks' home in the future she could think wistfully of the time a gorgeous young man took her out for a meal. Unless dementia had taken hold and she didn't even know who she was and wore her cardigans inside out.

The drive home was equally swift, the roof up as it was distinctly cooler now. Joe pulled into the driveway, killed the engine, and turned to Emily. Here it comes, she thought. The 'It's been lovely but' line that would flatten her fantasies and thrust her firmly back into reality.

'It's still quite early so, I wondered, would a nightcap be in order? Maybe just a cuppa for me as I'm driving but it seems a shame to call it a night just yet. Unless you've had enough of me already!'

Emily refrained from flinging herself bodily across the seats and indulging in a bit of mouth-to-mouth to complete the first aid experiences of the evening. Steady girl, she chided herself.

'That sounds like a good idea to me. Shall we?'

She slipped off her seatbelt and exited the car, Joe following close behind. Turning the key in the lock, she opened the door and headed towards the kitchen, flicking on a couple of lamps as she went. She headed straight for the kettle, checking there was sufficient water before turning it on.

'Emily?'

Joe was inches away from her. She could feel his body heat, the warmth of his breath on her cheek. Her heart was thumping as she turned and saw the look in his eyes. Not one of disgust or disappointment but of pure, unadulterated longing.

'Would you mind terribly if I kissed you? Because it's what I've wanted to do all night. And before that, actually.'

He reached out and gently tucked a stray strand of hair behind her ear before leaning in towards her. His lips grazed hers, ever so gently, his arms pulling her closer. The kettle was coming to the boil, Emily almost matching it on the temperature scale. She surrendered completely to his embrace, linking her hands behind his head and matching the increased fervency of his kisses. Every part of her was on red alert, her long-dormant libido fully awakened and crying out for attention. The lower sections of her anatomy felt like they'd been defibrillated, strange but delicious sensations flooding her mind and body. Had it ever felt like this before? Possibly not. Was she going to put a stop to it now, even if she regretted it in the morning? *Hell, no.*

Joe had moved back slightly, a question writ large on his utterly irresistible face. Emily gave her answer, taking him by the hand and leading him towards the stairs.

'Are you sure? I don't want to pressure you. If it's too soon please say and I'll go. We can just have a cup of tea and—'

She reinforced her response by grabbing him by the bottom and grinding his hips against hers. No room for doubt there.

'I'm sure. There's just one thing I think we really need to do before we go any further.'

Joe looked slightly abashed. He grappled in the back pocket of his jeans and produced a condom.

'I know, I know. Really presumptuous but I just wanted to be prepared. Sorry. Kick me out now, if you want.'

Emily could not have been more flattered than if he'd said she was the double of Angelina Jolie. Which she wasn't but he had clearly wanted to have sex with her and had thought ahead enough to consider contraception. Since her last period was over a year ago a pregnancy scare was highly unlikely but …

'Not that, you lovely, lovely man. I just think we really need to remove these bloody bibs, don't you?'

Both Joe and Emily glanced down and realised they were still sporting the protective garments from Chez Jacques. Explosive laughter followed, bibs were duly torn off and they proceeded to remove the rest of their garments en route to the bedroom.

CHAPTER 12

Susan had contemplated cancelling book club. She'd started her cancer treatment two weeks ago and it had left her tired, irritable and in considerable discomfort. The only thing that had prevented her doing so was the knowledge that it was the social highlight of her month. Terribly sad but true. She envied the other members and their busy and fulfilling lives, or at least the impression they gave of filling their days with work, hobbies or just relaxing with family and friends. Her days and nights never varied: juggling numbers for her clients and drowning out her loneliness with a combination of TV dramas and food.

A leaflet had dropped on to her doormat a couple of months earlier, advertising a new gym and offering a free trial session. She'd tossed it in the bin, only to fish it out a few hours later. Maybe it was worth a go, she'd thought in a rare moment of positivity. Before her courage deserted her, she'd picked up the phone and booked herself in for the following day.

Arriving at the gym, she'd felt shaky and sick. She'd watched a couple of women in their forties make their way through the revolving door, immaculate in their tight-fitting leggings and fluorescent tops. Both wore make-up, their hair tied back in high ponytails. Susan had glanced down at her own gym wear – a saggy T-shirt with an indeterminate stain on the hem and jogging bottoms she only ever used when gardening – and fought the urge to turn and run.

Inside she was greeted by a young trainer named Joseph who exuded good health and exuberance. He practically bounced on the spot as he waited for Susan to fill out a health questionnaire. She fudged a few of the questions: *How many times a week do you exercise?* (Real answer: none); *What is your current weight?* (No idea, the thought of stepping on scales was too awful to contemplate), and *What are your long-term gym objectives?* She'd wanted to write: *To stop being either invisible or the source of people's amusement* but settled for: *To lose weight and get fitter*. Which was probably the expected answer, after all.

In the gym, Joseph had started her off on the treadmill at a gentle walking pace. Within ten minutes she felt hot and sweaty, the well-worn elastic of her jogging bottoms chafing at her skin. Relief when Joseph returned and switched it off was replaced with horror when he guided her to a corner lined with floor mats and proceeded to demonstrate a series of exercises. She'd tried her best to copy his moves, painfully aware of every aching muscle and her inability to manage the ten to fifteen repetitions he urged her to do. 'You're doing great, Susan, keep going!' he'd said in an almost-convincing tone.

In the changing room Susan had tip-toed around the women who were totally naked and chattering away as they smoothed in various body creams or towelled themselves dry. She found a curtained cubicle and slunk inside, desperate to change into her day clothes and make a hasty exit. She'd decided to shower at home, making do with a quick wipe around with a damp flannel she'd stuffed in her toilet bag. As she'd pulled on her underwear she heard laughter outside, followed by a muffled 'Shush!'

'Did you see the state of that one? Honestly, I'm amazed people let themselves get in that state then expect a miracle in the gym. Personally, I wouldn't set foot in one if I was that size.'

Susan had struggled to do up her bra, her cheeks still warm from the exercise now red-hot with shame and embarrassment. Fumbling in her bag for her jumper she heard a second voice, fainter this time, but the words seared her as surely as if the speaker had yelled them in her face.

'I know! She reminded me of that *Star Wars* character. You know, Jabba the Hutt!' And with another peal of laughter they were gone. Susan left minutes later, never to return.

* * *

IT WAS NOW a quarter to eight, the book club ladies due to arrive in the next fifteen minutes or so. Some – like Emily – were always on time whereas others drifted in late or sent last-minute texts apologising for not being able to make it. Although, so far, it looked like everyone was going to turn up.

Susan had laid out the customary nibbles on her tiny dining table. She'd tried her best in the last few days to cut down on her eating, spurred on by the appalling realisation that her clothes were becoming increasingly tight. Size twenty would soon become size twenty-two. Nowadays most of the major stores stocked large sizes but Susan always felt mortified rifling through the rails, pushing aside the tens and twelves and gazing in awe at the sixes and eights. Surely women who wore those sizes must be missing an internal organ or two?

Despite her good intentions, she found herself slathering several crackers with home-made hummus. A bit too much garlic and not enough lemon juice. Gulping down a glass of water she eyed the Greek semolina cake she'd picked up at the patisserie. Revani, to give it its proper name. Susan was quite sure book club would give a resounding thumbs-down to her choice – *Beyond the Blindfold* – but she thought some Greek-themed food might make up for its shortcomings. Even by her standards it had been pretty atrocious. The writer clearly thought she was reworking *Shirley Valentine,* when the truth was she would struggle to make the cut in one of the teen-romance stories Susan had devoured in her bedroom when she wasn't doing her homework. Usually whilst she worked her way through a packet of biscuits. Just a small slice of cake, just to try. It was delicious. Of course it was. Everything always tasted good until the revulsion kicked in.

Checking she had enough wine glasses laid out and opening a couple of bottles of red and white, Susan thought about what she'd seen – or rather, *who* she thought she'd seen – as she'd left the patisserie. It was just the briefest glimpse of a man speeding past on a bicycle, a blur of colour before he disappeared around the corner. But it had been enough to quicken her heartbeat momentarily and she'd stood on the pavement for at least a minute in case he came back. Looking back now she berated herself for her foolishness. Jonathan was long gone, probably happily married with an adoring wife and adorable children. No less than he deserved. A man like him deserved so much more than a woman like her. She'd made the right decision – of course she had – and lived with it every day since.

* * *

'Fabulous cake, Susan, did you make it yourself?' Nancy Edwards was uncharacteristically chatty this evening, perhaps because of the third glass of wine she'd knocked back in under half an hour. Normally she drove to book club but apparently her son, home on a rare visit from Canada, had dropped her off along with Esther who lived a few doors away.

'No, it's shop-bought but I *did* make the hummus although I'm not too impressed with it. And I have to confess I wasn't too impressed with the book either, sorry.' Susan looked apologetically at the ladies who were all occupied with filling their plates and glasses.

'Oh, it wasn't *that* bad, although I thought the sex scenes were a bit tame to be honest. I'd expected a bit more *detail*, if you know what I mean. In my experience ...' Celeste had stopped suddenly, a look of what could be construed as embarrassment on her face. Strange, thought Susan. Had she been about to reveal intimate revelations about her sex life with Michael? She barely knew him but he always struck her as a bit old-fashioned and stuffy; not the kind to get experimental in the bedroom, anyway. Still, there was no telling what people got up to in their private lives, was there? Just because her own was relentlessly dull didn't mean others might not be more adventurous than surface appearances suggested.

Emily was peering at her Kindle, her face screwed up in concentration. Despite only really knowing her through book club, Susan liked her and wished they could become friends but didn't know how to make that happen. Why would someone as pretty and popular want to be friends with *her*? She tried her best to fit in at these meetings but always felt like the mongrel in a gathering of pure breeds. The fat kid sitting on the sidelines while the cool kids sashayed on by, barely acknowledging her existence.

'I quite liked the bit when Martha and Demetrios went on the picnic and got bitten alive by ants just as they were getting on with it!' said Emily brightly. Both Nancy and Celeste nodded in agreement, whereas Esther – who hadn't even pretended to read the book – looked blank. Susan sighed and cut herself another slice of cake. Maybe it was time to boost the book club numbers, not that she had a bulging contacts list to draw upon. Before she'd joined there'd been around eight or nine members but several had dropped out for varying reasons.

Before she could make the suggestion, Celeste had taken centre stage, any further discussion of the book replaced by potentially far more entertaining gossip.

'Believe me, those two'll be in the divorce courts before the month's out,' she decreed to her captive audience.

'But they always seemed such a nice couple,' said Nancy. The couple in question were Janet and John Jones, known locally for being members of the local amateur dramatic society and holidaying every year in Tuscany. John worked for the local council and Janet was a part-time librarian with a penchant for steamy bodice rippers. She was one of the book club drop-outs, in fact, citing 'too many other things to do' as her reason for quitting.

'Ha, she certainly did have other things to do!' said Celeste, eyes glittering as she was reminded of Janet's excuse for leaving. 'Like having her own bodice ripped open by Stan Woolford on her days off!'

Susan was vaguely familiar with the name. A local handyman, he had once called at her house to put up a few shelves. She couldn't remember much about him, only that his price was reasonable and the shelves hadn't fallen down.

'It all began when John hired him to put in a new shower. Apparently, the old one dribbled so badly they had to run around inside the cubicle just to get wet,' Celeste continued.

'He finished that job two months ago but I see his van outside theirs at least twice a week. And I'm *quite* sure it's not the plumbing he's tinkering with.'

Moving off to the kitchen to stick the kettle on, Susan felt sorry for Janet. Listening to Celeste there didn't appear to be a lot of concrete evidence of her alleged infidelity, just hearsay and supposition based on the presence of his van. Which might be completely innocent, after all. Perhaps they'd struck up a friendship and he popped in for a cuppa now and again? Not that he'd ever popped in to hers after the shelves were fitted. And – if they were having an affair – his van with 'Stan – The Man Who Can' proudly painted in bold blue letters was hardly the most discreet mode of transport.

Having taken orders for two cups of green tea, a decaf coffee and more wine for Nancy – making the most of her chauffeur for the evening – Susan returned to the living room. She passed one of the green teas to Emily who thanked her profusely. She even patted the sofa seat next to her, gesturing to Susan to sit down.

'It's been a lovely evening, Susan. And what a great idea, choosing food to match the theme of the book. No pressure on the rest of us, eh!'

Always vivacious and generous in her actions, there was something undefinably *different* about Emily that evening. Susan couldn't quite put her finger on it. It was like … like she'd been lit up from the inside, a low-wattage bulb replaced by a Hollywood-style spotlight. It was as if, on the surface, she was a willing participant in the light-hearted banter, whilst deep down something else was occupying her thoughts. A *good* something, judging by the way she smiled at random moments. Whatever was distracting her, it gave her a glow that no amount of make-up or restful nights' sleep could achieve. *I wouldn't mind some of that,* thought Susan wistfully. Her inner glow – if she'd ever really had one – had long been extinguished.

* * *

TIDYING up after the ladies had departed, Susan wondered – not for the first time – if she should move away. Pack in her job, sell the house and start somewhere new. Maybe a place by the sea. Some of her happiest childhood memories were of trips to the seaside with her parents. Donkey rides, building sandcastles or simply floating in the water and daydreaming for hours on end. Perhaps a change of scenery would inspire her to change her whole life. She could work in a shop or a café, take up a new hobby like painting or pottery. Closing her eyes, she imagined herself sitting on a little wooden deck with a brush in her hand, adding details to a simple landscape of sand and surf. She could try again to lose weight; perhaps it would be easier in a different environment? Away from people who knew her or at least *thought* they did. She could reinvent herself – no more sad, fat Susan – and become the person she had to believe existed somewhere inside. She imagined herself running (or at least, jogging) along miles of shoreline with the wind in her hair and happiness in her heart.

OK, who was she trying to kid? Drastic life changes demanded courage which was something she lacked, along with willpower and a sense of self-worth. Over the years – as her weight ballooned – her confidence had shrunk. Other people could start afresh, take on whole new identities but Susan knew she was stuck in a rut too deep to escape.

Turning on the TV she flicked aimlessly through the channels. Yet another programme about would-be dieters being put through their paces by an ex-military sadist; a soap opera – who knew which one? – featuring a delightful incest storyline, and a more appealing comedy-drama about a famous writer's upbringing on a Greek island. Settling for this one she cut herself another slice of cake and poured a glass of wine. Another hour or so and she'd head to bed. Where sleep offered her a few hours' respite from the mundanities of her existence.

CHAPTER 13

Meryl was merrily whizzing her Hoover around her flat, ABBA's greatest hits blasting out in the background. She hummed along contentedly, pausing only to gulp down a mouthful of her fennel tea. *So* good for the digestion, even if it reminded her of liquid liquorice.

Cleaning her small pad took very little time. Situated directly above the shop, it consisted of a decent-sized master bedroom; a tiny guest room that doubled up as her office; a combined lounge cum dining area and a galley-style kitchen. There was only one bathroom with an overhead shower and access from both the main bedroom and living area. Small but cosy, it suited Meryl perfectly and she had done her utmost to stamp her personality all over it. Twinkly fairy lights festooned the place all year round, luxurious velvet throws in shades of chocolate and maroon were artfully draped over her cream leather sofa and chairs and the walls bore an eclectic mix of prints and photographs that added a splash of colour throughout. Her lighting was subtle, just a few table lamps with low-wattage bulbs. It might not be a palace but it was hers and she didn't even have to worry about driving to work every day.

The main reason for today's domestic duties was that Miroslaw was coming round for dinner that evening. It was a Sunday and the only day that The Little Shop of Treasures was closed. This would be their sixth date and Meryl was more than a little nervous. Not that she feared anything bad would happen – he had always been the perfect gentleman – it was more a question of if something 'good' might happen. So far, they'd kissed several times, latterly with infinitely more ardour and a hint of tongue. Which meant sex could well be on the cards, although she suspected he would wait for her to give the green light. Was she ready? She wasn't completely sure. It had been a few years since her last relationship which had been a bit of a damp squib, both of them plodding on with half-hearted enthusiasm until they mutually agreed they had little in common. Her online dating experiences had nearly put her off men for life until Miroslaw came along. She certainly found him sexually attractive and she did miss feeling wanted and desired in that way. And she was only forty-eight – yes, she did fib a little about her age – and not ready to settle for a life of celibacy and only singing Swedes for company.

Switching off the vacuum cleaner Meryl straightened a couple of cushions and gave the room a liberal spray of Seduction, one of a range of essential oil blends that were very popular in the shop. She'd light a few candles this evening too, both to set the mood and ensure she looked her best. She'd picked out her outfit already. An old favourite, a silky black top with a sequinned trim around the neckline coupled with wide-legged black trousers that disguised the odd lumpy bit. She had considered putting on her control pants to suck in the aforementioned flab but decided against it. They were the most hideous-looking item of underwear she possessed, and took about ten minutes to wriggle into. And probably a good half hour to remove, by which time Miroslaw would have given up and gone home, defeated and deflated by their utter lack of sex appeal. Nope, she'd stick to her old faithfuls which could be whipped off and tossed aside in the time it took for him to strip off his boxers. Or his G-string. She prayed fervently it was the former.

After a quick shower, Meryl was ready to hit the shops. She'd chosen a simple menu, big on taste but easy to prepare. Miroslaw was keen on cooking so she wanted to impress, but equally didn't want to end up a sweaty and stressed heap in the kitchen. So it was smoked salmon salad with a crème fraiche dressing to start, lamb cutlets with leek mash and mustard sauce for the main and tarte citron from the high street patisserie. With coffee and brandy to finish. Or to set the scene for some postprandial hanky panky.

It was a crisp and clear day as Meryl strode purposefully around town. She'd picked up the starter and main ingredients in the supermarket, along with a decent bottle each of white and red. At least, she hoped they were decent. She always went for the deeply scientific method of choosing the ones with the prettiest labels. Just the dessert to deal with and she could head back with hours to spare before show time.

'A tarte citron, please.'

The patisserie was busy as always, Meryl reaching the front of the queue after a good ten-minute wait. They were open seven days a week and produced a mouth-watering and calorific selection of sweet treats that could derail the most dedicated dieter. She didn't mind. Desserts had never really been her speciality and their selection was always top-notch. As she paid and accepted the proffered plastic bag containing its lemony sinfulness she noticed another customer she vaguely recognised. A plump lady standing by the shelves of hand-made petit fours, lifting up one box, then another. She looked distracted, distressed even, her movements jerky and her hands shaky as she selected then rejected the choices. Who was she? And how did she know her? Then she remembered. She was a friend of Tabbie's mum. She'd met her once or twice when Tabbie had invited her back to the family home. If she recalled correctly, on one occasion it had been just before book club, which Emily – Tabbie's mum – hosted from time to time. They'd had to run through some possible new stock items for the shop and had decided to have a quick tête-à-tête at her mum's because Tom was hosting a boys' night and made it clear that women were categorically not welcome. Unless they came bearing six packs, takeaway pizzas and the promise of a pole-dancing routine.

'Susan? Hi, you probably don't remember me but I'm Meryl. Tabitha's boss? I run The Little Shop of Treasures. We met at her mum's, Emily's, a while back. And some other time, I'm sure, but anyway… Are you OK?'

The other woman stared blankly at Meryl, with red-rimmed eyes and a trembling mouth. She was now clutching a box of mini éclairs and looked in danger of squeezing the life out of them. It was clear something was wrong but Meryl was unsure how to proceed. Not a meddler by nature she was reluctant to appear nosy or pushy but, equally, she felt unable to simply walk away.

'Look, I can see you're upset and it's absolutely none of my business but if there's anything I can do? Here, let me take those for you.'

Meryl slid her plastic bag up her outstretched arm as she gently removed the slightly crushed box of éclairs from Susan's grasp. As she did so a solitary tear slid down Susan's cheek and she gave a little sob. Meryl turned to the thankfully empty counter and hurriedly paid for the goods, slipping them into the basket at Susan's feet.

'In my opinion you need a sit down and a cup of something good and strong. I'm a good listener if you feel like talking, but I'm just as happy to sit in silence if that's what you prefer. I just think you could do with a bit of company right now. What do you think?'

Moments later they were seated in a little bar around the corner. Meryl had ordered herself a small glass of white but Susan had declined alcohol and was nursing a mug of hot chocolate with marshmallow sprinkles. She still hadn't spoken, aside from a whispered 'thank you' when Meryl guided her gently out of the patisserie and along the street a few hundred yards.

She quietly surveyed her companion as they each sipped their drinks. Susan seemed a little calmer, a milky moustache adorning her upper lip which gave her a vaguely comical air in contrast to her earlier despair. Meryl decided against pointing it out, the poor woman clearly having bigger issues on her mind than a bit of unintended facial adornment.

'So, would you like to share what's troubling you? I promise I'm completely non-judgemental. If you're actually a man trapped inside a woman's body or you harbour a desire to rid the world of Z list celebrities with a Kalashnikov, then I'm all ears. I have to confess I'm a die-hard ABBA fan and have been known to wear dungarees and ogle pictures of Pierce Brosnan on the internet. He's even on my screen saver. How sad is that?'

At this point, Susan looked up and laughed. Actually laughed, a proper, from-the-belly, chortle that lit up her face and showed a hint of the real person within.

'None of the above, sadly. The truth is ... I have cancer. And I don't quite know how to deal with it. And there's not a person on earth I can share it with. Except you. And why should you care? You don't know me. You've been so kind but I can't burden you with this.'

Susan rose as if to leave but Meryl beckoned for her to stay. Her head said to walk away but her heart went out to this lonely lady who had spilled her darkest secrets and so clearly needed a friend to confide in.

'What kind? If you don't mind me asking? I've known a lot of people who've faced the big C and everyone has dealt with it in different ways. If I can help …?'

Susan looked at her with a mixture of despondency and desperation. She was clearly split in half, wanting to spill out all her worries and fears yet afraid to do so with someone she barely knew. Who could laugh at her behind her back, poor fat lady with a disease so prevalent yet it took her months to pick up the signs because she hated her body so much?

'Breast cancer. Early stages, thankfully. Had a small op, just going through some intensive radiotherapy. It's not been too bad, a bit like a nasty sunburn really. It's just, my fiftieth birthday's fast approaching and I never imagined my life would turn out like this. Then again, whoever knows what's going to happen to them? It's only another date on the calendar, so who cares?'

You should care, thought Meryl. Someone should care. This was a lady with little self-esteem facing a tough regime of treatment and with no-one to support her at the other end.

'When's your birthday? I'm a Leo. King of the zodiac and all that crap.'

Susan grimaced. Wiped a napkin across her mouth, removing all traces of hot chocolate residue.

'It's on the ninth of May. Taurus the bull. Seems quite appropriate for an old heifer like me!'

Both Meryl and Susan laughed a little nervously. It was time to leave yet neither knew what to say or do next.

'I haven't planned anything. I don't exactly have a long list of people who'd want to celebrate with me. So, it'll probably be me, a cake and an early night.'

No, it won't, thought Meryl as she swallowed the dregs of her wine and slipped on her coat. I may not really know you but I will do everything in my power to give you a party to remember.

They parted ways outside, after Meryl had keyed Susan's number into her phone and taken note of her address. She'd offered to accompany her on some of her hospital visits but Susan had politely but firmly declined.

'That's really kind of you but there's no need, honestly. Maybe we could meet up again for a coffee or something? If you're not too busy, that is.'

Meryl promised to ring her soon, watching as her new friend disappeared from view. Still a forlorn figure but with a more purposeful stride than before.

Back at the flat she quickly unpacked her groceries. Still a few hours until Miroslaw arrived so she decided to strike while the iron was still hot. She had Emily's phone number in case of any emergency involving Tabbie but had thankfully never had to use it. Until now.

'Emily? Hello there, it's Meryl, Tabbie's boss. Sorry to bother you but I just wanted to run something by you if you have a minute.'

Meryl quickly outlined her meeting with Susan, carefully omitting any mention of the cancer diagnosis. She didn't feel it was her place to share such information and, judging by Emily's responses, she was pretty sure Susan hadn't confided in her.

'She just seemed really down and when we were having a drink she mentioned her fiftieth birthday was coming up but that she wasn't planning on celebrating it. It just struck me as really sad so I was wondering …'

Before she could finish, Emily jumped in.

'I had absolutely no idea it was her birthday soon. Or even what age she was. The truth is, I only really know her through book club and the odd social gathering. I've always found her a tad irritating to be honest. A bit of a gossip-monger who knows everything about everyone. I don't really know who her friends are or if she has any. I think it was Esther Thompson who introduced her to me but they never struck me as particularly close. I know she's never been married and she works from home but that's about it.'

There was a brief pause as both women contemplated what appeared to be a rather sad and lonely existence compared to their own busy and generally happy lives. Emily broke their reverie first.

'Here's what I think we should do. I can send out an email to all the book club members saying I'd like to host a special meeting on the evening of Susan's birthday. Esther was supposed to host April but I'm sure she won't mind making it a bit later. And we can say something about finalising the timetable for the year, getting ahead with book choices before we take a break for the summer. Except I'll flag the others that it's actually going to be a surprise party for Susan's birthday.'

'Are you sure she'd come? She did say she'd probably stay home alone and have an early night, poor love,' questioned Meryl. She had visions of her and Emily having to physically drag Susan in her pyjamas out of bed, pausing only to pin a glittery '50' badge on her chest.

'I get the impression that book club is maybe the only real social activity she has, apart from the odd yoga class at the local community centre. So yes, I'm pretty confident she'll turn up. I can do some nibbles and bits and maybe ask the others to bring a plate of something too.'

'And I'll rustle up a few bottles of bubbly and some party hats and decorations from my shop. Maybe a nice birthday banner and some balloons? I've got some lovely fiftieth ones in bright pink and silver. I could come by a little earlier to get things organised if you like. Ooh, what about a cake? We can't have a party without a cake!'

There was silence on the line again for a few moments until Emily came to the rescue.

'You said you bumped into Susan at the patisserie? They do amazing birthday cakes, made to order. If we each contributed something – say £10 or £15 per person – we could easily order one...'

'And probably have money left over to buy a little gift too!' added Meryl. She was starting to feel distinctly excited at the prospect of staging a surprise party. As long as the intended recipient felt the same way.

They ended their chat with a promise to meet up soon and finalise the details. Meryl felt quite chuffed with herself, suffused with a warm glow at maybe, just maybe making someone's life a little brighter. Her own hadn't been sunshine and roses all the way but she was a glass half-full kind of girl and hated to see other people gazing bleakly into an almost empty vessel.

Another brief hose down in the shower and she was nearly ready for the main event. Still wrapped in her favourite fluffy bathrobe with a towel around her head she headed to the kitchen. Smoked salmon shredded and wrapped in cling film. Check. Dressing assembled, ready for a final whisk before pouring. Check. Lamb cutlets out the fridge to come to room temperature, chilled ready mash (a cheat, but even Delia cheated sometimes) on standby with chopped leeks to add at end, check.

Grainy mustard awaiting lamb juices and a spoonful of redcurrant jelly and seasoning to finish, check. Tarte citron needing nothing more than a sharp knife and a dollop of cream. The only finishing touches remaining were to herself.

There. All done. Meryl turned this way and that, pleased at her reflection and glad she hadn't gone for the suck-it-all-in underwear. Apart from being deeply unattractive, they also forced the unwanted flesh upwards creating a virtual second bosom beneath her already not insubstantial real one. She was confident that if they made it as far as the bedroom then Miroslaw would be happy not to be confronted with a four-breasted freak show contender.

'Meryl! You look spectacular. Truly, you take my breath away. Let me kiss you.'

Meryl duly obliged, submitting happily to a prolonged and tongue-tinged kiss which ended only when she slapped him playfully on the shoulder.

'Steady on! I have a gourmet feast prepared and a tummy that's rumbling. So, if you'd care to take yourself through to the lounge ...'

She took Miroslaw's coat and deposited it on her bed. Freshly made just in case. Music was playing quietly in the background. Not ABBA but A-ha. Norwegian but similarly Scandinavian. 'Take On Me' was her favourite. She'd loved the video when she was younger and had had a bit of a crush on the lead singer. In some ways Miroslaw reminded her of him. Maybe the chiselled cheekbones.

'Be a darling and pour us a glass of something while I put together the starter. Maybe the white as we're having fish,' said Meryl, opening the fridge and removing the salmon and jug of dressing. Miroslaw deftly squeezed in next to her and took out the bottle, sneaking another kiss as he did so. Meryl giggled and bent over to retrieve the mixed leaves from the salad drawer. As she began to plate up their entrees, he served the wine. They clinked their glasses and each took a satisfying mouthful.

'Very nice indeed,' remarked Miroslaw. 'A good choice, Meryl, and I have no doubt the food will be equally enjoyable. I have been looking forward to this all day.'

Not just the meal, prayed Meryl. Hopefully he had also been looking forward to taking their relationship to the next level. Now that he was here she could feel her earlier doubts fading, to be replaced by a distinct tingle of anticipation.

Seated at her bistro-style dining table which she'd set with her finest linen, cutlery and glasses they tucked into the first course. Miroslaw enthused over every morsel, declaring it worthy of any fine restaurant. Meryl blushed at his effusiveness but was extremely pleased at his compliments.

For the main course, she pan-fried the lamb cutlets and sautéed the leeks in butter, before beating them through the microwaved mash. Miroslaw laughed when she apologised for not making it from scratch.

'There's nothing wrong with a little helping hand now and again. Since I came to this country I have developed a liking for porridge and often use those instant sachets. So much quicker and just as good, I believe!'

They'd moved on to the red wine now, Meryl returning the half-drunk bottle of white to the fridge. She wasn't sure if Miroslaw was quite as impressed with this one, but he gamely swirled it around and proclaimed the lamb a triumph.

Taking a break before dessert they chatted easily, 'Hunting High and Low' playing away at low volume. Meryl filled him in on the latest goings on in the shop, including a funny episode the day before.

'So, I'd just arranged a display of cute baby bibs that had arrived earlier in the week. You know the kind of thing. Well, maybe you don't but anyway... they've got silly sayings on them. Things like 'Feed me or nobody sleeps tonight' and 'Someone put my cape on backwards'. Not something I'd usually stock but I've had quite a few young mums coming in recently and thought they'd sell well.'

Miroslaw had reached across the table and was stroking her hand in a rather seductive fashion. She felt her train of thought slip away as his thumb caressed her palm, fingers entwining hers. *Hand sex*, she mused. OK, on with the story.

'Well, the next thing is this little old lady comes in and heads straight for the bib display. She must have been at least eighty. She's flipping through them, chuckling away to herself. I figure she's looking for a present for someone, maybe a great grandchild? Finally, she takes one and brings it to the counter. "I drink till I pass out", it says. She pays, I ask if she wants it gift wrapped, and she shakes her head.'

'No need, love. It's for my Albert. I'm that fed up with him dribbling half his dinner down his front of an evening. Costs me a fortune in Vanish, he does! This should do the trick.' 'And off she trotted, pledging to return for a few more soon. Poor man!'

Miroslaw was smiling, his fingers now wandering up her arm and fondling it through her sleeve. Meryl felt little bubbles of excitement frothing up inside her. It looked like passion could very well be on the cards.

'Dessert? I picked up a very nice tarte citron. Cheating again, I know but—' She was silenced as Miroslaw pressed a finger to her lips before drawing it slowly down her chin and towards her chest.

'I only want you, my beautiful Meryl. Right now.'

Straight to the point then. They rose to their feet as one, Miroslaw drawing her into his arms and kissing her with an intensity that literally took her breath away. With lips firmly locked he steered her in the direction of the bedroom and the bed itself. Her head was slightly spinning as he perched her on the edge and began removing her top. She lay down and took a few deep breaths as he moved on to her waistband, unhooking the button and guiding her trousers southwards. Then proceeded to kiss her from top to toe, still fully clothed himself. Should she start undressing him too? Not that he was giving her much of a chance, the weight of his body pinning her to the duvet.

'You are so perfect, just like I imagined,' he whispered, fingers now playing with the edges of her bra. Hardly, thought Meryl, who was trying simultaneously to suck in her stomach and get some much-needed air into her lungs. Which was well-nigh impossible as he'd resumed full-on snogging interspersed with groans of pleasure and mutterings of 'Oh, Meryl'. Ah well, the tarte would still taste good tomorrow, she figured, then mentally rebuked herself for thinking such a thing when she was minutes away from her first sexual encounter in ages.

'Do you want me too?' Miroslaw murmured, his hands creeping round her back in pursuit of her bra clasp. She was about to reply in the affirmative when suddenly he stopped. Oh help, don't say she'd put on the wrong one! She had a couple of bras with so many hooks and eyes they would challenge Houdini himself.

Miroslaw was now sitting bolt upright, his face turned away from Meryl. She sat up too and touched his cheek, shocked to see tears glittering in his eyes when he finally looked at her.

'What's the matter? Miroslaw, have I done something wrong? Of course I want you too, you must know that.' Meryl felt herself trembling both with cold and nerves. She took a few steps to the door and grabbed her dressing gown before sitting down again.

He didn't reply for what seemed an eternity but had taken

hold of her hand. Finally, he spoke; his voice laced with regret and sadness.

'It's not you, it's me. I am so sorry, Meryl. I so wanted this night to be perfect. You are perfect but I have something on my mind and it is troubling me greatly.' He let out an enormous sigh and looked so forlorn that Meryl pulled him into a hug.

'Whatever it is you can tell me. Maybe I can help? Please, Miroslaw. I don't know if you know the expression "a problem shared is a problem halved" but I really believe it's true.' She waited, he sighed again and then he poured out his heart to her.

'Because these bastards – please excuse my language – have not made payment to me I have run into a little cash flow problem. Business has always been good but I know I have not always been the best at pursuing people who owe me money. And now I owe others money and they will not be – how do you say? – as accommodating as me.'

Over coffee and a slice of tarte citron Miroslaw completed his tale of woe. Meryl felt a mixture of anger and sadness as he explained how he'd built up his business from nothing but could end up losing it all.

A short while later he left, apologising profusely for spoiling the evening – which Meryl assured him wasn't the case – and promising to see her the next day when he returned for his car. With one last, lingering kiss he was gone in a taxi she'd insisted on calling for him.

Sitting in the half-light of the lounge with a second slice of tarte and a small glass of white Meryl pondered the situation. He hadn't stated how much money was involved and she hadn't liked to ask. But she had been building up a rainy-day fund over the years which now amounted to a not insubstantial sum. Should she offer to help? Would he even accept it?

Time for bed she decided, scooping up the last crumbs from her plate. She hadn't expected to be sleeping alone – or even sleeping at all – but she needed time to gather her thoughts. They could talk again tomorrow and hopefully she could find a way to ease his situation. First Susan, now Miroslaw. It had been an exhausting day.

CHAPTER 14

It had been a long process, some days filled with doubt that it would ever be finished. But – two weeks ago – to Celeste's total delight and amazement, she had written the closing paragraph of *Beyond the Bounds of Ecstasy*. Just shy of 50,000 words, every one of them her own creation. She was incredibly proud of herself and dying to share the news with someone but had decided to wait and see the outcome of the competition. If she was unsuccessful she'd probably hide it away in a secret file, never to shown to anyone. But if, by some miracle, she actually *won*, then she wouldn't be able to contain herself. She knew Michael would be delighted for her and as for Emily ... Well, she'd probably be completely gobsmacked that her under-achieving big sister had managed to put pen to paper. Or at least fingers to keyboard.

All that had remained was a final run-through for grammar and punctuation errors and to ensure the formatting matched the strict criteria issued by the magazine. They'd asked for submissions to be made by email with a covering letter giving details about herself, including which name she'd like to be published under. After a great deal of thought she'd opted for Astra Du Bois rather than her own name, figuring the former sounded far more exotic and in keeping with the mood of the book. It had taken her a long time and considerable Googling before she'd figured out how to attach the sizeable file. Then she'd spent another good half an hour composing the letter to go with it. Satisfied that she could do no more she'd taken a deep breath and hit 'send'. Now she spent a ridiculous amount of time each day checking her in-box to find out if Leo and Seraphina were just the tantalising ticket for the *Tea Break* faithful.

Michael had been gone for almost two hours despite the less than delightful weather. Grey clouds had been gathering all morning and now the rain was coming down in torrents. Silly man, he'll be soaked through. She closed her computer and decided to make herself a belated lunch.

As she sliced a wholemeal loaf and mixed chopped boiled eggs with mayonnaise and a sprinkling of chives she wondered if she should get one of those fitness bands too. Not that just *wearing* it made you lose weight and get fit. Wouldn't that be wonderful? Just strap it round your wrist and – hey presto – several pounds lighter and down a couple of dress sizes. Nope, obviously some serious effort was involved, particularly in the putting one foot in front of the other department. Celeste was well aware that exercise wasn't really her thing. She drove virtually everywhere and always sought out a parking spot as close as humanly possible to her destination. She'd tried a Pilates class once but kept falling off the Swiss ball thingy and she detested the thought of swimming or aquarobics. All that getting hair wet and make-up smeared everywhere.

Michael had always kept himself in good shape, whereas Celeste knew she'd let the weight creep on in recent years. She was far from obese – goodness, she'd never allow that to happen – but tightening waistbands and blouses that gaped between the buttons were irrefutable proof of her expanding figure.

Maybe she should pop out to the shops now, treat herself to a band? She'd picked up Michael's at the local sports store after looking at several models and opting for the one recommended by the friendly assistant. What was it called again? Something Up, if she rightly recalled. Jawline? Wish-bone? No matter, she'd recognise it when she saw it.

It would have been a brisk twenty or so minutes' walk to the shop but Celeste reasoned it was too wet. In any case, there wasn't much point in clocking up steps just yet when she didn't have the necessary equipment to log it, was there? She parked her beloved bright red Audi TT right outside, a space fortuitously available as another customer drove off.

'Hello there! I'm not sure you'll remember me but I bought a fitness tracker here a few months ago for my husband. And I've decided it's time to get one for myself!' Celeste beamed at the same helpful assistant who'd served her before. Probably in his mid to late twenties with a physique that suggested he took part in triathlons and scaled mountains on a regular basis.

Paul – as written on his name badge – claimed that of *course* he remembered her and exactly which model she'd bought. 'I've got it in a few different colours but I think the white one with the gold strip would really suit you. It's a limited edition so a bit more expensive. Try it on.' He handed her one from the display stand, helping to fasten the tiny clasp and adjusting it to fit correctly. Celeste was pleased to see it co-ordinated nicely with her Omega watch. Who'd have thought, a fitness band as a fashion accessory?

After helping her to download the relevant app and synch the band with her phone, Paul gave her a quick rundown on what the band could do. 'It monitors your heart rate, both resting and passive, and also records your sleep patterns. And, of course, it keeps count of how many steps you take each day. The optimum number is 10,000 but I usually manage at least double that!'

Well, hooray for you, thought Celeste a little sourly. Did that involve nipping out on his lunch break and speed-walking around the local park, knocking wobbly toddlers and grannies on zimmer frames out the way as he strode his way to stepping glory? She wondered if this piece of technological wizardry also barked out criticism if the wearer failed to meet its goals. 'Move it, fatty!' or 'Step away from the chocolate, now!' Probably not and just as well, or she'd end up stomping on it in a fit of pique.

Back home and still no sign of Michael. The rain had abated, the sun daring to peep out from behind the clouds. He was obviously on the same wavelength as Paul, the pair of them dead set on getting an electronic pat on the head from their fitness buddy.

Celeste gathered up a pile of dirty laundry and made her way to the basement utility room. Duly loaded and set in motion, she headed back upstairs and wiped down the kitchen worktops. Not that anything was particularly dirty, just a few stray crumbs from her sandwich. She had a cleaner who came in once a week and dealt with the more distasteful jobs like scrubbing the loos and cleaning the windows. Next, she made her way to the bedroom and spent a pleasant half hour rearranging her shoe collection according to colour, heel height and frequency of wear.

She checked her laptop to see if there'd been any response from *Tea Break* yet. There hadn't, although she'd received an automated message when she sent it saying that her submission had been received and would be considered in due course. She read through a few other emails but most were junk and she deleted them.

Right, time to check in with *Big Brother* and see just what she'd achieved so far. Ooh, she reckoned at least 5,000 steps. After all, she'd been up and down the stairs a few times and had walked from the shop to the car and from the car to the house. Which wasn't far but every little counted, didn't it?

'You moved 749 steps,' decreed the screen, with a graph displaying her inertia in colourful detail. Celeste slammed the phone down in disgust. No wonder Michael pounded the pavements for hours in order to reach his target. She clearly had some serious work to do in the walking department. Otherwise her new toy was going to break into hysterical laughter and broadcast across the internet that its owner was a total sloth who would only reach 10,000 steps with a rocket inserted in her rear.

Where was Michael? Maybe she should call him, check everything was OK. She had sudden visions of him keeling over on some isolated path, only to be discovered cold and stiff hours later by an inquisitive labrador.

As she picked up her phone and scrolled through the directory, something caught her eye. Sitting on the coffee table, partly covered by that morning's newspaper, was Michael's phone. He'd obviously put it down while having his daily fix of coffee and headlines and not noticed it when he left.

Celeste put down her own phone and picked up his. It was an older model in a rather battered black leather case but he'd insisted it was good enough and resisted her attempts to get him to upgrade it. She pushed the button and the screen sprang to life, prompting her to enter the pass-code. She hesitated, even though she was pretty sure she knew what it was. Whenever they holidayed anywhere Michael liked to pop their valuables in the room safe – pass-ports, her jewellery, his iPad and so on – and he always keyed in the same four-digit number. 1066. Michael was a bit of a history buff and prided himself on an encyclopaedic knowledge of key dates, The Battle of Hastings being just one of them.

She trusted him completely, had never been one of those women who felt compelled to rifle through their husbands' pockets or scrutinise their credit card statements for unexplained purchases. Likewise, she was sure Michael would never stoop to snooping through her things, although she had recently changed her laptop password. But only because she was fiercely protective of her book, not because she thought for one minute that Michael would go near it.

Celeste realised she'd been holding her breath. She exhaled loudly then typed in the passcode. Up popped all the colourful icons, including the one they now shared with their his and hers fitness bands. She pushed away her feelings of guilt, reasoning that she was just curious about how many steps he managed on a regular basis. She touched the icon and looked at bright orange wedge which displayed his grand total for today. 4,927. That didn't seem a lot considering he'd been out walking now for several hours. She scrolled back through the preceding days. A couple around the 8,000 mark, one at almost 11,500 – that was the day they'd hit the big shopping mall on the outskirts of town. She'd certainly *felt* like they'd covered a lot of ground that day. But it had been well worth it, garnering her a few new outfits and a set of golf clubs for Michael. Maybe the phone and band had to be in close proximity to record the steps? No, she was pretty sure that wasn't the case. When was his last epic walkabout? She racked her brains. It was the day she'd chatted to Emily about the chimney episode. Exactly one week ago. She located the relevant date with the backwards arrow. 3,072 steps. That simply didn't make sense. Unless …

Celeste sat down hastily on the sofa, still clutching

Michael's phone. Her heart was beating too fast, to the point she felt sure her band would start vibrating and flashing to warn of imminent cardiac arrest. There had to be a reasonable explanation, she told herself. Perhaps the band had come loose – Paul had told her they were sometimes prone to undoing themselves, although usually during the night if the wearer tossed and turned a lot – and he'd forgotten to put it back on. She thought this unlikely, however, given his dedication to the bloody thing. Maybe it was faulty, but she dismissed this possibility instantly. Michael would have noticed the discrepancy in the step count and been down the shop to have a word with the ever so obliging Paul. No, there was really only one answer that added up. Michael had been doing considerably less walking than he claimed. Which begged the question, what *had* he been doing instead?

Just as Celeste was thinking the unthinkable, she heard the front door open then slam shut. She hastily shoved his phone back under the newspaper, pasting on a broad smile as Michael entered the room.

'Hello, sweetheart. How are things? Sorry I was gone so long, decided to try a new route and got a bit lost so it added a bit to my schedule. Never mind, at least I'll have a pretty decent step total to add to my tally!' Michael beamed back at her, exuding rude health and the demeanour of someone with absolutely nothing to hide. Except, Celeste *knew* that something was amiss but was struggling to accept that Michael – her lovely, dependable, *faithful* Michael – might be hiding something from her. Something, or *someone*.

'I'm fine, darling, just been pottering around here. Oh, and I decided if you can't beat them, join them so I bought this.' Celeste thrust out her wrist, watching Michael's reaction at her new purchase. 'I know I need to get more exercise so now we have matching fitness bands and I fully intend to move more and get in shape. Maybe we can start walking together!'

Was it her overwrought imagination or did Michael pale slightly at this suggestion? If so, he quickly regained his composure and gave her a kiss on the cheek. As he bent down to do so, he spotted his phone peeking out from under *The Times*. He picked it up, looking abashed.

'I didn't even realise I'd forgotten this today. Goes to show how walking focuses the mind, clears away all the clutter of technology and those interminable beeps and pings signalling someone is after you for something. The only satisfying noise I want to hear these days is when this clever toy – he gestured to his band – tells me I've reached the magical 10,000!'

Which clearly hasn't happened recently, aside from their shopping expedition. She was still struggling to come up with a reasonable explanation, batting away dark thoughts of treachery and deceit as they crowded her brain.

'I expect it must have produced a fanfare today, you've been gone for ages! I had visions of you slumped over somewhere. In fact, I was about to call you but that wouldn't have done much good, would it?' she said, nodding at his phone. Although maybe he wouldn't have answered it anyway, not if he was indeed in a horizontal position, blood pumping through his veins as he… Stop, Celeste. She had absolutely no proof that Michael was up to anything underhand. But if the numbers weren't lying then *he* was. She just had to find out why.

* * *

MICHAEL HAD RETREATED to his study, telling Celeste he had some paperwork to deal with and the promise of dinner out that evening. He'd been taken aback by her surprise purchase, even more so at the suggestion they become fitness band buddies. Of course, there *were* days when he genuinely went walking. He liked stepping out in the fresh air, each mile covered clearing away the mental clutter of day to day life. But many of his alleged outings in recent weeks had been to meet up with Sophie and that was something he simply could not share with his wife. He could not even begin to imagine her reaction if she learned of their secret assignations. They had always been honest with each other; it would be like lobbing a hand grenade into their relationship. And he was far from sure it would survive the explosion. Not to mention the fact that Sophie loathed Celeste and blamed her – at least partly – for his decision to keep his distance all those years. Which he didn't think was entirely fair. No, he was the one who should have stood firm and insisted on seeing his only child. Celeste might not have been happy about it but it would have been the right thing to do. And given time she maybe, just maybe, would have grown fond of Sophie too. It wasn't as if she *detested* children – she'd always been fond of her niece, Tabitha, in a detached kind of way – she simply didn't have a maternal bone in her body. And Sophie was painfully accurate when she described him as weak and spineless. Whereas she at least was trying to mend some bridges even if they seemed beyond repair at times.

Michael could feel the beginning of a headache spreading across his temples. He didn't have the faintest idea what to do for the best. All he knew was that he had to keep seeing Sophie and her boys. And try to figure out a way to prevent his rock-solid marriage from crumbling apart. He could start by taking Celeste to her favourite restaurant and generating some enthusiasm about her newfound zest for pounding the pavements. Mind you, he'd believe it when he saw it. She had a positive allergy to exercise and would hop in the car just to pop to the corner shop. Getting wearily to his feet, he made his way upstairs for a shower, shave and a couple of paracetamol.

* * *

'So, when are we going to go on our first walk together? Not that we haven't *walked* together before, of course. I just mean now that we both have bands and can see how we're each getting on. It says on the app that there's nothing like a bit of support to spur you on. We can add each other as friends and track our progress. It'll be fun!'

Michael had just speared a garlic butter-oozing escargot into his mouth and narrowly avoided spitting it back out. How to dodge this bullet and come out alive, he wondered. He wasn't sure Sophie would be overly keen if he suggested they started taking long walks together. They generally met in unassuming little cafés, as far away as possible from potential prying eyes and wagging tongues.

'That's a sweet idea, my darling but it smacks a little of a competition and that's not how I see the band, for me at least. Of course, we can go for walks together but I don't really see the need to compare notes on who took the most steps or had the deepest sleep. Anyway, my ego would be deeply wounded if you racked up more steps than me!' Michael hoped his response came across as convincing and not too callous. Judging by the way Celeste's eyes narrowed and she savagely speared an olive with positive venom he feared not. As she popped it into her mouth her expression lightened and she smiled.

'OK, it was a silly idea. Forget I even mentioned it. It will be enough if we get to spend more time together and perhaps it'll help me shed a pound or two. Although I don't think there's much danger of me overtaking you in the stepping stakes!' Celeste dabbed at her mouth with her napkin, reaching across to squeeze Michael's hand. 'Still, I'm going to drop by the sports shop again and treat myself to some new trainers. Can't be getting into this fitness malarkey without the proper shoes, can I? What do you suggest, sweetheart? In terms of brand, I mean. Aren't Badedas meant to be good?'

Back home and Michael bid Celeste goodnight, citing fatigue after his long walk combined with a slap-up meal and a half-bottle of decent plonk. She'd pecked him on the lips, assured him she'd be up just as soon as she'd checked her emails.

She booted up her laptop but had no interest in the latest offers from M&S or John Lewis. She just needed a little quiet time to contemplate her next course of action. A trip to see Paul and get herself kitted out with appropriate footwear was a given. Maybe some comfy jogging bottoms too, and an all-weather lightweight jacket. Then she'd wait until Michael announced he planned a solo walking outing. Which she had no doubt he would, very soon. Except, this time Celeste would – quite literally – be following in his footsteps.

CHAPTER 15

Emily was floating in a most delicious way. Suspended between sleep and wakefulness, reluctant to open her eyes and discover it had all been a figment of her imagination. Which, if it *had* been, showed her imagination was capable of positions and strange noises her real self would struggle to conjure up. She stretched out an arm, made contact with something warm and breathing. Another person was in the bed with her. And had just rolled over and pulled her into an embrace that told her she wasn't dreaming, that all her torrid thoughts had been grounded in reality. Joe. She raised herself up on an elbow and dared to look at the man she'd spent the night with. And not the *first* night by any means. Since Bibgate, as they'd dubbed it, they'd seen each other many times, each one as wonderful and memorable as the one before. Which didn't stop her from continuing to marvel at waking up next to him.She prayed she didn't have a serious case of pillow face and cursed the fact she hadn't taken her make-up off. She'd been otherwise occupied, but smeared mascara and eyeliner did not bode well for morning seduction skills. She hadn't even combed her hair before they'd tumbled into bed. Emily was normally a stickler for pre-bed routines, and knew she'd failed spectacularly. Ah well, maybe his eyesight was a bit dodgy too. Doubtful though, given his youth and vigour. Maybe she could sprint – or at least shuffle – to the bathroom for a quick repair job and...

'Good morning, beautiful. How are you today?' Joe kissed the tip of her nose, hands sliding through her hair which probably had more knots than a macramé basket. Ouch! She wiggled away a little, still keeping her torso as close to his as possible. It was like a magnet, her bits drawn to his bits and quite unable to break the attraction. She'd thought last night's multiple couplings would have satisfied her for at least a decade, given the drought of recent years. She'd been wrong.

'We've been looking to expand the business. Cleaning chimneys brings in a decent income but it's not exactly sexy, is it?'

You certainly are, thought Emily dreamily as he ran a finger along her collarbone, sending shockwaves through her body.

'So, me and my dad – his name's Steve, by the way – did some research and found a great opportunity to expand. We've taken over a place called Where the Hearth Is – OK, another naff name – but it's working out well so far. They design and install really cool fireplaces. Even in homes where they don't think they've the space for one. Honest, Emily, you have to come and see for yourself. Meet my dad – I know he'll love you – and Adam. He manages the place and has a real talent for matching people with their needs and wishes.' By this point Joe was tracing butterfly kisses down her torso. She could barely recall her own name, never mind anyone else's. Right now she didn't want to think about life outside these four walls. Joe was now gently parting her thighs and, if she died right now, she'd be the happiest dead person on earth. Although the undertakers might need to manipulate her rictus grin into something more decorous.

Some twenty minutes later and Emily was lying back replete, Joe next to her with one arm coiled round her waist, the other smoothing her hair back from her face. She really should get up and get on with things. Like paying bills, doing the laundry and tackling a weightier than usual manuscript that had landed in her inbox. Strangely, she couldn't give a rat's arse about any of it. She was under no illusions that this was a long-term thing, but right here and right now was precisely where she wanted to be.

'Big plans for the day?' asked Joe. He was now nibbling her right ear in a provocative fashion. If she replied she'd be quite content to stay under the duvet for several repeat performances he might think she was a nymphomaniac. Or someone with nothing better to do with her life than experience multiple orgasms. Not that *that* sounded so awful, compared with tackling the ironing mountain or giving the toilet bowls a scrub. Neither of which had ever made her moan out loud with pleasure.

'Nothing exciting, just boring chores. What about you, don't you have lots of jobs to get to?' She fervently prayed that the answer was no, that every chimney in the vicinity was immaculately swept or that his dad was dealing with today's rota.

Joe leaned over her and looked at the bedside clock. 'I'm afraid I've got to get going soon. I've a few calls to make then I'll be working with Dad and Adam in the afternoon. There's a new consignment of fireplaces arriving and we need to figure out the showroom layout. But I've got time for a quick nibble ... breakfast, I mean!' He planted a smacker on her lips before clambering out of bed and heading off to retrieve the trail of clothes they'd discarded last night. Emily watched his departing bottom with unbridled lust. She pinched herself hard in the thigh – ouch! – just in case she was in the middle of yet another torrid dream. It was all too much to take in. And she was about to wake up to discover she was alone and had been sucking at the pillow all night. Nope, Joe was back – now fully dressed – and holding out a hand to her. 'Come on, lazy bones. After all that exercise, I'm *starving*!'

In the kitchen, Emily happily whipped up scrambled eggs while Joe sizzled some rashers of back bacon on the hob. A pot of coffee was on the table, along with glasses of juice and doorsteps of bread that Joe had sliced. They ate together contentedly, both hungry because of the calories they'd burned. When they'd finished, Joe patted his stomach – a six-pack for sure – and insisted on cleaning up. Duly done, he pulled Emily into his arms and kissed her until her head spun.

'So, I could well be working a bit late tonight. But could I see you tomorrow night? We could eat out again. Maybe not steak this time! Or ... you could come to my place and I'll make something? I'm no Masterchef but nobody's ever been rushed to casualty because of my cooking!' His eyes were twinkling with mischief and Emily felt another rush of desire.

'If you can rustle up something smooth and not life-threatening then I'm in. Baby mush?' *Oh help.* Why did she always come out with the most ridiculous things? Mentioning babies was *absolutely* not a good idea. Her reproductive system had most certainly called it a day, whereas Joe was in his prime for being a doting daddy. Not a subject they'd discussed, or – she reasoned – were ever likely to. But she didn't want to scare him off just yet.

'I'm sure I can come up with something more appetising than pureed carrots, thank you!' Joe showed no sign of mentally calculating the likelihood of them becoming parents and coming up with the obvious answer. No chance. Unless they adopted some poor little waif or spent a fortune on IVF treatment. Which would probably be ruled out on the grounds of her being the wrong side of fifty. And would she even *want* to be a mother again? Waving her child off to university in her seventies?

Thankfully Joe was a sex bomb as opposed to a mind reader. With a promise to text her later and pick her up the following evening for dinner à deux at his bachelor pad, he was gone.

Jim had always been more of an Oral B than an oral sex man. The few times she'd tried to initiate it he'd been very reluctant, preferring just to climb on board – so to speak – and thrust away until he was satisfied. Looking back, Emily had *rarely* been satisfied herself. Had lain there thinking, 'is that *it?*' as Jim descended into a coma. He'd been massively into dental hygiene, brushing and flossing and rinsing for several minutes morning and night. Guess he didn't consider getting his teeth entangled with her privates as effective as a good going over with waxed string. Crikey, she *was* getting crude in her old age, she thought with a chuckle. That's what happens when you get hot and horny with a fine young specimen. Speaking of hot and horny, it was probably time she got on with some work editing the latest racy saga that had arrived the day before. It was far bigger than the usual short stories or multi-part series' that she normally edited. The covering note from the magazine explained it was on the short list for a competition they'd run. Before making their final choice, they were sending out the frontrunners to various editors to give their expert feedback. Along with correcting the usual grammar, punctuation and presentation issues.

Fifty pages in and Emily was quite engrossed. Yes, it was pretty overblown, the writer clearly having spent too much of her life immersed in books featuring stallion-like heroes and swooning heroines. She'd had an amazingly orgasmic evening herself, but these characters took it to a whole new level. She felt exhausted, although that could also be to do with her nocturnal activities. Time for a long, restoring shower, she decided, then she'd get back to her editing.

Duly washed and dressed Emily returned to the job in hand. Despite herself she was enjoying the story which was tightly paced and with more twists and turns than a roller-coaster ride. The writer – who'd given herself the ridiculous pen name of Astra Du Bois – had both a vivid imagination and a deft way with words. Aside from a couple of spelling mistakes and misuse of quotation marks it was well presented, unlike some of the shambolic pieces she'd encountered in the past. She flicked back to the covering email from the magazine – *Tea Break* – but there was no mention of the writer's real name. Unless she really *was* Astra Du Bois and had a side line as a clairvoyant complete with headscarf and crystal ball.

Emily's mind drifted away from the manuscript and into the future. The very near future, as in the next evening. She wished she had a crystal ball of her own to foresee what was in store for her and Joe. Then again, would she *really* want to know? Her sensible and rational side said they'd perhaps date for a short time until Joe realised the age difference was too big a deal. They'd politely call it a day and, hopefully, remain friends. However, her wild and devil-may-care side – not often let off the leash – argued that nothing was impossible, that true love could conquer all as long as both parties felt the same. Or was she deluding herself, carried away on a wave of lust and influenced by Astra's torrid writing? Anyway, who said anything about love?

With the Joe Jackson song playing away on a constant loop in her head, Emily ploughed her way through the rest of the manuscript. Made her corrections and suggestions and fired it back to the publisher. Job done, what next? Maybe a trip to the shops, look for something new to wear tomorrow night. Her wardrobe badly needed an overhaul as Tabitha frequently reminded her. And much as she hoped to end the evening in her birthday suit it would be nice to start it in something reasonably alluring.

Emily parked Hamish just behind the high street and stuck the ticket behind the windscreen. She bypassed Bab's Boutique which she always thought was a little overly frilly and headed for Dressed To Kill which Tabitha assured her was a bit more 'edgy' and up to the minute. She wasn't convinced she was an 'edgy' kind of person – at least not in the fashion sense – but emboldened by her fledgling relationship she pushed open the door. To her great relief, no klaxons went off signalling the arrival of an older woman. The girl behind the counter – who looked in her early twenties – gave her a smile. 'Hi there. Just browsing? Give me a shout if you need anything.' Emily was relieved to be left alone to rifle through the racks. Too often assistants were immediately breathing down your neck, offering unsolicited advice and making polite chitchat. On her one and only trip to the US with Jim many years ago she'd wanted to beat them off with a big stick, so persistent were they in providing maximum customer service.

Emily was just stroking the sleeve of a satiny red top – scarlet woman! – when she heard her name being called. Seconds later she was being hugged by her friend, Christine. A rather awkward embrace as Christine was toting several shopping bags. Plonking them at her feet she looked Emily up and down then grinned broadly. 'Well, hello stranger! Haven't seen you in absolutely ages. How the hell are you, and why are you so rubbish at replying to texts?' Emily immediately flushed with guilt, stammering something about being very busy with work and stuff. The truth was, she was happy to meet up with friends from time to time but often made excuses when another coffee gathering or night out was mentioned. She'd never been one for meeting up on a regular basis to regurgitate previous conversations or indulge in wild speculation about other people's lives. This was another bugbear of her darling daughter. 'Mum, you spend far too much time home alone! It's not healthy, you know. You've got some nice friends, stop hiding away like a blinking hermit!' Maybe she was, but she enjoyed her own company and saw little need to change.

'Listen, do you have time for a quick cuppa when you're finished in here?' asked Christine. 'My feet are killing me and I could do with a sit down and a catch up.' Emily hesitated briefly, then nodded in agreement. She was fond of Christine even though – on the surface – they didn't have a lot in common. They'd met at a pastry-making course run by the local patisserie. Emily had signed up on a mad whim, with notions of creating delicious pies, quiches and éclairs. In reality, she couldn't get to grips with choux and her short-crust was more hardcore and virtually inedible. She resigned herself to ready-made from the supermarket but bonded with Christine who was similarly cack-handed. They generally got together every few weeks but Emily was embarrassingly aware it had been closer to three months since they'd last seen each other.

Sitting in a nearby café with a pot of mint tea, they got up to speed with their lives. Christine had been divorced several years earlier. Amicably, by all accounts. She was an attractive woman, if a bit forthright in her opinions, and incredibly sporty. Tennis, swimming, half-marathons – you name it, she sweated her way through it. Emily liked to keep in shape but would only run if something horrible was pursuing her. And her tennis skills left much to be desired. As did her breaststroke.

'I've been seeing him on and off for a few weeks now. Early days, who knows what'll happen? I'm not really looking for anything permanent. Been there, done that, got the decree nisi. Still, nice to know there's life in the old girl yet! Not ready for the vow of total chastity, if you catch my drift!'

Christine was chatting about the man she was currently seeing. A mid-fifties gym fanatic who had apparently run twenty full marathons and competed in several triathlons. Widowed fairly recently, he'd spotted Christine at the local sports centre smashing her opponent to pulp on the tennis court and asked her out. They'd been lobbing shots at each other ever since, neither apparently willing to concede an inch. Emily knew her friend well enough to know that everything was a contest and there could only be one winner. Probably the main reason her ex-husband had waved the white flag and beat a hasty retreat.

'So, what gives with the elusive Emily?' Christine swirled the teabags around inside the pot, then poured them a top-up. 'Anything or anyone I should know about? That was *quite* a sassy little number you picked up in the shop!'

Emily glanced at the plastic bag next to her, containing the red top with its cutaway shoulders. She hadn't tried it on, but knew it would look perfect with the slim-fitting white jeans she'd had for six years and still clung in all the right places. 'No, nothing. No one. All pretty dull really. Just plodding along, as you do.' Emily had no intention of sharing Joe with Christine. Or anyone else, for that matter. Not yet, not when it was all so new and shiny. Plus, she still wasn't sure what the general reaction would be when they went public. If they ever did.

CHAPTER 16

Tom was sitting in a darkened corner of Bar Belle, partly obscured by a large pillar. He alternated between taking nervous swigs of his pint and peering around the corner to check if Kate had arrived. He'd got there a little early, a few brochures and some print outs waiting in his briefcase.

Tabitha was having an at-home evening, which usually involved a hideous-looking face pack, her head shrouded in a comical zebra-print bath cap to maximise the effect of a hair mask. When he said he was going for a drink with the lads she was engrossed in flicking through Netflix in search of some trashy chick film to watch. 'Have fun', she replied, waggling her fingers in farewell. Except it came out more like 'aargh un' as said face pack was already setting like concrete.

Tom had felt horribly guilty – as well he should – but had tried to appease his conscience by telling himself that he was simply meeting a client. Admittedly a drop-dead gorgeous one who he could easily have dealt with at the office. Plus, his niggling fear that all was not rosy between him and

Tabitha grew a little stronger every day. Much as he'd been attracted to her when they first met, he hadn't felt anything like the *zing* when he first saw Kate.

Suddenly, there she was, her gaze searching the room until alighting on Tom. That dazzling smile again that made his insides go into meltdown. She was wearing the same red coat, open this time to reveal a short black dress. As she headed towards him several other men openly ogled her. Not surprising, she was a head-turning kind of girl.

'Hi Tom! This is so kind of you, giving up your free time to help me. Can I get you another drink?' She gestured to his almost empty glass, at the same time dropping her coat on a chair and fishing her purse out of her bag.

'Don't be silly, I'll go get them. Please, sit down. What's your tipple? OK, one glass of Pinot Grigio coming up.' He hastened to the bar which was mercifully quiet and was back at the table in under a minute. He handed her her wine and they toasted each other before settling back in their chairs. Tom put down his glass and picked up his briefcase, pulling out the relevant items. He spread them out before them, Kate leaning forward to take a look.

'Right, so based on what you said yesterday, I think Hong Kong could be a good option. It's considered very safe, even for solo female travellers. It's jam-packed with cultural things to do and see and the food is amazing. There are plenty of great hotel deals to be had at the moment as well as decent-priced flights. And if you like shopping' – Tom grinned in what he hoped was an engaging fashion – 'you're truly spoiled for choice with malls and street markets galore.' He felt a little thrill of excitement as he realised Kate was now staring at him rather than at the glossy brochures. Was there just a hint of personal interest in those mesmerising eyes, or was she simply daydreaming about steaming bowls of noodles and slinky cheongsams? God, she'd look *sensational* in one of those.

'It sounds amazing, Tom, and I can see you've come up with some other places too.' She gestured at a stunning collage of pictures of Costa Rica; a misty rain forest shot, a spectacular sunset and golden beaches lined by majestic palm trees. 'The thing is, would you mind if we chatted a little first, got to know each other a bit? Maybe if you know more about me it'll help to make the right choice.'

Privately Tom couldn't be more delighted at Kate's suggestion. Unless she'd suggested zipping back to her place so he could get to know her in a much more intimate way. Which wasn't likely – was it? Although she *had* wriggled her chair closer to his and he got another whiff of the same musky scent that had got him going last time.

Almost an hour later and Tom was pretty familiar with Kate's life story, and vice versa. Except he had omitted the minor detail of him living with someone. Which wasn't, of course, a *minor* detail, more like a gigantic African elephant with enormous flapping ears parading its way round the room. Luckily, Kate couldn't actually *see* this behemoth, nor had his nose grown Pinocchio-style. She hadn't *asked* if he was with someone, so he simply hadn't volunteered the information. What he'd learned about her was: she was twenty-eight; lived alone in a two-bedroom flat just outside of town; was the youngest of three, her older brother and sister in London and Leeds respectively, both parents still going strong and endlessly supportive, particularly when aforementioned bastard fiancé ditched her. His name was Arthur and she strongly suspected his protestations that there was no-one else were a pile of crap. She worked at a beauty boutique called De Luxe and enjoyed her job, but hated her boss, Caitlin, the one who'd refused to let her change her holiday leave.

'To be honest, I wouldn't be surprised if *she* was the one he was shagging on the side. She was always fluttering her stupid false eyelashes at him when he came in to pick up his products. That's how I met him. At first I thought it was quite nice that a man should take his skincare and hygiene routines so seriously. Now I just think he's an over-preening prat.'

Tom's version of life events to date was concise, if not entirely comprehensive. He'd talked about his own parents – they lived in the south of France and enjoyed a lively ex-pat way of life, renting out a gîte to supplement their pensions – and his siblings Jake and Rose. He'd never planned on being a travel agent – or exotic destination specialist, as Jonathan preferred to call them – but his history degree hadn't lent itself to many career options. Unless he became a history teacher. The thought of trying to teach the subject to classrooms of spotty teenagers who couldn't give a toss about Tudor times, only what time the pub opened and if their fake IDs would pass muster, filled him with horror. So, he'd stumbled into his current career, his knowledge of Incas, Etruscans and other ancient civilisations coming in handy when trying to map out itineraries for people keen on holidays with a difference.

'Not much else to add, really. It's not my dream job but it pays the bills and – as long as Jaws doesn't go in for the kill – I'll be fine there for a while.'

Kate snorted – ever so elegantly – at the mention of his boss's nickname. 'Is that what you call him? That's hilarious. I called in once before – you weren't there – and he *did* remind me of some deadly predator. All teeth and totally self-absorbed. He was actually *flossing* while he spoke to me. Eurgh! I'm *so* glad I came back and met you instead.'

Right. Tom knew his radar wasn't one hundred percent reliable but he was picking up major bleeps on the *I'm inter-*

ested in you wavelength. Kate was now twirling a lock of hair around her finger, one knee coming into close contact with his. He felt the heat, as powerful as the Kalahari Desert, just with no sand but scorching nevertheless.

'Another drink? Coming right up.' Leaving Kate flicking through some travel info he'd downloaded on Hong Kong he headed back to the bar, ordering their drinks as well as a couple of bags of posh crisps. Sun-dried tomato and Dijon mustard flavours. Clasping them between his teeth he hurried back to Kate. She thanked him, her fingers accidentally brushing his as she took the proffered wine glass. Or was it no accident? She was still seated very close to him, her body angled towards him and revealing a touch more cleavage than the average hot-bloodied male could handle. Luckily Tom had discarded his tie and loosened his top button before arriving at the bar, otherwise he felt sure steam would now be emanating from his entire body.

'I'm really tempted by the thought of Hong Kong, Tom,' said Kate. 'Have you ever been yourself?'

'Sadly, no,' replied Tom. 'I did visit Singapore once a few years back en route to Australia but it was only for a couple of days. Which, to be honest, was enough for me. It's pretty small and a bit too regimented for my liking. I think Hong Kong has a lot more to offer, especially if you've got a couple of weeks. Plenty of good day trips, that kind of thing.' Images of himself and Kate sipping ice-cold glasses of rosé as they cruised on a junk filled his head. Closely followed by a distinctly steamier one of them writhing on a petal-strewn four-poster bed. Strewth, he really was in dangerous territory now. And had also turned into an Aussie judging by his uncharacteristic turn of phrase. Focus Tom, he told himself. Whatever happened – and that might be nothing apart from bagging a new client – he needed to keep a cool head and a clean mind.

As Tom's thoughts wandered off to exotic and erotic places, Kate had scoffed all the Dijon crisps and was now licking crumbs from her fingers. Oh, God, she even made crisp-eating seem sexy as hell. She neatly folded up the empty packet and surveyed him thoughtfully.

'Listen, I hope this isn't out of order but it's after eight now and I'm starving! I make a mean spaghetti carbonara and it'd be lovely to cook for you. As a thank-you for going out your way to help me. Then we can finalise my plans. What do you think?'

What did he think? That he'd died and gone to heaven, that's what Tom thought. Where an angel in a figure-hugging dress was about to cook him one of his favourite pasta dishes. No revolting courgetti, just lashings of bacon, cream and parmesan. And who knew what might be for dessert?

It was a ten-minute taxi ride to Kate's place. They'd both driven to Bar Belle but agreed it was wise to leave their cars in the parking lot where they'd be safe until morning. Tom stressed that he would call another taxi for home after dinner. Kate was as inscrutable as the Mona Lisa, simply smiling enigmatically and whipping out her keys.

'It's nothing fancy but it's home. Make yourself comfy and I'll fetch some drinks and start on the food. Beer or wine?' Tom opted for the latter and she reappeared with a chilled bottle of Chablis and two glasses. Duly poured she returned to the kitchen whilst Tom scanned his surroundings. Small but chic, the living space was dominated by a curved screen TV and some impressive-looking speakers. He checked out her book collection. A hotchpotch of chick lit, crime thrillers and the odd weighty tome on such subjects as aromatherapy and homeopathy. He plonked himself down on a shabby but welcomingly squishy sofa and took a gulp of wine. Meanwhile the delicious aroma of sizzling meat permeated the air and his stomach gave a rumble of anticipation. Hearing the sounds of Kate clattering around in the kitchen he whipped out his phone and fired off a quick text to Tabitha. *Sofa at Clive's looks likely, beer flowing like lava. Soz xx*

Maybe he was being presumptuous and there'd be nothing more on the menu than a nice meal. In which case, he'd head home where Tabitha would probably be snoring gently, and tell her that he'd decided against another night tossing and turning on Clive's hideously lumpy couch.

Kate's flat had no dining area so they ate in the kitchen. It was a perfectly pleasant Ikea number with white glossy cabinets and dark wood round table above which hung a funky seventies-style light. It was on a dimmer and she'd turned it down low, giving the room an intimate feel. The carbonara was delicious and the conversation relaxed and easy. They shared the bottle of wine, Kate getting gigglier as he topped up her glass.

'Ooh, I'm feeling a wee bit tipsy,' she said, lifting her hair from her neck and effortlessly twirling it upwards and securing it with a chopstick she grabbed from a drawer. With tendrils hanging loose on each side she looked even more delectable. Almost Oriental. All she needed was that sexy cheongsam and… Hang on, she was getting *really* close now, her face inches from his …

'You've got some sauce on your chin. Here, let me wipe it.' Brandishing her napkin – OK, piece of kitchen roll – she cleaned off the offending blob. Damn, for a minute there he'd thought she was going to … aah, *now* she was. Kissing him, that is. Those full, pouty lips moving in harmony with his, those slender arms snaking their way around his neck. Dreams really do come true. It looked like there'd be no way he was heading home tonight. Except— a dark little voice in his head reminded him that, while Kate was no longer attached, he most certainly was. And had neglected to mention that fact when he'd had the chance earlier. The sole reason for the omission was he'd *hoped* something might happen between them. Revealing he was shacked up with someone would have killed their fledgling romance stone dead. What did he do now? Carry on and confess at some later date? Make some excuse to leave now, dump Tabitha, then rush back as soon as possible to take things to the next level? Nope, that wasn't a very noble thing to do. If – or rather – *when* he broke the news to his girlfriend that he wanted out he owed her more than a garbled explanation and then legged it through the door. Which left him with really only one other option. Bugger.

'Kate? Sorry, can we just pause for a minute?' He regretfully removed his lips and disengaged himself from her embrace. Her face was flushed and her eyes sparkled with desire. Tom suspected it wouldn't take long for the flush to change to red-hot anger and the sparkle to be replaced by revulsion.

'What's the matter, Tom? I thought you wanted this too. I knew there were sparks between us as soon as we met. Is it because you haven't known me long enough? Honestly, I don't normally leap in on the first date but it just felt *right*.'

It certainly did, Tom thought sadly. And now I'm going to make it the complete opposite. 'Listen, I wasn't completely honest with you early. I'm truly sorry about that. The thing is, I have a girlfriend. We live together. Have done for a while.'

Kate looked shocked but thankfully didn't pick up the remains of the carbonara and dump them on his head. She simply took a small sip of wine and nodded for him to continue.

'It's going to sound like a total cliché but things haven't been great between us recently. We both know it but we've been tiptoeing around it, not talked about it. Stupid, I know, but I guess neither of us was brave enough to put it into words. Anyway, I know I've screwed things up with you now. I just couldn't sleep with you knowing that I lied and equally I need to break up with my girlfriend. It's not fair to drag things out. Especially when I've met someone like you who makes me feel so amazing and alive. I'm so, so sorry.'

Tom got up to leave. Kate got up too, no doubt to shove him out the door and deadbolt it behind him. Instead, she took his hands in hers and kissed him lightly on the lips. OK, that was *so* not what he was expecting. A hard slap or a nifty right-hook, perhaps.

'I think you've just been incredibly brave, Tom. Fine, maybe you should have said something before but I *do* understand. We were getting on so well. I probably wouldn't have invited you back here if I'd known but if you're really telling the truth about your relationship being on the rocks …' Tom nodded furiously like a demented dashboard toy, 'then I believe you. My fiancé was a first-class prick but not all men are like him. My gut feeling tells me you're not. I think you're a kind-hearted, considerate and *very* attractive man who I'd like to get to know better. *Much* better.'

There were days when Tom thought that somebody up there didn't like him. Today wasn't one of them. He felt like he'd just scored the winning goal in the cup final, instead of being booed for missing a penalty. If Jeremy Clarkson himself had appeared in a puff of smoke – or exhaust fumes – and offered him the keys to a new Ferrari he could not have felt more elated.

'I promise you Kate, as soon as I get the chance I'll tell Tabitha – sorry, that's her name – that it's over. Hand on heart. Thank you for believing me. And thank you for a wonderful evening. Could we see each other again soon? Very soon, please?'

Kate crinkled her perfect little nose and gave him a quizzical look.

'Well, I was rather hoping you'd stay. Unless that would cause a problem at home? No? After all, the night's still young and I'm not the slightest bit sleepy. And, as I said, I want to get to know you. *All* of you.'

As she went in for another killer kiss, Tom told the annoying little voice in his head to go stuff itself. Tonight was filled with magic and the promise of rafter-raising sex. Tomorrow could bloody well wait.

CHAPTER 17

'Happy birthday, dear Susan, happy birthday to you!' The whoops and cheers of the book club ladies died down as they awaited her reaction. Which was to promptly burst into tears. Meryl rushed forward and gave her an enormous hug.

'Oh Susan, I really hope we haven't upset you. We just wanted to give you a little surprise on your special day.'

Susan drew back from the embrace and broke into a huge smile. It was a bit like the sun peeking through grey clouds and transformed her face from downcast to delighted.

'I'm just completely stunned that you've done all this for me.' She waved her hand around the room which was bedecked with balloons and banners, a small but beautifully wrapped pile of presents arranged on the coffee table.

To think she'd almost not come! When she'd read the email from Emily about a book club meeting on the evening of her birthday she'd immediately fired off a reply saying she couldn't make it. Within minutes Emily had called her and wouldn't take no for an answer.

'I know I'm a bit of a sergeant major but if we don't rally

the troops and sort out what we're reading in the coming months then there'll be mutiny! Esther gets downright tetchy if she can't stock up in Waterstones months in advance. Please come, there'll be cake!'

She hadn't been expecting this. Not in a million years. Susan felt her eyes fill again as Emily appeared from the kitchen with a tray of champagne flutes and bottles of Prosecco. Celeste and Esther followed bearing trays of canapés: mini quiches; a selection of sandwiches, smoked salmon blinis and sausage rolls. Everyone took a filled glass and raised them in toast to Susan.

'Cheers!' said Meryl. 'Here's to new beginnings and happy days ahead. You know fifty is the new thirty so seize the day, my dear girl.'

Plates were distributed and food eagerly devoured. Susan's appetite had waned in the course of her treatment but she gamely nibbled a few things. There weren't *many* good things to say about having cancer but she'd dropped quite a few pounds. Every cloud and all that, she thought wistfully.

'Pressie time! Come on Susan, get stuck in,' urged Emily. She did with gusto, tearing off the shiny wrapping paper to reveal a treasure trove of gifts. A bottle of perfume; a pretty pair of earrings; a voucher for a manicure, and a beautiful scarf in shades of lime green and gold.

'You really shouldn't have. You are all too, too kind. Thank you. Thank you *so* much.'

Everyone was chattering away happily. Susan found herself telling them all about her cancer treatment which prompted another round of big hugs. Nancy Edwards then revealed – to everyone's astonishment – that she'd had breast cancer too and had recently been given the all-clear.

'It's a tough road, for sure, but when they catch it early – like you – then the prognosis is good. If you ever want to talk to me about it please, just call. In fact, we're looking for new members for our mahjong club so if you're interested ...'

Not really, thought Susan, but she appreciated the kind offer. There'd been a couple of others too. Alice Johnson was a keen movie goer, 'but him indoors hates the cinema so if you ever fancy a night out with a bucket of popcorn then give me a shout.' This was much more Susan's thing, as was Emily and Celeste's suggestion that they meet up once a week to go walking.

'Got to get the steps in now I've got this little monster keeping an eye on me,' announced Celeste, waggling her wrist to show off her band. It would do her the world of good to get some exercise, maybe even help to shed a bit more weight.

Susan was well aware that the party and all the proposed social activities were borne out of pity for her. Poor, lonely Susan with her cancer and her sad little life. But did it really matter *why* they were doing it? For the first time in years she felt content and included. It was about time she stopped hiding from the world with only mountains of food for company. What was it Meryl said? To seize the day. Carpe diem, her new motto from hereon in.

As she'd been caught up in her own thoughts, Susan hadn't noticed that the lights had been dimmed. She looked up as Emily made her way carefully to the dining table, a cake on a silver platter in her hands. Space had been cleared and she set it down with a flourish, producing a lighter to ignite the two candles – a five and a zero – which took centre stage. Beneath them, stark against the white icing, were the words *Happy birthday Susan* in bright pink.

'We did think about having fifty small candles but decided against it. Didn't want another fire hazard!' joked Emily. Everyone gathered around, singing loudly again as Susan bent down and blew the candles out. 'Make a wish! Make a wish!' they all commanded. She did, sending up a silent prayer to whoever might be listening. 'Please, let me beat this awful disease and – if I can have one more – maybe some happier times ahead.'

The cake was dismantled and sliced, each of them pronouncing it another triumph by the patisserie. Susan took a small portion and politely declined seconds and to take the remainder home.

'Please, divide it up between you. I'd just end up devouring the lot and that wouldn't be a good way to kick off my good resolutions for the next year!'

* * *

TWO WEEKS later and Susan had undergone another couple of rounds of treatment. She hated it and felt distinctly sick afterwards but viewed each appointment as another two fingers up to her cancer. Her consultant was a kindly man in his late fifties who always made her feel important and not just another case to deal with. 'You're doing well, Susan,' he'd said at her last visit. 'Keep up the good work!' She smiled, thinking it was the doctors and nurses who were doing all the work. All she had to do was turn up and let them zap those rogue mutant cells into oblivion.

In the meantime, she had been to the cinema once with Alice and thoroughly enjoyed herself. She'd also been on a couple of walks with Emily and Celeste and found the fresh air, exercise and company just what the doctor ordered. The pounds were still coming off, albeit slowly, as she was paying close attention to her diet too. No more late night snacking, just three sensibly portioned meals a day. She deliberately avoided passing the patisserie which she considered her Achilles heel. Satisfyingly, her clothes felt looser and she felt lighter both in body and in spirit. She no longer felt the need to indulge in idle gossip or wild speculation about other people's lives. This was *her* life and if she was being given a second shot at it then she had no intention of screwing that up.

Before heading home, Susan wanted to pick up a couple of paperbacks. Although many of the book club members used their iPads or Kindles to download reading material, Susan loved the look and feel of an actual book. Always had done and she saw no reason to change *that* aspect of her life. She could spend hours browsing, drawn to one book by its cover, another by the blurb on the back. Her taste certainly wasn't highbrow – romantic fiction and edgy thrillers were more her scene – but she loved to lose herself in a good story.

A new bookshop had opened in town a couple of months before. The old one had closed down when the owner retired and the premises had been turned into a pet emporium. For almost a year she'd had to travel further afield to stock her shelves, occasionally using Amazon, but again she missed the physical contact and ambience only a real shop could provide. She'd been delighted when an entrepreneurial young couple had transformed a former rundown ironmonger's into a cosy bookshop cum café. They'd managed to create a truly welcoming environment, complete with comfy leather chairs and sofas, old-fashioned chandeliers and a vintage coffee machine they'd imported from Italy.

Entering the shop, the delicious aroma of freshly brewed coffee and a hint of cinnamon from the pastries they had delivered daily assailed Susan's nostrils. The former she would order in a moment, the latter she would savour only by smell. Firstly, she would have a look at this week's Top Picks which were displayed in a beautiful oak cabinet by the door. A couple caught her eye immediately, and she removed a copy of each to study them more closely. She also spotted a sign saying that a well-known local author of grisly murder mysteries would be doing a book signing there the following week. Susan made a mental note to jot down the date in her diary. *Death Defiant* sounded worth a look.

With a cup of coffee in one hand and her books in another, Susan weaved her way through the other customers scrutinising the shelves and tables piled high with reading material. There was a free Chesterfield just ahead if no-one beat her to it. Damn! She was almost there when a male figure rounded the opposite corner and plonked himself down. Cursing under her breath, Susan swivelled around in search of somewhere else to sit. Then swivelled back again, coffee slopping over the saucer. It *couldn't* be ... could it? After all these years, it was *impossible*. As she stared in open-mouthed disbelief, the chair thief raised his head and stared back at her. Before Susan could find words in her paralysed throat, he got to his feet and stood before her. Observing that her hand was shaking and threatening to tip the entire contents of the cup on the floor, he gently removed it and placed it on the small side table. She clasped her books to her chest, feeling her heart thudding beneath them.

'Susan. It really *is* you. For a second I thought I was hallucinating. Or had accidentally slipped through some cosmic time warp. It's been – what – twenty years? Such a long time. How are you? God, this is totally surreal. Although I should have known the one place I'd be most likely to bump into you would be a bookshop!'

Aware she was still gawping like a deranged goldfish, Susan put down her books and reached out her hand. Jonathan ignored the polite gesture and pulled her towards him and into a giant hug. Feeling the heat rising in her cheeks she succumbed for a moment then pulled away. The feel of his body so close to hers brought back powerful memories she felt unable to process right now.

'Yes, it's really me. This is so weird. Gosh, you haven't changed a bit. How come you're here, of all places? I thought you'd moved away?'

After their split – or rather, her rejection of him – Susan had heard on the grapevine that he'd packed in his job and relocated somewhere up north. Manchester or Birmingham, she couldn't remember. He'd written to her a few times but she'd never replied and eventually the letters had stopped.

'I've been in Salford working with a chartered surveyor firm since I left, but I was headhunted for a job back here four months ago and decided it was too good to turn down. Plus, deep down I always missed this place, so it was great to come back. I did think of trying to contact you but ...'

His words tailed off, those familiar hazel eyes studying her intently. Susan felt her pulse quicken again as she took in his appearance. He really *hadn't* changed, aside from a slightly receding hairline and a few creases around the eyes. Just as handsome as always, still capable of creating butterflies in her stomach. Even after two decades and ...

'So, what's new? Sorry, that's a seriously dumb question. I'm sure a lot has changed since— 'Susan didn't know how to finish her sentence so let it hang in the air, laden with meaning and regret. No doubt he had met someone else, probably very soon after she'd treated him so badly. Men like Jonathan weren't meant to sit on a shelf gathering dust. Unlike herself, even if she had recently vowed to embrace a whole new world. She just didn't envisage a man in it. Ever.

'Look, this place is packed, your coffee's history – Susan glanced at the half-empty and rapidly cooling cup – and we have a heap of catching up to do. Why don't we buy what we mean to buy then find somewhere else to play Twenty Questions? Sound OK to you?'

Despite having barely glanced at the books, Susan paid for them, Jonathan waiting patiently by her side. He'd picked up a guide to the best cycling routes in Europe – 'Yes, I am still a bike devotee, once a nerd always a nerd!' – and they'd strolled a couple of doors down to a quieter spot with a free table in the window. Order taken, Jonathan had leaned back in his chair, a playful grin on his ever-youthful face.

'Right, who's going to start?' He held out an imaginary microphone which Susan smacked away. She'd forgotten – no, had pushed down into a hidden vault marked *do not open* – how easy it had been with him. How relaxed, how *natural* it had seemed. Until she had forced him away, carried on a tidal wave of her own self-loathing.

'*You* start! My life's been totally tedious. I don't want you nodding off while I try to drink this cup of coffee before it's stone cold.'

Jonathan had laughed, that wonderful from-the-belly laugh she'd dreamt of even after the years had passed and she'd found very little humour in her humdrum existence.

'Me? Well, truth be told, I don't think they'll be queueing up to turn my story into a Hollywood blockbuster anytime soon. Although I've always fancied being played by Tom Hanks, as long as he can do a convincing English accent!'

Susan had listened as Jonathan condensed the past two decades into a bullet point list of highs and lows, memorable moments and ones better consigned to the annals of history. He'd met someone, it hadn't worked out, so he'd never married and – much to his sadness – never had children. He'd travelled extensively to some of the remoter parts of the globe, always intent on pedalling his way through scenic splendour. His parents had both died within the past few years – Susan had never met them but knew they'd been very close – and he now viewed his own mortality as an opponent to be outwitted and outsmarted.

'That's enough about me. Tell me about *you*. By the way, you look amazing. Sorry, should have said that before but I was just so *gobsmacked* at seeing you again. The woman who broke my heart.'

He said this with levity in his voice but his expression told a different tale. If Susan didn't know better she would have sworn he still carried a candle for her. Which was ridiculous. Why would a man like Jonathan still hanker after a ghost from the past, when there were must be so many other women eager and willing to snap him up?

'I'm good. Well, apart from having cancer, I'm good.'

Jonathan had visibly tensed at her throwaway remark, his hand edging towards hers, her own fingers creeping of their own accord in his direction.

'Breast cancer. It's a bugger, but so far so good. Had some surgery and getting through a course of radiotherapy now. Not pleasant but not as bad as I'd imagined. Not that I *ever* imagined it. It happens to other people, so when it happens to you it's like an out-of-body experience. But I'll get through it. There's no other option, is there?'

Jonathan had said nothing. Just squeezed her hand a little tightly and gazed at her with increased intensity. Her insides were now pools of boiling lava, threatening to spill over and lay waste to all the barriers she'd erected over the years. Was this *right*? Could she possibly put aside all that had been said and done in the past and start afresh? Would *he* even *want* to, considering how callously she'd cast him aside? She felt like a completely different person now, but so was he. Was it remotely possible they could pick up the dropped stitches and knit themselves something new and sustainable?

As if in answer to her unspoken question, Jonathan raised his eyebrows and gesticulated towards the door.

'I think we still have a lot of talking to do. Which we can carry on at your place. Unless you have a doting husband who will punch my lights out if I turn up unannounced and with my arms wrapped round you. I'm assuming that's not the case?'

Susan gathered up her handbag, her purchases and her courage. It was now or never. She'd let him go once before, a second time would be madness.

'There's no husband. There was only ever you. Shall we go?'

* * *

IT WAS the middle of the night. Susan was wide awake, keenly aware of the sleeping presence next to her. They'd talked for hours, interspersed with tears, hugs and an overriding sense of making up for lost time. They could never claw it back, but they *could* move forward. Together. That was a scary word in Susan's vocabulary but one she liked the sound of. *Together.* Not alone, not afraid, no longer the laughing stock or the recipient of well-meant sympathy. A half of something that added up to something worth having. She saw herself all those years ago, convinced she was right to let him go. Now? She had looked down the barrel of death and realised what a fool she'd been. Jonathan loved her – he'd said there had never been anyone else who came close – and she loved him. It was that simple. They hadn't made love tonight, just cuddled up and shared more stories. By mutual consent they'd gone to bed, kissed and then drifted off to sleep. He would be there in the morning. She turned over and willed herself to sleep a little longer. Because the rest of her wonderful, unimaginable life was about to start.

CHAPTER 18

Tabitha had woken gradually, the dawn chorus heralding the start of a new day. She hadn't planned on waking *quite* this early but last night's evening alone had given her plenty of time for soul searching. When she'd gone to bed just after ten – not long after receiving Tom's text – she'd made up her mind. Staring at her deep-cleansed face in the mirror she had rehearsed the words carefully.

'I'm sorry Tom, but this just isn't working. I know it, you know it. There's no one else. I just think we should call it a day.'

She hoped he wouldn't be *too* upset – if he started crying she'd feel like a complete bitch – but it was better this way. Given time, he'd meet someone else and so would she. Hopefully. If her mother could start dating again then who knew what might be waiting for *her* around the corner? She didn't know what time Tom had rolled home. He was zonked out next to her, a beatific smile on his face as he snuggled up to his pillow. Oh dear, she was going to wipe *that* away pretty soon. She felt a pang of guilt as she eased her way out from under the duvet. Time for a slice of toast and a cup of coffee before she dropped her bombshell.

'Excuse me, but *what*! Could you repeat what you just said?' Tabitha felt like a character in a movie who'd slipped into an alternate universe. One in which everything had been turned upside down. Or maybe there was something wrong with her hearing. Had some of last night's gloopy hair mask got lodged in her ears? She prodded inside one but found nothing amiss.

'I'm sorry. I said I think we should split up. It's been on the cards for a while now. I really don't want to hurt you, Tabitha, but it's just not what I want anymore.' He'd looked at her with remorseful eyes. She resisted the temptation to gouge them out with the bread knife. How *dare* he? How *very* dare he? There she'd been, her script perfectly prepared, and he'd completely pulled the rug from under her feet. *She* was the one doing the dumping, not *him*!

'So, is there someone else? At least tell me the truth!'

Of course there was no one else. Tom might be ranking highly in the bastard scale right this minute but he absolutely *wouldn't* ... OK, now he was looking like a condemned man on the way to the gallows.

'Actually, there is. I'm sorry, Tabitha. She's not the cause, just a symptom.'

Which made this other woman sound like a rare medical condition rather than a brazen hussy who'd snaffled *her* man. Even if she didn't want him to be *her* man. She just didn't want him to be someone *else's* man quite so quickly. He could at least have had the decency to feign heartbreak, just for a moment or two. Instead, he now looked like a condemned man who'd been told his sentence had been quashed after a last-minute appeal. Obviously relieved to have confessed his sins and now free to go and fornicate with a clear conscience. Or at least a marginally less grubby one. Was that what he'd been up to last night? Not comatose on Clive's couch after a beer-swigging session but busting the bed springs with Miss Perfect Pants?

'Fine. Totally fine with me. It's a relief, in fact. Now I can focus on my future career and meeting someone who appreciates me.'

And my mung beans and lentils and other amazingly healthy pulsey things. Although right this minute she'd *kill* for a bacon buttie and something strong and alcoholic. A Bucks Fizz or a mean Bloody Mary. Anything to take the edge off her humiliation at being gazumped at the eleventh hour.

Several hours later and Tabitha was feeling slightly better. A glass or two – or three – had nicely numbed the pain. And chewing her way through two rounds of Tesco's finest smoked bacon encased in slabs of sliced white slathered in butter had helped too. Maybe not her cholesterol levels but who gave a flying fig about that right now? She was young, she was single and the world was her oyster. Or lobster, as Aunt Celeste was prone to saying.

She'd had a little snooze, curled up on the sofa like an ageing tabbie. Bollocks, not the cat analogy again! Woken up with a mild headache and a sense of being wounded but not defeated. Tabitha metaphorically prodded her heart. Definitely bruised, but broken? Probably not. Being dumped by Tom wasn't up there in her Top Ten moments to cherish but in a way, it was a relief. She was just a bit cheesed off she hadn't been the one to do the dumping. More wounded ego than anything else. Although the fact he was heading off on holiday with his newfound love did grate a little. More than a little.

'You're going to Hong Kong with someone you've barely known five minutes? Are you *kidding*? We were together eighteen months and the most I got was a dirty weekend in

Bath. Pardon the pun. And that was only because you had to attend that boring travel expo thingy. Remember? So, I saw you for about three hours in the evening and you were too shagged out – or pissed – to do very much.'

Tom had at least looked sheepish as she'd ranted on, furiously stuffing his clothes into a suitcase. He had disappeared into the bathroom, emerging with a pathetic handful of toiletries and a well-worn toothbrush. They hadn't accumulated much together as a couple. A few cheap wall prints, some DVDs, a set of kitchen knives. Tom had assured he didn't want any of it (and was certainly *not* going for custody of the spiraliser).

So, what now? She was officially single again and free to see anyone she wanted. The problem was, eligible, hunky bachelors weren't exactly queueing around the block, in her experience. Her mum had finally started dating again, although was being incredibly coy about the details. Meryl was totally loved up with Miroslaw and her aunt Celeste had always seemed very happy in her marriage to Uncle Michael. She'd just never been that close to either of them. She'd never quite understood her aunt's reluctance to having children (although she knew that not everyone was cut out for motherhood). The topic of Michael's first marriage and child was a touchy one, her mum warning her many years ago that the subject was taboo. Tabitha just knew that her own biological clock was ticking away in the background. Not loudly but ever-present. She adored babies and grew positively misty-eyed when a new mum wheeled her little bundle of joy into the shop.

It wasn't something she'd ever really contemplated for herself but Tabitha wondered if online dating was worth considering. She'd tried to persuade her mum – without success – but Meryl had eventually found her prince after a few frog encounters. Surely there was no harm in just looking, for goodness sake! It wasn't like she had to bare her soul – or anything else – in the first place. Just sign up, log in and fill out a few pertinent details. Then see what, or who, popped up.

Tabitha decided to steer clear of the site where Meryl had met more than her fair share of disasters. She opted for another, entitled Cupid's Bow, that claimed the highest match rate on the internet. Yeah, right. How could they possibly calculate that? Did its members have to pledge to supply a blow by blow account of their successful encounters, maybe even invite the company founders to their weddings? Still, the site *looked* impressive and was easy to navigate. It was offering a one-month free trial. All she had to do was complete a questionnaire and upload a photo. This was optional but Tabitha figured she scrubbed up pretty well. She had a good one of her and Tom together at a party a few months ago which was particularly flattering. A quick crop and the traitorous one was history.

OK, this might be a *little* naughty but Tabitha also created a profile for her mum, but without a photo. She was just curious who might pop up as potential life partners for both of them. She had texted Emily several times begging for details about her new man, but been fobbed off with excuses.

A lot on my plate, darling. Be in touch soon xx.

That was a few days ago so she didn't know about Tom, although it wasn't going to be a *complete* surprise following their last conversation. So, a lot to catch up with on both sides.

After a few minutes of the system processing Tabitha's data – her Five Point Test had come in handy as a guide to her wants and absolute turn-offs – a series of profiles became available for her perusal. She sped-read through them, immediately dismissing several as no-hopers. One listed a Crime Watch-worthy physical description of his ideal woman. As she had neither Pamela Anderson's boobs nor Gillian Anderson's hair colour they were destined never to meet. Another related his tales of romantic woe, including his recent divorce and how he'd been hurt countless times by heartless women in the past. There was one who looked promising from his photo – cute face, curly dark hair, nice smile – but his written profile was littered with grammatical errors and an abundance of LOLs. Like her mum, Tabitha was a stickler for good grammar and spelling. Maybe he had an awesome personality but clearly couldn't write for toffee. Another "no".

Grabbing a quick cup of tea, Tabitha returned to the screen and switched to possible candidates for her mum. She had no idea really how Emily would describe herself on a dating site but she'd tried to be as accurate as possible. Her mum was both attractive *and* smart, with a great sense of humour. She'd seen how men would look at her when they were out together. Not so long ago a thirty-something guy had asked if they were sisters! Emily had laughed and asked if he'd been to SpecSavers recently. Self-deprecation was another of her characteristics, not necessarily the best one when it came to meeting men.

Scanning the available photos Tabitha was grabbed by a distinguished-looking gent who was into rock climbing, fine dining and wanted to meet a lady 'who makes me laugh but isn't afraid to poke fun at herself. Nobody's perfect – least of all me – but I believe there's someone out there to share life's journey with. Bumps and all.' Ooh, promising, she thought. If things don't work out with Emily's current squeeze then … Tabitha accidentally hit the forward key and another image filled the screen. Hang on a sec, didn't *he* look rather familiar? She squinted at the photo. It was a bit blurry and dark. She peered closer. Oh shit. Oh no. It *couldn't* be, could it? She hastily read through the accompanying profile.

'My name is Martin and I'm looking for love. Who isn't? I'm keen on cooking, movies and romantic weekends in the countryside. Looks are less important than being on the same wavelength. I just want to meet someone who I can share things with and who feels like the missing half of me.'

Tabitha could feel herself shaking with a mixture of disbelief and rage. Calm down, she told herself. Perhaps this was an ancient profile and he'd simply neglected to take it down. She checked the date when it was posted. Less than two weeks ago. Right, officially a complete and utter cheating bastard. Martin – aka Miroslaw – was doing the dirty on the lovely Meryl. Which one was his real name? Maybe neither. Perhaps he had a long list of fake identities which he used to attract unsuspecting women. But why? What was his motive? Was he just a serial philanderer who notched up conquests and moved on? Or was there something more sinister going on?

She felt genuinely devastated for her boss and good friend. Meryl had a heart of gold and always saw the best in people and was forever performing little acts of kindness. Like knocking a few pounds off the price of an item in the shop if she suspected the customer was struggling to gather together change in their purse. Or, more recently, arranging a surprise birthday party for a woman she barely knew but had felt desperately sorry for. She would be *crushed* to discover the man she was seeing was a two-faced liar with a hidden agenda. Tabitha really, *really* didn't want to be the bearer of such horrible news. But she knew she couldn't keep her stomach-churning discovery to herself. That would be cruel and unfair. She prayed that it wouldn't be a case of shooting the messenger. That Meryl would ultimately be grateful and glad to see the back of Miroslaw/Martin/whatever else the slimy toad called himself.

* * *

Meryl had also woken early after a disturbed night of tossing and turning. Forsaking her fennel tea for an eye-opening double espresso she turned on her computer. Accessing her e-banking details she clicked on her private savings account. Current balance just over £25,000. Gosh, that was more than she thought. She'd set it up in such a way that a fixed sum from her current account was transferred over each month. Plus, she'd had a couple of wins on the National Lottery in the past couple of years. Instead of blowing the money on holidays or clothes she'd salted it away too.

There'd never been a grand plan as to what to *do* with the money, or when to dip into it. Perhaps if she was nearer sixty and still alone she would splurge it on a fabulous cruise or as a down payment on a little holiday pad in France. The Little Shop of Treasures was never going to make her a millionaire but it allowed her to live a comfortable life and she'd sensibly built up a private pension pot to ensure her later years were equally secure. Now that she'd met someone who really cared for her, her fears of ending up a lonely old pensioner had faded significantly. She closed her eyes and envisaged a golden sunset, walking hand in hand on a sandy beach with Miroslaw. Which might well be in jeopardy if he couldn't repay his creditors. If he lost the business would he stay here or flee to his native Poland? That thought filled Meryl with horror, and she felt panic take a grip. If there was *any* way she could ease his financial burden then she would do it.

Downstairs in the shop Meryl set about preparing for opening at nine. Tabitha had rung half an hour before. Full of apologies, she pleaded a bad headache but insisted she would be in for the afternoon shift, despite Meryl's insistence she take the day off.

'So, how was last night?' she'd asked, but not in her usual teasing tone. Poor girl, she was obviously in a lot of pain.

'It was lovely! Miroslaw really appreciated my cooking. I'll tell you more later but – please – stay home if you don't feel any better.'

A handful of customers drifted in and out during the first hour. One sale in particular – of a set of hand-painted wine glasses and matching decanter – made the till ring with delight as they were one of the more expensive items on the shelves. The rest either browsed and left or picked up small knick-knacks and greetings cards. The shop was empty when the doorbell chimed and in walked Miroslaw. Her heart leapt at the sight of him, then dropped when she saw how exhausted and drawn he looked. There was a visible layer of stubble on his chin and his shirt was clearly un-ironed.

'Oh, Miroslaw! You look done in, my poor darling. Look, I'll pop up my "Back in fifteen minutes" sign and we can have a cuppa out the back.' He smiled gratefully and followed her through.

'Listen, my beautiful Meryl. I should never have burdened you with my problems last night. It was selfish and unfair. I have done much thinking and … I think it best I go away for some time. If I sell my car – *no, not that divine leather-seated Range Rover!* – and a few other things I can perhaps keep the wolves from the door. But not for long. I have acquaintances in my own country who might be able to offer me some work …'

Before he could continue, Meryl had taken his hand and squeezed it tight.

'Look at me, Miroslaw. I've been thinking too and … here's the thing. I have some savings put away and I'd like you to have them. No, please don't argue. My mind's made up. It's only £25,000 but if it helps—'

She wasn't allowed to finish her sentence. Miroslaw had enveloped her in a gigantic hug, sniffing loudly. With a voice dripping in emotion he whispered, 'You would really do that for *me*? You are truly an angel sent from heaven. I count my lucky stars every day that I met someone as wonderful as you. Thank you. And I promise I will pay back every penny as soon as I can.'

Needing to get back and reopen the shop, Meryl told Miroslaw to email her his bank details immediately so she could arrange to transfer the money into his account.

'I'll try to do it this afternoon when Tabitha comes in to work, tomorrow at the latest. I just hope it's enough,' she said, kissing him goodbye at the door.

'It is more than I could have dreamed of, just as you are, my beautiful Meryl,' he replied huskily.

* * *

IF SHE'D BEEN EXAGGERATING her headache earlier, Tabitha could feel the beginnings of a full-blown one now as she entered the shop. Meryl was tending to a customer and radiating joie de vivre in that way only a woman in love can. Damn, bugger and blast. She was totally dreading this. It would be like slamming the cage door on an abandoned puppy who'd been convinced adoption was on the cards. Right now, she could cheerfully throttle Miroslaw/Martin and take the murder charge on the chin.

'Hi Tabbie! Are you feeling better? You still look a bit pale, are you *sure* you should be here?' Meryl eyed her with sympathy, Tabitha deliberately looking down in case she blurted out her bad tidings on the spot. She needed to psyche herself up, choose a moment. Not that there would ever be a *good* moment to say what she had to say.

'I'm fine, honestly. Had another snooze and popped some

pills, so fit and ready for action. What would you like me to do first?'

As Tabitha got stuck into more box unpacking and shelf rearranging, she decided that her news about Tom could wait. Her misery at discovering Meryl's newfound love was a treacherous cad – she loved that old-fashioned word, but hated that she had to use it – far outweighed her feelings about her ex-boyfriend. Besides, who knew what his game was? She'd read plenty of stories about women being physically assaulted or fleeced by men they'd believed were the loves of their lives.

'Sweetie, can you hold the fort for a little while? I just need to pop upstairs and deal with something on the computer. Won't be long.'

Tabitha nodded as Meryl bounded up the stairs to her flat. The spring in her step reminded Tabitha of a graceful gazelle in a David Attenborough documentary. Completely unaware that a salivating lion was about to tear her world apart.

There were no customers. Tabitha shifted some old stock to the side and began placing tree-shaped ring holders into an empty glass cabinet. A cold trickle of unease ran down her spine. She didn't know why, but she sensed something was terribly wrong. Swiftly turning the shop sign to "closed", she belted up the stairs, taking them two by two. Reaching the flat she burst in, a surprised Meryl looking up from her desktop.

'What's up, Tabbie? Are you feeling poorly again? I'll be there in a minute, I just have to …' Meryl hesitated, fingers poised over the keyboard. She took a deep breath, then gestured for Tabitha to take a seat.

'The thing is – oh, I was going to tell you all this later – last night *was* lovely but I discovered something.'

Tabitha held her own breath. Perhaps she already *knew*

and was contacting the police or something? Although being a cheating, lying scumbag wasn't yet a criminal offence, sadly.

Meryl continued, 'Poor, poor Miroslaw has been having financial problems. He was in *bits* last night when he told me. He could lose his business and everything! Anyway, I decided I was going to loan him some money, just to tide him over. I'm just transferring it right now and—'

'*Stop right there*!' shrieked Tabitha in true banshee fashion. A startled Meryl slid backwards in her wheeled chair, eyes agog like a petrified possum. 'Do *not* touch the computer! Step away from the keyboard, *now*!'

CHAPTER 19

The letter, when it dropped on the doormat, felt like an incendiary device. Celeste picked it up gingerly, as if afraid it might combust before she had the chance to read it. She'd seen the *Tea Break* logo on the envelope, felt her heart start to gallop as she realised the day of reckoning had arrived. Much sooner than expected – it had only been a little over two weeks since she sent off her story. Which might well mean it was a kindly worded rejection. Although she wasn't sure they would write to *everyone* who'd taken part in the competition.

Taking a deep inward breath, she ripped it open and removed the contents. Slipping her reading glasses into place she scanned the words.

'Dear Celeste. We are delighted to inform you that you are the runner-up in our romantic fiction competition. We received hundreds of submissions and were very impressed with your work. So much so, we intend to publish your story in instalments later this year as we are sure it will delight our readership. A cheque for £3,000 will be with you shortly and we will be in touch to arrange a short interview and photo session, as per the competition guidelines. Congratulations!'

Second place. She wasn't entirely sure how she felt about that. Disappointed to have been pipped at the post. Curious as to whose story had impressed the judging panel more, and why. Then she chided herself for being negative. She should be *proud*. If it were the Olympics she'd be destined for a silver medal, standing tearfully on the podium as they played the National Anthem. No, she had done remarkably well and *achieved* something in a life that had been comfortable but lacking in the personal achievement stakes. Wait until she told Michael! She could imagine his face now, stunned but delighted for her. Her well-kept secret could be brought out into the open ... Celeste clamped her hand over her mouth, a wave of nausea sweeping over her. Revealing *her* little secret was one thing, but uncovering Michael's was something else entirely. And tomorrow could well be the day she found out the truth about his mysterious walks that involved very little *actual* walking.

In the past couple of weeks, she'd donned her new fitness gear and headed out with Michael on a few occasions. If he wasn't happy about it, he'd disguised it well.

'Absolutely, darling! Fabulous weather for it. Shall we head for the park or would you prefer something more challenging?'

As Celeste still regarded exercise with trepidation and loathed having to wear trainers – *so* unattractive – she always opted for the park. At least it was flat there and she didn't have to contend with disgustingly healthy individuals bounding past her while she wheezed red-faced up a slight incline. She'd also walked a couple of times with Emily and Susan. Luckily, they were more into a relaxed pace with the promise of a coffee and a natter at the end.

She should have been ready for it – seen it coming – but

when Michael announced this morning he was going walking by himself the next day, Celeste had been taken aback. She'd tried to convince herself that her fears were irrational, that she'd got things all wrong, but all her paranoia and doubts had come flooding back.

'But *why* can't I come with you?' she'd wheedled, tightening her bathrobe around her as Michael flicked through the rest of the post. She'd grabbed it when he was in the shower and hidden her *Tea Break* letter.

'Sweetheart, there are times I just need to be alone.' Greta bloody Garbo, seethed Celeste inwardly. 'I love walking with you, truly I do, but you know I walk faster than you. And further than you.' He'd looked sheepish at his remarks which were valid but did nothing to quell her inner unease.

She'd wanted, *so* wanted to share her success but felt the words snag in her throat every time they made a bid for freedom. Dinner had been subdued, Michael full of forced bonhomie, Celeste incapable of joining in. All she could think of was the task ahead. Following the man she loved to find out if he was stepping out with someone else.

* * *

THE NEXT MORNING he'd gone, small backpack stocked with water and sustaining stacks. Celeste had waved goodbye, heart heavy as a stone. Within minutes she'd laced up her trainers, pulled on her lightweight jacket and headed out in pursuit.

He'd taken his car, claiming that the start point of his walk was too far to cover on foot. Celeste climbed into her TT, revved the engine and took a left, confident she would have him in her sights soon. She was right, his distinctive Audi A4 was a short distance ahead, stopped at traffic lights. There were a couple of cars between them. Hopefully enough to conceal her bright red vehicle which didn't exactly lend itself to undercover missions. Before long they were heading out of town, Michael keeping well within the speed limits as was his nature. At a crossroads junction he went straight ahead, finding a gap in the traffic. Celeste wasn't so lucky and had to wait an excruciating minute or so before she could safely follow. Fingernails tapping frantically on the wheel, she prayed she hadn't lost him already. No, he was still within her sights – just – as he rounded a bend. Where was he heading? They were now leaving the outskirts of town and heading into the countryside, the streets becoming sparser as rows of houses gave way to leafy lanes. As the buildings dwindled Celeste felt a wave of panic descend on her. She was now only a few cars behind and the one directly in front of her was signalling to turn right. She was quite sure she would be easily spotted then the game would be up. And no doubt Michael would have a perfectly plausible explanation – a new route he'd discovered – whereas she would have to explain why she was tailing him like an under-cover cop.

Keeping her head down low – as if *that* made a difference – Celeste gripped the wheel even tighter and prayed that Michael was so focused on what lay ahead that he wouldn't notice her. Or just assume it was another red TT. They weren't *that* uncommon, after all. Emily had laughingly told her several months ago how she'd waved manically at one, only to realise belatedly that it wasn't Celeste and some other woman who'd stared at her as if she were a lunatic. Who was the madwoman now, she thought to herself? This had to rate as one of her dumbest ideas ever, and she'd had quite a few over the years. She should have looked Michael in the eye and demanded an explanation, although that would have meant confessing to snooping on his phone. How had she gone from being a contented – smug, even – wife to a demented stalker? Was this retribution for all the times she'd gleefully told Emily of yet another marital breakdown, a husband who'd strayed or a wife who'd run off with her fitness instructor? That would *never* happen to her and Michael. They were a team, forging their way through life side by side. She thought they were the epitome of coupledom but perhaps one team member was playing away from home. A sob caught in her throat, tears blurring her vision. She blinked them away. Now was *not* the time to plough into a hedge and have to be pulled out by a friendly farmer and his tractor, Michael looking on in bewilderment.

Lost in dark thoughts, Celeste barely registered that Michael's car had disappeared from view. Bugger! She slowed right down, prompting the one car behind her to toot its horn impatiently. Giving them a one-fingered salute – not something she'd normally do but today it felt *good* – she scanned left and right and spotted a sign that said Barnswick Green Garden Centre. Unsure if that was where he'd turned off, she indicated and followed the gravelled driveway at a snail's pace. It continued some distance, twisting and turning until a large barn came into view. Decorated with colourful hanging baskets and overflowing urns surrounding its perimeter, it looked like nirvana for the green-fingered. Except neither she nor Michael were remotely green-fingered. They had a gardener who came on a regular basis to mow the lawn, plant things and generally make their outdoor space look appealing. Well-meaning friends had given them cuttings and potted specimens as gifts in the past, all of which had shrivelled up and died almost immediately. Celeste just had to *look* at a gorgeous bouquet of flowers and they committed suicide, even when she remembered to add the little sachet of stuff that was meant to prolong their freshness. Surely Michael hadn't suddenly discovered a passion for forticulture? Was that the right word? Celeste couldn't give a damn. His car was parked just ahead, only a few vacant spaces around it. She pulled in, shaking with nerves, as far from him as possible. As she climbed out, she noticed a blackboard announcing today's specials. *Pumpkin soup. Home-made scones with Cornish clotted cream & jam. Goats' cheese salad & frittata with feta and olives.* Not just a garden centre then, but an oasis of delicious food too. Celeste felt her tummy rumble. Not a good time to be salivating over a menu when she might be about to have her heart ripped out and trampled to pieces.

With her hand on the door, Celeste felt like she was teetering on the brink of something momentous. Would she find Michael browsing through herbaceous borders, sniffing scented blossoms or stroking silken leaves like Alan Titchmarsh on ecstasy? Or would he be stroking something – or someone – else entirely? Only one way to find out.

Inside, Celeste navigated her way through the vast displays of everything a keen gardener could possibly want or need. With no personal interest in secateurs or compost, she headed towards the rear of the building where an arrow pointed to the cafeteria. As she approached, the hum of conversation and clatter of plates and cutlery indicated that business was booming. Or blooming, perhaps. Pausing by the entrance, she wished she'd worked out some kind of strategy to deal with whatever she was about to face. She hadn't, although for a brief moment she considered popping back to the shop and arming herself with something sharp and lethal.

Forcing one foot in front of the other, she entered and cast her eyes around the room. There were young mums bouncing babies on their knees, older couples supping soup or sharing scones and pots of tea and a group of teenagers clutching clipboards who were engaged in loud conversation. A school outing, she guessed, as an older lady shushed them and dug into her salad with an air of resignation. She wondered what today's lesson was. How to grow your own fruit and veg? Clever ways to create a window box with some seeds and a whole lot of patience? They'd probably be happier with a lesson in cultivating cannabis. Not that she'd ever *tried* it herself, but right now some mind-numbing substance would be very welcome.

Just as she was wondering if Michael had actually *bought* something and left already, she saw him. Seated in a far corner, but not alone. He was with a young woman who was picking half-heartedly at her food, her fork coming to her lips then returning to the plate untouched. She watched, feeling a pain deep inside her rise to the surface, as Michael reached out and touched the woman's arm. The pain multiplied as she put down her fork and leaned inwards, Michael's arm resting on her shoulder. He stroked her dark blonde hair, the look on his face one of exquisite tenderness. Celeste could take no more.

'Nice to bump into you, Michael. Thought you were taking one of your *epic* walks but it seems you've developed a passion for something else. Anything you'd like to share with me?'

Celeste stood before them, simmering with a rage she'd never felt before. She had given years of her life to this man – made it her mission to back him all the way – and *this* was how he repaid her? By having an affair with some slip of a girl who probably only had her eyes on his bank balance and life expectancy.

Michael was staring at her with a mixture of incomprehension and terror. His bit on the side was staring too, but with more than a hint of hostility. Christ, did she *really* think they were going to skip off into the sunset leaving her behind to pick up the pieces? She straightened her shoulders, took a deep breath, and said the words that had been festering inside her since she'd first seen them together.

'You know what, you disgust me. What were you thinking? She's what, twenty-something? My God, she's young enough to be your daughter!' Celeste glowered at the girl, who looked back defiantly. Whoever she was, she certainly had confidence in spades.

Michael looked down at his hands, looked up at his young girlfriend, then raised his eyes to his wife. 'She *is* my daughter, Celeste. This is Sophie.'

Celeste was totally dumbstruck. She stared at the girl who stared back with barely concealed contempt. Now that she knew the truth she could see the resemblance. The same eyes, strong chin, hair colour. Michael had shown her a couple of photos in recent years but she'd barely glanced at them. 'Hm, pretty girl. Hopefully a nicer personality than her mother!' Now she cringed inwardly as she recalled her dismissive tone, her lack of interest. She'd never imagined, not for one minute, that she'd be standing in front of her husband's only child in a garden centre café in the middle of nowhere. It was patently clear their meetings had been going on for some time judging by the way the girl had placed a protective hand on Michael's arm. She whispered in his ear, something that made him sit upright and frown.

'Absolutely not. You are *not* leaving, Sophie. This situation has gone on for far too long. You have a right to be here and so do I. There's no way on earth I'm losing you again.'

They had reached an impasse. Celeste was stunned beyond belief that she was looking at her husband's only child, a person she thought he'd consigned to history as a result of his tumultuous relationship with her mother. A person she'd been *happy* to leave in the past, so keen was she to create a perfect marriage with no irritating outsiders to interfere. Yet, looking at them now, she felt a pang of guilt. More than a pang; more like a piercing stab deep within her gut. If Michael had felt the need to keep his liaisons with Sophie secret, what did that say about her?

Michael looked crushed, his arm still around his daughter's shoulder, his gaze upon Celeste. Feeling her knees about to give way, she pulled up a seat and attempted a wobbly smile.

'OK, I got everything totally wrong but what was I supposed to think? I find my husband with a younger woman, jump to the wrong conclusion, make an idiot of myself. I blame these things!' Celeste twirled her fitness band around her wrist, wishing she'd never bought the bloody thing. Michael looked perplexed and Sophie ignored the gesture completely. Instead, she looked at her watch and got up to leave.

'I have to go. I need to pick up the boys soon. Dad, I'll be in touch.' She bent down and kissed Michael on the cheek. Didn't acknowledge Celeste's presence, simply walked past her as if she didn't exist. Which was a state she would happily embrace right now. Disappear in a puff of smoke, pretend none of this had happened, rewind to just of the two of them. But that wasn't possible, was it? Michael and Sophie had found each other, clearly needed each other, and where did she fit in to the picture? Precisely nowhere. She'd shown her hand a long time ago, and it was a possessive and ultimately destructive one. She thought Michael needed only one person – herself – but she was wrong. So, *so* wrong. He needed his daughter and he had gone behind her back to make it happen. Which meant one of two things. He didn't want to hurt her so had kept Sophie a secret. Or he resented her so much for keeping them apart that he would leave her and concentrate on rebuilding his relationship with his daughter. Whichever way she looked at it, Celeste couldn't see a Disney ending. She was far past the wicked stepmother stage. You had to actually *know* the person before you got to wear that badge. And she couldn't fathom how she and Sophie would ever become close to being friends. Too much damage had been done. Most of it – she sadly accepted – on her part. If she'd just opened up a little bit, listened when Michael had talked about his daughter, shown the tiniest bit of interest. But she hadn't. Too wrapped up in me, myself and I.

'I'm going home now, Celeste. I'd offer you a lift but as you obviously followed me here, I assume you'll make your own way back?' Michael rose stiffly to his feet, his expression impossible to read. She stood up too, desperate to touch him but terrified of his reaction.

'I'll see you back there. You *will* be there when I get home?' Celeste pleaded with her eyes, begged for a chance to talk, to find some resolution in this awful mess.

'I'll be there. I'm just not sure how long for.' Michael scraped back his chair and marched off. Celeste watched his departure with blurry vision and a certainty that her marriage was officially over. And that she had only herself to blame.

CHAPTER 20

Fresh herbs in pots. That's what Tabitha was on a mission to find today. She was fed up binning half-used cellophane packs of basil, coriander and parsley from the supermarket. Yes, you could chop them up and freeze them but she never remembered to do that. She was always peeling their blackened and seeping remains from the fridge drawer, pledging to give it a good scrub. Except, she rarely did that either.

She headed to one of those out of town shopping places that offered a cornucopia of goods. Gardening items and implements, essentials for the arts and crafts enthusiast, everything your heart desired on the bathroom and bedding front. As she parked her car, one of the shop names rang several bells. Where the Hearth Is. It had probably been there for ages but never registered until she'd spoken to her mum the other day. When she'd *finally* got the lowdown on Emily's hot date. Which, come to think of it, had been ages ago, or at least a few weeks. They chatted regularly but her mum had been incredibly tight-lipped on the subject.

'Talk about keeping me in suspense! Have you ever

considered a career with MI5, Mum? Yes, I *can* keep a secret, and inflict torture. So, come on, spill!'

Emily had revealed that the date had gone well, despite the choking incident. She'd described in detail the ambiguous bibs which had Tabitha doubled over in laughter.

'I must go there! Even just to keep one as a souvenir. Tom would find it hilarious, except ...' Her voice had tailed off, Emily's motherly instincts immediately honing in on her daughter's change of tone.

'Is everything all right, darling?' she'd asked. 'I know you were a bit down when we last met. I'd hoped it was just a blip but something tells me it's more than that.'

'We've broken up. Well, he broke up with me but that doesn't really matter now. Because I was going to do it anyway. Turns out he'd met someone else which was a bit of a kick in the teeth. Anyway, I'm fine, honestly. Better now than years down the line when I'm old and crinkly like you!'

Her mum had feigned indignation, well used to Tabitha's good-natured teasing.

'Anyway, don't want to talk about Tom any longer. Too boring. I want more details about you and – what's his name again? – Joe. Did you go back to his? Or did he come back to yours? Spill the beans, *did* you?'

'For your information, he came back to mine. Beyond that, the beans are staying firmly in the can. And you can beg all you like. It was only a date, who knows if anything will come of it.'

What sounded suspiciously like a giggle came down the line.

'Mum? What's so funny? Did he suggest a romp and you said you'd forgotten how to do it? Honestly, it's like riding a bike but a lot more fun and you don't need to wear a helmet. Unless it gets *really* energetic ...'

Emily had sighed loudly in order to convey her exasperation at Tabitha's attempts at humour. 'One more wisecrack and I'm hanging up. Do you hear me? Let's talk about something else.'

It took another ten minutes of probing before Tabitha dropped the subject of Joe. Clearly unwilling to reveal anything much about her date, Emily had, however, mentioned the name of his company – cue another fit of chortling from Tabitha – and how they had bought over another business as part of ongoing expansion plans.

'It's called Where the Hearth Is and he's really excited about it. Apparently designer fireplaces are big business. You can get hole-in-the-wall ones, suspended ones, even ones for outdoors. Tabitha, *please* stop with the snoring noises. You are a rude and horrible child.'

Tabitha had been about to wind up the conversation when she remembered about Meryl. She'd let out an involuntary shriek, apologising when her mum complained of a ruptured eardrum.

'Oops, sorry about that. Didn't mean to startle you. I just remembered something completely *awful* that I thought you should know about.'

Tabitha proceeded to fill Emily in on the Miroslaw/Martin saga, describing how she'd found his details on a dating site but omitting to mention she'd been checking out possible matches for her mum. She didn't think she'd appreciate *that* little nugget of information.

'Thank God I was there and managed to stop her sending him the money! Lying toad, I wonder how many other women he's scammed over the years.'

Emily had voiced her genuine shock and sadness for Meryl.

'That's awful! She seemed so thrilled to have met someone she believed could be Mr Right. She was positively *radiant* at Susan's surprise party, telling everyone about him and how happy he made her feel. How did she take it when you told her?'

Tabitha continued the tale. 'Well, she was totally distraught, of course. I don't think she really believed me at first, until I showed her his dating profile. Then we decided to look at a few others and ...'

'Let me guess. Miroslaw aka Martin had spread himself around a bit more in the hope of ensnaring other unsuspecting females? Am I right?'

Meryl and Tabitha had found two other profiles, both added very recently. He'd used the same photo but the accompanying blurb was different each time. As was his name. Marvin and Maurice.

'What's with all the Ms? Or has he already worked his way through the rest of the alphabet?'

The two women had paused for a moment, both wondering how many others he had duped.

'So, what's she going to do? Has she been in touch with him?' asked Emily.

Tabitha explained that – once Meryl had stopped crying and calmed down – they'd concocted a plan. 'She was going to ring him and demand an explanation but I figured it was better to confront the bastard face to face. So she texted him and said there'd been a slight hitch with the money transfer but it would go through in a couple of days. And that she was *really* busy with the shop but they could meet up to celebrate very soon. He texted back immediately gushing like a burst pipe. Made me want to throw up. Anyway ...'

She told Emily she had the day off in a couple of days and planned to do a bit of shopping.

'I persuaded Meryl that I'd pick her up from the shop if she closed up a little early and we'd head to his building company. She said he'd always been a bit cagey about it – fobbed her off when she mentioned dropping by – but he let slip the name one day. It's only a half hour's drive away. I thought we'd put him on the spot, let him know the game's up. I can't *wait* to see the look on his face when he realises he's been rumbled!'

Something was clearly niggling at the back of Emily's mind. 'But didn't Meryl ever visit him at his place? They've been dating quite a while, I would have thought ...'

Tabitha interrupted. 'No, he always made the excuse that he had a crappy flat above the business, didn't want her to see it until he'd spruced it up a bit. Told her it wasn't good enough for an elegant lady like her but that he had grand plans to modernise it or buy something better. Presumably with someone else's money.'

The pieces of the puzzle were clicking into place. Miroslaw – or the M man – deliberately kept the women in his life at bay until he'd done the dirty on them. Which begged the question from Emily: 'In that case, wouldn't they just track him down at work too and contact the police? How long could he possibly keep this going without being caught?'

Neither of them had an answer to this, unless his previous victims had been too embarrassed or ashamed to admit their gullibility. What they *did* know was that Meryl was no pushover and would put aside her heartache in order to retain her dignity.

Tabitha was about to push a coin into a trolley and head into the garden centre when she found herself hesitating. Curiosity about her mum's mystery man won the day and she made her way towards the fireplace shop. There was no guarantee Joe would even *be* there as he was a chimney sweep by profession. But Emily had indicated that he spent a lot of time at the new business and was in the process of combining the offices to cut down on overheads.

Pushing open the door, she was amazed at the vast array

of fireplaces displayed before her. In every conceivable shape, size and configuration they twinkled and sparkled with warmth. No doubt fake but impressive nonetheless. Some were classic in style, others ultra-modern and a million miles removed from her childhood memories of hanging a stocking on Christmas Eve. Explain to your children how Santa was going to squeeze his way down *that* one she thought, eyeing a futuristic number snaking its way down from the ceiling.

'Can I help you?' A voice broke her reverie and she turned to face its owner. Oh, wow. It wasn't only the fireplaces that were smoking hot around here. Tabitha gulped and tried to regain her composure as she took in the easy-on-the-eye man who'd addressed her. Well over six foot, a body made for sin and a face that would make angels weep in envy. So, obviously taken or – more than likely – gay. Damn it.

'Erm, I'm just having a look. Thank you. If that's OK. *At the fireplaces, not at you,* she wanted to add. Just in case her tongue had inadvertently lolled out and she was drooling in a most unseemly manner.

'No problem. Take as long as you like. I'm Adam and I'm here if you need anything. If you see anything you fancy ...'

'You!' screamed a voice inside Tabitha's head. 'I fancy *you*! My boyfriend's just dumped me and I know I shouldn't be contemplating another relationship so soon but ...' She tried but failed to dampen her enthusiasm. Every cell in her body was on red alert, not helped by the fact he was looking at her in a very interested way. A very *heterosexual* way. Unless he swung *both* ways but – hey – she was an open-minded person.

'Actually, I was rather hoping to bump into the boss. He's a friend of my mum's and I was just passing and thought I'd drop by and say hi. My name's Tabitha, by the way.' She extended her hand and Adam shook it warmly. Nice grip, she thought. Very nice hand. Attached to other very nice body parts.

'I'm not sure if he's around but … hang on, you're in luck! Here's the man himself.' Adam disengaged himself from her grasp and gestured towards another man who'd appeared from a backroom area. Tabitha took in his solid but well-toned build, his cropped but full head of hair laced with strands of silver and a handsome face that spoke of a life well-lived and enjoyed. *Thumbs up, Mum,* she thought.

'Hi! Oh, I'm *so* pleased to meet you! I'm Tabitha. Emily's daughter. I know this is really bad of me – my mum will *kill* me when she finds out – but I was just passing so I thought I'd drop in and say hello. I hope you don't mind, I just like keeping an eye on things. Ridiculous, I know, she's a grown woman and all that, but you never stop worrying about them. Mums, that is, just as they never stop worrying about their children!' Tabitha ground to a halt, aware that Joe was looking at her with something like bafflement creeping across his craggy features.

'I'm pleased to meet you too, Tabitha. But I think we're talking at cross purposes here. You said your mum's name is Emily? But I'm afraid I don't know any Emily.' He looked over at Adam, who shrugged, giving Tabitha another smouldering look that half-convinced her they were batting for the same team.

'But, you're *Joe,* aren't you?' Tabitha was now beyond confused, as well as hot under the collar as Adam sent her another sizzling stare. Any more of this and she'd be a molten pile of embers they'd have to sweep up and dump in a wheelie bin.

'No, I'm Steve. I'm Joe's dad. He's out back if you'd like to meet him. Or he was. Here he is now. Joe? There's someone here who'd like to say hello. Tabitha? Meet Joe.'

Tabitha felt like her whole world had tipped on its axis.

The man standing in front of her, looking about as stunned as she felt, was thirty, maybe a year or two more. She could see his physical likeness to his father – both incredibly attractive men – but she could not begin to make sense of what was in front of her. Her mother was dating – maybe even *sleeping* with – a man young enough to be her son. Unless she'd got it all wrong, misunderstood names, misread information. That must be it, she'd been more upset about the Tom break-up than she'd realised, had got hold of the completely wrong end of the stick.

'You're Joe? The chimney sweep? So, you know my mum? I'm just a little confused, think I might have got things mixed up. Always been a bit of a ditz. Once a blonde, always a blonde, eh!' Tabitha had swung her head from side to side to demonstrate her blondeness. Stopped abruptly when Joe had taken her by the arm and steered her towards a corner spot. Pointing to a seat, he had poured her a cup of water from a dispenser and gestured for her to sit down.

'Tabitha. I've heard a lot about you. Well, not a *lot*, but your mum adores you. And I know she's been worried about telling you about us. I completely get it but here's the thing. I really, *really* like your mum – Emily – and I think she feels the same way. It's early days but … I think we have a future. And I know there's an age gap but it honestly doesn't bother me. Does it bother you?'

Did it? Suddenly Tabitha wasn't sure. Yes, she'd been stunned when she learned that her mum's new boyfriend was more her own age than what she'd imagined. Yes, she was having a hard time coming to terms with this fact. She'd always hoped that her mum would meet someone else, she'd just never foreseen it would be a *toy boy*. Yet, looking at Joe's earnest, worried face and thinking of her mum's evident joy and – understandably now, her evasiveness – she wondered if it really mattered. Did a distance in years mean a distance in connection? Could two people transcend a couple of decades and come together if it was meant to be? Or maybe it was simply meaningless sex and they'd wake up, move on and no harm done?

Steve – the dad – was looking uncomfortable, as well he might. Joe was still watching her, trying to gauge her reaction. Adam, meanwhile, was delving into a drawer and produced – with a flourish – his business card.

'Voila! In the midst of all this soap opera drama I thought you should have this. In case of a burning desire – sorry – to contact me. You have my home number, mobile number and email. I will answer all and sincerely hope to hear from you. Soon.'

She took the card and tucked it into her purse. Joe walked with her to the door, his dad and Adam discreetly sloping off to attend to business elsewhere.

'Tabitha, I'm sorry if this has all been too much to take on board but, believe me, I'm not messing about. Emily is special and I would never hurt her. Hand on my heart.' He made the gesture and something inside Tabitha pinged painfully. Tom might not have been The One but she knew that he had never come close to the intensity of feeling that she sensed Joe felt for her mum. Which made her – what? Sad for herself? Happy for them? Completely confused? Time to go home, she thought.

'Bye, Joe. It was good to meet you. Take care.' She kissed him on the cheek and left, all thoughts of herbs in pots wiped from her mind.

CHAPTER 21

It was D-Day. Or rather, M-Day. As arranged, Meryl had shut up shop early and she and Tabitha had set off like Holmes and Watson in pursuit of Moriarty. Except his name was probably something much more mundane. Like Eric or Kevin. Unlikely to be Xavier as he had a considerable way to go alphabetically.

Behind the steering wheel, Tabitha glanced across at her boss and friend. She was ghostly white and gripping her handbag as if her life depended on it. She'd assured Tabitha she was OK, that this was the right thing to do, but her demeanour suggested otherwise. Seeing Miroslaw again and facing the truth about his treachery was clearly something Meryl was dreading. Understandably. To meet a man you thought was your soul mate, only to discover he was a conman with only your bank balance in mind, was a bitter pill to swallow.

Indicating left, Tabitha pulled into the yard with the sign McArthur's Builders in bright red letters against a white background. A few vans with matching logos were parked out front, alongside piles of paving slabs, bricks and miscellaneous materials. When quizzed, Meryl reluctantly admitted she didn't know Miroslaw's surname. Tabitha suspected *McArthur* wasn't it, but didn't push the point. She now firmly believed he was about as Polish as the Queen but saw no need to rub more salt into an already painful wound.

'Are you ready?' Tabitha squeezed Meryl's hand, after prising it from her handbag and noting the definite tremor as she responded. Part of her wanted to put the car in reverse and get as far away as possible from this place and that man. Find someone genuine and lovely who would worship and adore Meryl, not treat her with such contempt and callousness. But she knew closure – another word she loathed – was only a few steps away. Until Meryl slammed the door on this doomed relationship she would be unable to open the way to another.

'Hi! We're looking for the boss. At least, we think he's the boss. Miroslaw?' Tabitha addressed the man behind the desk, who was cleaning his left ear with the tip of his Biro. After scrutinising the results – and wiping them down on his overalls – he deigned to look at them.

'Sorry, love. Didn't quite catch what you said. Got a bit of an ear infection. The missus says I should get drops but I figures there's nowt you can't fix with a good old scour. How can I help you?'

Tabitha took the lead, Meryl quivering by her side. 'I was asking if we could see Miroslaw. I believe this is his company. If you could please call him, see if he's free to come and talk to us.'

The man – whose name badge said "Bert" – scratched his head. A fine dusting of dandruff settled on his shoulders. Tabitha tried not to visibly recoil. They were here for information, not to assess the dubious habits of a staff member. But if he so much as cleared a lung or scratched his balls she swore she would ...

'Miroslaw? Never 'eard of him. Sure you've got the right place?' Bert was definitely going in for a groin adjustment. Before he could realign his tackle, Tabitha whipped out a photo from one of the websites. 'Do you recognise this man?' She waited, aware that Meryl was leaning on the counter, her face contorted with angst and apprehension.

Bert removed his hand from down under and swivelled the photo from left to right. Took out a pair of glasses from his breast pocket and looked again. Sighed deeply, then sighed again. This time, with genuine regret.

'Sorry. I *do* know this guy but he ain't the boss. Never was. Think he's been leading you up the garden path. He worked here for a few months. Seemed OK at first but then money started going missing. Couldn't quite pin it on him but he always had an answer. A bit too slick, if you know what I mean? Anyway, he legged it, probably a couple of weeks ago. Haven't seen him since. Hope he hasn't been doing the dirty on you too?'

Tabitha wrapped her arm around Meryl's shoulder. She was still shaking, but with shock or with fury, it was hard to tell. She had to get her out of there. A stiff drink or two was a given. They'd head back to the shop, park the car, and take it from there. Just one small question was dying to leap from Tabitha's mouth.

'So. You *do* know him but he didn't call himself Miroslaw. What *did* he call himself?'

Bert had another scratch. Another snow globe moment of whiteness followed.

'Malcolm', he replied. 'Said he came from the West Country but I never bought the accent. Never trusted him, truth be told.'

* * *

BACK AT THE Little Shop of Treasures, Tabitha ushered Meryl upstairs. She hadn't said a word on the return journey, just stared ahead as if all the answers to the universe were etched on the windscreen. Time for some serious action. She headed for the fridge, located a bottle of white and grabbed two glasses from an overhead cupboard. Thankfully it was a screwtop as Tabitha hadn't a clue which drawer might contain a corkscrew. She poured two generous measures and brought them over to where Meryl had collapsed in a crumpled heap.

'Here. Get this down you. It won't cure anything but it'll help numb the pain. I know the advice is to "drink responsibly" but right now I think you need be a bit irresponsible. Oh Meryl, I am so, *so* sorry.' Tabitha took a generous mouthful of her wine. Waited as Meryl raised her glass, then proceeded to knock it back in one. Go, girl!

Spluttering slightly, Meryl signalled for a top-up. Tabitha duly obliged, already prepared to crash on the couch if their drinking session showed signs of continuing.

'You know, I should have known it was too good to be true. All those years in the desert and along he comes, my Lawrence of Arabia. My knight in shining armour. Sweeping me off my feet, making me believe I'd found my happy ever after. But it was all a big, fat *fucking* lie.'

Tabitha winced, not least because she had never heard Meryl swear before. It was a bit like watching *The Sound of Music* and hearing Julie Andrews drop the F bomb. She bit her lip and watched as Meryl downed another substantial measure. Thankfully there was a second bottle in the fridge. And she would happily stay the night and open the shop in the morning if needs be.

'Is it me, Tabbie? Do I just attract the wrong kind of men? Am I so dumb, so *stupid* that I can't see when I'm being played for a fool? I'm not getting any younger, and clearly not getting any wiser. Should I just give up? Cash in my savings and sail off into the sunset? Where I'll probably meet another smooth-talking bastard with his eye on my assets. And I don't mean *these*!'

Meryl looked down despondently at her cleavage, which was heaving considerably less since she'd consumed the best part of a bottle of wine. She was calmer, that was for sure, but her morale had been dealt an almighty blow. Tabitha didn't know *how*, but she knew she had to find a way to put her boss back on her feet, restore her faith in humanity – at least, the ones with penises – and ensure the Dancing Queen was back at the top of her game.

A second bottle down and Meryl swayed her way to her bedroom. Tossing a pile of bedding and pillows in Tabitha's general direction, she hiccupped gently and weaved her way back for a hug.

'You're an angel, Tabbie. I don't know what I'd do without you. You're like the daughter I never had. Your mum's the luckiest woman on the planet, having you. Sleep well. See you in the morning.' And she was gone, leaving Tabitha to arrange the covers and pillows on a sofa that was clearly not designed for slumber. More like chronic back pain and rampant insomnia. Ah well, she was still young, free and single. Which suddenly reminded her. Adam. With all the drama of Meryl and discovering her mum's much younger lover (if they'd got that far yet, who knew?) she'd neglected to contact him. And the ball was firmly in her court as she had all his details. She pulled his card out of her purse and located her phone. Time for a text. She squinted at her watch. Definitely not too early. Or too late. After a few misjudged attempts she managed to type : *Hi there! It's me! Tabitha! How are you! Would you like to meet up sometime?* She hit send then squinted at what she'd just written. Far too many exclamation marks. Bugger. Too late now. He was probably sniggering at her message then hitting delete. All that flirty stuff at the showroom and she'd blown it by firing off a text fuelled by alcohol and empathy for her boss. Not the best way of launching a fledgling relationship. Tabitha slumped back on the sofa, resigned to a restless night plagued with nightmares of Miroslaw and Adam poking her with pitchforks and cackling demonically. Then her phone beeped.

Hello there! It's me! Adam! I'm just fine, happy to hear from you! Are you free tomorrow evening! Drinks at Bar Belle, say 7pm! That would be great! PS I think I trounced you with the exclamation marks!

Tabitha suppressed a giggle, stuffing a corner of duvet in her mouth in case she disturbed Meryl. Just when her faith in mankind was hitting an all-time low, there was someone out there who could make her smile.

The next day, after a surprisingly good sleep, Tabitha woke at just after seven. There was no sign of Meryl and a couple of hours before they needed to open the shop. Dressing quickly and gathering up her bits, she headed home to shower and change.

Back at her flat, she made a strong pot of tea and scoffed a round of toast dripping with butter and marmalade. Then she hopped in the shower, feeling better than she deserved after the wine consumption. After blow drying her hair and painting on a layer of slap she was all set.

Meryl was already busy putting price tags on some new stock when Tabitha walked in. She put down her stickers and pen and rushed to give her an enormous hug.

'Sorry about last night. Too much wine always makes me maudlin and tearful. Particularly when I've had a day like yesterday. But I can't thank you enough for being there for me. And *with* me. I think I'd have collapsed on the spot if you hadn't been there to take care of me.'

Tabitha hugged Meryl back with fervour. 'You've nothing to apologise for. I'm just glad we know the truth now and you can get on with your life and meet some delicious hunk who'll treat you like the goddess you are.' Meryl laughed, and patted Tabitha on the cheek. 'I'm hardly a goddess, sweetheart, more of an ancient relic. And I don't need to be worshipped, just treated with kindness and respect. Anyway, I'm having a sabbatical from dating for a while. Just need time to lick my wounds and ... damn it. I completely forgot!' Meryl slapped her hand on her forehead, her smile gone.

'What did you forget?' asked Tabitha, her own face creased with puzzlement. 'If it's about placing that order for those fancy wallet things then I did it already ...'

Meryl shook her head and let out an exasperated sigh. 'No, I was supposed to text Miroslaw about the money transfer and to arrange a night out to celebrate. Ha! As if *that's* going to happen. Over my dead body, or rather, *his.* The thing is, if nothing shows up in his account he'll no doubt appear spouting his usual bullshit and I truly never want to see his conniving face ever again.'

Tabitha decided this required some careful thought and more tea. She popped to the loo first – empty then refill – with a promise to return with refreshments and a suitably cunning plan. A few minutes later and she was back, bearing two steaming mugs and a broad grin. 'I've got it!' she announced in a tone that suggested she had just discovered a cure for something horrible. 'Let me just grab a bit of paper and a pen ...'

Meryl watched curiously as Tabitha scribbled away, occasionally crossing something out. Finally she stopped and pushed the piece of paper in front of her boss. 'There. What do you think?'

Meryl put on her glasses and read the words out loud:

Dear Miroslaw. Or should that be Martin? Or Marvin? Or

Maurice? My sources tell me it might even be Malcolm. Whatever your name ***really*** *is, I just wanted to let you know that you won't be seeing a penny of my money. If you ever dare to show your slimy, deceitful face around here I'll be calling the police. And I'll be letting all the dating agencies you've signed up with know what a cheating bastard you are. Meryl.*

She turned to Tabitha, her mouth wide open. 'You really think I should do that? Contact the dating sites, I mean?'

Tabitha nodded with conviction. 'Absolutely! Fire off that message to him now and, when we get a break later, I'll help you to email the ones we found. They might not do anything but maybe they have a kind of blacklist of creeps like him. If it stops him scamming someone else ...'

The rest of the morning passed pleasantly. Unsurprisingly, there was no reply to Meryl's text, not that she expected or wanted one. Time to draw a line under the whole sorry experience and move on. Onwards and upwards, that had always been Meryl's motto when life didn't go to plan.

At just after midday, when a couple of customers had departed laden with goodies, she turned the shop sign to 'Closed'. Tabitha had just returned from the loo – all that tea had got to her – and she raised her eyebrows in surprise. Normally they stayed open at lunchtime, with one of them manning the shop while the other nipped out for sandwiches or a takeaway salad. 'What's up? Are you feeling all right?' she inquired, worried that Meryl was still in shock and wasn't really up to a full day's work.

'I'm absolutely fine, Tabbie. All the better for having my golden girl around to look after me. And, on that note, I'm taking you out for lunch so grab your coat and let's go!'

Seated in a booth in Wine O' Clock, one of Emily's favourite hang-outs, they perused the glossy menus. Meryl had insisted they have a glass of bubbly each – 'to celebrate getting rid of M Man!' – so they toasted one another before placing their orders. Seafood risotto for Meryl and Cajun chicken salad for Tabitha.

'It's lovely in here, isn't it?' said Meryl, forking up a mouthful of rice and prawns. 'I can't believe I haven't come here before. Didn't you say your mum's a regular?'

Tabitha took a large gulp of water before replying. The chicken was *extremely* spicy but very tasty. 'She comes every couple of weeks with my aunt Celeste. Ooh, there's something *I* completely forgot to tell you about. You are *not* going to believe this!'

She proceeded to relate how Emily had started dating but been very reluctant to share many details. How she'd found the shop where the mysterious Joe was based, only to discover ...

'Your mum's dating a thirty-year-old? Oh, my goodness, that must have been a shock for you. Although, why the heck not? As long as he's not after her money, only her mind and body! Let's face it, Tabbie, your mum's a good-looking lady who's spent far too long alone. If they're happy together who are we to judge?' Meryl gave her a stern look, obviously anticipating a long list of reasons why it wouldn't work.

Instead, Tabitha gave a hands-up, "who knows?" gesture and forked up the last bits of salad. 'You're right. It's none of my business and if she's OK with the age difference – and *he* certainly seems to be – then who am I to interfere? All I've ever wanted is for my mum to be happy and find someone who really cares about her. If Joe's the one, so be it.'

Suddenly feeling a bit emotional, Tabitha dabbed at her eyes with her napkin. Wouldn't it be strange if her mum ended up living with – even *marrying* – the undoubtedly handsome and charming Joe while she remained resolutely single. Destined to be the bridesmaid but never the bride. Except ...honestly, Tabitha wondered if she had some kind of early onset dementia, so many things seemed to slip her mind these days. "Senior moments" was how her mum jokingly referred to them when she couldn't find her car keys or came back from a food shop minus a vital ingredient.

'Meryl, with all the drama of the past twenty-four hours I forgot something else. Or *someone* else. Not only did I meet Joe, I met the *very* attractive Adam!'

As Tabitha related the tale of their flirtation at the shop and their text exchanges last night, Meryl called the waiter over.

'Two more glasses of fizz, please. Don't look at me like that, Tabbie. I promise to drink nothing but fennel tea for the next few days but I think we should kick back a little and mark the fact that two very special ladies have found themselves some hot men. If you could just find one for *me* then we could celebrate a triple victory!'

On the way back to the shop – both a little giggly and praying they weren't inundated with demanding customers – Tabitha found her thoughts returning to her trip to Where the Hearth Is. Meryl's mention of luck coming in threes reminded her of the third person she'd spoken to that day. Steve, Joe's dad. A fine-looking specimen and – if first impressions were accurate – a genuinely nice man,too. She had no idea if he was married, divorced or widowed but she could find out. And a chat with her mum was well overdue, if only to reassure her that her relationship with Joe wasn't an issue.

Unlocking the door of The Little Shop of Treasures, Meryl turned to Tabitha. 'You look very pleased with yourself, young lady. And you've been humming away since we left the restaurant but I couldn't quite name that tune. What was it?'

Tabitha looked at her with an expression of pure innocence. 'Oh, nothing. Just a silly song I heard on the radio the other day. Come on, let's get ready for some serious selling!'

Following her boss into the shop she resumed her discreet crooning: *Matchmaker, matchmaker, make me a match...*

CHAPTER 22

Tabitha had never been to Bar Belle. Come to think of it, there were lots of places locally she'd never been to. She and her friends tended to stick to familiar, established places. Where they'd been served under age, the staff pouring them a shandy in the knowledge they weren't going to get blind drunk and create a scene. She hadn't been ID'd in years but her mum *had* been some ten years ago in a bar in Miami. Much to her delight and her dad's disgruntlement. 'I'm forty-two Tabitha, and they asked for proof of age!' She'd been totally chuffed, her enthusiasm somewhat dampened by Jim's comment that her oversized sunglasses concealed a multitude of sins. The teenage Tabitha had hated him at that precise moment. For deliberately crushing her mum's evident joy. And for what reason? Jealousy, perhaps. Her dad had faded over the years, age taking its toll in many ways until he collapsed and died. Emily, on the other hand, seemed to grow into herself. She was ten years older now but looked incredible. Slim, trim and effortlessly stylish, she knocked spots off women twenty years younger. Which was presumably what had drawn Joe to her. Maybe he'd tired of vacuous twenty-somethings with all the conversational skills of an amoeba. Maybe he'd had enough of fake breasts, fake tans and obsessions with boybands and reality TV shows. God knows, Tabitha couldn't be bothered with any of that stuff. She was no intellectual but she knew she wanted more than that.

As she was a little early, she fired off a text to Derwyn and Fiona. *On a hot date! At least, I hope it's hot! When you guys free to meet up? xx*

She'd updated them on the Tom front, messages fired back expressing sadness with a hint of "saw that coming!" Both replied within seconds, demanding a summit meeting the following night. She'd just replied in the affirmative when a denim-clad groin reached her eye line. Lordy! Raising her eyes from her phone, she took in all of Adam in his absolute glory. Fitted white shirt showing just enough chest hair to induce instantaneous meltdown. Dark jeans clinging in all the right places. Face cleanly shaven, skin gleaming and eyes twinkling with merriment, mischief or mayhem. Enough with the letter M, thought Tabitha.

'Hi. Mind if I join you? You look thirsty and I could absolutely annihilate a pint right now.' Those eyes were now positively dancing with devilish delight. Two could play at that game, thought Tabitha.

'You may indeed, but only if you bring me a white wine spritzer and a shot of Sambuca. Flaming, of course.' Crikey, where had *that* come from? The only time she'd witnessed a flaming Sambuca was when Aunt Celeste had ordered one and poured half of it down her sleeve. She'd been rushed into the restaurant kitchen, arm ablaze, emerging minutes later with an icepack and steely determination to finish her veal saltimbocca.

Adam returned with the drinks, Tabitha grabbing the Sambuca and raising it in the air. 'What shall we drink to?

World peace? An end to global warming? No more crap about Kardashians or other nonentities on the tabloid pages?'

He raised his pint and clinked her glass. 'Let's drink to new adventures. You and me, Tabitha. Let's start at the very beginning...'

A very good place to start, thought Tabitha, stifling a giggle. She was back in Julie Andrews territory, except this time she wasn't the only one in on the joke. Adam was already on his feet and singing slightly off-key about "Doe - a deer, a female deer."

'You're far too young to know *The Sound of Music*. Unless...'

'It's true. My mum force-fed me some of the old classics. I know all the words to The *Wizard of Oz, Mary Poppins, The Sound of Music* and *The Lion King*. Which is much more recent, admittedly, but I was hooked the first time I heard it. "Hakuna matata..."

Tabitha joined in with enthusiasm. 'It means "no worries", for the rest of your days. Wouldn't that be nice? Improbable, but nice.' She looked directly at Adam. He looked back at her. Gave her a smile that would have melted ice caps. And proceeded to burst into a rendition of "Follow the Yellow Brick Road" complete with Munchkin-like voices. People were staring from all directions. Tabitha decided she didn't give a monkey's. Even a flying monkey's. She got to her feet too and joined in. "We're off to see the Wizard, the wonderful Wizard of Oz." Linking arms with Adam she realised that the whole bar was singing along. Not *quite* in tune but with energy and enthusiasm. It was a strangely uplifting and life-affirming moment.

'If we left now do you think they'd be upset?' whispered Adam in her ear. They'd come to the end of the yellow brick road and the crowd were baying for more. Tabitha knew all the words to "Supercalifragilisticexpialidocious" but was damned if she was going to engage the audience in another singalong.

'Who cares? Let's get out of here.' She grabbed his hand and hauled him towards the exit, aware of booing and cries of "don't go!" behind them.

Out on the street Tabitha was aware of two things. One – she was absolutely starving and two – she really, *really* liked Adam. He made her laugh. He definitely had a good head of hair and his teeth were worthy of a dentistry ad. She didn't know if he could cook or if he was a genius in bed but she was prepared to wait and see. And she *was* going to wait. Much as she'd like to lure him back to her place and put him through his paces she knew she'd regret it in the morning.

'Fancy a quick pizza or something?' They'd stopped outside an Italian restaurant which had a decent reputation. Adam folded his arms and gave her a stern look. 'It goes without saying what I fancy, but you have the look of a famished lioness who's just watched several wildebeest disappear over the horizon. So, let's go and get some serious slices of pepperoni or whatever your heart desires.'

As they were guided to a table in the dimly lit interior, Tabitha did a double-take. It *couldn't* be, could it? She peered into the darkened corner, then attempted to retreat, nearly tripping over Adam who was right behind her.

'Are you OK? You look like you've seen a—'

Tabitha didn't hear the rest of his sentence. She was now staring at Tom, seated at a cosy table for two with a disgustingly dark-haired harlot beside him. OK, maybe she was a perfectly nice girl but she was still the one who got to go to *Hong Kong*. Bitch.

'Hi Tom. Nice to see you (Lie). Looking good (Truth, damn it). So, this must be? (Wait for name of shameless tart).'

Tom looked appalled, the woman next to him cooler than an iced cucumber. She ran her fingers along his thigh,

Tabitha wanting to shout: 'Get your hands off! He's mine!' But he wasn't, not any more. She felt Adam's hands on her shoulders, gentle but supportive.

'Tabitha, this is Kate. Kate, Tabitha.' If he was expecting a sisterly embrace or a high five, he was destined to be disappointed. The two women gave each other cursory glances, Tabitha desperate to sit down and eat something, Kate clearly feeling she had the upper hand.

'Sweetheart, it's been a long day so let's go and have some dinner. Tom, Kate. Nice to meet you. Enjoy your meal.' With those well-chosen words, Adam steered Tabitha to their table, placed an order with the waiter and sat back. Tabitha tore off a piece of bread, dunked it in some olive oil, and gave him her most glacial of stares.

'Why did you do that? Call me sweetheart when you've known me for five minutes? I get that you figured out he's my ex but *why* did you do that?' Tabitha felt like she was unravelling like a ball of string, being attacked by a band of manic kitties.

Adam said nothing. Nodded politely when the food arrived, carved up the pizza and slid a couple of slices in Tabitha's direction. They ate in silence for several minutes, both acutely aware of Tom and Kate's presence just yards away.

'Yes, Tabitha. This is *not* quite the date I imagined.' Adam peeled off a slice of pepperoni and pushed the doughy part to the side of his plate. 'I never imagined bumping into your ex, but I don't think you expected that either. I called you *sweetheart* because I wanted to you to feel confident. I wanted you to show him that you'd moved on. I hope you have. And I'm here if you want me to be.'

Tabitha was speechless. Was this man for real? Should she have him stuffed and mounted as rare exhibit at the British Museum? Roll up, roll up. Genuinely nice guy. Thoughtful, caring and exceptionally easy on the eye. Yes, they do exist in this selfish, greedy and narcissistic century. On second thoughts, Tabitha had no desire to share him with anyone. If he really was as lovely as he seemed the rest of womankind could form an orderly queue. She had a priority pass and fully intended to use it.

'It's fine. Sorry I overreacted. It was just a shock, you know, running into them. But I'm OK with it. It's history now. Honestly.' Tabitha smiled in a way she hoped conveyed she was absolutely over Tom and more than a little bit into Adam. He smiled back in a way that suggested they were on the same page, with many chapters still to be revealed. Phew! She cast a sideways glance at love's young dream as Adam dissected another slice of pizza and felt nothing. No sadness, no envy, no bitterness. Just a sense of moving on and going with the flow.

Almost an hour later and they had shared some more wine, laughed a lot and confessed to a mutual liking for *Joseph and his Amazing Technicolour Dreamcoat*. Bill duly paid – Adam refused to split it – they headed off into the night singing in harmony. Admittedly neither knew all the words but passers-by smiled indulgently as they warbled away. Tabitha couldn't recall when she'd had so much fun, felt so at ease in someone's company. It was a night to remember, not one to go in for the casual fumble and flaming cheeks in the morning.

They'd reached her doorstep. She already had her keys to hand, prepared to part with – hopefully – the promise of another date to follow. She sent up a silent prayer as she opened the door and turned to face Adam. 'Thank you. For a lovely evening, despite the awkward bit. Can we do it again? If you'd like to?'

By way of reply Adam placed his hands on her face and kissed her. A soft, barely-there kiss but enough to give her serious goosepimples and cause her to question her vow of chastity. 'Take that as an affirmative,' he replied, Tabitha's lips still tingling from their all-too-brief contact with his. 'We've still got a truckload of show tunes to work our way through, haven't we?'

Tabitha grinned and stuck her key in the lock. 'Absolutely. I think we should move on to *Oklahoma* next, then maybe *Les Miserables*? Although that always makes me cry.' As she opened the door she wondered if Adam would invite himself in. Her virtuous side – not the dominant one – hoped he wouldn't. Her wicked side was screaming "Go on! You know you want to!"

Whether he could read the agonising dilemma on her face, or was simply a perfect gentleman, Adam stepped back and gave a little bow. 'Personally, I'm a big *Oliver* fan but we can argue the toss next time. Would tomorrow be OK, or do you need more time to get into character? Belt out some numbers in the shower? I can be patient, but only up to a point. If I have to wait more than twenty-four hours until I see you again I may well spontaneously combust. And that would be messy and massively inconvenient for my boss.'

At the mention of Adam's boss, Tabitha's brain went into hyper drive. She'd meant to quiz Adam about Steve during the evening but had been somewhat distracted. Yes, it could wait until tomorrow but suddenly she needed to know where he stood on the availability scale. 'Erm, just curious and all that but is he single? Steve, I mean.'

Adam gave her a look that suggested her query was as unexpected as Hugh Jackman announcing he was gay and shacking up with Russell Crowe. Presumably to serenade each other in sexy French accents. 'Please, don't tell me you have a thing for older men. I couldn't bear it. Plus, I happen to know that Steve is a very good singer but not really a fan of musicals so that would probably put a nail in the romantic coffin. I know he's extremely good-looking but—'

Tabitha cut him off with a glare worthy of a school-teacher facing a classroom of belligerent teenagers. 'I am *not*, repeat *not* interested in your boss in that way.' She ignored Adam's overly dramatic sigh of relief and continued. 'I just wondered. You see, my boss, Meryl, has had a really shit time with men recently and I saw Steve and I was just thinking...'

'You were just thinking you could pair them up? Before I spill, you need to tell me a bit more about your boss. Is she cute, funny, not prone to stalking innocent men and boiling bunnies?'

Tabitha gave a quick rundown on Meryl, wondering why they were conducting this conversation on the doorstep when it would be much easier inside. But she knew if they both went indoors her wicked side would win the day and her clothes would fall off all of their own accord.

'Sounds perfectly nice. OK, Steve is widowed. His wife – Joe's mum – died around five years ago. Cancer, I believe. They both took it hard. I think Steve's dated on and off in the past couple of years but nothing serious. He doesn't really talk about it, why would he? All I know is he's a great guy and if he met someone who made him happy that would be fantastic.'

Tabitha was now a woman on a mission. Both to somehow introduce Meryl to Steve and to keep Adam in her life. As well as checking that all was well with her mum and Joe. Crikey, she almost needed a spreadsheet to manage all the potential love lives in the frame. 'So, if I somehow managed to introduce Meryl to Steve, do you think ... ?'

Adam nudged her inside, a finger pressed against her lips. She fought back the urge to open her mouth and lick it. Her wicked side was definitely going for gold and a few victory laps.

'Off to bed with you, scheming wench. I'll pick you up tomorrow around seven and we'll eat, drink and plot devious ways to ensure global peace and harmony. Sweet dreams, *sweetheart.*'

With a giggle and a final kiss – slightly less chaste than the previous one – Tabitha closed the door. Her head was a complete jumble, thoughts of Adam at the fore, thoughts of the other cast members in her life shouting for attention. Sleep seemed a remote possibility, so she headed to the kitchen and made herself a cup of hot chocolate. On the way, she scooped up the morning's post and dumped it on the counter. Bills, bills and more bills. And another that caught her eye. "Party People Inc." Wasn't that the company who'd hired her for the wrap party for that mad Scottish reality show? She ripped open the envelope and scanned its contents. Oh. My. God. It seemed that Big Tam had bigged her up with the powers that be (despite her aversion to artery-clogging choccie delights) and now they were offering her a job! Well, at least an interview for a job. A *proper,* event-planning job involving planning events from the ground up. Everything she'd studied for but had had little chance to put into practice. The interview was scheduled for a week's time in London. She'd have to tell Meryl, take time off work, polish up her resumé and dig deep for confidence she knew existed but was buried under layers of self-doubt and abject fear. You *can* do this, she told herself. The hardest part would be leaving Meryl. If she even *got* the job, that is.

Sipping her hot chocolate and rereading the letter, Tabitha couldn't help but dwell on the vagaries of life and how things could change in little more than a heartbeat. One minute she was living with Tom and an increasing sense of dissatisfaction, the next she was singing and feeling totally connected with a man called Adam and possibly embarking on a new career. Maybe even managing to match her beloved

Meryl up with a man who seemed to be everything the website weirdos were not.

Tucked up in bed, Tabitha could feel another ear worm coming on. 'Love Changes Everything'. She wasn't sure of the show – something Andrew Lloyd Webber – but it seemed right. She drifted off to sleep, contentment written all over her face.

CHAPTER 23

It had been almost a week since Celeste had confronted Michael and discovered his rekindled relationship with Sophie. An agonising, terrifying week with the two of them passing like ships in the night. Michael had moved his things into the guest bedroom by the time she'd returned home, the door firmly closed behind him. They'd barely exchanged more than a handful of words and meal-times were tense and punctuated only by the clatter of cutlery or scraping of plates.

Celeste desperately wanted to make things right but she hadn't a clue where to begin. Or if the gulf between them was too great and Michael was just biding his time before telling her he was leaving. Every time she imagined the words she felt sick to her stomach. Even more so, because she'd had the power all those years ago to change the course of their history. If she'd encouraged her husband to see Sophie, welcomed his daughter into their lives, everything would have been so different. Berating herself for the hundredth time she wished she had done things differently. She might never have come close to being a mother to Sophie but maybe they would have become friends. And Michael would have revelled in his role as doting dad and grandfather. He was clearly doing that now, but the chances of Celeste and Sophie ever picking up the pieces were virtually nil. Judging by Sophie's expression when Celeste saw her for the first time, she made Disney villainesses look like paragons of virtue and loveliness.

Michael was out. She'd heard the front door slamming a little earlier. He'd offered no explanation as to where he was going. Not that she needed one. She'd heard him murmuring on his phone about an hour ago and it was clear he was speaking to Sophie. No need to hide it anymore. The ugly truth was out there. Michael was with his family and there was no place for Celeste in their cosy unit.

For want of something to keep her mind occupied she switched on her computer. There were several new messages in her inbox. One was from *Tea Break*, asking if she could be available next week for the interview and photo session. The cheque had arrived a couple of days ago and Celeste had shoved it in her bedside drawer. There was no way now she could share her news with Michael. All her joyous thoughts of celebrating becoming a published writer with him had been reduced to dust. She was half-tempted to contact the magazine and withdraw her story. Return the cheque and forget the whole sorry affair. The thought of having to smile for a photo shoot and babble away about her wonderful life to some hack journalist filled her with dread. 'Yes, I'm *delighted* to have come second in the competition. It's just a shame that my lovely husband is about to divorce me because I'm a self-centred old bitch who thinks the world revolves around her. But hey, you reap what you sow!' No, that probably wasn't *quite* what they expected. Although the *Tea Break* readers might experience a frisson of –what was the word again? – Sigmundfreud. Something about getting pleasure from someone else's misfortune.

Aware that she was in danger of sliding deeper into a pit of misery, Celeste figured there was only one person she could really talk to. Who might actually be happy for her small success and take a slightly less harsh view of the situation she was in. Emily. As sisters went they weren't exactly close – was she close to *anyone*, except Michael? – but Emily had a kind heart and a non-judgemental take on life.

Driving to Emily's house Celeste knew it would have been better to call her first but she'd been afraid of bursting into tears on the phone. There was every possibility she would be out but she'd take the chance.

Pulling into the driveway, Celeste was surprised to see a van with 'Up Yours' written on the side parked just in front of the garage. What a rather rude name. What kind of business *was* it, she wondered. Still, its presence meant that Emily was probably at home having something or other repaired. She rang the bell and waited. Nothing. She tried again, still no sound of approaching footsteps. Glancing upwards she saw the bedroom curtains twitch a fraction. How strange. Maybe 'Up Yours' was a plumbing company and they were currently inspecting her u-bend or a faulty shower head. Which didn't fully explain why someone had just peeked through the curtains instead of answering the door.

Finger at the ready to ring again, Celeste could make out a shadowy figure approaching the door. It swung open and there was Emily. Looking, it had to be said, rather dishevelled. Her hair looked like it had been attacked by a garden rake and – hang on a minute – her T-shirt appeared to be on back to front.

'Hi! Celeste! What a surprise! What are you doing here?' Emily's tone of voice suggested her sister's visit was about as welcome as a bunch of leaflet-wielding Jehovah's Witnesses. Something was definitely amiss.

'Sorry, Em. I should have rung but I just needed to get out the house. I really need to talk to you but if it's not a good time ... ' Celeste halted as she heard the distinct sound of footsteps descending the stairs and approaching the door. Emily stepped back, clearing the way for whoever it was to pass. Celeste took a step back too as a tall, dark and very handsome young man appeared before her. He also looked distinctly flustered, although his clothes seemed to be on the right way round.

'Celeste, this is Joe. Joe, this is my sister, Celeste. Joe was just leaving, weren't you, Joe? Had another spot of bother with the chimney but all sorted now. Thank you, Joe. See you soon ... I mean, if I get another blockage, that is.' Joe had shaken Celeste's proffered hand, glanced at Emily, then sped to his van with indecent haste. Luckily Celeste's Audi wasn't blocking him in and he performed an expert manoeuvre before vanishing from view.

A stunned Celeste followed a clearly flustered Emily into the house. 'Give me two minutes and I'll be with you. I just need—' She bolted up the stairs, leaving Celeste gazing in bewilderment at her departing back. Unsure what to do, she wandered into the living room. Took in the sight of the fireplace looking spotlessly clean and clearly unused recently. Plus, hadn't Joe been upstairs as opposed to working in the living room? She knew there were no fireplaces there. Which meant either he did other jobs on the side or ... Oh my goodness! The whirring cogs and gears in Celeste's brain clicked into place. She sat down hastily, all thoughts of her own news driven away by this shocking revelation. At that moment, Emily burst into the living room, her T-shirt righted and her hair marginally tidier. 'Cup of tea? Coffee? Or would you like something cold? I've got a really nice juice blend with beetroot in it; it's meant to be good for lowering blood pressure.'

Celeste couldn't decide whose blood pressure was the highest at that precise moment. Emily's neck and cheeks were suffused with a deep red flush and she could feel her own heart pounding away as if she'd just completed a 10K run. 'Emily, are you having *sex* with that man?' No point in beating about the bush. She didn't need to be a genius to work out what was going on. It was written all over her sister's face.

'Yes. I am. I mean, we were. But it's not what you think,' stammered Emily. 'I know you're probably thinking I'm having some mid-life crisis and decided a quickie with the chimney sweep would spice up my life but it's not like that. We've been seeing quite a lot of each other – *evidently, thought Celeste, judging by their rapid dressing* – and I really like him. Really, *really* like him. And he feels the same way.' Emily now looked less flustered and more defiant, her chin raised as if daring her sister to voice her criticism.

'But – darling – he's just so *young!* I'm all for you dating someone, Lord knows it's been long enough since Jim passed away but don't you think it's a little ... inappropriate?' That wasn't the first word that had come to mind. Sordid, sleazy and downright disgusting had all been contenders but she'd bitten them back, aware that they would not be well received. Not that *inappropriate* had gone down well either. Emily's face was thunderous as she sat down opposite her, balling up the hem of her T-shirt with hands that looked equally capable of grabbing Celeste by the throat.

'Yes, he's young. And don't think for a minute that doesn't worry me too. I've had many sleepless nights stressing about it. Wondering if everyone will laugh at me behind my back. The merry widow making hay with her toy boy lover. The thing is, *he* asked *me* out. On a date. I didn't lunge at him like some sex-starved suburban housewife who fancied a bit of rumpy pumpy because she was bored and desperate. We have fun together, we chat all the time, he tells me I'm beautiful and when I'm with him that's *exactly* how I feel. I know you don't approve and I'm not asking for your approval. Just bear in mind we can't all be like you and Michael, so loved up and snug in your own perfect little utopian world. Forgive me but, if being with Joe makes me happy, who are you to pass judgement?' Emily had apparently run out of things to say. Now it was Celeste's turn to speak, and to shatter her sister's illusions. She cleared her throat and began, her voice shaky and hoarse.

'You think I have the perfect life? Maybe I did up until a week ago but it was a life built on lies and a woeful lack of communication. Now it's all blown up in my face and I don't deserve an ounce of sympathy. I *know* I don't but I wanted to speak to you about it. There isn't another soul in the world I can talk to. Michael's going to leave me and I honestly don't think I can go on without him.'

Deciding against hot beverages and juice in favour of a large glass of red each, Celeste and Emily faced each other over the kitchen counter. A box of tissues was between them, along with a bowl of stuffed olives and slivers of parmesan drizzled with balsamic vinegar. Neither had any appetite for food. Celeste had filled her sister in on the whole Sophie story, how she sincerely regretted her actions but could see no way of putting things to rights. Emily had always known about Michael's family history but assumed he and Celeste had talked it over, made their peace. She often wondered if Michael missed his daughter but seeing him and Celeste together convinced her that they were that rare thing. A truly contented couple inhabiting a world largely untroubled by the wants and needs of others. Hearing Celeste now, she realised her view of their world was that of an uninformed outsider, privy to little more than scraps of information. If they'd been closer all those years ago perhaps she would have persuaded her big sister to bring Sophie into the fold. To hell with the bitter and twisted ex-wife. Why did people muck things up so badly? Were we all so fixated on looking after number one that we forgot to look at the bigger picture? Emily didn't think she was a selfish person. Her focus over recent years had been Tabitha, her proudest achievement and biggest cause of concern. She'd never really worried about Celeste and her circle of friends was small and unchallenging. Until she met Joe she'd resigned herself to a mundane life of work, socialising and counting off birthdays on the calendar. Then she met Joe and it was like being lit up from within. Not just the sex – incredible as it was – but the sense of being in a good place. A happy, positive and uplifting place. She still couldn't predict where it was going, but the journey was one she would never regret. What was the saying? *Better to travel hopefully than arrive.*

Second glasses poured, Emily was relieved that Celeste was less tearful but still twitchier than a drug addict on methadone. There was clearly something else on her mind, aside from the whole Michael/Sophie thing.

'I get the feeling there's something you're not telling me. And you absolutely don't have to but I'm listening. It's been quite a day of confessions so step up and fess up.'

Celeste swirled her glass around. Should she tell Emily about her writing? Why not? It was time she shared it with someone, even if her success was now tainted by her misery. 'I know you're going to laugh but I've been up to something. Something I kept secret from Michael. No, I haven't been having it away with the window cleaner' – cue nervous laughter on both sides – 'I've been writing. A book. Well, a novella, at least. Not as long but still bloody hard work. It's won second place in a competition. I never thought I could write anything worth publishing. Never thought I could do *anything* of note, to be honest. Right now, I should be happiest woman in the world but I've never felt more wretched. You're the smart one; I'm the pathetic big sister who screws everything up.'

Emily leaned over, grabbed Celeste's hand and squeezed it tight. 'That is *amazing*! Well done, you! Tell me more. What's it about and where's it going to be published?'

As Celeste outlined the plot of her opus, Emily sensed a feeling of deja vu. The character names were so familiar, the storyline as fresh as a newly-blossomed daisy in her mind. It couldn't be ... could it?

'So, did you write it under your own name, or did you ... ?' She waited, still unable to process what her brain was yelling at her.

'No, I used a *nom de prune.* Figured my own name was a bit dull, so I went for Astra Du Bois. Nice touch, don't you think?' Celeste looked gratifyingly pleased with herself. Emily swallowed back the urge to laugh like a demented hyena. What a day so far! Her sister had discovered she was sleeping with a stripling of a lad, she'd learned that Celeste's enviable marriage was coming apart at the seams and now she knew the sex-stuffed manuscript she'd edited and admired was actually the product of her sister's fertile imagination. What next? Probably a text to Joe apologising for the interruption earlier and suggesting a rematch as soon as possible. The very thought took her back to Leo and Seraphina territory. Her *sister* wrote that? Just went to show you never knew someone. Not really. Which led her back to the whole Michael/Sophie issue and what – if anything – she could do to help.

'Have you thought of contacting Sophie directly? No, hear me out.' Emily saw the raw panic in Celeste's face and cut her off before she could protest. 'Why don't you ring her, suggest you meet? What have you got to lose? Michael's never going to give her up now. You won't get through this unless you actively *do* something! I don't believe Michael wants to let you go, but he's completely torn between the past and the present. *Do* something, Celeste. You have to.'

* * *

CELESTE WAS on her way home. Her initial shock at Emily's younger lover had given way to an acceptance that different things worked for different people. She could no more imagine sleeping with a thirty-something than chartering a rocket to the moon but that was how she was made. Michael was engrained in her like the wording on a stick of Blackpool rock. Bite off a piece and the message remained the same. Together for always.

Pacing around the bedroom – Michael was home but closeted away in his study – Celeste scrolled through her contacts. She wasn't proud of herself but she'd accessed Michael's phone again a few days ago and found Sophie's number. To dial or not to dial. That was the excruciating question. She'd probably hang up the instant she knew who was calling. And she wouldn't blame her. Not in the slightest. Roles reversed, she knew what her reaction would be. Still, nothing ventured, nothing gained. She pressed 'Call' and waited.

'Hello? Sophie here. Who's calling?' Celeste counted down silently from ten to zero. This was it. 'It's Celeste, Sophie. Probably the last person in the world you want to talk to. I know we have nothing in common but there is one person we both care about. Your dad. I completely understand if you want nothing to do with me but I'd like to meet up with you. Try to explain my side of things. Which is feeble and grasping at straws but it's all I have. I don't like myself and I don't expect you to like me either but could we please at least try to chat? Then, if you still hate me I'll disappear and let you get on with your lives.'

Total silence. But no tone that indicated she'd hung up. Celeste felt sure she would faint if she had to wait a moment longer.

'Sure. The garden centre where we ran into each other? How about lunch there tomorrow? The quiches are excellent and the salads not too shabby either. I'm a bit tired of all the pretence and bullshit. Let's just see how it goes?' She ended the call, Celeste feeling like she'd had her head in the noose only to receive a last-minute stay of execution. Sophie was willing to see her. Baby steps for now. She headed up to bed, pausing to say 'Goodnight' to Michael. No reply. Her chest tightened. Everything hinged on what happened when she met up with Sophie. Emily could be sleeping with every tradesman from Bucks to Berks but that had little bearing on Celeste's life. She had to find a way to fix her marriage – and fast.

CHAPTER 24

Dinner at Joe's had been amazing. He'd whipped up a delicious concoction of chicken wrapped in bacon and stuffed with an oozing mixture of cheeses and mustard. With a side of saffron-tinted tagliatelle. Washed down with some rosé wine and followed by a raspberry pavlova.

'You made this? You *actually* made a meringue?' Emily was incredulous as she took another mouthful of crispy but meltingly soft-in-the-middle dessert. She hated to think how many calories she'd consumed but was confident she'd burn them off a little later.

'Indeed I did, oh doubting one. I find whisking egg whites until they form stiff peaks quite therapeutic. Just because I'm a sad old bachelor doesn't mean I dine on ready meals and toast!' Joe gave her another of his pulse-raising smiles, leaning over to caress Emily's exposed shoulder. The red top fitted like a dream, perfectly complemented by the white jeans which she'd managed to avoid spattering with food. When Joe had picked her up he'd done a double-take, before pronouncing her good enough to eat. 'It's almost a shame we're not going out, because I'd be the envy of every man in the room with you looking like that.'

His flat was immaculate, all gleaming surfaces, polished wood floors and huge windows that overlooked an area of parkland. It wasn't big but it felt like a proper home. An L-shaped squashy sofa dominated the living space, there were rugs and cushions galore and the open-plan kitchen was light, bright and fully equipped with all the aspiring cook could want. The bedroom and bathroom were equally impressive if a little masculine in their furnishings. Luckily, Emily had managed to add a few feminine touches, if a hot brush, tubs of cleanser and moisturiser and her favourite fluffy slippers counted.

It was only their eighth date but Emily felt totally at ease in Joe's company. Of course, they had got as intimate as humanly possible on the first date but there was no sense of awkwardness or embarrassment. Just a sense of "rightness", of somehow fitting together. It was an altogether new and exciting feeling that made Emily feel like a giggly teenager instead of a menopausal housewife. When she'd looked in the mirror earlier she swore she looked younger too. No amount of expensive anti-ageing products could replicate the radiance that came with dating a seriously hot young man.

'Can I fix you a coffee? I've got a half-decent decent bottle of brandy if you fancy one?

Settled down on the comfy sofa with their coffees and brandies Emily and Joe chatted about everything and anything. He'd been reticent about his past but revealed he'd studied computer science at university and worked briefly for a software company.

'It was OK but my heart wasn't really in it. I'd helped my dad out with the business when I was younger and really enjoyed it. Getting my hands dirty, meeting people, learning the tricks of the trade. So ... when he asked if I'd like to join him I jumped at the opportunity. And now we've got Where the Hearth Is, it's pretty full-on. We're a good team. Adam works like a Trojan sourcing new fireplace designs from all over the world and I've put together a pretty impressive website, if I say so myself.'

Emily fetched her laptop and found the site. They navigated through it together, Emily suitably impressed at its easy-to-follow layout and the sheer volume of fireplaces on offer. At the top of the home page were photos of Steve, Joe, Adam and their part-time accountant Rosemary. She was immediately struck by the resemblance between father and son, both fine-looking male specimens. And Adam wasn't too shabby either in the looks department. He had a cheeky twinkle in his eye and for a fleeting moment she wondered ... no, she was *not* going to interfere in Tabitha's life. If things weren't working out with Tom it was up to her to figure it out. In any case, Adam was probably married or at least seeing someone. Rosemary - who appeared to be in her late sixties with a mop of frizzy grey hair - looked like a retired headmistress. But Joe assured her she was a great laugh and super-efficient at her job.

'So, tell me more about your work,' asked Joe, who now had his arm around Emily's shoulders and was stroking her shoulder again. She pushed the laptop aside and took a sip of brandy. Very nice. They hadn't shared much in terms of their working lives up until now. Just the basics, content instead to talk about light-hearted topics and enjoy each other's company.

'There's not much to tell, really. I just edit short stories and the like for women's magazines. Make sure they're fit for publication. It doesn't make me much money but I can work from home and pretty much suit myself hours-wise, unless there's a tight deadline.'

'Have you never thought of writing something yourself?

You said you studied English at uni, so you've clearly got a talent with words. How cool would it be if you knocked out a bestseller? Then I could boast that my girlfriend was famous and accompany you to book signings up and down the country.'

At this, Emily choked back a laugh and almost spat out a mouthful of brandy. 'Not much chance of that, I'm afraid. I have started a couple of books but never got beyond the first chapter or two. I love reading but I just can't seem to find my voice when I'm writing. It all seems too contrived and derivative. I'll stick to what I'm good at which is knocking other people's scribblings into shape.' She snuggled up closer to Joe, secretly thrilled that he'd referred to her as his "girlfriend". Although what else was he going to call her? His lady companion? Bit on the side? Ageing bimbo? She wasn't in bad nick and while her IQ might not be genius level she considered herself reasonably intelligent.

'What shall we do now?' asked Joe, polishing off the dregs of his brandy. 'Fancy watching a movie or something? I've got Netflix so hopefully there's something on there we both like the look of.'

Emily nodded and reached for the remote control on the table. Watching a movie together seemed such a chilled, *coupley* thing to do. She and Jim had rarely watched anything together, aside from the odd episode of *Antiques Roadshow* and his beloved *Channel 4 News*. On the odd occasion they'd gone to the cinema, he'd inevitably nodded off halfway through. He'd mocked her viewing choices, discounting them as frivolous or banal. She'd secretly got her fix of quirky comedy or tear-jerking romance when he was at work, battling through the ironing pile as she laughed or sobbed. Since he died Emily had feasted on a diet of fun and frothy fare, with no-one to criticise her choices. She and Tabitha had spent many a girly giggly evening gorging themselves on snacks and chocolate and arguing over which male lead was the most fanciable. Emily had a bit of a soft spot for Paul Rudd – not a classic matinee idol but undeniably cute – whereas Tabitha favoured Ryan Reynolds but had come to terms with the sad fact that they were destined never to meet.

They settled on a romantic comedy starring some soap actress who'd hit the big time in recent years and an older actor. It wasn't an Oscar contender but it provided some laughs. If Joe had any thoughts on the reversed age gap he chose not to comment. Emily, lying alongside him and happily sharing the odd passionate kiss, felt no need to comment either. She felt utterly at ease, and Joe's body language said he felt the same.

When the final credits rolled, Joe switched off the TV and pulled Emily even closer. 'Without seeming presumptuous, would you be up for a sleep-over?' Emily giggled and pointed to her small overnight bag parked by the door. 'Does that mean we stay up all night doing our hair and nails and consuming our body weight in sweets?' Memories of Tabitha and her friends high on sugar and surrounded by hair straighteners and crimpers came rushing back. All bleary eyed and monosyllabic the next day. Joe raised an eyebrow and went in for a tickle. 'Much as I pride myself on being in touch with my feminine side, I don't think sparkly nail polish and marshmallows are quite my thing? Convulsed with laughter Emily pushed him away and went to fetch her bag. 'I think I'm the presumptuous one. Toothbrush, toiletries and a change of clothes. Do you think I'm utterly shameless?' By way of reply Joe took her bag and grasped her hand, leading her towards the door. 'Absolutely. And utterly irresistible. Let's go and get naked. Unless you brought us matching onesies?'

* * *

THE MORNING after and Emily was feeling absolutely bloody amazing. Like a warrior queen who could slay dragons, rally troops and still have time for a quickie before mounting her trusty steed. Admittedly she felt like she'd been through the wars but then, it had been a physically exhausting night. Joe had youth on his side. Emily realised she might need a few gym sessions to keep up with his stamina. Or some female Viagra. Nonetheless, she felt amazing if a tad saddle sore. Joe was sleeping soundly beside her, his beautiful features relaxed with a look of sheer contentment etched upon them. Emily contemplated grabbing her phone and taking a quick photo for posterity. Posting it on Facebook with the caption: *Who's been sleeping in my bed?* and a series of grinning emojis. That would certainly trounce some of the mundanities that popped up from friends and acquaintances. Pictures of newly-clipped pooches, smug boastings of their offspring's latest achievements and endless dumb quizzes that were meant to reveal deep and meaningful character traits. Or not. She rarely posted anything on Facebook, and she *certainly* wasn't going to share Joe with the salivating masses. But there was one person she really should come clean with. Her daughter. Tabitha. She'd been skirting around the subject, dodging the inevitable showdown. Maybe now was the time to bite the bullet – why was she thinking like a Wild West cowboy? – and confess her sins.

Emily was wriggling out of bed when Joe snared her round the waist and pulled her back again.

'Sneaking off without a good morning kiss? Shame on you, woman.' She pecked him on the lips, conscious that morning breath was a distinct possibility.

'Just needed the loo then I thought I should give Tabitha – my daughter – a call. Just to catch up. The thing is –'

Emily hesitated, unsure how to frame the words. The last thing she wanted was for Joe to think she was embarrassed to be seeing him. Or ashamed. The more time they spent together, the more convinced she was that they'd found that elusive "something". And it wasn't just about the sex, incredible as it was. They had a real connection, never had she felt more at ease with a man. Not that she had a great deal of worldly experience – she could write it down on the back of a postage stamp – but it felt *right*. Even if a large percentage of the population would take an entirely different view.

'What's the thing?' enquired Joe. Who was now looking extremely sheepish, like a naughty schoolboy who'd been caught copying his neighbour's exam paper. Very cute but definitely wrong-footed.

'Well, I haven't been completely honest with Tabitha. I haven't *lied*, as such, I've just been a little economical with the truth. About us, I mean. You and me. Us. And I hate that I'm deceiving her. It's just I don't know how she'll react.'

Emily felt as tongue-tied as a fellow student seated in the headmaster's office with a set of mathematical equations biroed on her forearm. Joe was now looking as if expulsion was on the cards. What was going on?

'Emily, I'm really sorry, but I haven't been completely honest either.' His expression had gone from sheepish to downright guilty as charged. 'The thing is, and I know I should have told you before, I've met Tabitha. And she already knows. About us. I *was* going to tell you but there never seemed the right moment. I was hoping she'd call you but clearly that hasn't happened.'

Emily's stomach roiled and she sat back down abruptly, unsure if she was going to throw up or pass out. Tabitha *knew?* Joe had *met* her? When had this all happened? And why was she the last person to know about it? It could only mean one thing. Her daughter had somehow found out the truth and was so horrified and appalled she couldn't bring herself to talk about it. Or – a second, even more stomach-churning thought – she'd met Joe and been attracted to him. After all, they were of the same generation who'd grown up with smartphones and internet and endless TV channels, even if it was still well-nigh impossible to find anything to watch. In her humble opinion, at least. IMHO was what they'd type. Along with LOL, LMFAO and other strange codes that Emily tried to decipher but gave up on. No, that wasn't possible. Them being attracted to each other. Joe wouldn't be sharing her bed right now and Tabitha … Oh God, what was going through her mind?

Joe had taken hold of both her hands and was gazing imploringly at her. Begging her to listen, hear his side of the story. Did she really have a choice?

Some fifteen minutes later and Emily was fully up to speed with the unexpected visit, the case of mistaken identity with his dad and Tabitha's reaction. Or plural *reactions*. As Joe told it, she'd been taken aback at first but seemed to come round. Had even kissed Joe on the cheek when she left, rather than slap him in the face and call him all manner of names. Maybe she was saving the name-calling for her mother.

'I feel terrible, Emily. I was so sure Tabitha would be straight on to you when she found out. Then I thought maybe she had been but you were worried about telling me what she said. Although I didn't get the impression that she was shocked. I told her how I felt about you. At least, I said you were special. And you *are*. Please believe me.'

Emily felt like her head had been removed and replaced backwards. Tabitha had met Joe and – if she accepted his version of events – wasn't about to force her mum to enter a nunnery and take a vow of eternal chastity. *And*, Joe had just called her *special*. Which no one had ever called her before.

Jim had treated her like a pleasant but only mildly interesting sidekick. Handy to have around the home and to adorn his arm at business functions but *special*? That accolade was reserved for his wine collection and assortment of gardening gadgets. There'd been no one before and her handful of dates since his death barely warranted a second thought.

Aware that Joe was still gripping her hands and awaiting a response, Emily made a snap decision.

'I'm going to call her now. Tell her I know *she knows*. Ask her why she didn't tell me she knew. I'll deal with you later.' Emily fixed Joe with her best school mistress glare. He pouted back, still naughty schoolboy but facing detention rather than expulsion.

'Tabitha? It's mum. And a not-very-happy mum. Just when were you planning to tell me?'

CHAPTER 25

Tabitha gulped as she heard her mum's tone of voice. She rarely got cross with her – the last time she could remember was when she was about sixteen and got horribly drunk on cheap cider and threw up all over an expensive Chinese rug. She certainly hadn't done *that* recently and only two possibilities of what she might be concealing came to mind. The fact that she was seeing the delectable Adam, or the fact that she knew Emily was seeing the equally easy-on-the-eye Joe. Somehow, she doubted it was the former.

'Sorry, mum. I guess you know I've met Joe and— ' She struggled with what to say next. How to explain her initial shock but subsequent realisation that Joe *seemed* the real deal, despite the age difference.

'But why didn't you call me? Tell me that you'd met him? Was it because— ' Her voice suddenly went from angry to fearful, betrayed by a distinct wobble.

'Mum, it's OK. Really it is. I met Joe and – the truth is – I liked him.'

That clearly *wasn't* the reaction Emily had been expecting, judging by the sharp intake of breath.

'All right, I'd imagined someone a bit older – well, a *lot* older – to be honest. I met his dad first and I just assumed he was the one you were seeing. Mind you, they're both very attractive. Not that I *fancy* either of them, but you wouldn't kick them out of bed for eating crisps!'

Her mum had snorted with laughter, no doubt amused by the charming turn of phrase. Tabitha knew she could be crude at times but she didn't mean to be. She just said what came into her head and sod the consequences.

'So, you don't disapprove? I was so worried you'd be completely horrified. But … the thing is, I think we could have a future together. It scares me to death but it's also the most amazing feeling in the world.'

Tabitha found herself unable to speak, words failing to shift the emotional block in her throat. It was a bit like watching a romantic movie and struggling not to cry when all you wanted to do was bawl like a baby. She straightened up her shoulders and willed herself to keep it together.

'That's exactly what he said to me. He said you had a future, and that the age gap didn't bother him. And I absolutely believed him. So … if you're totally fine with it … then I am, too.'

The conversation had continued for another ten minutes, Tabitha keen to bring her mum up to speed on the luscious Adam – Where the Hearth Is was certainly a hotbed of hotties – and her cunning plan to hook Steve up with Meryl. She was pretty proud of that one, although Emily seemed less convinced of it being a success. In any case, she was dying for the loo so brought things to a close.

'Don't worry, mum. I'm *totally* cool with you and Joe. Just as long as I can be chief bridesmaid at your wedding!'

* * *

EMILY SAT QUIETLY for several moments. Delighted as she was that Tabitha wasn't filled with revulsion, she knew there were still many obstacles in the way of a happy-ever-after. Not least, the small matter of babies. Or, rather, the impossibility of them. Neither she nor Joe had ever raised the subject but she knew it had to be broached. And now was as good a time as any. Strike while the iron's hot, wasn't that the expression? Although she'd rather be branded with a hot poker right now than ask the question that could blow her shiny new world apart.

Joining Joe in the kitchen, Emily struggled to form a sentence. She watched his broad shoulders as he located pots and pans, retrieved a pack of bacon and a carton of eggs from the fridge. What was the old joke again? *How do you like your eggs in the morning? Unfertilised.* Ta da. She pulled up a chair at the counter, inhaled deeply and said: 'Babies?'

Joe turned from his labours, one eyebrow raised in question. 'Sorry, Emily, I'm not sure I heard you correctly. Did you just say 'babies'?'

You complete and utter idiot, thought Emily. For a supposedly educated and well-read woman her stunted vocabulary was pathetic. Another deep breath and try again. 'I was just wondering if – you – wanted them. Babies, that is.'

His other eyebrow rocketed upwards with its partner. 'Well, I've never had one for breakfast. Prefer a good fry-up myself but—' He faltered as Emily's face crumpled and tears began to fall. And not delicate, lady-like ones but full-on snotty, gasping-for-breath ones. Enough to put any man of his breakfast, never mind anything more profound. Grabbing a handful of kitchen roll Joe rushed to her side.

'Em, I'm sorry. I seem to be saying that a lot today but I am. Truly sorry. Please, calm down and let's talk about this.'

He thrust a wad of paper towel in to her hands and she swiped at her face, thanking the gods of small mercies that she hadn't got around to putting make-up on. Because molten mascara combined with nasal secretions was *not* a good look.

'It's just – we haven't talked about it. Children. Because I'm past it and you're in your prime. I guess I never thought we'd get this far. Maybe I'm jumping the gun but if we were going to continue – if we *were* going to take this any further – we *have* to talk about it. Because it would break my heart to get in the way of you being a father. It would just be *wrong*.'

Emily's tears subsided as Joe took control of the tissue situation and dabbed gently at her face, all the time maintaining eye contact. She could lose herself forever in those eyes, drift away like a piece of flotsam caught on a rising tide. Why was life so bloody *unfair?* You meet the man of your dreams only to be roundly smacked in the chops by Mother Nature saying, 'time's up, move along, make way for women with child-bearing hips and functioning ovaries.' She might still have the hips but the ovaries had packed their bags, written their postcards and disappeared over the horizon.

'Em. Emily. Listen to me. Very carefully.' A hugely inappropriate snigger rose deep within her as she recalled an eighties sitcom she'd been forced to watch with her parents. *I shall say zees only once.* Not that Joe would remember it. He was of a younger generation, the ones who viewed reality TV as a normal part of life, not a shocking indictment of how low society would stoop in the pursuit of 'entertainment'. Except she *did* have a soft spot for those two Geordie lads and the exploits of various dubious celebrities in the Australian jungle. Kangaroo testicles, anyone? Oh for God's sake, woman, focus!

Joe finished dabbing and pulled Emily on to his lap.

'Right, let's get one thing straight. I do *not* want – have *never* wanted children. Cross my heart and hope to die. Well, not literally. But it's the truth, Emily. Since my early twenties, maybe even before, I knew that babies were not on the cards for me. Don't get me wrong … ' Joe paused, clearly seeing the bafflement on Emily's face. 'It's not that I don't *like* them, of course I do, I just never saw them as part of my life. The world is over-populated as it is. Maybe I'm weird or just downright selfish but I've only ever wanted to meet the right woman and not have to share her. Which might not go down well with other people but I've always been honest about it. Except with my last girlfriend but she didn't have a maternal bone in her body anyway. My dad's a bit miffed he'll never be a granddad but he understands. Just because you *can* father a child doesn't mean you *should.*'

Emily looked at this earnest expression and realised he meant every word he said. Surprised as she was, her uppermost emotion was one of relief. They could carry on seeing each other as long as it lasted and she wouldn't feel she'd metaphorically stamped on his biological desire to procreate. And if he changed his mind in the future …

As if reading her thoughts, Joe wrapped his arms around her and planted a kiss on the top of her spinning head.

'And I *won't* change my mind, Em. I always vowed when I met the perfect woman I'd tell her how I feel and just pray she felt the same. Now I have, and I really hope you understand. Because – the thing is – I love you.'

If Emily's head had been spinning before, it was now whirling away at warp speed. Did he just say he loved her? Did she love him? The answer was simple. Yes, she did. With all her heart. He'd come into her life in the most unlikely way, blown away the dust – in more ways than one – and made her feel cherished and adored. And loved. She'd been given a real shot at happiness, and what happened next was up to her.

'I love you too.' There, she'd said it. And it felt *amazing.* Like crawling parched through a desert, then stumbling across an oasis. Or fishing a crumpled lottery ticket out of the bin only to discover you'd misread the numbers and the jackpot was yours. Or—

'So, Mrs Hardwick. Do you think you can put up with me and my peculiar ways? I'm fairly house trained and not too shabby at DIY. Oh, and I can cook pretty well and dispose of dead creatures if necessary. There's just one other thing—' Joe lifted Emily's left hand to his lips.

'What's that?' replied Emily, her whole body zinging as if hardwired to the National Grid.

'Well, I was kind of thinking that Emily McKenzie has a certain ring to it. Don't you?'

CHAPTER 26

'But *why* do I need to look at new fireplaces?' Meryl looked at Tabitha as if she'd suggested shopping for elasticated stockings. 'I have a perfectly nice one already.' Which was true, although she'd never actually lit it. It was currently home to a display of dried flowers and a couple of rather ugly china dogs she'd inherited from her mother and couldn't bring herself to bin.

Tabitha rolled her eyes in impatience. Meryl wasn't playing ball and her dastardly cunning plan to introduce her to Steve depended on them *actually* meeting. She'd considered setting them up on a blind date then vetoed that idea. One – Adam was unconvinced Steve would agree – 'I really don't think it's his thing. Joe said he went on one once and she turned out to be a New Age nutter who wanted to align his chakras. He told her very politely no one was touching his chakras, especially on a first date.' Two – with Meryl's woeful experience on online dating she would balk at the very thought. Only the other day she'd declared she was thinking of becoming a lesbian. Or a nun. Although she wasn't overly enamoured by the idea of wearing a wimple.

'Ah, come on, Meryl. Where's your sense of adventure?' she urged. To which Meryl gave an even more spectacular roll of the eyes.

'Sorry, Tabbie, but looking at fireplaces isn't really up there on my bucket list of things to do before I die. Visiting Machu Picchu maybe, or swimming with dolphins in Florida but not oohing and aahing over cosy inglenooks or gleaming grates.'

Deeply frustrated, Tabitha decided to play her trump card. If this failed, she vowed to leave Meryl's love life in destiny's fickle hands.

'But you'd get to meet Adam! He's definitely working today and he promised to take us out for lunch.' And – fingers crossed – Steve would join them if there was so much as a spark of interest between him and Meryl. She'd physically drag him along if she had to. 'You don't have to buy anything, just have a quick wander around the showroom and then off to Chez Jacques for a slap-up meal! Pleeeease!' Tabitha fixed her boss with her most beseeching look.

Meryl finished folding origami-style a brightly coloured paper napkin for this week's Japanese-themed window display. 'Damn, it looks more like a turkey than a swan. Never mind, at least the stacking Geisha dolls and chopsticks look more authentic.'

As did both she and Tabitha who had – very reluctantly – agreed to wear a kimono in keeping with Meryl's latest attempt to draw in the customers. She found it incredibly uncomfortable and was reduced to walking in a shuffle within the confines of the heavy fabric. And going to the loo was a complete nightmare. Meryl, however, was in her element and had been muttering about a fairy tale theme next, having ordered a consignment of sparkly wands and glittery wings to appeal to the Disney-obsessed little girls whose idea of a birthday party was to outdo each other in the dressing up department. There was no way Tabitha was going along with that one. Meryl would probably have her in a mermaid's tail and scalloped bra, waving alluringly at passers-by. And completely unable to walk or pee.

'So? Are you coming or not? It's almost midday and we could easily close up for a couple of hours. Adam's dying to meet you!' *And Steve will take one look and realise he's just met the woman of his dreams.* Although seeing the pair of them done up like extras from *The Mikado* might not have quite the desired effect.

'OK, OK! You win. But only because I want to meet your new man. And I never say no to a free lunch.' Meryl wiggled her eyebrows to show she was joking – she'd have her purse out ready to do battle over the bill – and made her way upstairs. 'I'll just get changed quickly and we can head off.'

Tabitha followed her – waddling like an incontinent penguin – and grabbed the bag containing her civvies. 'Just one other thing, Meryl,' she said as her boss teetered on the bottom step. 'Please don't wear your dungarees.'

Arriving at Where the Hearth Is, Tabitha felt like she was going on a blind date herself. Her earlier conviction that Meryl and Steve would take one look at each other and think: 'Where have you been all my life?' had been replaced by a fear that they would be totally indifferent. Or, even worse, take an instant dislike to one another. She couldn't imagine that happening but she felt the weight of responsibility bearing down on her shoulders. Still, nothing ventured, nothing gained. And neither of them need ever know they'd been set up.

'Tabitha! Aren't you a sight for sore eyes!' Adam was waiting by the door as they walked in, looking criminally gorgeous in his trademark dark jeans and white shirt. He kissed her enthusiastically, prompting a passing female customer to murmur, 'I didn't get one of those!' but in a good-natured way.

Meryl stood a little behind, waiting to be introduced. Tabitha reluctantly drew apart from Adam – God, his kisses were incredible – and pulled Meryl forward.

'Adam, meet Meryl. Meryl, this is my boyfriend, Adam.' Ooh, the sheer thrill of saying 'boyfriend'! Especially one who wouldn't look out of place smouldering on the cover of GQ. Not that looks were everything – she wasn't completely shallow – but dazzling personalities didn't quite compensate if your loved one made Quasimodo look like a bit of all right. OK, she was officially shallow.

'Lovely to meet you, Meryl.' Adam moved as if to shake her hand but went in for a French-style kiss on each cheek instead. Meryl – looking pretty as a picture in her favourite floral dress – took it in her stride.

'And you, Adam. I've heard so much about you. Honestly, Tabbie hasn't stopped talking about you. It's Adam this and Adam that and … ouch!' Meryl was brought to a halt by Tabitha swiping her hard on her upper arm.

'Sorry, Meryl! Thought I saw a wasp moving in for the kill.' And I'll bloody kill you if you don't shut up, she intoned under her breath. Thankfully, Adam merely winked, linked arms with Meryl and guided her off for a whistle stop tour of the finest fireplaces in the south east of England. Leaving Tabitha with time to put the next stage of her cunning plan into action.

'Steve! How are you?' Having knocked at the door of his office and been instructed to enter, Tabitha marvelled again at the resemblance between father and son. What if Steve had been the one to turn up at her mum's the day after the book club incident? Would the same chemistry have existed?

In many ways, it would have been easier. Same generation, no worries about people whispering behind their backs, tut-tutting about predatory older women and gold-digging younger men. Not that her mum had zillions in the bank attracting twenty-something chancers like moths to the flame. She was just Mum, a beautiful, talented and very special lady who'd met Joe, made a connection and decided to sod the consequences. No, Tabitha decided. If Steve had turned up it would never have worked. What made people fall in love had nothing to do with age, religion, background or musical tastes. Well – maybe the latter was a factor. If Adam had professed to hate musicals she wasn't sure they would have a future. Tom had been indifferent about them – preferred heavy metal and weird rap stuff that made her ears spontaneously bleed – whereas Adam always had a song in his heart and a show tune ready to share with an inebriated bar. He was cute, funny and made her feel on top of the world. Lookin' down on creation. Help, time to move things on a little.

'Tabitha. How are you? Steve gave her a fatherly hug which reminded her a little painfully of her awkward relationship with Jim, her real dad. Steve had taken the whole Emily/Joe thing in his stride. When she'd asked him – a few days after they first met – how he felt about the relationship, he'd paused. Scratched his head – thankfully, no dandruff unlike the delightful Bert – and looked her straight in the eye.

'Truthfully? I was worried. Joe's my boy. My only son. Since his mum died ...' Steve had hesitated, clearly unsure how much to share with Tabitha. She'd nodded for him to continue. 'Well, he's had quite a few girlfriends in the past. There was one – Caitlin I think she was called – whom he seemed pretty serious about. Until she dumped him for another fella. Can't say I was too upset, mind. Always thought she was a piece of work and there's no way on earth his mum would have approved. Whereas Emily clearly makes him happy, and vice versa.'

It had been a good answer. No, scratch that. The perfect answer. Now all she needed to do was make Steve and Meryl realise they too were a match made in heaven. Or at least take a tentative step or two on the ladder to love.

'I'm great, Steve. In fact, I've got an interview for a job in a few days. Right up my street, although I haven't quite got around to telling my boss yet. Of course, I might not even get it but—' Tabitha clamped her mouth shut as the office door bounced open and in walked Adam, a clearly smitten Meryl still clinging to his arm and giggling coquettishly.

'I take it all back, Tabbie. Adam has convinced me that a new fireplace would transform my place! I've taken loads of photos and he's going to come and measure me up!'

Tabitha shook her head in mock exasperation as Meryl clamped Adam to her ample bosom by way of gratitude. Coming up for air he winked at Tabitha.

'Don't worry, gorgeous. It's only the vital statistics of the fireplace I'll be checking out. Although if I wasn't already spoken for—' Cue another bout of girlish giggles from Meryl. Right, time to put her cunning plan into action.

'Meryl, this is Steve, Adam's boss and Joe's dad. Steve, this is Meryl, my boss and newest devotee of Where the Hearth Is.' Tabitha felt Adam's hand slip into hers and give a reassuring squeeze as the unwitting players in her self-penned romance greeted each other with warm smiles and handshakes. A few minutes of chitchat followed before Adam glanced purposefully at his watch.

'You know, my stomach thinks my throat's been cut. Why don't we adjourn to Chez Jacques for lunch and seal the deal with a bottle of bubbly? You too, Steve. Live dangerously and skip the Pot Noodles just this once, eh?'

Steve grinned at Meryl who was looking slightly concerned at his alleged dining habits, whereas Tabitha knew that he was an accomplished cook.

'Please ignore young Adam. He knows full well that such culinary atrocities have never passed my lips. But I do have a soft spot for a medium rare steak and a side of French fries. What are we waiting for?' Extending a gentlemanly arm which Meryl, without hesitation, took, they left the office. A few steps behind them Tabitha smirked at Adam, who kissed the tip of her nose.

'See, I knew they'd hit it off! Just look at them!' She watched as Steve opened the main door for Meryl, flipping the sign to Closed and retaking her arm as they headed to the car park. Adam took Tabitha's hand and began to sing quietly under his breath. 'Getting to know you, getting to know all about you.' He paused, kissed her again. 'You shouldn't read too much into it yet, oh scheming one. Steve is naturally gallant and holding open doors and proffering arms doesn't mean you should be buying boxes of confetti just yet.'

Tabitha nodded as if suitably chastened, but inside was a growing conviction that she had just helped to create a vital spark between two people dear to her heart. Now she hoped that nature – and a glass or two of fizz – would fan the flames.

Jacques welcomed them with his usual manic enthusiasm. For some bizarre reason, he was sporting what Tabitha knew was called a 'Jimmy hat'. Big Tam had been at great pains to explain this unorthodox headgear during their encounter at the *Scots Wa Hae* wrap party.

'Ya see hen, it's like a tartan bunnet wi' ginger hair attached. Great fur parties an' that if ye wannae look like a true Scotsman.' He'd gestured to a few crew members –

'Sassenachs, the poor souls' – which Tabitha later learned through Google meant English people. Everyone had been wearing the aforementioned hats and looking distinctly uncomfortable about it. Whereas Jacques wore his with all the pride of a coronated king.

Seated at a corner table and kitted out in their ambiguous bibs, they placed their orders. Steaks all round with fries and a large mixed salad to share. Tabitha had toyed with the idea of goats' cheese salad but the sizzle and whiff of other diners' orders soon changed her mind. She plunged a piping hot chip in the accompanying pot of garlic dip and took a bite. Heaven! Next to her Adam was slicing his slab of meat with all the fervour of a serial killer while across the table Steve and Meryl seemed to be getting on very well.

'No, I've never been married,' announced Meryl who had quickly drained her first glass of bubbly and smiled as Jacques hurried to top her up.

Crikey, thought Tabitha, it didn't take them long to get down to the nitty gritty. Although she guessed Meryl had quickly clocked Steve's wedding band – he'd explained he still couldn't bring himself to take it off – and was keen to ascertain his current status. Given her recent experiences with the male species she couldn't blame her.

'Seems to be going well, doesn't it?' whispered Adam who had already polished off more than half his steak and all his fries. Tabitha slapped his hand away as he attempted to pinch one off her own plate.

'Oi, get your paws off my food! How you stay so slim is a mystery to me. Do you have hollow legs? Or maybe a tapeworm?' She'd never met anyone who could eat so much – third helpings were commonplace – and still have room for dessert. Although he did work out at least three times a week and their handful of encounters of the carnal kind had been energetic to say the least. With Tom, sex had been lovely but there had been something fundamentally missing. Adam didn't just pass the Tabitha Five Point Test, he ticked off boxes she hadn't even considered before. Like total musical compatibility, willingness to co-operate in her madcap schemes and zero interest in overgrown schoolboys larking around in fast cars.

Jacques reappeared bearing a small chalkboard listing the desserts of the day. 'Ze crème caramel eez magnifique but the cherry cheesecake eez no' bad' he proclaimed in his inimitable fashion. Adam – surprise, surprise – went for the crème caramel. The rest of them declined, opting instead for coffees all round.

'So, what do you get up to in your spare time, Steve, when you're not flogging gorgeous fireplaces or poking your brushes up people's chimneys? Although Mum says you leave most of the dirty work to Joe these days. Oops, I mean—' Tabitha felt an unbecoming flush rise from her chest and spread to her cheeks. She really hadn't meant to imply anything sordid between her mum and Joe, just that he liked the actual sweeping side of the business. Which brought her back to the charming and eloquent Big Tam. 'Hae ye had yer lum swept recently, hen?' he'd enquired when she'd called to thank him for recommending her for the job. She'd briefly mentioned splitting from her boyfriend but hadn't had a chance to mention the arrival of Adam on the scene. 'Sorry, you've lost me there, Tam,' she'd replied, with no clue as to what a "lum" was and why it would need sweeping. It was only later – thanks to good old Google again – she discovered it was a Scottish slang term for a lady's private parts and he'd been asking about her sex life. Eek! She'd suspected Big Tam had a bit of a crush on her but – sadly – her lum didn't feel the same.

Steve just grinned to indicate he'd caught the double entendre with no offence taken. Adam had nearly spat out a mouthful of dessert while Meryl gave her one of her finest headmistress looks. *That's a detention for you, young lady.*

'Not much free time on my hands these days, sadly. The business keeps me pretty occupied, although I do squeeze in the odd game of golf when the weather's decent. I enjoy going to the cinema and I read a fair bit, mainly crime thrillers and the odd biography. All pretty dull, I'm afraid.' He looked apologetic, as if he'd just confessed to being an ardent train spotter or collector of porcelain figurines. Meryl looked happy at his response, even if she secretly thought golf was second only to cricket in the 'watching paint dry' stakes.

'No, not dull at all!' chirruped Tabitha brightly. 'Maybe you could introduce Meryl to golf, I'm sure she'd take to it like a duck to water. You'd like that, wouldn't you, Meryl?' Ha! Revenge for the kimono and all the other atrocities she'd put up with for her darling boss.

'Thank you, Tabbie. But I'm sure Steve has plenty of willing and able partners on the golf course. Right, Steve?' Meryl fluttered her eyelashes at Steve, while no doubt mentally figuring out another hideous and embarrassing outfit for Tabitha in the future. Please, please, please let me get this job, prayed Tabitha.

Adam was virtually licking his bowl clean. Lucky he was perfect in so many other ways, thought Tabitha wryly.

'Any deep, dark secrets, Steve?' Meryl was fluttering her eyelashes so hard it was a wonder Steve wasn't propelled backwards with their sheer force. How many glasses had she had, wondered Tabitha? Shy and retiring weren't words she'd normally apply to her boss, but now she was making a bull in a china shop look light-footed.

Steve again took it in his stride, topping up everyone's glass from the second bottle that had materialised at the table. Despite Meryl's sledgehammer approach, he seemed genuinely taken with her. Tabitha was no body language expert, but she'd noted his chair moving ever-so-slightly closer. The way he lightly touched her arm when making a point. Definite chemistry there.

'Ah, well. If it's "show and tell" time, maybe you should go first, Meryl.' His twinkly eyes sparkled even more. Adam nudged Meryl with his elbow.

'Come on, Meryl. Let's hear it! There must be some juicy story you can share with us. A hot lady like you must have got up to some shenanigans.' Everyone leaned forward expectantly. Jacques, who'd arrived to clear plates, was lingering within earshot. He'd even adjusted the ginger bits to ensure maximum hearing ability.

'OK, fine. If you really must know I once worked as a kissogram. It was when I was in my early twenties and money was a bit tight.' Stunned silence around the table. Aside from a tiny snort from Adam, who quickly disguised it as a coughing fit.

'Crikey! That must be where you get your fondness for making us dress up in the shop.' Tabitha eyed Meryl with a mixture of incredulity and respect. Even if she was down to her last penny, there was no way she'd ever don a French maid's outfit and plant a kiss on a sozzled groom-to-be.

'So, what was your weirdest costume and song and who did you have to deliver it to?' enquired Adam. Steve had placed his arm around the back of Meryl's chair, not touching but clearly offering moral support.

'Not my proudest moment, but I had to wear a bumble bee costume. And sing 'Honey Honey' by ABBA to a man retiring after thirty years in the bee-keeping business. He kept tweaking my sting and managed to pull off one of my wings when he went in for a full-blown snog. Urgh, it was revolting.' Meryl shuddered at what was clearly a best-forgotten memory.

'Well, I'm sure you made a delightful bumble bee. I'm sorry we made you bring that one up, but it does sort of lead to my own misadventures in my misspent youth. In a convoluted kind of way.' Steve had squeezed Meryl's hand in a gesture of support, but was looking distinctly agitated. What next, thought Tabitha? Was he about to reveal a past life as a male stripper? Or a drag queen? Little did she know she was closer to the truth than she could imagine.

Steve inhaled deeply, exhaled loudly then began.

'It was back in the early eighties and me and a few friends decided to form a tribute band. It started as a bit of a joke but we ended up playing quite a lot of gigs and making reasonable money. Who knows, it might have led to bigger things, but a bunch of Aussies had the same idea and went on to be a huge success all over the world. So, it just petered out for us. Probably just as well, really.'

Meryl, Tabitha and Adam were deep in thought; each trying to figure out which band Steve and his mates had paid homage to. The lightbulb moment came – not surprisingly – to Meryl.

'Oh my God! You were an ABBA tribute band, weren't you? It just dawned on me; the Aussie ones who made it big were Bjorn Again. Am I right? Ooh, please tell me I'm right!'

Meryl was clapping her hands in glee while Adam and Tabitha exchanged a look that said, who'd have thought it? Privately, both would have guessed some hairy, heavy rock combo with a young Steve smashing guitars and thrusting his pelvis with great gusto.

'Spot on, Meryl. We did indeed impersonate the fab four Swedes. It lasted a couple of years but work commitments got in the way and eventually we just drifted apart.'

'Which one were you, Steve? I bet it was Bjorn. I always thought he was cuter than Benny. You remind me of him a little bit, although without the beard. This is so amazing!

Tabitha, does Steve know I'm one of ABBA's biggest fans? No, of course he doesn't, silly me. Go on, tell us more!'

Meryl was practically fizzing with delight that she and Steve had established such a special connection. Tabitha was delighted – hadn't she prayed they'd hit it off? – but there was more to come, if Steve's furrowed brow was anything to go by.

'Well, the thing is … we thought it'd be fun to mix things up a little. As I said, it was all a laugh to begin with. We were four blokes which meant two of us performed as the girls. And I was one of them. Agnetha, the blonde one. Complete with wig and blue eyeshadow.'

Fifteen minutes later and they were in the car park of Where the Hearth Is, still contorted with laughter. Adam was begging Steve for photographic evidence of his brief career as a female singer. Steve maintained no such evidence existed and refused to divulge the name of the group lest they were uncovered on the internet in all their spangly, platform-soled glory.

As Meryl and Tabitha bade their farewells, Steve gave them each a big hug in turn. Tabitha noticed that his embrace with Meryl lasted slightly longer and that her boss was positively glowing. So, Steve's previous penchant for short kimonos and dodgy make-up hadn't put her off.

Climbing into the car – Tabitha had stuck to one glass of bubbly – she turned to Meryl.

'That seemed to go rather well, don't you think? Bit of a surprise, Steve's confession but he is a lovely man, isn't he? And I hope you liked Adam. You certainly seemed to hit it off!'

Meryl giggled again – there'd been a lot of giggling in the last couple of hours – and swiped Tabitha playfully and rather tipsily with her hand.

'Adam is divine and as for Steve … I knew what you were

up to, my darling Tabbie. Trying to fix me up with a new man. I'm not completely daft, you know! But I think you might just have succeeded. Not only is he charming and good-looking but he likes Abba!' With a contented smile, Meryl settled back in her seat. *Mission accomplished,* thought Tabitha.

CHAPTER 27

High noon, weapons drawn, dust thingies bouncing across the heat-baked soil. Shame it was about eleven degrees, drizzling and the best they had to arm themselves with were slices of quiche Lorraine or a smoked salmon and cream cheese combo. The good, the bad and the calorie-laden. If it all went horribly wrong, they could club each other over the head with the complimentary bread sticks.

Three breadsticks later and Celeste spotted Sophie conversing with the earnest young woman in charge of tables. She pointed enthusiastically towards Celeste – yeh, old dear in need of company – and Sophie made her way across. With a face that resembled a bulldog who'd just chewed a wasp then decided a squirt of lemon juice was the perfect chaser. Oh dear. Was this *really* a good idea?

'So. You wanted to talk? I'm not sure what the point is but I'm all ears.' Sophie was also chewing on a breadstick and fixing Celeste with a look that said, 'Don't mess with me or I'll zap you with my death ray. Which means you'll be a pile of ashes in seconds. And I'll have no qualms about scooping you into a hankie and depositing you in a bin when I leave.'

Come to think of it, she did have quite distinctive ears. Volcanic, was that the word? Certainly pointy and quivering with emotion right now.

'Look, Sophie, I'm as amazed as you are that we're sitting here like this. Thank you for agreeing to come. I just thought we should have a chat, clear the air a little.'

Two pink spots flared like beacons on Sophie's cheeks as she snapped another breadstick in half with brutal precision. Celeste gulped and clutched her throat nervously.

'Clear the air? Clear the air? It'll take a bit more than flinging a few windows open and squirting some air freshener to clear up this sorry mess. Metaphorically speaking, of course. Have you really grasped the damage you've done? I've spent all these years desperate to have a father while you did everything in your power to keep us apart. It's all about Celeste with you. Cocooned in your safe little world, Michael catering to your every whim. Fine, you didn't want children. But he already had one. *Me*! But you made sure that door stayed firmly closed.'

And if they hadn't bumped into each other, would that still be the case? Would Celeste and Michael have been able to preserve the status quo? Suddenly, like an explosion in her head, Celeste knew her world would have collapsed eventually. If not this year or next, then sometime in the near future. Maybe when the boys were a little older and started asking questions. Do we have a granddad? Where is he? Can we go see him? Sophie and her sons were part of her husband, their DNA interwoven for eternity. She was a mere side road, a diversion. She loved Michael – and believed he still loved her – but if it came down to a straight choice there was no doubt who held the winning hand. Sophie and her boys were the aces in the pack, Celeste the Joker. And not a particularly clever or amusing one. More the hapless court jester whose inability to entertain the king would soon lead to her grizzly demise. Sophie certainly looked as if a hooded axe man would be a welcome addition to their table right now. Celeste decided a spot of lunch would be preferable.

'Shall we order? I'm really quite peckish.' Which was an outright lie as her stomach was churning like a washing machine on spin cycle. Plus, she'd forgotten her reading glasses so everything on the laminated menu was a total blur. 'What do you fancy, Sophie? I'll just have what you're having, if you don't mind.' She stared hopefully at the younger woman, who was beckoning to the waitress on the other side of the room. She hurried over, pen and pad at the ready.

'So, what can I get you ladies? Today's pea and mascarpone soup is totally fab and I can also recommend the courgette fritters with goats' cheese and red onion chutney. Or we do a pretty spectacular frittata with mixed salad and the best home-made dressing you'll ever taste!'

Before Celeste could comment, Sophie turned to the waitress with a smile that completely transformed her pale little face. From bulldog to beauty in the blink of an eye.

'We'll both have the soup and a smoked salmon sandwich on wholemeal bread, thank you. And a large bottle of mineral water. Sparkling OK?' She waited for Celeste to nod her assent, the smile retreating as quickly as the waitress's departing back.

'This is a nice place, isn't it?' Celeste felt the need to fill the awkward silence that had descended in the minutes since their order had been taken. 'Funny, I'd never have found it if I hadn't followed your dad that day ...' Her voice wavered as Sophie gave another of her Medusa-strength glares. Probably *not* the wisest move, harking back to the memorable moment she'd accused father and daughter of having an affair. If she was to get Sophie on side – OK, at least persuade her that Celeste wasn't a malevolent old bag hell-bent on ruining her life – she needed a more tactful approach. Think, Celeste, think!

'How are the boys? Have they settled in at school? It must be so hard for you, coping on your own.' Oops, another own-goal, judging by the expression on Sophie's face. The last time she'd seen such a pained look was when Michael had serious constipation, only alleviated by industrial quantities of prunes.

'Actually, I'm *really* curious to know *how* you found us. Dad never told me and, to be honest, I didn't give it much thought until now. Did you, like, bug his car or something?'

Celeste suppressed a snort of laughter at the very idea of her planting a tracking device on Michael's Audi. She wasn't totally technically inept but anything electronic often defeated her. She needed to dig out the instruction manual every time the clocks changed to reset her oven display. Although she hadn't fared *too* badly with her fitness tracker sleuthing, even if the end result had short-circuited her safe little world. What would Sophie think if she revealed the truth? That she'd snooped on Michael's phone, deduced that something was amiss and pursued him like a latter-day Miss Marple, albeit clad in lycra and trainers rather than brogues and tweed.

'Well, it's a bit embarrassing actually but it all began when I bought myself a fitness tracker.' She waggled her left wrist in Sophie's direction. Not that she'd bothered checking the daily data much recently. In the days and nights following her discovery she didn't *really* need an app to tell her she was barely sleeping and was lucky to pass the 4,000-step mark. Sophie gave it a cursory glance just as the waitress arrived with their food. They both picked up their spoons and gave the soups a desultory stir.

'I'm not quite following you.' Sophie had a pained expression, although that could be the result of taking a large mouthful of the steaming-hot soup. Celeste nibbled the corner of her sandwich and contemplated her next move. Would Sophie loathe her even more – if that was even possible – or might she feel a smidgeon of sympathy for a woman convinced her husband was doing the dirty on her? Truthfully, she had no idea but very little to lose.

'Well, I just *happened* to have a peek at Michael's phone and—' For the next ten minutes Celeste related the whole sorry tale. Soups cooled and sandwiches remained barely touched. Sophie leant across the table, chin rested on her clasped hands, expression worthy of an ace poker player.

'So that's how I ended up making an absolute fool of myself. My intention was to find a hobby I could share with your dad but instead I trampled all over our relationship.' Celeste felt tears welling and fumbled in her handbag for a tissue. Before she could undo the clasp, Sophie reached over and handed her a paper napkin. Dabbing her eyes, she continued.

'I set out with the best intentions, truly I did. I thought walking together would be good for us, for me in particular. I thought I'd lose a few pounds but the only thing I've lost is the man I love and now you both hate me. And I really don't blame you. I know I'm responsible for keeping you apart and what I did is unforgivable. I've had plenty of time alone to think about what I've done and I have no excuses. I'm a selfish, self-absorbed woman and you have every right to want nothing to do with me.'

Sophie appeared to have stopped listening. Having peeled the top layer of bread from her sandwich, she was now removing pieces of salmon with all the intensity of a pathologist performing a post-mortem. Celeste's already meagre appetite had vanished completely, along with any hope of a happy ending. She decided enough was enough, pulling out her purse ready to pay and go. As she did, she realised Sophie's head was bowed and her shoulders were shaking. Oh, crap, now she'd reduced *her* to tears. Except ... wasn't that a guffaw of laughter?

'That is one of the funniest things I've heard in ages.' Sophie was shaking her head in disbelief but with what looked suspiciously like a large grin breaking across her previously inscrutable face. 'Seriously, my life's not been a bundle of laughs recently but the thought of you tailing Dad like that ... and all because of a step counter thingy. It's like something out of a TV show. I know! Jessica whatsername, that amateur detective who outwitted the authorities and always caught the bad guy. Mum used to watch it when I was little.' Mention of her mum shrank the edges off her grin. Clearly mother-daughter relationships were far from harmonious, no doubt due to Sophie's newfound cosiness with Michael.

'*Murder, She Wrote*. I watched a few episodes myself back in the day.' Much as she admired Angela Lansbury as an actress, Celeste had always thought the number of dead bodies uncovered in a relatively small community defied belief. Unless Jessica herself was the killer. Hmm ... As long as Sophie wasn't harbouring a secret desire to bump *her* off. She didn't *look* like a cold-blooded killer but who knew? At least she hadn't nipped off to the loo, leaving the way open for Sophie to lace her soup with weed killer. Which was in plentiful supply here, although disposing of a body during the lunchtime rush might prove a little challenging.

Sensing a slight lightening in the tension between them – murderous tendencies notwithstanding – Celeste decided it was time to share another little secret with Sophie. Her success as a writer. She still hadn't been able to raise the subject with Michael. The interview and photo session were scheduled in two days' time. A *Tea Break* writer and photographer would turn up on her doorstep, expecting Astra Du Bois in all her overblown glory. Waxing lyrical about Leo and Seraphina and carefully concealing her disappointment about not being the rightful victor. She'd read the winning story and been singularly unimpressed. The sex scenes – in her humble opinion – were far too restrained. Definitely pre-waterworks or whatever they called it. More flannelette nighties and pyjamas than togas and eye-watering contortions. She wasn't *quite* sure where it had all come from – she and Michael were quite traditional in their routines – but she was proud of what she'd written. What she lacked in real-life experience, she more than compensated for in fictitious filthiness.

'You've written a book? Seriously? Oh, my God. Celeste, you are revealing hidden depths I never imagined. Honestly, I thought you made puddles look shallow.'

Celeste tried not to look offended at *that* little barb. She knew she wasn't particularly intellectual or well-read but at least she'd given the writing a go and achieved some modicum of success. OK, *Tea Break* wasn't exactly *The Times Literary Supplement*. Last week's issue had featured articles on removing nasal hair and unblocking sinks but it had its faithful followers. Still, at least her revelation had lightened the mood which could only be a good thing. Sophie now looked less like a person with bowel issues and more the rather pretty young woman she clearly was. She could see now the likeness to Michael. Not so much the physical one she'd noted that awful day but more of a similar sparkle in the eyes when they laughed. The way Sophie crinkled up her nose when she was thinking. And they both appeared to share the habit of dissecting their food. It drove her mad when Michael would push his food around the plate, dividing it into individual mounds of ingredients. Sophie was now nibbling a piece of salmon, the bread reduced to virtual crumbs.

'Nice salmon. Much better than that over-dyed and flabby stuff you get in the supermarket. I wonder where they source it from?' She licked her fingers enthusiastically before wiping them clean on her napkin.

'We can always ask the nice waitress, I suppose,' replied Celeste. Not that she gave a stuff where the fish came from. It tasted just the same as any to her, not that she was a particular fan of anything that came out of the sea. Peeling prawns made her feel sick and the very *idea* of tipping a raw oyster down her throat …

'So, does Dad know about your foray into the writing world? He hasn't mentioned it to me, but then you're not exactly our main topic of conversation. Sorry, don't mean to be rude, just stating facts.' Sophie polished off the last gleaming slice of salmon and gazed guilelessly at Celeste. Face of an angel, ability to wither with a well-chosen word worthy of Jeremy Paxman in full flow. Just smile, Celeste, keep smiling and – most importantly – keep the conversation going.

'No, he doesn't know and I'm not sure when – or if – I'm going to tell him. We haven't really been communicating much in the past week. Although, I suppose I'll have to say *something* if a bloody journalist and photographer turn up on the doorstep. Unless I pretend they're doing a feature on cold-hearted cows who keep fathers and daughters apart. Come to think of it, they *did* do something similar in the past. Except it was about fathers who'd scarpered then turned up years later when their offspring became famous or won the lottery.'

Sophie was signalling to the rather flustered waitress, currently dealing with a group of elderly women all fiddling gamely with their hearing aids.

'Thought we'd have a coffee. What do you fancy, Celeste?'

Although she – thank God – didn't need a hearing aid herself, Celeste wondered for a moment if she'd heard correctly. Did Sophie just address her by her *name*? And in an almost friendly way, as opposed to spitting it out like an unwanted fish bone.

'Hi again.' Sophie smiled at the waitress, who was now clearing away their plates. 'Can I get a soy milk cappuccino and ...' She looked expectantly at Celeste.

'Erm, I'll have a regular coffee, please. With cow's milk.'

Before the waitress could depart, Sophie quizzed her on the provenance of the salmon which was apparently wild – was it normally tame, wondered Celeste? – and lovingly oak-smoked to perfection somewhere in Sussex. Sophie eagerly keyed the details into her phone, clearly intent on stocking up herself. Job done, she settled back in her chair.

'I gave up meat and most dairy products a couple of years ago,' she informed Celeste. 'I'm a pescatarian, actually.'

Celeste wasn't quite sure how to respond. Ah, well. If Sophie was now divulging personal information she had better join in.

'Interesting. I'm a Leo which accounts for a lot but—'

Right, she might have hoped for a thaw in relations between them but having Sophie howling in mirth yet again was a little disconcerting. She had no idea what was so amusing about comparing star signs but Sophie's reaction would have delighted any stand-up comedian. She waited – a little grumpily – for her one-woman audience to stop thumping the table which was attracting attention from other customers. Finally, Sophie resumed her composure, just as their hot drinks arrived.

'Sorry, I didn't mean to laugh like that. It's just ... well, never mind.' Before she could finish, her phone began to ring. She squinted at the screen, frowned, then picked it up.

'Hi. Dad. How's things? Yes, I'm fine. What's that? No, he's fine too. It was just a touch of the cold. He's back at school now. Yes, George is OK. Just a little miffed he didn't get two days in bed and had to do his spelling homework while his brother watched telly. I'm heading back to pick them up soon because Angie,' – *the childminder* – she mouthed to an anxious Celeste – 'has a doctor's appointment. Yes, it looks like the settlement will be made any day now so that's good news. It's taken the miserable bastard long enough.'

Sophie hesitated, her nose crinkled in true Michael fashion. Celeste swirled her spoon around in her coffee, her nerves jangling like wind chimes in a breeze. What would Michael think if he knew who was sitting opposite his daughter? What would he *do*, more to the point?

'Where am I now? Well, believe it or not, I'm having lunch with Celeste. No, Dad, I'm not joking. She called me up and we agreed to meet and ... here we are.'

Another pause. Celeste lifted the cup to her mouth then put it down, her hands shaking too much.

'It's OK, Dad. Honestly. I didn't have high expectations' – Sophie gave a half-smile/half grimace in Celeste's direction – 'but we've survived. Even had a few laughs. Dad, are you still there?'

Celeste pictured Michael's usually gentle and kindly face contorted with fury and disbelief that she – the viper in the nest – had attempted to worm her way into Sophie's affections. Any faint hope of reconciliation shrivelled up inside her. It was over. Except—

'Sure, she's right here. I'll just pass you over. Hang on.'

Sophie held her phone out to Celeste. Celeste eyed it with all the enthusiasm of a toddler being offered a spoonful of cough syrup. Hands still a-tremble, she tentatively took it and raised it to her ear.

'H...hello? Michael?' She waited, certain his words would be cold and dismissive.

'Celeste? You're really there? With Sophie? Sorry, stupid remark, of course you are. It's just ... I didn't expect ... oh, darling, I'm so, so sorry.'

As Michael's achingly familiar voice came down the line, Celeste felt a warm tingle spread from her head to her toes. He was speaking to her, *really* speaking to her. But – wait a minute – had he just *apologised*?

'I've been a complete idiot. Blaming you for everything and letting Sophie do the same. The real bad guy in all this was me, not having the courage to keep in contact all those years. Just burying my head in the sand and convincing myself that all I needed was you. And I *do* need you, Celeste. I've missed you so much these past days but I just needed some time to sort my head out.'

'But, Michael, I went out my way to keep you to myself. You know that. I'm so ashamed of myself but I can't turn back time. If only I could. I called Sophie because I wanted to try and make amends.' She glanced at Sophie, who merely nodded. The unreadable look was back, but minus the edge of hostility.

'I don't think I've done a very good job of apologising so far but I'll keep trying. For all our sakes.' Celeste halted, unsure what to say next and still reeling at Michael's contriteness. Did she deserve it? Or was it truly the case that they shared the blame, neither willing to shatter their tranquil little existence? They were all suffering the consequences now, but no one more so than Sophie and her boys. But ... maybe, just *maybe*, there was a glimmer of hope for some kind of resolution.

'Listen, darling. I am so happy you and Sophie have met. And I promise I'll talk to her properly now, explain that I take responsibility for my own pathetic actions,' continued Michael. 'But, for now, can you just hurry home to me?'

Saying her goodbyes, Celeste handed the phone back to Sophie who was now signalling to the waitress for the bill. She pulled out her own purse and shooed away Sophie's attempt to place a bundle of notes on the table.

'This one's on me. I'm just glad we got together and … let's just see what the future brings. But I would like to see you – and the boys – again. Please?'

As the waitress reappeared with the bill, Sophie stood up and shrugged on her coat. She hesitated for the briefest moment before shuffling around the table and giving Celeste a quick hug. Celeste felt as if she'd just won the Nobel Prize for Literature.

'I think we can arrange that. And, by the way, make sure you tell my dad about your writing. If you don't, I will!' said Sophie with what could only be construed as a proper, from-the-heart, smile.

Counting out the change, the waitress looked between Celeste and Sophie. Thanking them for the generous tip, she turned to leave then turned back again.

'You know, it's so lovely to see a mother and daughter out having a nice lunch together. I saw the pair of you laughing away earlier and it proper made me happy. Me and my mum just don't get on. She thinks I should have gone to uni, got myself a degree, instead of working in a café. But I like what I do and one day I'll open my own place. Anyway, have a good day.'

As she zoomed off to the next table, Sophie looked at Celeste. Celeste felt the corners of her mouth twitching. Then they both burst into peals of uncontrolled laughter, vaguely bordering on hysterics.

CHAPTER 28

Tabitha twirled this way and that. Checked out her reflection in the mirror. Looking pretty damn hot, she decided. The satiny fabric clung in all the right places; her hair was piled up in an artful way that suggested done but with wispy tendrils hinting at ever-so-slightly undone. Make-up just right, not too much, not too little. Yes, all perfect for a very special day.

'You look amazing.' Adam was standing in the doorway, looking pretty amazing himself. Normally dressed down in jeans and casual shirts, he was resplendent in formal attire, even if his top button was undone and his tie languishing in his pocket. 'Are you ready for this?'

Tabitha took a step towards him, slightly hindered by the tightness of her dress. She envisaged him unwrapping her later, like a much-wanted Christmas present, and couldn't suppress a smile of sheer, unadulterated joy. 'Never been more ready in my life. Let's get this road on the show!'

Adam gave her a look as he drew her close, careful not to crease her outfit or smudge her face. 'Methinks someone might have had a glass too many of bubbly in the preparation stages. Getting your words a little mixed up, my gorgeous girl?'

Tabitha hiccupped gently – OK, she had downed a couple between showering and dressing – but ... hey ... wasn't that what champagne was invented for? Celebrating the golden moments in life. Like when she'd gone for the interview in London and actually bagged the job. Which she loved with a passion, even if it meant spending prolonged periods of time away from Adam. It involved travelling all over the country, meeting new people, doing precisely what she loved and had dreamed of for years. Leaving Meryl had been hard but her beloved boss had been a total rock. Possibly aided by the fact that she was stepping out – her words, not Tabitha's – with Steve and all seemed to be going well. *Very* well, in fact. And all due to Tabitha's magical powers (or inability to keep her non-twitchy nose out of other people's business if you accepted Emily's viewpoint).

Speak of the devil, or at least a wickedly besotted pair, judging by the way Meryl and Steve approached with their hands tightly clasped together. Meryl was a vision of loveliness in a shot silk mauve dress, perfectly complemented by Steve's charcoal suit and lilac shirt. She hurried towards Tabitha, who had been joined again by Adam after a hectic round of introductions and hand-shaking.

'Tabbie! You look stunning, my darling girl. Doesn't she, Steve?' She hugged Tabitha enthusiastically, before giving Adam the same treatment. He responded with equal enthusiasm, having grown immensely fond of Meryl in the past twelve months.

'She does indeed. Pretty as a picture as always.' Steve gave Tabitha a kiss on each cheek, before exchanging a manly backslap/hug with Adam. 'What a perfect day for a wedding. Speaking of which, when are the happy couple due to arrive?'

Minutes later and the cast was beginning to assemble on

the steps of the registry office. Tabitha liked to think of them in that way – players taking their positions, rehearsals over, the production finally ready to be staged. Hard to believe where they'd all been a year ago, how far they'd all come in both individual and collective ways.

'Susan! I hardly recognised you.' Tabitha gave her mum's friend a warm hug, turning to embrace the beaming man by her side. 'And you're looking pretty dapper too, Jonathan.'

The pair of them shuffled closer together with a slightly embarrassed but emphatically chuffed expression on their faces. Susan knew that a large part of her changed appearance was down to shedding over two stone – and still more to go – but the decreasing numbers on the scales only told part of the story. She was free of cancer, although regular checks were still necessary, and beside her stood the man she'd loved, lost and – miraculously – found again. As an accountant she was used to making sense of numbers but she'd given up on counting her blessings. Was just grateful she was alive, with good friends and a man who made her feel everything she'd failed to feel in the past.

More and more people were arriving, the official photographer huddling them into groups on the steps of the registry office. Smile! Click, click went the camera, capturing each moment for posterity. The weather had decided to behave itself after several anxious days of downpours and dark clouds. Now the sun had made a welcome appearance, bathing the guests in its warm glow.

Tabitha spied her aunt Celeste and uncle Michael making their way from the parking area. She suppressed a giggle as Celeste tottered across the gravel driveway in her vertiginous heels, clinging to Michael lest she come a cropper. She was wearing a bright orange dress which almost matched the colour of her fake-tanned skin, hair styled in an elaborate chignon with an enormous fascinator that appeared to have been plucked from some exotic bird.

'Tabitha, darling! Don't you look totally ravishing.' Still clinging to Michael's arm, she carefully leant in for an air kiss. Just as well, thought Tabitha, who didn't particularly want to be smeared with gloopy tangerine lip gloss.

'Hi Aunt Celeste, Uncle Michael.' Tabitha exchanged a quick hug with her uncle, Celeste now safely on level ground. 'You both look wonderful. Didn't you come with Sophie and the boys?' Just as the words left her lips she heard the unmistakable sound of two tiny terrors approaching at breakneck speed. Scuffing their highly polished shoes through the stones, one wielding a toy aeroplane and making appropriate noises, the other clutching a plastic dinosaur head on a stick.

'Boys, would you *please* slow down! And George, stop snapping at your brother's ear with that damn thing!' Looking rather flushed and harassed, Sophie caught up with the dynamic duo and grabbed the offending T Rex from her youngest's hand, prompting a wail of outrage. Sensing imminent meltdown – Edward was rubbing a rather inflamed ear with a distinctly wobbly lower lip – Tabitha delved into her beaded purse and produced a bag of jelly beans. 'Here boys, look what I just happen to have on me!' Like starving velociraptors, they pounced on the sweets, cramming handfuls into their mouths. Sophie sighed, then squeezed Tabitha's hand in gratitude. 'Not sure a ton of sugar and additives is *quite* what the doctor ordered but at least they're quiet for now. Thank you.'

Tabitha watched as Sophie and the boys walked towards Celeste and Michael. Her uncle embraced his daughter warmly, before bending down and hugging each of his grandsons in turn. Stepping back, Sophie smiled at Celeste then gave her the briefest peck on the cheek. Celeste in turn ruffled the hair of Edward and George in a slightly self-conscious manner. They'd come a long way in the past year, but if Rome wasn't built in a day then repairing years of damaged relationships and deep-rooted animosity would take considerably longer. Privately, Tabitha thought her aunt a singularly selfish person, her uncle a virtual saint for putting up with her 'me, me, me' ways for so long. When the whole painful Sophie saga came out she'd fully expected Michael to walk away and build a new life with his daughter and grandsons. But – to give Celeste some credit – she'd extended an olive branch to Sophie. Who – to give her massive respect – didn't tell Celeste which orifice she could shove it in. Tabitha could never imagine them having cosy stepmother/stepdaughter tête-à-têtes but at least they'd achieved some workable level of acceptance.

Suddenly the low murmur of the crowd turned to excited whispers then cheers.

'They're here! Look, everyone. They've arrived!' Indeed, a powder-blue vintage Austin Healey had swung into the driveway. Tabitha sent up a silent prayer of thanks that the roof was firmly up. Artfully tousled was one thing, dragged through a hedge backwards quite another.

As everyone watched, Joe emerged from the driver's side and made his way around the car to open the passenger door. He was wearing a slate-grey suit and gleaming white shirt, accentuated with a deep purple tie. He really was a stunning-looking man, thought Tabitha. A collective roar of approval went up as Emily emerged from the car, clutching a small posy of flowers in one hand, her other held firmly by her husband-to-be. Tabitha felt a flood of emotions wash over her, not least pure joy that her wonderful, amazing mum had found true happiness.

'Och Em, you look like an angel!' Her friend Kirsty – who'd flown over from Australia for the occasion – looked

Emily up and down, her face alight with pleasure. Emily self-consciously smoothed down her cream dress, appliquéd with swirls of bronze and taupe. She'd spent hours browsing for it with Tabitha, discarding many for being too over the top or too 'young'. But she'd been immediately smitten when she set eyes on this one. As had Tabitha, judging by the way her eyes had filled when she emerged from the changing room.

'Aye, but you're a wee devil for 'no telling me about your man sooner,' scolded Kirsty good-naturedly. *That* had been an interesting Skype chat three months earlier, with Kirsty shrieking like a madwoman to the point her husband Dave rushed in fearing some medical emergency. He dutifully fetched a hefty glass of Springbank and she toasted Emily and Joe, who she'd demanded step into view of the camera and went a vivid shade of crimson when Kirsty pronounced him 'well braw'.

Dave appeared next to his wife and gave Emily a kiss on each cheek. 'Looking a knock-out as always, Em,' he said before slinging his arm around Kirsty's shoulder. 'And this one doesn't scrub up too badly either!' With mock exasperation Kirsty nudged him in the ribs. 'Less of your cheek, Dave, or I'll be trading *you* in for a younger model! Has Joe got a dishy brother by any chance?'

It was time for the ceremony to begin. As neither Joe nor Emily were particularly religious, they'd opted for a secular service with an officiant recommended to them by Rosemary at Where the Hearth Is. They'd written their own vows which had caused a great deal of hilarity. Emily was adamant there was no way Joe was going to 'promise to be with you through the toughest trials in our live and cry with you. Except when you're sobbing at some sappy soap opera storyline. Then, you're on your own.' Equally, Joe put his foot down at Emily's pledge to 'learn how to check the oil in my car and master the offside rule. Actually, forget that one. Ain't gonna happen.' They'd settled for a simple declaration of their lasting love for each other no matter what life threw at them. Till death did them part. The traditional ending had sent a little tremor of fear down Emily's spine. With their age gap, wasn't it more than likely she'd be the one to die first? Completely understanding her concern, Joe had kissed her tenderly before reminding her of the famous Joan Collins quote.

'When she was asked about the thirty-two-year gap between her and her younger husband, she simply replied, "If he dies, he dies." There are no guarantees, Emily. But I'm in it for the long haul. You won't get rid of me that easily!'

Stood together at the front, Emily and Joe faced the officiant, a kindly faced man in his mid-sixties called Andrew Black. They'd met him a couple of times beforehand to discuss the proceedings, united in their desire to keep things simple. She'd already done the full-blown wedding thing and Joe was happy to go along with her wishes. He'd confided in her about Caitlin, how he'd thought she might be *The One*.

'There I was, imagining some exotic location. White sandy beach, awesome seafood banquet, hot and cold running waiters. When, the truth was, all I needed was the right person. And I've found her.'

Tabitha was dabbing at her eyes with a tissue, aware of other sniffling sounds around her. And not just the women. Steve – sitting to her right with Meryl – looked distinctly misty-eyed. Even her normally wise-cracking and wonderfully manly Adam had produced a hankie, although he'd mumbled something about a 'dodgy contact lens'. Yeah, right.

'I now pronounce you man and wife. You may kiss the bride.' As she had no veil to lift, Joe simply took her in his arms and kissed her. Thoroughly and expertly, only coming up for air when some wag at the back yelled, 'Oi, get a room!'

It was official. They were married. Mr and Mrs McKenzie. Emily pinched herself hard on the fleshy part below her thumb. Ouch! No, it wasn't a dream. Or, rather, it *was* but a real-life, wide awake, this has *actually* happened, one. Who could have imagined all those months ago that a dead pigeon could have led to this?

'Are you all right, Em?' Joe's words shook her out of her reverie. She rubbed the still-throbbing piece of skin before taking his outstretched hand. Those strong, capable fingers, always immaculately clean. She felt the warmth of his touch, the now-so-familiar yet always electrifying sensation of making physical contact. Mrs Emily McKenzie. Without a doubt, the happiest woman on the planet.

Turning to face their friends and family, Emily was aware of Adam gesturing to Mr Black, who scuttled off to the side. A split-second later, something burst out over the loudspeakers.

'**De**-de-de-de-de, **De**-de-de-de-de, **De**, boom, boom, boom... Congratulations, and celebrations...'

To loud whoops and applause, Emily and Joe made their way towards the exit, serenaded by Cliff Richard in his heyday. Passing Adam and Tabitha she attempted a frown but the moment was so surreal, so totally bonkers it somehow felt *right.*

'It was *his* idea, honest, Mum,' hissed Tabitha as Emily kissed her before passing her the posy of flowers. 'Wait, aren't you supposed to throw those outside, and whoever catches them is next down the aisle?'

Emily patted her indulgently on the cheek before moving off. Her parting shot was aimed at Adam. 'Thought I wouldn't leave it to chance, darling. And, don't worry, Adam. Revenge *will* be mine. Maybe a little "I Should Be So Lucky"?'

Leaving Tabitha clutching the flowers and blushing profusely, Emily and Joe made their way to the car, now festooned with a Just Married sign. Liberally covered in confetti, they clambered in and headed into town.

The reception was at Bar Belle. They'd negotiated a good deal on a delicious buffet and free-flowing champagne, wine, beers and soft drinks. Tabitha had taken charge of the organisation and decoration. All the tables had silver and gold heart-shaped balloons as their centrepiece, and Meryl had sourced some flame-shaped place cards bearing everyone's name. Adam had sorted out a DJ and a small area had been cleared as a dance floor. He'd promised – hand on heart – to play at least a few Abba tracks but any more Cliff Richard and he was a dead man.

'Grand do, Mrs Hardwick. I mean, Mrs McKenzie. Kind of you to invite me. Not often I get out of an evening these days. Not since before the missus passed away and we had our weekly trips to the bingo.'

It was Ken Crompton, the car mechanic who'd kept Hamish roadworthy over the years. She hadn't *really* meant to invite him. She'd just felt sorry for him when she took her beloved Mini in for a service and spotted his supermarket bag stacked with unappetizing ready meals for one. Maybe Tabitha could fix him up with someone. Although that *someone* would need a sense of humour bypass and intimate knowledge of axles and brake pads.

Before she could get embroiled in deep conversation about sprockets and suspensions, Joe appeared by her side. He'd discarded his jacket and taken off his tie. He proffered a glass of champagne which Emily gratefully accepted and nearly downed in one.

'Steady on, Em! We've still got the whole reception to get through. Unless you're drowning your sorrows, having realised you married the wrong man.'

He winked at Ken, who was munching on a mini cheeseburger, waitresses circulating now with plates of nibbles. Narrowly avoiding spearing his upper lip with the cocktail stick, he muttered something about needing a beer and shuffled off.

Several hours later and the party was winding down. There'd been laughter, music and a fair bit of dancing. Meryl had persuaded Steve to bust some moves Abba-style and Adam had raised temperatures performing a steamy Argentine tango with Tabitha. Despite having two left feet, she'd managed to follow his lead and avoid falling on her bottom. Emily and Joe had taken to the floor for the first dance. 'Top Of The World' by The Carpenters. Joe had insisted upon it after hearing about a rowdy school trip when Emily was fifteen which involved sneaky cigarettes, stolen kisses with young Italian studs and a burnt nightie ditched in a bin in the centre of Rome.

'You little devil!' he'd exclaimed. 'But I'm not sure where the squeaky-clean Carpenters come into all this debauchery.'

Emily had explained that a Carpenters tape was all their coach driver had, hence the reason she knew every one of their songs off by heart.

'That was probably my favourite. It still takes me back if I hear it on the radio. And I thought the lyrics were beautiful. I still do.'

Which was why they twirled and whirled around the floor, lost in the moment, as the song played: *'Everything I want the world to be, Is now comin' true especially for me. And the reason is clear, it's because you are here. You're the nearest thing to heaven that I've seen.'*

It was time to leave. They had both changed into casual clothes and a taxi would pick them up in minutes to take them to the airport. Ten days in Mauritius lay ahead. Joe would get his pristine beach and breath-taking sunsets, but this time he knew it would be with his perfect match.

Saying their farewells, Emily found herself swept into hug after hug. Her darling Tabitha and the delightful Adam. Meryl and Steve. Celeste and Michael. Even Sophie gave her an unexpectedly heartfelt embrace. Susan and Jonathan had left a little earlier, both thanking her profusely for a wonderful day and with promises to meet up soon.

Surveying all the friends and family around them, Emily marvelled again at the difference a year or so could make. Life could be cruel but, right now, all she could see was a great, big bubble of joy. Speaking of bubbles of joy, here was the effervescent Kirsty, who wasn't so much a 'glass half-full' girl but a 'bring on the next one.'

'I'm *so* happy you could make it, Kirsty.' Emily swiped away a stray tear as she wrapped herself around her friend. 'I just wish we had more time together. We'll have to visit you in Oz one day soon.'

'Och, Em, I widnae have missed this for the world! Didn't I always say, Dave, that this one was destined to get snapped up sooner or later? But a hunk like Joe? You really *are* a wee jobby!' Dave duly nodded in embarrassed agreement, just as someone called out that the taxi was waiting.

As Joe approached Emily, ready to embark on their honeymoon and all that lay ahead in their life together, his handsome face said it all. Happiness radiated from him more effectively than the heat from any state-of-the-art fireplace.

'All set, my beautiful wife? Your carriage awaits.'

Yes, thought Emily. *I'm all set.*

THE END

AFTERWORD

A Clean Sweep was a labour of love (and a fair amount of sweat and tears). I'm so, so happy you've read it and I can't thank you enough for supporting me.

Word of mouth is crucial for any author to succeed. If you enjoyed the book, *please* leave a review on Amazon. Just pop over to your preferred site. And on Goodreads too, if you can spare an extra minute. Even if it's just a sentence or two, it would make all the difference and would be very much appreciated.

My second romantic comedy novel, The Haunting of Hattie Hastings is also available and my third will be published in June 2020. If you'd like to keep up to date with all my writerly news, please visit my website www.audreydavisauthor.com Enormous thanks again and happy reading!

ACKNOWLEDGMENTS

This book is dedicated to all my wonderful friends who put up with my endless rambling and gnawing doubts that it would ever see the light of day. Lindsey, Kirsteen, Fiona and Marguerite, thank you for reading and giving me much-needed moral support.

Special thanks to Matilda who came back with a long list of suggestions as to where and how it could be improved. I took *most* of them on board, honest.

Huge thanks to the wonderful Debz Hobbs-Wyatt for her detailed critique and advice on formatting and other issues I wasn't even aware of. Any mistakes that remain are entirely of my doing!

Special mention must go to the amazing Start Writing Fiction course offered by Future Learn, a free on-line offshoot of the Open University. It gave me the much-needed push to get writing instead of just daydreaming. The feedback from other students and tutors boosted my confidence and convinced me that anything was possible.

An enormous thank you too to the super-talented Lisa Firth at Oliphant Author Services for her stunning cover design. She completely captured the essence of the story when I wanted to give my debut a face-lift!

This book simply wouldn't have happened without the visions of loveliness that are my chimney sweeps. Not just one, but two of them. You're obliged by law in Switzerland to have your chimney swept and it was their good looks and charm that inspired this story. Everything else is entirely a work of fiction, I promise!

Finally, it is dedicated to my husband and two sons who cheered me on every step of the way, even when the words dried up and my confidence shrivelled away. Thanks guys, love you. Are you ready for the next one?

* * *

ABOUT THE AUTHOR

Audrey Davis is a former journalist, born and raised in Scotland but now living in Switzerland. Much as she'd like to claim to be an expert skier and skilled mountaineer, she is more at home on the sofa watching Netflix and drinking red wine. She speaks French – badly – but cooks rather well. Years of devouring romantic fiction finally persuaded her to try her hand at writing a book. This is the result.

audreydavisauthor.com

Printed in Great Britain
by Amazon

85464989R00181